PAUL REIDINGER

GOOD BOYS

A PLUME BOOK

PLUME
Published by the Penguin Group
Penguin Books USA Inc., 375 Hudson Street, New York, New York 10014, U.S.A.
Penguin Books Ltd, 27 Wrights Lane, London W8 5TZ, England
Penguin Books Australia Ltd, Ringwood, Victoria, Australia
Penguin Books Canada Ltd, 10 Alcorn Avenue, Toronto, Ontario, Canada M4V 3B2
Penguin Books (N.Z.) Ltd, 182–190 Wairau Road, Auckland 10, New Zealand

Penguin Books Ltd, Registered Offices: Harmondsworth, Middlesex, England

Published by Plume, an imprint of Dutton Signet, a division of Penguin Books USA Inc.
Previously published in a Dutton edition.

First Plume Printing, June, 1994
10 9 8 7 6 5 4 3 2 1

Ⓟ REGISTERED TRADEMARK—MARCA REGISTRADA

LIBRARY OF CONGRESS CATALOGING-IN-PUBLICATION DATA
Reidinger, Paul.
        Good boys / Paul Reidinger.
            p.   cm.
        ISBN 0-452-27220-3
        1. Friendship—California—San Francisco—Fiction.   2. Young men—
        California—San Francisco—Fiction.   3. Gay men—California—San
        Francisco—Fiction.   4. San Francisco (Calif.)—Fiction.   I. Title.
        [PS3568.E479G65   1994]
        813'.54—dc20   93–48610
                                                                            CIP

Printed in the United States of America
Set in Bodoni Book and Gill Sans
Original hardcover designed by Steven N. Stathakis

PUBLISHER'S NOTE
This is a work of fiction. Names, characters, places, and incidents either are the product of the
author's imagination or are used fictitiously, and any resemblance to actual persons, living or
dead, events, or locales is entirely coincidental.

BOOKS ARE AVAILABLE AT QUANTITY DISCOUNTS WHEN USED TO PROMOTE PRODUCTS OR SERVICES.
FOR INFORMATION PLEASE WRITE TO PREMIUM MARKETING DIVISION, PENGUIN BOOKS USA INC.,
375 HUDSON STREET, NEW YORK, NEW YORK 10014.

For Jocelyn B.
and Thomas P.

acknowledgments

The author extends his thanks to Richard Hersh, Steven Wiesner, Billy Abrahams, Christopher Schelling, and especially Liza Mundy for their invaluable help and encouragement.

"Yes," I say to Carl, "he is still very handsome."

There is a whisper I can't quite make out. Drew is still very handsome. Michael too. Ten years seem hardly to have touched them, though it does look like they shave every day now. Drew skips the occasional day or two. Tonight he had a bit of George Michael-ish stubble, which usually turns me on (like that boy from last Thursday, a sweet twenty-year-old who told me he loved me before the clock struck twelve; I shooed him out as gently as I could) but didn't tonight, thank God. This had been a concern beforehand.

"You're being very prurient tonight," I say to Carl, removing the blue blazer and tie (museum pieces, really) and tossing them onto a box of books I've packed but not yet taped shut. (Ran out of tape this morning.) He doesn't answer, because he hates it when I call him prurient, but I do hear the wind sighing in the window frames and the chimes tinkling from the balcony next door.

"I don't blame you for being prurient," I add, anxious to make amends, though I use the offending P word again. Carl is silent. This may mean that I'm forgiven, or that I'm not, or that the question of whether old college chums are still attractive now bores him. I wish it bored me. I wish I felt something, other than the sense of being totally remote. Maybe I should be thankful.

I love them still, I think, and yet, and yet. Hard to put a finger on it. Here's Michael, an M.D. now, licensed and certified, married with child, owner in fee simple of an actual piece of God's green earth (with two and a half baths and central air). There's Drew, repatriated from D.C. under mysterious circumstances, living now with his brother in L.A. and working for a TV production company. I know their résumés, but all that has really happened to them, I haven't seen. All that has really happened to me, they haven't seen.

"I told them," I say to Carl. "About us. About you."

More silence. It can be like this. Sometimes it's like I'm talking to myself. (Which is still better and cheaper than the phone-sex lines. They are absurd.)

I did tell them, though it pretty well shattered the evening's American-Express-ad patina. On the Metro ride to the Civic Center, I thought about not telling them—because who, after all, wants to hear such things, especially over grilled swordfish with red-pepper aioli? And who, after all, would really want to tell, when telling brings back all these memories one has spent years digging fire lines around, so that even if they never burn out, they won't burn out of control, either?—and then I thought about what the point was of seeing them at all if I planned not to tell.

Way back when, as a twenty-two-year-old neophyte adult abruptly and unwillingly expelled into the world, I would never have guessed that my life (or at least the large chunk of it presently under review) would eventually be defined quite so sharply, so thoroughly, by what happened so quickly to someone other than me. *Wasn't life supposed to be incremental, a coral reef that assumed a shape over time? That's what it used to be. So I was taught, so I believed, being dutiful and credulous.*

"They were shocked," I tell Carl. *They were shocked. Slack jaws and sputters into silence.* "I mean, it's understandable. Wouldn't you be?"

He murmurs, but I can't make it out over the rustling wind. Probably he's saying, Well, no, Christopher, I wouldn't be. Probably he's right. I would have been shocked if I'd been Drew or Michael, but being shockable is me. ("One of your many charms," *Carl told me early on, before we moved in together. We were leaving the baths at Eighth and Howard at my insistence after a courtly older gentleman asked us to piss on him in the showers.*)

"Should I move to Los Angeles?" *I ask Carl.* "Drew wants me to move to Los Angeles." *This time I don't wait for Carl's answer.* "I'm not moving to Los Angeles," *I say.* "That's the last thing I'm doing."

"You should move to L.A." *were practically the first words out of Drew's mouth when we met.* (The first actual words were "I'll have a vodka gimlet.") *He and his brother have fabulous digs, et cetera. West Hollywood. By the end of the evening, when Michael had driven off in his rental car and it was just the two of us, I didn't think I'd have to explain why West Hollywood isn't as alluring a place as it once might have been. I did have to explain, or I felt the need to explain, why I'm moving where I'm moving, which is not to L.A., but he didn't get it, and I was too tired to elaborate, or to argue with him about my plans. I found myself thinking, please just stop talking and take me in your arms and hold me. Please. He didn't.*

"I should have asked him to," *I say aloud, more to myself than to Carl.* "We should have touched."

Real men don't touch. Don't cry or kiss. Too faggy. They are stone and steel, have heart attacks and die.

Maybe I'm not a real man, but all I'm thinking about as

I peel off the final cotton layer of civilization and slip between the cool sheets is how I am longing to be touched, to be held, to feel the simple warmth of him next to me. That is what the whole evening reduces to. Not sex, desire, lost love. Just human contact.

"Please just hold me," I say, softly, into the pillow, so he won't hear.

a PARTY

"If Trina's there," Drew said, "you're not to take her off and drill her before I've had a chance."

"Whatever you say, butch," Michael said. He always tried hard to be agreeable.

"I know I can trust Christopher here," Drew went on. He had already had three beers and seemed to be walking several feet above the damp sidewalk toward the big white frame house where a Christmas tree's lights twinkled in the bay window. "The most he would do is cave in her head with a baseball bat. Am I overstating?" he asked, turning to Chris. "Or are we mellow tonight?"

"We are extremely mellow," Chris said. He had had two beers. Michael, being Jewish, had had a slice of pecan pie and a cup of cocoa. It was in his responsible pocket that the car keys nestled. They had parked a block and a half away so that Michael wouldn't have to parallel park. It wasn't his best thing. Dents and scratches on the Fiat so attested.

"You're drunk," Drew declared. "Admit it, and I shall be quick and merciful. Episode?"

" 'Arena,' " Chris recited.

"And I am?"

"The Gorn."

"Correct."

(Chris and Drew had been freshman roommates and had bonded on the first day by listing all the episodes of *Star Trek* by title. Drew, though he had short blond hair and looked like a cross between a water-polo star and a storm trooper, could raise one eyebrow at a time, just like Mr. Spock, and was a fanatical rationalist.)

"Please," Michael said. "We're going to a party. We're supposed to have a good time." He hated *Star Trek* lock, stock and barrel and was apt to become sullen when episodes were named and favorite lines recited from memory. Chris and Drew, out of deference, reserved this amusing pastime for indulgence when they were alone, except when they were drunk, like now.

Trina was Drew's on-again, off-again girlfriend. On or off, Chris hated her with a zest and consistency that was mostly absent from the rest of his life. As to why he hated her, therein lay the question.

"I thought you said this was an orgy," Drew said to Chris. "A holiday orgy. You distinctly said orgy. Didn't he say orgy?" Drew asked Michael. "I am so horny and so drunk, it's unbelievable. God only knows what could happen." He gave Chris a nudge that nearly drove him into the leaf-strewn gutter. "Wink-wink."

"You think Trina'll be there?" Michael asked. "I thought she was living down in Sunnyvale or someplace like that. I haven't seen her in months."

"Trina can be found wherever people are dissipating themselves," Drew said. "In the metaphysical sense. Mountain View is the name you're looking for, butch. Haven't seen her in months! I like that. If I know you, you've probably spent many an afternoon together surreptitiously humping like bunnies whilst I toiled in the stacks."

"Should we tell him the truth?" Michael asked Chris solemnly. "He might freak."

"Let him," Chris said. Immediately he felt stupid and reckless for not knowing to what truth Michael adverted and, with Chris's consent, was about to disclose.

"I knew you two kids've been keeping something from me," Drew said. "Let me guess. You are partners in sodomy."

"Yes," Michael said.

"Oh God!" Drew said. "I knew it! I feel so left out. No one ever asked me if I'd like to be a partner in sodomy. Well, once. I name no names. Did I mention I have a marijuana cigarette in my back pocket? Shall we?"

"Definitely," Michael said. Chris shrugged.

They slipped between an old madrone and an old garage and had a smoke.

Naked, Drew made Chris uneasy, and since Drew was often naked when they were alone together in the series of rooms they had shared since freshman year, this was an issue. At first Chris assured himself that it was just his stiff Midwestern upbringing in collision with the wild and woolly ways of the West Coast. When that got old, he admitted to himself that he felt inadequate, not because Drew had a bigger dick (he didn't seem to, but precise comparison was a tricky proposition) but because the balance of him—pecs, thighs, ass, et cetera— seemed to be more impressively developed.

("Have you ever measured yours?" Drew asked near the end of their first term freshman year. It was late at night and they were tanked on cheap beer. One final to go, each. "You have to measure from the top when it's hard. Not that cord by your asshole. That's how guys are always ending up with eight inches. You should hear my brother. I think he starts at the small of his back."

Stunned silence from across the room.)

Chris was attractive, though he did not think so; this made him more attractive, though he did not know it. He made every effort to ignore his genitals and his heart, those untrustworthy ungovernables that were always threatening upheaval and anarchy, and he hoped they would ignore him. Lie, you sleeping dogs. Love and sex to age nineteen was an unwritten chapter, a blank sheaf of pages he was torn between wanting and fearing to fill, or at least mark slightly. Or at the very least open. Maybe tomorrow, next week, next year. Meanwhile he wondered if the people around him could hear the bomb ticking away inside.

There had been a romance here and there since the chaos and disruption of puberty—a few French kisses, a grope and a fondle, plenty of hanging around at the mall eating french fries and talking on the telephone long into the night. But he always felt like he was acting in a mime show. This was stuff you were supposed to do, what everyone else was doing, so you did it the way they did it. When his parents told him to go to Sunday school or clean out his closet, he did that, too. He was a good boy, not a rebel. And he always covered his nakedness.

Not Drew. Parading around in the buff was something he did apparently without even thinking about it. While Chris slept in his underwear and always woke up with a hard-on that took several minutes to tame before he could make a seemly exit from the sheets, Drew slept in the nude and bounced out of bed with missile-like morning glory. Chris tried not to notice, but who couldn't notice such a thing? He felt like asking Michael, a premed and a scientist, if this was normal, Drew's parading and Chris's noticing, but he thought better of it. Michael might misunderstand.

Michael naked was less intimidating. He was shorter than Chris and Drew (both of whom were in the six-foot range) but

Chris assured himself this wasn't it. It wasn't that his dick was smaller than theirs, either, though Chris had never seen it hard (had never seen anyone's hard, for that matter, other than his own and Drew's). Michael wasn't as shy as Chris about stripping, but at least after squash and shower he didn't dress himself from the top down, waiting until the last possible moment to slip on his underwear. That was Drew's shtick.

It went without saying that Chris's disquiet on the matter of naked males was purely one of propriety and decorum. It had nothing to do with the fact that, though he had gone out several times over the past nine months with Meredith (tonight's hostess) and had even referred to her as his girlfriend once or twice, the extent of their physical intimacy had yet to proceed beyond a bout or two of French kissing. This odd development was not discussed with Michael, certainly not with Drew.

"Man," Drew said. "Phasers on stun." He staggered slightly as he said this.

"We're lost," Chris said.

"It was right there," Michael said. He pointed in the direction Meredith's house had lain in before Drew produced his malodorous joint and they detoured to smoke it.

"We are deeply disoriented," Drew said. "Meanwhile, while we stumble, the fucking, sucking and sodomy proceed apace as the centerpiece of the orgy to which you, Christopher, promised to lead us, your hard-up flock, emphasis on *hard*. Have I ever mentioned that I am much better sex when I'm blitzed?"

"You are not. Don't believe him," Michael said to Chris.

"That was a fluke," Drew said. "Anyway, I wanted to try again but you said it was going to be too big and you had a headache."

Chris dared not look at them, for fear they would read on his face the thoughts that were going through his mind. *Drew*

and *Michael?* No, not possible, couldn't be. True, Drew floated
through this region of life on a magic carpet of ambiguity, but
not Michael. He had had so many girlfriends that neither Chris
nor Drew bothered to learn their names anymore unless he introduced them a minimum of three times. It had been this way
since freshman year, when Michael lived across the hall with
a roommate who always seemed to be flying to Los Angeles for
the weekend. Many were the times when Chris or Drew or the
two of them together had approached Michael's door to solicit
the pleasure of his company on a pizza run or a flick, only to
see the telltale MAID SERVICE sign hung on the doorknob, indicating that Michael was in session with somebody.

"That guy," Drew had said once, when he and Chris had
ricocheted off MAID SERVICE toward a kegger at one of the frats.
"He is something else."

"Maybe he wasn't in there. Maybe he just forgot about the
sign," Chris suggested.

"Maybe the pope is Jewish," Drew said. "Get a clue,
please. His bill for bedsprings is going to be more than tui-
tion."

"I wonder who it is this time."

"Doesn't matter," Drew said. "The man deals in volume.
If it breathes, he pokes it."

"You don't know that," Chris said, but his tone was so
doubtful that Drew didn't bother to respond.

Unlike Michael, Drew had enmeshed himself in what they
all called "a relationship," which sounded adult and meant
sustained if not exclusive fucking. The co-enmeshee was Trina,
who had introduced herself to Drew at a home football game
sophomore year by standing one bleacher level below him and
turning to embrace. *Voilà:* face in crotch. Drew gave a dizzy
grin. Chris went up in smoke and stormed out of the stadium,
but no one paid any attention.

And so it went. Drew, having been Chris's constant com-
panion, suddenly was coming home at four in the morning with

his shirt untucked and his button fly tangled. Adding two and two, over and over, night after night, kept Chris sleepless. He blamed her for existing. He wanted to blame Drew for the whole mess but couldn't. Notes were exchanged on pillows. Drew pled lust. Chris fumed and sulked.

Eventually summer came and Drew went off to Washington, D.C., as an intern and Trina just went off somewhere and the whole evil spell was broken. Hurt feelings healed some. When fall came, Drew saw her, but discreetly, so as not to upset Chris.

Meanwhile, Chris met Meredith on a field trip for an oceanography class that satisfied, in part, the vexatious science requirement. At first he asked her out to take revenge on Drew. Then he decided he liked her. Then he decided that they should do more than kiss, but what exactly that would be, and when, he couldn't decide. Since the beginning of fall term they seemed to be adrift, but bobbing decidedly in the direction of friendship. Chris liked to think they were "soulmates" and was proud that their relationship transcended the carnal, though he kept that detail secret, Drew being the beast he was.

"The great thing about Trina," Drew said—they were back on course, at the house, mounting the steps to the porch—"is that she swallows. Most girls don't like to. She's like a sump pump. Does Meredith swallow?" he asked Chris. "Or does she spit it out into a Kleenex? I hate that! Or does she just jerk you off?"

"I think," Michael said, "we should change the subject." He pointed toward the front door, which was open and full of people.

"I mean, most girls try to get you to wear a rubber anyway," Drew went on blithely. "Then they can say, Sorry, don't like the taste of rubber—got to give them that much—and then it's like, why bother with this at all?"

"We've taken a vote and decided to have your mouth temporarily disconnected," Michael said. "Right, Christo?"

Chris nodded. He spotted Meredith standing near the door, talking to people as they ebbed in and out. Next to her stood one of her two roommates, another undergraduate woman. The third roommate, a spectral art-history graduate student who dwelt in the stuffy attic, was shy of undergraduates and had arranged to spend the evening in the library stacks.

"If I were a girl, I'd swallow," Drew continued. "Even if it is icky, it's part of the job."

"You're being gross," Chris said. "Let's say hi to Merry."

"Ah, Merry," Drew said. "Yes, let's. I've been wondering when you were going to introduce us properly. Maybe I'll just pop my little question directly to her and wait for an answer from those lovely lips."

"Don't you dare," Chris said. "You're drunk and fucked up and completely out of control."

"And damn proud of it," Drew said.

Meredith smiled when she saw Chris, and he shepherded his flock toward her. Chris leaned forward and kissed her on the cheek. This felt adult and sophisticated and Southern, all at once. She was from western Virginia.

"Glad y'all could make it," she said. "I know you're Drew," she said to Drew, offering a hand, "and I know you're Michael. You were in my Art One class freshman year."

"I thought you were in *my* Art One class sophomore year."

Meredith laughed. "We were in the same class. You always sat way to the right, near the front, and you had that wine-colored backpack."

This was all true, even unnerving. When Michael was unnerved he smiled, and because he came from a prosperous family of Northeastern suburban Jews the teeth displayed in his smile were well-to-do suburban: white, straight and perfect. The more unnerved he was, the wider the grin, the brighter the glow. At the moment he was a human searchlight. "And you sat—" he began, as if he remembered.

"At a vantage point," she said.

"I liked that class," he said. "I wish I could take more classes like it."

"What stops you?"

"Oh," he said, shrugging his shoulders. "I'm a science person, I guess. Most of my classes have been bio, chem, stuff like that."

"You're premed."

"Yeah," Michael said. "Don't say it like that."

"Are you sensitive about it?"

"I don't want to be a barbarian," Michael said. "You don't think I am, do you?"

"Not yet."

During this exchange Chris could feel Drew getting antsy beside him. He followed Drew's gaze to a serving table inside, atop which were arrayed wines of several colors and a lot of little plastic cups.

"I thirst," Drew said.

"We're going to partake," Chris said to Meredith. "If he asks to take your pulse, call the police."

"He's stealing your woman," Drew said when they had reached the serving table and were examining the wares.

"She's not *my* woman."

"She has to be somebody's woman. She is utterly babe, in that cut-stone way. Dr. M. is afoam at the mouth. What's going on with you two, anyway? I think you should fess up, so I can help you develop a plan before it's too late."

"Why does something have to be going on?" Chris said. "We're friends. Is that hard to understand?"

"Men and women are never friends," Drew said. "Don't kid yourself. They are different species and mortal enemies."

"Well, Merry and I are friends," Chris said.

"I think she's making a new friend."

"What's that supposed to mean?"

"The M man swoops for the kill. You stand in danger of losing the Darwinian struggle to spread your seed."

Chris was trying not to notice that Drew was right: Michael and Merry were gabbing away. He tried to convince himself that he was jealous. There was some sort of uncomfortable feeling down there, in the locked closets of his heart. It felt more like panic, but maybe that's what true jealousy felt like. He told himself that what he felt about Drew vis-à-vis Trina was *not* jealousy, just an especially virulent strain of disdain. Everyone knew that feelings were a hopeless jumble anyway, so why bother trying to sort them out and name them? He concentrated instead on stemming the tide of anxiety that rose in his throat.

"Red or white?" Chris said. "Or champagne. There's champagne too," he added. "And rosé champagne."

"All of the above," Drew said. "There's that faggot David Rice."

"Let's try the rosé," Chris said. This was definitely panic. David Rice and his friend Katherine had been in Chris's freshman English class. They were always together. It was so like Drew to conclude that David was gay despite Katherine, but deep down Chris knew Drew was right.

"He's looking at you," Drew said, a shade loudly, Chris thought. "Turn around so he can see your ass."

"Michael was right," Chris said. "Your mouth should be disconnected from your brain. But permanently."

"I wonder if *he* swallows."

"For God's sake," Chris said. He handed Drew a little cup of sparkling rosé. Drew scarfed it and helped himself to another.

"You yelled at me," he said to Chris, downing the second. "I need it. I deserve it."

"He's not coming over here, is he?" Chris asked, trying not to sound panicky.

"As a matter of fact, *ja,*" Drew said. "He's got that look in those bedroom eyes of his. I can't decide if I should defend your honor or leave you alone with him."

"Stay right where you are," Chris said. "He makes me nervous."

"He's just a fag," Drew said. "He probably doesn't bite."

"Christopher," David Rice said. *"Quelle bonne chance."*

"Hi," Chris said as casually and masculinely as possible. "Hi, David. Haven't seen you in a while."

"No," David said. He turned to Drew. "I don't believe we've met."

"This is Drew Hopewell, my roommate," Chris said. "David Rice. Fellow freshman English survivor."

David and Drew shook.

"You're Geoff's brother?" David asked.

"He's my brother. And you're Katherine's chum."

David smiled.

"And where might she be?" Drew asked.

"Possibly in the ladies'," David said. "You know Katherine?"

"By reputation."

"Ah," David said. "Then you know all the news that's fit to print."

Chris was understanding very little of this. Somewhere to his right he could feel Michael and Merry still chattering away—falling in love at first sight, let's face it, just like in the movies—so he didn't dare to look over that way. He looked instead to the left, over Drew's shoulder, where, in the middle of the living room, he saw the back of the familiar blond head that was the head of the last person in the world he wanted to see.

"And then some," Drew was saying. "You two are the objects of considerable speculation."

"Yes," David said. "I suppose. So are you two."

Drew stared at him for an instant, a funny little smile on

his face. Chris felt as though he'd been slugged in the belly. It had never occurred to him that David could be impudent. In two quarters of freshman English, he'd hardly said boo to anyone except Katherine. They always seemed as though they were about to whisper to each other or had just finished whispering to each other.

Chris waited for Drew to say something clever or outrageous that would pop this unexpected bubble of tension. Or perhaps there would be recourse to fisticuffs. Drew and David were physically comparable, so one could not really say who might prevail.

"He's the man," Drew said at last. "Right, daddy?" he said to Chris.

"I'll spread the word," David said. "Excuse me. I see madame. Good to see you," he said to Chris, who nodded shyly.

"Prick," Drew said when they were alone again. "I don't know what it is about those girls, but they can be so nasty."

"Does he know Geoff?"

"There's no telling who knows Geoff," Drew said.

"I hope you don't start a brawl," Chris said. "I've got a final on Sunday."

"Did you know people whisper about us?" Drew said. "That's hysterical. I should have told him we were into golden showers and fist-fucking. He would have believed it. They're so decadent, these faggots."

"I wish you wouldn't say that word," Chris said. "It's rude. How do you know he is, anyway? Why would she spend so much time with him if he were? That doesn't make any sense."

"He's the palace eunuch," Drew said. "An unthreateningly limp dick in her presence. If you're a slut like Katherine, you need a breather once in a while."

"That's unfair," Chris said. He took two tiny steps to the table for another cup of wine. When he retraced the same tiny steps to the place he'd left Drew only seconds before, he found that the dread blond head was now there with him.

"Oh," Chris said. "Hi."

"I'm to do as I'm told or I'll be severely dealt with," Drew said. "Is that a promise?" he said to Trina. "Is the bullwhip in your car?"

"I brought the cattle prod," she said. "Hi, Chris." She had that glassy-eyed, dizzy look and was unsteady of foot. Drew had slipped an arm through hers for bracing purposes. Chris drank his wine in one gulp. "I just saw you guys standing here so I thought, like, hey, join the party."

"How's the stop-out life?" Chris asked. Trina had suspended her academic efforts at the end of last year to take a part-time position in the entertainment industry (she was a night cashier at a record store). For this and many other reasons she was deeply alienated from her family—a real-estate dynasty in San Francisco—but even bêtes noires can have trust funds, and so she did.

Chris had often asked himself just what it was that drew Drew to this particular package of femininity. Trina was lovely enough to look at, blond like Meredith though fuller and less aristocratic of feature (with the corollary danger of blowsiness somewhere down the road). She wasn't stupid, despite Chris's best efforts to make himself believe otherwise. There wasn't really anything wrong with her except that he didn't like her, and he found it impossible to accept that Drew could and did. Chris held fast to his belief that somewhere out there, the perfect someone awaited him who was patient and discerning.

"I'm a bad student," she said. "I never really belonged here in the first place. I only got in because both my parents went."

"How's the record business?"

"I don't really pay that much attention," she said. "I just sort of show up and they make me do stuff."

"What kind of stuff?" Drew asked, suddenly alert.

"What's going on at this so-called record store? You've never mentioned stuff before."

"It's nothing filthy," she said, "so get a grip. It's just been so long since I've seen you guys, I thought I'd say hello."

Chris nodded.

"I want to hear about this record store," Drew said to her. "Something is going on there I should know about, I can feel it."

"Well—" Trina said.

"Christopher is very squeamish about these sorts of things. You guard the wine," he said to Christopher. "And try to keep you-know-who at bay," he added, casting a glance in Michael's direction. "If he's like this sober, imagine what a little tipple might do."

They were gone.

"Do you like *any* wine?" Meredith asked.

"Mogen David."

Meredith made a face. "You *are* a barbarian. That's not wine, it's sugar water."

"I like sugar water."

"That's sweet," she said. He laughed. "I do feel that people shouldn't live in California if they don't appreciate wine," she said.

"I only have a temporary visa," Michael said. "I'll be deported eventually."

"How do you know Chris?"

"Freshman dorm. How do *you* know Chris?"

"Field trip to Point Reyes," she said. "I like him. He's kind of shy. Drew is a major presence."

"Drew," Michael repeated.

"I see them together a lot."

"They're roommates."

She nodded. "He's told me a lot about Drew. About you, too."

"You seem to know him better than he's let on. He can be very secretive."

"We've really become good friends," she said. "He's been the best guy friend I've had so far. When I was breaking up with Patrick—this guy I'd been going out with last year," she added in response to Michael's quizzical uplifting of his eyebrows, "Chris really helped."

"Okay, now I feel stupid about the wine," Michael said. "I should learn to like real wine, right? Teach me."

"Let's go into the kitchen," she said. "That's where I keep the really good stuff. And it's quieter."

"Fancy meeting you here," Drew said.

"I know like almost nobody at this party," Trina said. "So I've been getting really sloshed."

"Excellent."

"You haven't called."

"Sorry. Plate is full. Exams. You know. Plus Christophe has not been scarce."

"Christophe," she said. "What is it with that guy? He looks at me like he'd like to give me a good whack with his Louisville Slugger."

"Not Christophe," Drew said. "He's gentle as a pussycat. Just a bit shy around sensual women, that's all."

"Flattery will get you everywhere," she said.

"Let us rendezvous," Drew said. "Thirty minutes? Mountain Mike's? You have wheels?"

She nodded.

"And all requisite keys? Including apartment?"

She nodded again.

"*Parfait*. Thirty minutes. I'll make the necessary excuses, throw Christophe off the scent. Make sure he sees you leave. I'll hang around a bit, then feign the rupture of a small aneurysm in my brain and reel into the mean streets."

"That's a brilliant plan," she said. "A brain aneurysm."

"Don't be snotty," Drew said. "It drives me wild when you're snotty. You worry about your end. I will do what must be done."

"He went outside to throw up," Chris said to Katherine. "That's what he told me." That had been more than twenty minutes ago. The explanation had seemed plausible at the time, even welcome, but now Chris, consulting his watch, asked himself if any person, even one capable of such exuberant coarseness as Drew, could throw up for twenty minutes. He decided it was remotely possible.

(Drew had gotten sick in their room one night freshman year after a late-night binge of beer, Twinkies and devastatingly overmixed screwdrivers.

"I have a cast-iron stomach," he reassured Chris when Chris cautioned against too bold a mixture of solids and liquids.

In the middle of the night, apocalypse. Drew made a few wobbly steps toward the door and the bathroom somewhere beyond, but he made it only as far as the scrap of shag carpeting they used as a throw rug.

"Your cast-iron stomach is rusty," Chris couldn't resist saying as they hauled the ruined rug down two flights of stairs to the Dumpster. Drew reluctantly put on a pair of shorts for the expedition. The room smelled peculiar for days.)

"If you ask me," Katherine said, "he's flown the coop. Typical." She had bumped into Chris at the serving table, where she was gathering up little cups of wine as if they were going out of style. "I'm sorry," she said, when Chris looked at her. "I'm hogging them, aren't I. But they are so small." She set two cups back on the table in a gesture of contrition. Chris drained them.

"Yes!" she said approvingly. "À votre santé. Isn't it just like Meredith to give a party and serve the grog in little doll cups? David has been dispatched to find the most elephantine steins he can find. You've spoken to him?"

Chris nodded.

"He's been missing for a bit, too," she said. "Hmm. Let us think this through, rationally and carefully. Drew is missing. David is missing. David has a monstrous crush on Drew." She nodded to herself. "You check the bedrooms and closets," she said to Chris. "I'll check the shrubbery."

"Whoa," Chris said. There was a lot here to absorb.

"Ah-hah!" she said, over Chris's shoulder. "There you are, you bad boy. We thought you'd made off with Drew."

"I wish," David said. He shot Chris a smiling glance. "I thought you had."

"*Please,*" Katherine said. "Never again. I've only just begun to drink."

"No steins," David said. Now he looked sheepish as he produced two spotty water glasses. "Just these."

Katherine examined them, nose in a critical wrinkle, but she said, "They'll do. We always liked your last name, didn't we, David. Halloran. Irish, yes, isn't that right?"

"Yes."

"I'm right," she said triumphantly to David. "I knew it. And you said it was Greek!"

David shrugged. "So where *is* Drew?" he asked.

"He told Chris he was going outside to puke," she said. "We were speculating that you had somehow lured him into the bushes for purposes of molestation."

"Not me," David said. "Lousy bushes around this house. I notice that the girl he was with is gone, though."

"She left a long time ago," Chris said hopefully.

Katherine made a cheerful harrumphing noise. "Is *that* who he's seeing these days?"

"Oh no," Chris said. "They broke up over the summer."

Katherine went on as though she hadn't heard and wouldn't have cared if she had. "A mindless strumpet," she said. "Exactly the sort of dreary tart I knew he would end up with. Drew doesn't care for girlie brains, has he ever mentioned that to you? Superior women threaten him." She handed the water glasses to David. "I'll have more of the white," she said. "Fill 'er up."

"I didn't know you knew Drew," Chris said while David poured.

"Oh, Drew," she said with a roll of the eyes. "I know far too many people." David returned and handed her a water glass brimming with wine. She took a long slug.

"Did I hear the name Drew?" David asked.

"He's absconded," Katherine said. "I've explained this already. So stop pining. We're embarrassing Chris. I'm sorry," she said to Chris.

"Not at all."

"David is obsessed by straight men."

"Am not."

Katherine scowled at him. "It's not his fault he's a crazed monster," she said to Chris. "Some of us just have difficulty with reality from time to time."

"Who says Drew isn't available?" David said. "We have his roommate right here. Let's ask him."

"I don't think so," Katherine said, but she shot Chris an inquiring glance as she spoke.

"Is Drew, you know," David began, trying not to falter, "is he—"

"Why do you think Chris would know?" Katherine demanded. "They're just roommates."

"Roommates," David repeated, making the word sound deliciously lewd.

"I apologize on his behalf," Katherine said. "We are experiencing temporary hormonal difficulties. Aren't we, dear?" she said to David. "Now don't sulk. It's not your fault."

David sulked anyway.

"It's past his beddy-bye time," Katherine explained to

Chris. "I should take him home. Do you need a ride some-where? I got my license back this week."

Chris surveyed his prospects. Drew had vanished; that was now plain. Michael was missing in action. Even if he was still in the kitchen with Meredith, the car keys and the car were his and the likelihood that he would be leaving anytime soon seemed dim. Outside, a light winter rain. Katherine's re-marks about driving and hormones gave little comfort, and Da-vid looked pouty and predatory, but there was no choice. Chris said okay, and away they went.

Twelve days later, on a foggy Sunday afternoon, the three of them milled around together at the airport. Finals were over; the holidays loomed. Michael was waiting to board his flight to the East Coast. Chris's flight for Chicago was to leave about an hour later. Drew, having delivered them and their luggage as per custom, was driving to Los Angeles in his red 1966 Mustang.

"You're being coy," Drew said to Michael. "We have in-sufficient data."

Michael smiled. "She was sorry she didn't get to say goodbye to you," he said. "To both of you. We were sorry."

Chris shrugged. "It worked out okay," he said.

"You're blaming me that the faggot breathed hot on your neck while that slutty bitch weaved all over the road," Drew said. "Aren't you."

"No," Chris said. "I'm blaming you for coming in at three in the morning and turning all the lights on."

"I said I was sorry!" Drew said. "I was sick. I got lost. Anyway you were sound asleep and snoring. You slumbered peacefully right through my heartfelt offer of sodomy."

"You're obsessed by that word," Chris said.

"Do I dare leave you two alone?" Michael asked as his flight was announced.

"Sodomy, sodomy, sodomy," Drew said.

At the gate Michael set down his backpack and slipped his arms around Chris. Some gift of Jewishness made this physical gesture easy and unself-conscious for Michael and for the uptight Anglo-Saxon on whom he bestowed it. He wrapped his arms and gave a squeeze and said, "Take care. See you in two weeks." Then it was on to Drew.

"You love her, don't you," Drew asked when they separated. "You're bored with me. Men are so fickle!"

Michael grinned. "One thing I never am with you is bored," he said.

"What a relief," Drew said to Chris after Michael had given one last wave and slipped out of sight down the jetway. "I'm not boring."

"It's true," Chris said. "You're rarely boring."

Drew glared at him. They walked to Chris's gate.

"You don't have to wait," Chris said. "It's getting late. Long drive for you."

"This must be one of my rare boring moments," Drew said. "You're trying to get rid of me. What is it? My haircut? My antiperspirant?"

"Be careful. Say hi to Geoff."

"Geoff," Drew snorted. "Probably won't see him. He'll be hanging around the boys' locker room at Hollywood High."

"Say hi to him anyway."

"I don't really want to go home," Drew said after a moment, during a lull in the flight information that was being read over the loudspeakers.

"You can visit me," Chris said, trying to sound genuine but not too eager.

"I might," Drew said. "It's cold there, though. I wouldn't want to bore you."

They faced each other. At least they should shake hands.

"Well," they said, almost in unison. They swayed and shuffled to let each other know that they had not *absolutely* ruled out a hug but that it was no big deal either way.

"I'd better take off," Drew said.

"Yeah. Okay."

"Don't shovel. You'll have a heart attack."

"I won't."

For an instant Chris thought Drew *was* going to shake his hand, but as he passed he brushed close and gave Chris's arm a little clasp.

"Live long and prosper," Drew said.

"You too."

"Two weeks. Be there."

"Aloha."

Drew walked away. As he did, he raised his right hand and, without looking back, split his fingers into the Vulcan salute. Chris returned the gesture, knowing that Drew, without looking back, knew he had.

YOUNG doctors IN LOVE

Michael's roommate, Joe Zaccardo, wears a gold stud. It glints in his left ear with piratical splendor.

"I like it," Meredith says. "Maybe you should get one."

"I thought they were for if you were gay," Michael says. Is Joe gay? He seems much too tall to be gay. He's never hit on Michael (so far as Michael knows) or any other guy. Then there are all those unfamiliar girls whom Michael has bumped into over the months as they've scuttled into and out of the bathroom on their way to or from Joe's room. Plus Joe is soon to be a surgery resident, and who's ever heard of a gay surgery resident? Joe can't be gay.

"They're not," Meredith says. Her nose wrinkles. "When was the last time you took out the trash?"

Michael looks guiltily and irrelevantly at the sink. "It was Joe's turn," he says. "I don't smell anything."

"Phew!" she says. "It smells like something died in there."

They are standing in the kitchen. She is arranging another load of noshables on a large serving platter: bite-sized ham-and-spinach quiches, Triscuits and Brie, florets of raw cauliflower and broccoli with a spicy mustard-yogurt dip. He is trying to decide which wine is sweetest. They all seem snobbishly dry. When he thinks she isn't looking he pours some 7UP into his glass of chardonnay.

"I saw that," she says, not looking at him.

"I couldn't help it," he says. He takes a slug.

"What *are* we going to do with you?" she says. "I don't see Joe adulterating his wine."

Of course not. Earring or no, Joe is a real man, a surgeon-in-waiting, tall. He is also the birthday boy, star of the small but sassy surprise party Michael and Meredith have staged for him. He gave a gratifying yelp when he came through the front door and switched on the lights and caught his first glimpse of the assembled guests, all of whom were sitting cross-legged on the bare floor (there was no furniture in the living room except a card table erected for the occasion and some pillows and a television) with paper grocery bags over their heads. (This last detail was Michael's idea: "It prolongs the surprise," he reasoned.)

The party was also Michael's idea. He is Joe's roommate and ex-first-year lab partner. He is the beneficiary of Joe's failure to complain about Meredith's frequent and extended stays. At the moment, not counting Meredith, Joe is Michael's best friend. Friction cannot be risked.

Michael has always had a man in his life. Until college— until last month's visit to D.C., in fact—this man was Drew. Drew was the man Michael studied with and identified with. He was another preprofessional who understood what Michael was going through, because he was going through something similar. Michael didn't have to explain. Such a man was necessary. It had to be a man. Women, by virtue of their being sexually attractive, were disqualified. Michael needed that *friendship*, simple but sturdy.

For a couple of years Michael resisted elevating Joe to the number-one position, even though they had gone through the first year of medical school together, were basically inseparable and looked so much alike that people mistook them for brothers. Drew remained a sentimental attachment and a token of a life Michael had enjoyed more than medical school. Drew was still his best friend, really. There was no need to make a ranking.

Then the October visit, which promised to be uneventful but wasn't.

"For your information," Michael says, "Joe carries little packs of sugar in his wallet. Just in case."

"Very funny," she said. "Is there any birthday cake left? I see you smacking your lips."

"I couldn't help it," Michael says. "You weren't looking." This is a lie: There's plenty left. She knows.

"I know," she says. "I saw you. Help me carry this out, will you?"

They are the perfect couple. Everybody thinks so. Everybody likes them, jointly and severally. Even Drew and Dana, Drew's law-school girlfriend, who disapproves of a great many things with tremendous ferocity.

Even Michael can't help wondering if he and Merry truly are perfect. It seems perverse to be searching for proof to the contrary. There is a logic at work. They complement each other in so many ways. She is tall, he is short. She is blond, he is dark. She is Anglo-Saxon, he is Jewish. She is a Southerner, he is a Northerner. They are inevitable.

Still, they hang in limbo. When he starts his radiology residency in a year and a half, will he stay in Chicago? How long will she work for her art museum in Philadelphia? Since he graduated from college they have lived a jetway romance, meeting for a week here, a few days there, talking constantly on the telephone. When she graduated, a year after he did, he half-hoped she would just call up one day and say, I'm at O'Hare, come and get me.

She actually did call one day the first week of August of his second year. She actually was at O'Hare. He picked her up at the airport and they had a late-evening pizza at Lou Malnati's. He wanted to ask her how long she planned to stay, but suddenly it occurred to him that she might say "indefinitely" or "forever" and he wasn't ready for either answer. They talked about other things.

Three days later she got off the phone with her father to announce that there was an art-museum job in Philadelphia. One of the museum's trustees was an old law-school chum of her father's. Next day she was gone. He was relieved and upset at the same time. Now she's back.

The worst thing about being the perfect couple is that there's nowhere to go but down. People aren't interested in hearing the doubts and complaints of a twosome in which they've invested all their fond hopes and expectations that sometimes things *do* work out. Their own personal lives can be and are ruinous and wretched, but the perfect couple's cannot be, because then everyone's is, and the game of life becomes pointless and hopeless.

This is suffocating, especially since Michael has no outlet for frustrations along these lines. Joe has made himself perfectly clear on the question of Meredith. ("If you don't want her, I'll take her." Ha ha.) Meredith might understand, but on the other hand she might get the wrong idea if he brought up the topic. She *really* might get the wrong idea if he brought up Dana, lately the source of most of the unvented pressure.

So there is no exit.

Joe has a nurse in tow: Liz, from the eighth floor. Michael recognizes her as he circulates the plate of hors d'oeuvres. Probably she recognizes him, though no sign is given. They were on the same service over the summer, much of which Meredith spent traveling through Europe with her parents.

"So what do you think of Liz?" Joe asks when he and Michael are alone in a dim corner, far from the madding crowd. "Should I marry her?"

"Come on," Michael says. Even jokes about marriage (and he's not sure Joe is joking) make him uneasy.

"She's a fox," Joe says. He takes a sip of Michael's wine. "God," he says. "It tastes like somebody poured sugar in there."

"I like it," Michael says.

"I'm speaking to Meredith about it," Joe says. "She'll read you the riot act. How about beer? Ah yes," he says, spotting the bottles on the table. "What I like about Liz," Joe continues while popping the top, "so far, is that she's really tough. She's already called me an asshole twice to my face for honking at people."

"You shouldn't honk at people. Everybody's got a gun now, you know," Michael says.

"Right. We know that from the E.R. I know I shouldn't do it but it's just the way I am. They do something stupid, I honk. *Somebody* has to. Anyway, she calls me an asshole and I'm thinking, You're absolutely right, I am."

"Haven't I told you this?" Michael asks.

"Yeah, sure, but it's not the same," Joe says. "It's sort of hot when she says it. You know what I mean? It's hard to explain."

Michael nods in agreement, though Meredith has never called him an asshole or anything else of the kind. Partly this is because he's milder than Joe and doesn't blow a gasket at every red light or abrupt lane change. Partly it's because of Meredith herself. She's never called *Joe* an asshole, even privately to Michael, though Joe has given them more than one white-knuckle honky-honk ride from the airport to the city.

He's never heard her call anyone an asshole. Michael and Meredith, mellow forever.

"What does Sue think?" Michael asks Joe. Sue is another nurse (fourth floor) Joe has seen on and off for a few months.

Joe shrugs. "Haven't seen her," he says. Swig of beer. "I think that's kaput. She wants to move to Seattle anyway. Do you think I'm immature?" he asks. "I mean—you know what I mean. I mean, look at you two. I wish I felt that way about somebody. Maybe I'm really in love with you and just don't know it."

"Come on."

"What if I'm in love with both of you at the same time? Is that possible? I can't handle it. I'll be right back."

He goes off toward the kitchen. Michael can't tell if he's drunk or not. Joe always seems to be in control.

"What was *that* all about?" says a voice. The voice belongs to Liz, whom Michael recognizes when he turns.

"Hi," he says as casually as possible. "How've you been?"

"How've *you* been?"

"Okay."

"Me too. You were surprised to see me."

"I didn't know."

"About me and Joe. We're recent. He tells me I'm the first girl who's called him an asshole to his face. I don't believe it. That's Meredith?" she asks, inclining her head toward a corner of the room where Michael knows Meredith is making everyone feel at home.

He nods.

"I can see why you like her. I'll bet she's not a nurse."

"No."

"You doctors," Liz says. "I don't know why I bother."

"Joe likes you," Michael says.

"Is that what he was telling you?"

"We talked. He's under a lot of pressure lately."

"I forgive you for blowing me off," Liz says.

To Michael it sounds as though she's spoken these words through a megaphone to the entire gathering. He wills himself not to flinch.

"I thought it was you," he says carefully.

"She's not looking," Liz says. "She can't hear me. Don't worry. Maybe it was mutual."

"Whatever," Michael says, meeting her eyes. "It's okay."

She nods. "I'm going to go find him," she says. "I just wanted to tell you."

"Okay."

In a moment, just as he is relaxing again, there is a tug at his elbow.

"All roads lead to Rome," Meredith says. *"Buon giorno."*

"That was Liz," Michael says. "She came with Joe."

"I know," Meredith says. "She introduced herself while you and Joe were talking. She reminds me of Dana, a little."

"Drew's Dana?"

"They have the same nose and mouth, don't you think? And they're both sort of blunt."

"I guess. Joe says she's tough."

"Joe needs tough. *Joe's* tough. Putting up with a doctor is a full-time job."

Michael feels small. "Am I being criticized?"

"I'm tough," Meredith says. "You have noticed, haven't you? Have we talked to Joe yet about you-know-what?"

"Not yet. He did most of the talking."

"Maybe I should."

"No," Michael says firmly. "I'll do it. It won't be a problem."

Before midnight a gaggle of law students crash the party and finish off the last of the food and drink. By twelve-thirty the guests and interlopers have fled and the apartment is empty except for Meredith and Michael and Joe. Liz was one of the last to go, leaving on the arm of a woman who had shown up at the same time as, but not with, the law students, though this distinction was not immediately apparent in the hubbub.

"That was Annie," Joe explains. "Her roommate."

"Also a nurse," Michael explains to Meredith.

"They have to go in early tomorrow," Joe adds.

"Since when has Annie been hanging around with law students?" Michael asks.

"I don't think she is," Joe says. "Liz had called her for a ride and I think she just showed up at the wrong moment. Now everybody hates her because they think she's friends with law students."

Joe settles himself on one of the pillows near the TV set, which is tuned to WGN but is muted. An old Western in black and white flickers on the oversize screen.

"So you two have me all to yourselves tonight," Joe says, draining the last of his bottle of beer.

"You're not going in early tomorrow, are you?" Michael says. "It's Saturday."

"No," Joe says, "not until seven. Autopsy."

"Sheesh," Michael says.

"He's getting soft," Joe says to Meredith. "Keep an eye on him."

"Constantly," she says.

"So you both met Liz," Joe continues. "You already knew her, though, didn't you, Doctor?"

"She was on my service in August."

"She seemed very nice," Meredith says.

Joe laughs and bangs a fist on one of his knees. "Nice!" he says. "Yeah. She bites the heads off nails. I love it."

"Some guys go for that sort of thing," Michael says. "It's perfectly normal. Nothing to worry about."

"Will you come to the wedding?" Joe asks.

"Sure," Michael says. "We'll bring a box of nails."

"Then again, she is a whore," Joe says. "Half the guys in the hospital have slept with her."

"How do you know that?" Meredith asks. She sounds completely calm, curious in a detached way, but Michael can tell she's pissed off about the word "whore."

"She's told me," Joe says. "They've told me."

" 'Whore' seems a little strong," Meredith says in a moderate tone. "She's not doing all this alone, don't forget."

"Are you interested in your present?" Michael asks. "We got you a present. Meredith wrapped it."

"I like presents," Joe says.

"First you have to tell us how you like being twenty-eight," Meredith says. "Some of us are thinking about turning twenty-eight."

"We decided to let you go first," Michael adds.

"Liz is thirty," Joe says, a little hazily. "I don't usually go for older women. The thing is," he continues, focusing his attention on Michael and Merry once again, "twenty-eight, it's not *that* old, but, you know. Look at you two. How do you do it?"

"We're perfect and have no flaws," Meredith says. "Right, champ?"

"I know *that*," Joe says.

"It's just that simple," Michael says. "Be perfect and have no flaws and life will be a bed of roses."

"It's really something to see how you guys have stuck together," Joe says. "I really mean that. All these years in different cities. Most people don't last very long in the same city."

"Better get the present," Meredith says to Michael. He nods and gets up and starts toward the back bedroom.

"Will you marry me?" Joe asks Meredith while they wait. "Remember, I asked first."

"How do you know?" she says, but with a smile.

"I don't," he says. "I'm just hoping out loud."

"I like this place," she says.

"Yeah. It's okay. It's close to the el and Ann Sather's. We're addicted to Ann Sather's cinnamon rolls. So will you?"

"I'm thinking."

"Don't think. Then you'll say no. My hours will be hell and I'll have affairs with lots of different women."

"So *you're* a whore," Meredith says.

"I'm a normal male person," Joe says cheerfully. "We can do whatever we want."

"What are you two talking about?" Michael asks. In his hands he holds a carefully wrapped package of vaguely cylindrical shape.

"Joe's proposed," Meredith reports. "While I weigh the proposal, I make the counterproposal that I live here awhile to see how things work out."

"This is for you," Michael says to Joe. He hands him the package. "It's a lifetime supply of Grecian Formula."

"Thanks," Joe says. "I was wondering. You don't mind if I marry her, do you?"

"Not at all," Michael says. "Why would I mind?"

"Because I'll keep sleeping with you, too. That way everybody'll be happy. She does know about us, right? You have told her?"

"Sure," Michael says. "I tell her everything. Besides, the earring is a dead giveaway."

"I thought so," Joe says. "I couldn't remember if you're supposed to wear it in the right ear or the left. I read about it in Ann Landers once."

He rips the paper open to reveal a box of Godiva chocolates and, taped to the side, a little pouch labeled ONE-NIGHT STAND KIT. Immediately Joe opens the kit and produces a small vibrator, a pack of condoms with ribbing and reservoir tips, and several flavors of lubricating jelly.

"Now you have to marry me," Joe says to Meredith. "Look what I've got."

"I hope everything's the right size," Michael says. "We didn't have all your measurements."

"I still think we should live together first," Meredith says. "There's plenty of room here, don't you think?"

"Only one bathroom," Joe says. "Of course, Mike and I never shower, and we can always piss off the deck. Like we did last weekend, remember?" he says to Michael. "Or maybe you don't."

"I wasn't even in town," Michael says.

"Anyway, I did," Joe says. "It can be done. Another bathroom would be nice, though. What am I going to tell Liz? Maybe you can go out with her," he says to Michael.

"I don't think so."

"The bathroom is not a fatal problem," Meredith says. "We'll all just have to be careful."

"She means flush for a change," Michael advises Joe.

"Are you really coming to live here?" Joe asks.

"I think so," Meredith says. "If it's okay with you."

"My God," Joe says. "Wild. We can all see each other naked. We'll get a see-through shower curtain."

"You're sure you won't mind sleeping in the broom closet?" Michael says to Joe.

"Not if you're there with me," Joe says.

"You two," Meredith says.

During cleanup, while Michael lugs bags of trash down three flights of narrow, dark, uneven stairs, Joe puts a battery in his new vibrator and turns it on. It gives a low hum. He presses it against the upper arm of Meredith, who is standing at the sink washing glasses in soapy water. She gives a little shriek, and suds fly.

"Oh!" she says. She looks at the vibrator, which Joe turns off. "I really should chew you out for doing that, but since it's a gift we gave you jointly, I really can't, can I?"

"Was it good for you?" Joe asks.

"It was fine," Meredith says. "Just never do it again."

"Sorry," Joe says. "Don't want to get the new roomie p.o.'d before her time. I think it's cool you're coming here. I really do. You'll love Chicago. It's a great city with a great climate. And don't worry about Mike and me. We're real discreet and hardly anybody knows."

"Very discreet, I can certainly believe that."

"You don't mind group sex, do you? I knew you wouldn't. I told Mike everything would be fine."

"Did you," Meredith says faintly.

"Sure. Because you're cool. I was talking to Liz about this the other night and she was getting really crazy about it, like, why would we be interested in this. I told her, because it's fun, which it is. Maybe it's a guy thing. Hey, Mike," Joe says to Michael, who has just trudged up the stairs to fetch another load of trash, "Meredith wants to have group sex."

"You know me," Meredith says.

"Maybe I should put Joe out with the trash," Michael says.

"Whatever," Joe says. "As long as I'm ready to go at six-thirty a.m. sharp."

"He reminds me of Drew, in some ways," Meredith says later, in the dark. "Isn't that funny? He reminds me of Drew, and Liz reminds me of Dana. I guess that means Drew and Dana have been on my mind."

"I told you Joe could be lippy."

"Oh, he's harmless," Meredith says.

"Did he really propose?"

"I hope not," Meredith says. "I'm not ready for that, I'm pretty sure."

"I hope not too," Michael says. "I hope you said no," he adds more cautiously. "There are other voices to be heard."

"Yes," she says. She licks one of his nipples. It tickles, and he laughs. Can Joe hear?

"Joe's lonely," Meredith says. "He's afraid he's not going to find someone."

"He shouldn't be lonely," Michael says. "He's tall, dark and handsome. And soon to make scads of money. I mean, surgeons. Come on."

"It's not so simple," Meredith says. "Just going in to watch an autopsy at seven on a Saturday morning in November—think about that for a minute. You'd have to be a pretty special kind of person to put up with that."

"We've never fooled around, him and me," Michael says, whisking the sentence in one piece past the lump in his throat. "I wasn't seriously worried."

"It's just that I've never heard him talk quite like that."

"It's his way of saying he wants to be a part of something," Meredith says. "It's his way of telling us he wishes he had something like what we have."

"It's an original way of telling," Michael says.

"He's original."

For a while they lie there in the quiet dark. He is thinking about Drew and Dana, Liz and Joe, oh what a tangled web he has woven. It keeps him up nights. Drew will never find out. Dana won't tell. It will be as though it never happened. He is pretty sure Meredith has gone to sleep under her landslide of pillows, but then she speaks.

"*Have* you ever messed around with another guy?" she asks.

"Once," he says. "Okay?"

"I'm curious," she says. "I'm always in search of your secrets. Tell me about it. I'll bet you've never told anyone. I'll bet you've never told Drew or Chris or Joe."

Of course she is right, but he doesn't feel like admitting it.

"I was fifteen," he says. "At summer camp. There were a bunch of us in a cabin for a week. Our cabin counselor was this older guy—Ralph. Seventeen, I think. I slept on a bottom bunk. He had a regular bed right across from mine. The kid above me got food poisoning the first day and went home in an ambulance. So at night Ralph would ... you know. And I had eyes and ears, and one night he just whispered, Come on over, so I did."

"What was it like?" she asks.

"I didn't like it, if that's what you're asking."

"You're supposed to say that," Meredith says.

"You're right," he says. "It was actually okay. During the day we pretended that nothing was happening, but we did it about five nights in a row."

"That's sweet, really," she says. "Innocent."

"We didn't think we were innocent," Michael says. "I'm pretty sure he wasn't. He knew what he was doing. I was scared for months I was going to turn out to be a faggot. Then DeeDee Kaplow gave me a blow job in her basement while her parents were upstairs watching *Charlie's Angels.*"

"Now I know two secrets I didn't know before," Meredith says. "DeeDee Kaplow and Ralph."

"They're probably married somewhere," Michael says. "I'm tired, aren't you?"

"Sort of."

They drift.

Deep in the orange city night the sugary chardonnay pools, and Michael treks bleary-eyed and naked to the toilet, where he finds release with the lights off. He is not quite sure if he's awake or asleep and dreaming. Will he awaken from this inky pleasantness to find himself afloat in a sea of warm piss and a vexed Meredith alongside?

Behind him, the shower stall. It should be empty, but he senses a presence. It can't be Dana, because she's in Washington, D.C., in Drew's arms and bed. He turns his head to check it out, just to make sure, and in the doorway there is a shadowy presence. He starts. The presence speaks.

"Sorry," Joe says. He isn't seeing much, either.

"It's you," Michael says.

Joe flips on the light, and they both squint.

"Nice ass," Joe says. "You sleep naked. I'm telling your mom." He rolls down the elastic band at the front of his Jockey shorts. A moment later, the water flows. "I do too, usually. But, you know, mixed company and all that. I guess this wouldn't be something you'd have to worry about."

"I don't want you telling my mother."

"If Merry's really going to live here, you have to tell her that there is some risk of seeing all of me at some point."

"You really don't mind?"

"No," Joe says. "I'm an exhibitionist. You mean her being here? No. It gives me a good excuse to stay at Liz's." He finishes and snaps everything back into place.

"Right," Michael says.

"Liz seemed to have a lot to say to you."

"Not much," Michael says. "We talked about you."

"I'll bet," Joe says. "And we talk about you. Two."

"So we're even."

There is a moment of silence. Michael stands there looking down at his dick, which has run dry. It looks shriveled and vulnerable and woeful. He prays to God Joe doesn't think so.

"You know what I'm wondering," Joe says.

"Not really."

"Come on."

Michael flushes.

"It's three in the morning," Joe says. "I'm thinking. Liz. Eighth floor. August. Meredith far far away. Liz a tramp, let's speak frankly. You have the face of an angel, I admit it."

"What are you saying?" Michael asks.

"I know you can't be *this* innocent," Joe says. "I'm just wondering. Just out of curiosity. You know. I mean, stuff happens. You're not married, you're not engaged. Liz obviously goes for this certain look. Do I have to draw a map?"

There is another moment of silence in which water flows into the toilet tank. Michael feels trapped, like a deer caught in oncoming headlights. Just a few more seconds and splat. Joe stands between him and the door, foreclosing the possibility of easy escape. Mixed with the urge to flee is another: to tell.

"You're asking if I slept with Liz," Michael hears himself saying.

"Well," Joe says, shuffling a foot, "yeah."

"What does she say?"

"I can't ask her that!" Joe nearly exclaims in a voice still hoarse with sleepiness, but still loud enough, Michael supposes, to be heard by preternaturally perceptive Meredith.

"Let's get out of here," Michael says. He switches off the light. "It doesn't look good."

They move in train to the darkened living room, which is still redolent of festival. Michael squats on a pillow. Joe reclines on another. There is dim light from the streetlamps outside the bay windows—an eerie glow that twitches and shifts on the white walls as a cold autumn wind rattles the bare tree branches. The radiators crackle and hiss.

"She didn't tell you anything," Michael says.

"No," Joe says, "scout's honor. What could she tell me?"

"Why do you want to know this?"

"I'm not sure," Joe admits. "I'm sick of these, excuse me." He lifts his hips and peels off the briefs. "There. Free at last. Now we're even."

"This could look a little strange," Michael says.

"Don't care," Joe says. "We know we're not fags. I can't decide if I want you to be perfect, or if I want you just to seem perfect and secretly be flawed like the rest of us."

"You don't really think I'm perfect," Michael says. "No one's perfect."

"No one's perfect," Joe says, "true. But I wouldn't bet the farm."

"I'm doing rays instead of surgery. My parents think that makes me imperfect."

"And you sleep in the nude and jack off every morning before you get out of bed. Big deal. None of that little shit counts."

"I did sleep with her," Michael says. "See? I'm not perfect. I am so not perfect."

"Wow," Joe says in a tone that seems to Michael to be nearly reverential.

"It just happened," Michael continues. "She just came on to me one day after work and it just happened."

"Does Meredith know?"

"Are you crazy?" Michael says. He doesn't want to mention that Meredith seems to know everything about him. He knows she can't and doesn't, but he is afraid that even bringing the subject up will make it seem less implausible and therefore closer to being true.

"You think she'd flip."

Michael nods. Joe nods with him in sympathetic vibration.

"Was it good?" Joe asks, in a whisper Michael can barely hear.

Michael keeps nodding, but he's not thinking about Liz now; he's thinking about Dana and how much he wants to tell Joe about her, too. Liz doesn't really count, nor do any of the others. In his moral calculus there is a difference between simple romping and feeling something for someone. He has tried to be careful about that. He tried to be careful about it with Dana, but he was caught unawares and thrown off balance by her violent desire, and everything has been out of control since. He is burning up from the inside, and no one can help him.

"She is hot," Joe agrees, on the matter of Liz in the sack.

"It's over," Michael says. "It was never really anything. You know what I mean? It was physical."

"You're saying it had nothing to do with Merry."

Michael nods. "Exactly. That's exactly right."

"But you don't think Merry would see it that way."

Michael shakes his head.

Joe's next question hangs in the air between them, unspoken: Tell me more. Tell me about the others.

"I'm really wrecked," Michael says. "Have to get to sleep. Are you really going in at seven?"

"I'm dedicated," Joe says. "What can I say? You get along to bed. I'm going to hang around the bathroom and see if something else interesting happens."

"Please don't," Michael says. "It doesn't look right." He is afraid Joe and Meredith will bump into each other.

"Relax," Joe says. "These lips are sealed."

"I couldn't have told anyone else," Michael says.

"It's not that big a deal," Joe says. "It happens. Life goes on."

"It just seems weird, you know, that this happened, and now you're seeing her. It's like, me and your girlfriend, even though she wasn't at the time. What does that make us?"

Joe shrugs. "We'll break up sooner or later anyway, so we'll both be Liz rejects. She dumped you, right?"

"I can't remember," Michael says. "It got very weird."

"Whatever," Joe says. "I always take a long hot shower afterwards so I'm not worried."

"I'm going to bed," Michael says again.

"If you're interested in going in with me in the morning . . ."

"I'll think about it."

"Right. Well, then, I'll see you at dinner, maybe."

"Deal. Moti Mahal."

"Tandoori chicken, sag paneer."

"Okay," Michael says. "Sounds good."

"And one last thing," Joe says. "*Great* glutes."

"Fuck you."

"You ought to be in pictures."

"All you surgeons are psychopaths," Michael says. "Flush before you leave in the morning."

"As if you had to ask."

They go their separate ways. Michael, padding down the corridor toward the back of the apartment, hears Joe's door click lightly shut. His own door opens with a squeak, and he slips inside. By the faint blue light of the digital clock he makes his way to the bed and lies down beside her. She seems to be in a deep sleep, her breathing slow and regular. He is certain that the last twenty minutes with Joe belong to Joe and him alone.

But even so, the pressure remains. The heart of the secret remains inside him. As he lies there in the dark next to her he hears it beating in his chest, alongside his own heart, growing bigger and bigger.

l'affaire CARL

Carl is the first man Chris has enjoyed getting fucked by.
Who knows this, other than Carl? Not David, who is pretty
much in a constant state of hysterical self-pity these days
(*Can't we at least be friends*—*he* what?); certainly not Chaz and
the rest of the gang from college—lately discovered as fellow
postgrad migrants to the city—who dart around like a school
of pretty neon tetras, bar to bar, Endup to Troc to Alta Plaza
to the Balcony. Then everyone would know, and it is none of
their business.

Older men have come to hold a certain attraction Chris
had not anticipated when he was taking his first tentative steps
into the queer new world where destiny seemed to have deposited him. The fresh freshman face of Wade, whose doubts and
insecurities were even more profound than his own, was irresistible at first; to be with him was to take a vicarious loop
back through the wasteland of his own adolescence, with the

comfort of knowing that, whatever happened, he would never have to be a completely confused eighteen-year-old again.

The young are unstable, jittery, fickle, critically ill with their own youth; Chris has never considered himself one of their number, even if the count of years says otherwise. Inside he has always felt older and more sober than his peers; he is drawn to the world of adults. That, he thinks, is where he belongs—among people who have an idea who they are and where they are going. Their world, with its fixed points, is navigable.

So far he has not hit upon a way to tell all this to David without seeming to condescend not only to him but to his own past selves (especially the one that got involved with David in the first place). They are, after all, the same age, the same class. How do you say, Classmate, peer, I find you callow? I want someone with a rough beard and a mustache and a good job. I like men, not boys, no offense.

Facial hair represents everything Chris believes he is looking for. Desperately seeking mustache: the stability of tomorrow and the day after. He has even come to find mustaches sexy in themselves, a glimpse of what lies below the belt, another sexual tool to be skillfully deployed.

(Chaz is always shrieking about the horrors of clones; Chris can already hear him shrieking about Carl.)

Most of the few men he's slept with since he started making his forty-five-minute voyages into San Francisco have been clones, with, by definition, mustaches. David is the glaring exception—clean-shaven David, with whom the sex was glaringly unexceptional. The connection is obvious to Chris, but not to David, who has been whining furiously since the demise of whatever there was between them. (David insists on describing it as "our relationship"; Chris thinks of it as a "fling" but is willing to compromise on "affair.")

Today is Carl's thirty-third birthday; tomorrow is their three-month anniversary—reckoning from the party at which

they met, not the first time they slept together, which techni-
cally was a day later, and including the two weeks' hesitation.
If Chris had the money he would commission a fireworks display and a champagne brunch for thousands in Golden Gate
Park; then *everyone* would know, Chaz and the gang included.
They are bound to find out eventually, anyway, if they don't already suspect. Sooner or later everyone knows everything
worth knowing about everyone else. The whole party saw the
two of them trick out.

But the budget is $25, or maybe a little more. That will
buy a big tub of flavored Lube and a dildo from Jaguar Books
(returnable, if he already has one Chris doesn't yet know
about) and a little something *leather*, along with a card featur-
ing naked men and a pizza at Marcello's or the Sausage Fac-
tory. Someday, when his career as a technical writer for the
genetic-engineering firm on the Peninsula rockets him to fame
and glory and riches, he will buy the fireworks.

A curious development of their sex life (curious, at any
rate, to Chris, who absorbed from Drew a certain fondness for
categories): He has begun occasionally, but more and more fre-
quently, to fuck Carl. The first time Carl rolled onto his back
and guided Chris between his legs he wasn't sure quite what
was happening, what to do; but the deed itself crackled with
the upside-down thrill of inversion and role reversal. It was
like wearing lace panties, Chris imagined; it was, in a way, like
getting fucked. He finds himself liking the new arrangements.

Carl, to Chris's surprise, has seemed equally pleased.
Maybe he is glad that the burden of performing, the weight of
having to be in charge, is sometimes lifted from his muscular
shoulders. In those first days and weeks all he did was lead
the way while Chris followed. Now they are more nearly equal,
and Chris cannot help thinking—when Carl's burly body is
squirming beneath him, subject to his control—that he has become more of a man than he ever expected to.

·   ·   ·

Chris's first solo foray into gay San Francisco, late in the summer that began with the temblor of graduation, took him to the Midnight Sun, where the first face that caught his eye was a shockingly familiar one. He ordered a beer and looked the other way.

For graduation his parents had bought him a car—a four-year-old Accord with a manual transmission, which it took him some time to figure out how to shift without stalling the engine. The first benefit of the car was that he was able to get to his job. The second was that it gave him social freedom, which he was glad to have even if he didn't exactly know what to do with it. All revved up, don't know where to go.

The face belonged to David Rice, although Chris needed a few moments of desperate memory-searching and a few more sips of beer to recall the name. He was Katherine-from-freshman-English's friend, and he kept looking in Chris's direction. Chris could feel the laser burn of David's glance on the side of his neck and the back of his head. As carefully as he could he made for the safety of the wall, eyes fixed on the video screen overhead.

Chris had been in one San Francisco gay bar before (with other people, dancing; there was safety in numbers and movement) and in the vicinity of Castro Street gay bars, but never *in* a Castro Street gay bar. It had taken him forty-five minutes just to find Castro Street, another ten to park the car, still another ten to make up his mind about which bar to go into and work up the nerve to do it. Badlands was too dark and smoky. There was a line in front of the Sun (meaning: time to reconsider), leading to an open door from which emanated the friendly sounds of a Hall & Oates song he had heard on the radio. A line, Chris thought, must mean it's popular. Not without feeling slightly like a Muscovite joining the queue for whatever item happened to be available that day, he took up station at the rear.

No matter that he was in San Francisco, anonymous and

alone, pondering the complete freedom it was his to exercise (until his contact lenses told him it was time to drive home): The specter of Drew still hung heavy. College itself might be a memory, a gilded galleon the tip of whose mainmast was just now dipping below the horizon astern, but Drew remained burningly alive, an issue unresolved, a feeling unspoken, a truth unexpressed.

This was the truth: Chris was totally, completely in love with Drew—still, despite the hundreds or thousands of miles that now separated them (was Drew still in L.A., or off for his year of life in Munich before law school?), despite the basic impossibility of things. The night after they graduated, when the world of college went dark forever with the abruptness of a light being switched off, they cried like babies in each other's arms.

He stood by himself in the Midnight Sun, thinking about that moment to keep himself from thinking about David and whether he, too, had made the connection. Chris hoped not, but halfway through his second beer and in the middle of a Joan Rivers clip about San Francisco's being so gay that even the traffic lights were pastels, the inevitable happened. There was a tap on his shoulder, and a voice said, "I know you." Chris swung his head around, trying to look pleasantly surprised instead of mortified. They shook hands and made what chat they could in the bar's din; after not too many moments David made the inevitable proposal. *My place . . . drink . . . if you want to.*

Chris had had sex before, but even with Wade it had been, after the thrill of anticipation and the shedding of the first few outer garments, disappointing. He hadn't really been in love with Wade or any of his handful of other partners (he was convinced that this was a far larger element of the problem than was really the case), and he found it impossible not to be self-conscious about his inept fumblings and thrustings. Maybe it would be different with David; Chris had been fascinated by him—although not enough to do anything about it—ever since Meredith's party. That was already almost two years ago. Anyway Chris was too shy to say no.

"Okay."

David's body, revealed after brief preliminaries, turned out to be a miracle: bigger than the others, more muscular, long and white, the skin so soft and smooth and warm that the mere touch of it amazed Chris; he ran his hands along the trim flanks as though he were a blind man. The dark hair on top of the head was thick and short, the shadow of a one-day growth of beard more pronounced in the dim light. Pecs that had been worked on, worked on, worked on rose gently, hard and lightly thatched with hair; he ran his hands down to the flat belly and a darker, more substantial trail. On down. Ground zero; its rich perfume made him queasy with desire. The sturdy legs were arcs of muscle wrapped in a ghostly mat of fleece.

Eventually, after an hour of out-of-sync messing around, they came; then Chris was depressed. David, instead of dozing off like a decent person, became even more insistent and passionate, wanting to try something new before even a fraction of a proper interval had passed, but the harder he tried the less interested Chris was in him. Yes, this is a gorgeous guy, he told himself, but . . . But what? He was mystified by his detachment from a body and a general aura so like Drew's—what had attracted him to David in the first place, he realized with a start. It all became clear in the darkness. How could he not have seen it before? Drew was blond, but they could have been brothers. (Except Drew already had a brother.)

"What's wrong?" David whispered.

"Nothing," Chris whispered back, trying not to be annoyed that David could ask such a question within seconds of their having exhausted themselves all over everything.

"You seem far away."

"I'm right here."

"I'm glad," David said. "I've wanted this to happen for a

long time, but I never thought it would. I was kind of surprised to see you tonight. At the Sun, I mean."

Chris nodded, thinking about Drew, about how David, in the end, wasn't Drew, wasn't even close. What was the point of being here? He didn't love David and he never would; he didn't even believe David loved him, although there was an appalling note of coo creeping into his words.

Love, being in, is the issue with Carl: Are they or aren't they? It shouldn't be such a difficult question to answer, Chris thinks as he walks toward Carl's flat on Twentieth Street. Yes or No. Chris is prepared to give *his* answer.

If you can't say it, can you be in it, or be it? What are they to each other? *(Lovers?)* After three months a relationship, if it is to live, must be evolving into something, growing and changing, becoming better and deeper. The last thing he wants to hear—the fear of which has kept in check his urge to force Carl to talk about the two of them—is a kind and gentle statement that they are friends and fuckbuddies, but not lovers. That would mean Carl has not seen and heard and felt the bond between them the same way Chris has. That he has missed the point.

Chris knows he is in love with Carl, totally and completely, and he is not afraid to say it if he gets a chance. He knows because he no longer thinks about Drew during sex, or after; when he does think of Drew it is with the comfortable warmth with which one regards old, dear, irrelevant friends. It is Carl who obsesses him, Carl upon whom the stream of Chris's romantic energy is now showered, Carl who has become the center of his life even if he's being coy about it.

One tiny step in the right direction was Carl's surprise presentation to him two weeks ago, unprompted, of a key to the apartment.

"For your very own," he said in a lighthearted tone that warned, Don't take it too seriously; but Chris was exhilarated anyway and immediately put himself in charge of locking and unlocking the door whenever they were going out or coming back.

But a key does not a kingdom make, or even a household. That, after all, is at least a plausible goal—cohabitation—although even Chris, filled with an exuberance he did not know he possessed before he met Carl and something actually worked out for a while, hesitates a bit at the momentousness of it. Living together. Every time he leaves Carl and Carl's and makes the drive home down the freeway, he is torn between the urge to press the relationship to the limits of what it will bear, and to be satisfied with what they already have and with the incremental progress they're making into whatever future awaits them.

Friday evening. Carl won't be expecting him for a while because Chris didn't tell him he was taking the afternoon off to come to the city for the birthday shopping. The weather is clear and mild for July, the bank of ocean fog quiescent off the beaches beyond Twin Peaks. As he works the key in the lock he hears voices and laughter coming from the living room, and he feels a knot tighten in his stomach.

It's not that he suspects Carl of trashing around when he has the chance, or that he suspects every male friend of Carl's of being an ex, a smoldering wick ready to burst into flames once again without notice, like one of those trick birthday candles. Full-blown sexual paranoia hasn't struck him yet.

But he is still jealous and suspicious of Carl's friends—that group of men older than he is who've known Carl longer than he has, who sometimes seem to treat Chris as an odd fancy in their friend's life, a passing distraction. That is the message he reads from their bantering condescension: We will still be here, with Carl, while you are back trolling the bars, you vanilla twinkie munchkin.

There are only two of them, thank God, Chris notes as the door swings open and he quickly surveys the living room.

Bruce and Martin, who are said to be lovers, sit on the couch together. Carl is sitting in a chair across from them.

"Hi," Chris says, shifting the packages so he can close the door. "You've got company."

"It's the kid," Martin says. "Bearing gifts."

"Anything for us, doll?" Bruce says, reaching into his shirt pocket for a cigarette.

"You're early," Carl says, standing to greet him. "Very. Did you soar on wings of gossamer?" They kiss lightly on the lips, and for an instant Chris feels less alien.

"Sorry," he says. "I had some errands to run. I guess I should have called."

Bruce looks at him, eyebrows raised in a campy but mute invitation. Martin supplies the sound.

"Does he give good call?" he says to Carl in a throaty, breathless voice before bursting into a low chuckle. Carl smiles but says nothing. Chris doesn't know what to say.

"Maybe we should leave the loverboys alone," Bruce says to Martin in a stage whisper. "They seem to be *enraptured.*"

"Will we see you later tonight, doll?" Martin says to Carl. "We're paying, don't forget. It's your present."

"Bring the kid, too," Bruce adds, blowing smoke out the side of his mouth in Chris's direction. "On the house."

"We'll see," Carl says.

"Oh, honeybun, that's old-girl talk," Martin says. "We'll see! You're still in your *prime.*"

"USDA *Choice,*" Bruce says.

After they are gone, Chris asks, "Why do they call me the kid?" He means to make Carl defend the indefensible moniker, make him feel uncomfortable enough about it that he will ask them not to use it anymore.

"Why do you think?" Carl says. "You're young, they're not. It's a compliment, really."

"I don't like it."

"They're just jealous," Carl says, putting a hand on each

of Chris's shoulders and blowing the hair back from his forehead. "You're beautiful."

"What's happening later tonight?" Chris asks, following
Carl into the toilet and standing behind him while he pees.
"That they were talking about paying for?"

"Mmmm," murmurs Carl.

"Tell me," Chris says, sticking his tongue into Carl's ear
and tickling his underarms, which he knows to be sensitive.
Carl convulses. "Ve haf vays."

"You do."

Not the baths, please, Chris is thinking. I won't go even
if they do pay, please not there. The baths represent what he
most dislikes about gay life: anonymous, promiscuous sex with
people for whom you feel nothing, while, in a little office somewhere above the cubicles and lockers and showers and
steamroom, an accountant with a green eyeshade hunches over
the books, calculating the profit of sex as industry.

They fool around for a while on the sofa in the living
room, under the Miró print. Chris is hot for it; the sex eases his
jealousy, his apprehension about what the night will bring. He
wishes that the two of them were the only people in the world,
that no matter where they went, no matter what time it was, the
phone would not ring, friends of Carl's would not invite them
to things or invite themselves along on expeditions meant for
just the two of them. He knows this is nothing more than a fantasy but can't help indulging it.

"You still haven't told me," he says during a break in the
action.

"Told you what?"

"What's on for tonight."

"I thought you were taking me out for rack of lamb at
Fournou's Ovens."

"Pizza at Marcello's. After that. What Bruce and Martin
were talking about."

"Oh, that."

"Yes, *that.*"

"You won't like it."

It *is* the baths.

"Try me."

"They're going to the Troc," Carl says.

"Are we?"

Carl shrugs. "They said they'd pay. If you want to."

"What if I don't?"

"We'll see."

Chris's aversion to Trocadero and the city's other dance pal-
aces, bars and assorted loci of gay nightlife is rooted in his belief that nothing good (which means, to him, nothing durable)
can come from them. They lie in the realm of drugs and drinking, smoking and sex, till-the-dawn dancing and endless taxi
rides to strangers' apartments.

Although he isn't much fonder of parties—which are organized around essentially the same principles but enjoy the
virtue of being, for the most part, private rather than public,
and better lighted—he has been forced to take his harsh position under reconsideration by dint of the fact that he met Carl
at a party.

And such a party.

"You'll love it," David insisted, the eagerness in his voice
betraying the hope that at this party Chris would finally soften
and their relationship/fling/affair would return from the dead.
Why he thought this, Chris could not understand. Chris said
yes, even so.

"Great!" David had said, sounding like a fourteen-year-
old who has just committed glorious suicide by asking out the
prettiest girl in the class, only to hear her accept.

Chris's reasons for agreeing to go to the party with David
had nothing to do with David, other than the fact that David's
presence would protect him from the stigma of being alone in
an unfamiliar crowd; David could introduce him to people. The

main reason was simple curiosity: This was a college-family party, for alumni (mostly young), staff and, with any luck, students. Chris couldn't help thinking that at such a gathering the odds of meeting someone worthwhile would be considerably enhanced.

It didn't take Chris and Carl long to catch one another's eye. Their paths crossed at the giant bowl of guacamole, where Carl introduced himself and said, "I don't usually like guacamole, but this looks yummy." Chris nodded, trying not to stare at Carl's small, perfectly straight teeth, which, under his thick dark mustache, seemed brilliantly white. "Yummy" was not a word Chris had heard grown men use; Carl's saying it arrested his attention. He felt a sudden surge of physical attraction and felt, too, that Carl was attracted to him. He didn't care that Carl had nothing to do with the school he was still so attached to; that he had been brought to the party by a staffer (whose pedigree was therefore equally suspect). When Carl asked him if he wanted to walk the three blocks to Polk Street for ice cream, Chris was barely listening. He would have agreed to anything. David's furious face flared briefly in the fog that now flowed around them, but it quickly disappeared. They said goodbye to the host, who, resplendent in a black tux with fuchsia bow tie, was kissing people at the door as they came and went, and were off.

Two weeks later, it was Chris whose face was a screech of fury and anger and humiliation. He had let himself be *rimmed* and *fucked* by a complete stranger who, after making him toast the next morning, taking a shower with him and kissing him goodbye, promptly refused to return his calls, respond to his notes (even those he drove all the way into the city to place, along with bags of fresh doughnuts, on Carl's windshield) or in any way acknowledge that he existed. It was as though *it* had not happened, as though nothing had happened.

In desperation and lust, not knowing where else to turn, Chris turned and returned to the Midnight Sun, where the hours disappeared as if eaten by acid. He drove to the city one, two, three nights in a row to stand under the video screens; he felt like an addict.

One night, two weeks and a day from the night they met, Carl was there, too. They both looked away, pretending not to have seen each other. Carl was with some other people; Chris was determined not to retreat. He bought beer and watched the video and laughed and drank and talked to the boy standing next to him (quite attractive, Chris thought, the tide of his emotions sloshing noisily in a new direction), getting more and more ripped. However embarrassing his performance, he was determined to make Carl see it.

By the time Carl stuck a finger into his back and said, "Draw, Sheriff," he was far enough gone to think for a moment that the police were actually raiding the bar and sticking guns in people's backs. He reached behind for the pocket where he kept his now-half-empty wallet and his driver's license, and found his hand brushing, not a gun, but a finger that was attached to the rest of warm Carl. He blushed, sighed a short "Hi," and turned away.

"How've you been?"

"Okay," Chris said, nodding, half-looking.

"I got your notes."

"Oh."

"And the doughnuts. They were sweet. The notes and the doughnuts. Both. I ate the doughnuts. I hope that was all right. I didn't know what to say."

"You could have said *something*," Chris said, turning away as he said it, lowering his voice, feeling self-righteous but fearing confrontation. He wished Drew were there to say something really snotty and awful.

"I didn't mean to hurt your feelings," Carl said. "If I did. I guess I did. Yeah. I just got the feeling that maybe we were looking for different things."

"What are you looking for?" Chris asked.

"A new job," Carl said with a low laugh, which Chris did not join. "Sorry. You're so serious! We had fun. We liked each other."

Chris nodded.

"Maybe you'd like to go get something to eat?" Carl said. "I'm kind of hungry. We can talk a little. It's hard to have a conversation in here."

Chris nodded again. "Okay," he said, against his better judgment.

"Back in a minute. Have to say so long to some people."

Chris didn't expect him to come back, but he did.

Carl came from Iowa. His family lived on a farm near a village of a few hundred people; Des Moines lay two hours away, north by northwest across the cornfields. The farm had been in the family for four generations, and, despite Carl's living in San Francisco, it would pass, in the person of his younger brother—married, with children—to at least a fifth.

At age eighteen Carl went off to Iowa City for college. His parents, though unschooled, were prosperous, and they believed in the value of education. They did not balk, at any rate not openly, at their eldest son's going away to school, or his announcement, four years later, that he had decided to go to business school in Los Angeles. That was the way you got ahead in the world, and Carl was too restless and ambitious not to try.

Gilded with the M.B.A. and the glory of being twenty-five, he came north to San Francisco almost immediately after graduation. The ostensible reason for the move was the job he had accepted with Crown Zellerbach; that's what he told his family. What he didn't tell them was that he was gay, knew he was gay, needed to deal with being gay, however you did that. He wanted a gay ZIP code, a gay grocer, a gay pharmacist, gay friends, gay lovers. What better place than San Francisco?

Finding gay lovers turned out to be far easier than he had

feared during the long years of sterile study; he had frantic sex with as many men as he could. He discovered the groves of Buena Vista Park, alive day and night with possibilities; the tea rooms in Macy's and Golden Gate Park, the playground at the Collingwood school, the back rooms at Jaguar Books, the balcony at the Century Theater, the baths at Eighth and Howard. He learned how to pick people up just walking down the street, or in a bookstore; how to suck someone off at two in the afternoon in a stand of trees, or in a toilet stall; how to get fucked repeatedly at the baths, without having to look at individual faces; or, if in the orgy room, how to get fucked and sucked simultaneously while sucking someone else. Fisting, scat, and water sports he left to the wildly adventurous, but there wasn't much else he didn't try. He carried a little tub of Vaseline and a clean handkerchief wherever he went, and, other than to work, he seldom wore underwear.

Naturally these escapades made him feel guilty. You were not supposed to enjoy sex, certainly not have it two and three times a day, every day, not in public places, not with all these different people you don't even know and don't want to, not even their names, not with *men.* It was a sin, he was damned and he knew it—but that recognition only made him more obsessive.

Two years after he first came to the city—and a year after he'd left Crown Zellerbach to take a job as marketing director for a small gourmet coffee company on Potrero Hill—he moved in with a man he thought he loved and who, he thought, loved him. Tim was blond and don't-have-to-work rich and drove a Triumph convertible; although they were the same age, Tim looked at least five years younger. They met standing in line for a movie at the Lumière and went home together that night. A month later Carl moved in.

For several months all was peaceable, but it was Tim's apartment and Carl could not quite make himself comfortable in it. Tim, moreover, never broke his slutty stride, did not interrupt his long-standing habit of entertaining young men during the day, while Carl was off coordinating shipments of Kona beans. Several times he returned home to find Tim *in flagrante delicto*. Fights, tears, reconciliations—until one day Tim asked him to move out so a nineteen-year-old trick he had met on the sidewalk in front of the Hibernia Bank could move in.

Carl believed in love, but not for himself. Love required a purity of body and soul he had long since lost; corruption had been hard at work inside him, eating away his goodness, from the moment he first set foot in the city. He packed his things and resumed the life he thought he and Tim had saved each other from—the machine-gun encounters, flashing vividly, fading to nothing—but never quite gave up the hope, deep down, that someone, somehow, someday, would redeem his sins, the countless faceless fucks; would clean and press his soul and give it back to him and hold him forever.

Even now, Chris does not grasp the full reality of Carl's self-doubt, his lack of faith. To the extent that he does, it frustrates him and he fights it. Gently Carl has alluded to the squalor of his life, past and present, but Chris doesn't really want to hear and isn't really equipped to cope with it. Romance, in his own life, remains an overwhelming imperative, the stuff from which tomorrow's happinesses will be fashioned. Existence without it is inconceivable.

Some of this they talked about that foggy night they left the Midnight Sun together, Carl's hand on his shoulder; topics were gingerly parried over hamburgers and, later, between bouts of intense sex.

"You just think," Chris said, staring blankly at the white ceiling, "that the other person has to be like you, if it's going to work out. Has to come from the same background. Childhood," he said, saying no more, because he didn't need to. His point, he thought, was perfectly clear; surely Carl agreed with him.

"Don't you think people outgrow their pasts, where they came from?" Carl asked.

"No."

"Haven't you?"

"My best friend from college always made fun of me because I was from the Midwest. But it doesn't really bother me."

"I think every faggot in this town is trying to get away from wherever it is he's from," Carl said.

"You aren't," Chris said. "That's why we get along so well, don't you see? We come from the same culture." For an instant he felt embarrassed; why was he analyzing, theorizing? Magic was meant to be enjoyed, not analyzed.

Carl replied by kissing him on the mouth, and they stopped talking for a while.

Chris has touched something soft inside Carl—a tender cleft of childhood that lies deep in the muscular, scented, suave folds of a full-grown faggot. At heart Carl is a little boy, sad and vulnerable, wanting to be taken care of. He knows it's there of course, this vestige of innocence and dependency, but until he met Chris he thought it had no more power over him than to make him affectionate toward puppies or, occasionally, to yearn for chocolate-chip cookies and milk.

The adulterations of city life have not yet touched Chris, even though he looks like just another cute queerboy out to dish dirt and toss hair. Only when Carl first held the trembling body in his arms, felt the eager, shy kisses, did he understand how new Chris was to the game, how beguilingly unfamiliar with its Darwinian rules, how precious not yet to have been scarred by it (as he was). He was *tabula rasa;* he was soft clay waiting to be molded.

And yet—the life plan permits thinking about love, mourning its absence, even seeking it, but not falling into it. That window, if it had ever been open, has long since been closed, bolted, shuttered. After Tim and one or two others, after a years-long sex drunk that brought him to some kind of physical intimacy with, it seems, half the men in the city, he is persuaded that love, if there is such a thing, is beyond him. Or he beyond it; what does it matter? It isn't going to happen, isn't worth serious worry. That energy is reserved for the making of money and the accumulation of property, for family, for wrestling with the unanswerable question of whether to stay in San Francisco (hellish paradise) or move on. Not that any other city beckons.

It is two a.m.; chilly fog seeps through the city, blurring the streetlamps. Chris is feeling bitterly sorry for himself. He stands alone in the parking lot of the bank across the street from Trocadero and watches the double-parked taxis and limos disgorge their avid passengers. The building itself, an old warehouse, throbs with the heartbeat of disco music, its pulse strong as an Olympic athlete's.

Somewhere inside, on the city-block-sized dance floor, under the flashing strobes and the chrome railings, amid shirtless bodies and bottles of poppers and rags soaked in ethyl chloride to enhance the natural rush of the place (not to mention the drugs ingested through various orifices), Carl is dancing. He is dancing with Bruce and Martin, with Chaz and The Gang, with friends whose names Chris does not even know. He is the center of attention, the birthday boy—his own shirt probably off by now, Chris supposes, knotted around his waist, pecs drawing lustful stares, inviting glances from the very wired people nearby.

Does he even know I'm gone? Chris wonders. *Did he even notice how uncomfortable I was?* Probably not. There had never been a moment's doubt in his mind that the evening would end this way: in a druggy dancing frenzy, crushed out of shape by people who cared about Carl but not about him, who in truth were anxious to see this wobbly affair finally collapse so they could get back to the business of being disco faggots with their humpy friend Carl.

At some point fairly soon, he knows, he must make a decision. It is getting cold and a bit windy; inside, the dancing made him sweat, and now he is shivering. The choices are to go back inside or not to go back inside; if not back in, then to find some way back to Carl's, or straight to the car for the drive home down the Peninsula. This last choice would be an emphatic echo of the way he told Drew what he thought of Trina's practically giving him a blow job in the stands at the infamous football game.

Going back inside—to the nightmare of noise and people and darkness ripped by heart-attack flashes of light; a world tolerable only if you're on serious drugs—is out of the question. It would be as though he had never left, never signaled anything, and they will be here all night anyway. Home it is. He flags a cab and names a street corner near Carl's. The Accord is parked half a block away. He checks his pocket for the keys.

Dawn pales the eastern sky when Carl finds him, crumpled on the couch like a thrown-away doll. All his clothes are on except his shoes, which are lined up neatly by the door.

The energy kick of the MDA is beginning to wear off now, but Carl's senses are fully alive: He is aware of himself. Chris: A beautiful thing, even tangled up as he is. Carl feels a tremendous surge of hot affection for the boy. So this is where he went! At first Carl thought he had just gone for a glass of juice; by the time he failed to return, Carl was already buzzing from hits of this and that (plus the MDA, which he'd taken in the bathroom, up the ass, shortly before they'd left the apartment; Chris did not know this). From time to time, it flashed across his eyes that he hadn't seen Chris in a while, but like a firefly's light, recognition of the absence quickly faded, and he went back to his dancing and his friends, speeding the night away.

"Sweet prince," he murmurs, bending to kiss Chris on the lips. Hunger and the urge for caffeine command him, however, and in a moment he is in the kitchen, grinding Guatemalan coffee beans in the Braun grinder and rummaging through the refrigerator for omelet ingredients. As the sun finally peeks above the Berkeley hills, its first light glinting red off the miniblinds but soon growing warm and white, he loads his big breakfast onto a tray and takes it into the bedroom so he can watch a porno movie while he eats.

Ever since the terrible crackle-screech of the coffee grinder Chris has been awake, groggy at first and uncertain of where exactly he is, then remembering, feeling utterly degraded, trapped in the apartment of a man he no longer wants to have anything to do with. He pretended to be asleep while he was trying to figure out how to escape; now Carl is in the bedroom, and if there is to be a window of opportunity, this must be it.

Shoes are by the door—right where he left them. He can pick them up and rush out into the morning without putting them on, without having to deal with Carl; he can put them on in the car. The plan is terribly simple, foolproof, impossible to bungle. He sits up and eyes the shoes.

Last night he told himself he was too tired to drive the forty-five minutes to his own place, even though it wasn't even three o'clock and he wasn't the least bit drunk and had often made the drive even deeper in the night, when all the circumstances were far worse. It made sense, he told himself last night, that he should sleep at Carl's—carefully establishing himself on the sofa to emphasize *at Carl's*, not *with Carl*.

It makes sense, therefore, to leave without saying anything. There is nothing to say. The evening was a predictable catastrophe. Only the final indignity of Carl's coming home with some other man in tow has been avoided; he seems to be in there alone.

Yawning, Chris gets to his feet and pads into the toilet, where he pees quite audibly. *I don't care*, he says to himself. *Let him listen.* Having made up his mind not to play dead anymore, he is filled with reckless defiance. The whole thing has been a grievous mistake—three months wasted.

"Three months wasted," he hears himself saying. He looks up from the porcelain bowl and sees Carl's face reflected in the mirror over the washbasin. It is a haggard and white face, dark rings under red eyes: drugs warmed over. Carl's expression is infinitely sad, but peaceful, like a martyr's. Calmly, Chris buttons himself up and flushes, wondering how he is going to deal with this new obstacle. It's one thing just to disappear—here one minute, gone the next; quite another to barge wordlessly past someone you've been sleeping with for weeks, as if he didn't exist.

In that moment of hesitation, Carl speaks. "I'm sorry," he says.

Chris glances at him in the mirror, conscious of a sudden weakening in his knees. Carl looks vulnerable, tired, in need of a hug.

"Me too," Chris says, turning.

"I didn't know what happened to you."

"You didn't even look."

"No," Carl says, mortified. "I kept thinking you'd come back. We were all pretty fucked up. I wasn't sure you weren't right behind me somewhere."

"I wasn't."

"I know that. I'm sorry."

"I just can't stand this," Chris said. "You did it deliberately, so you wouldn't really have to be with me. You let your friends take over so you don't have to deal with change in your life. You're afraid of your own feelings."

Carl's head droops, but he holds out his arms toward Chris. "I really am sorry," he says in a pathetic whisper.

For an awkward moment they stand like that: Carl with his arms extended, Chris frozen next to the toilet. Gradually Carl's arms sag, as though the muscles, like those in his neck, are leaking air.

"I love you," Chris says in a flat, hard voice—a challenge. Carl does not look up. "I wish I didn't. I mean, it's hopeless. But I do. I don't know what to do." He steps through the narrow space between Carl and the doorjamb, expecting Carl to touch him, which he does not. He sits on the low bench by the front door and works the laces of his sneakers.

"I know it's mostly my fault," Carl says. He has followed at a contrite distance and is now sitting on the opposite end of the bench. "This isn't easy for me, you know. I like my bad habits! I've had them a long time. I'm perfect at them. What am I supposed to say to all these people I know? Sorry, can't see you anymore? They're like family."

"You don't even try."

"Nothing I could try would satisfy you anyway," Carl says. "Face it. You have this rigid idea of what we have to be. You can't see it any other way."

"I love you," Chris says, "and you don't love me."

"You know it's not that simple."

"It is." The shoes are laced and tied; he is ready to go, but he doesn't.

"You're wrong."

Chris stands.

"Please don't go," Carl murmurs. "Please don't leave me."

You're too fucked up on drugs to know what you're saying, Chris thinks—but something stops him from saying it. Carl is shuddering softly, making strange sniffly noises, and after a perplexed instant Chris understands that he's crying. He watches the bare shoulders quiver and heave, the muscles in the nape of the neck tense. Slowly he sinks back to the bench, one arm sliding involuntarily around Carl, the big warm mass settling under his shoulder. It is only decent to settle him down a little before leaving, Chris thinks, trying to ignore the sensual duet the two of them cannot seem to help playing, even when all hope is lost. Only decent.

WILLS

"Maybe we should get married," Dana says.

Drew assumes she is making a joke, not a very funny one at that, and drives on. The traffic back into town is stiff. Or maybe he misunderstood. Maybe she said, "Maybe they should get married." This is more likely. In fact it seems inevitable. They will get married. Not to say they should, but then they don't need his approval. A black Cadillac De Ville with diplomatic plates cuts him off, and he says "fucker" in a conversational tone. The Cadillac careens on, back to the Bulgarian embassy or wherever it came from.

Stress rules. Driving around D.C. drives him into a state. He is convinced he will die in a car accident that will be caused by his having a heart attack behind the wheel. He will have the heart attack at a moment like this: driving home from the airport after dropping off old friends from the past who've been visiting the present; being swerved at by some Balkan maniac.

They cause stress, these old friends. Who are they? They jump into existence after months and years in telephone and Christmas-card limbo, and, just as you are getting used to the idea of their actually existing, they jump out again, back to limbo. The emotional compression and decompression make the ears of your heart pop. Before they arrived he had been eager for their visit, eager to see the two of them together, eager for them to meet Dana; but his disappointment at their leaving— that crestfallen sense that they were leaving before he had quite figured out where they belonged in his life—quickly gave way to relief at the return of routine.

Routine: That is law school. For two years routine has consisted of study and Dana: Those are the two irritants around which the pearl of his life has formed. Ha! He hates the unfortunate association of metaphor with poetry, but this metaphor he likes, because it reflects his view that beauty and pleasure are not transcendental but arise from the grit of every day and cannot be separated from it. (Also because he thought of it himself instead of picking it up from the assigned reading.)

They are the oddest couple in their class. He hates all her friends—"the communists," he calls them, the school's politically correct crowd, forever agitating against oppression and hierarchy and racism—and loves to try bending their various inflexible orthodoxies. They hate him. Many a get-together has burst into flames after Drew, inadvertently the first few times but deliberately as he draws a bead on what galls them, utters one heresy after another. Affirmative action is reverse racism. English should be the official language. Homosexuality is a preference, not an immutable trait. The invasion of Grenada was necessary and just. The list is long.

So they disagree about everything and should be mortal enemies, except that they have somehow managed to sustain an affair that is more than sexual, less than intimate. When they are alone, away from her gang of zealots and the group of white males with whom he plays basketball two days a week, their ideological differences are suspended, and they skate along on a very smooth, very lovely surface. There is the strange comfort of knowing one's foe. There is the zest of making an unlikely alliance. And there is momentum.

Marriage?

One of the few things he thought they agreed on (outside of food and bicycle trails) was the dilapidation of marriage—"a failed institution," she once declared in the heat of studying for her final in Domestic Violence. Marriage was for the hordes, those countless sheep who needed to be told what to do, when, with whom. She saw it as an instrument of domination by penis; he saw it as the death of freedom. Either way, it wasn't for them.

"Don't you think?"

"I'm sorry?"

"You haven't heard a word I've said."

"I'm driving."

"You always say that when you're not paying attention," she says. Then, slowly and clearly, "I wonder about us."

Stopped at a red light, he finally permits himself to absorb the thought. "Like, you and me," he says.

"Like, yeah. You and me."

"Babe," he adds.

"Sing it," she says.

"Are you saying you *want* to get married?"

"I wonder."

"It's bourgeois," he says, deploying one of her favorite pejoratives, hoping to start a fight that will change the subject. "Won't marriage be abolished after The Revolution?"

"Oppression of women will be abolished," she says. "Not marriage per se. There'll always be a place for partnerships between loving equals."

"Like us."

"Theoretically."

"Or Mike and Merry."

"I barely know them," she says. "Only what you've told me, and I'm not sure you're reliable."

"They're perfect," Drew says. "Everyone thinks so. You saw for yourself."

For a moment she says nothing. Drew likes it like this: on the offensive, in control, telling people what they're really thinking. Any prospect of discussing The Revolution—that vague but definitive event somewhere in the near future in which the white patriarchy will be bloodily overthrown and replaced by justice and fairness forevermore; so she describes it—fills him with glee; he culls her many remarks on the subject in search of contradictions, inconsistencies, implausibilities.

"I didn't know you read minds, too," she says.

"Sure," he says. "I'm on law review."

At the end of his first semester he had flown west for Christmas feeling that the law, if not exhilarating (never a serious expectation), was at least satisfying, or at the very least a surmountable hurdle in the steeplechase of career. It was applied history, in which your knowledge of past problems and their solutions was adapted to modern circumstances. He was comfortable with that. Thinking like a lawyer meant thinking effectively rather than expansively, being sensitive to history and language but *using* them as well. It gave a sense of movement and purpose: We are going somewhere.

But where? He had not anticipated the changes law school would work in who he thought he was, in what he believed and felt. He had come ready for an intellectual exercise, for rigorous training in reason and logic; this had been expected. Each step flowed naturally and easily from the last. Every problem was thought through and analyzed in light of the relevant statutes and cases, while the people whose difficulties formed the basis of the analysis were reduced to a few syllables: Plaintiff and Defendant, Appellant and Appellee, Petitioner and Respondent. That impersonality did not bother him.

What did bother him was the understanding, which came to him in the early weeks of his first semester, that there really was *no such thing* as justice or fairness. His emotional resistance to the fact lingered, but there it was. Every side had an argument, a set of precedents, a policy angle. You sorted and weighed. Somebody won and somebody lost. The trick of the law was to make outcomes seem inevitable, "fair," "just." The real trick was when the balance was close, as it always was in the professors' hypotheticals; when "weighing the equities" of a case left you in a Solomonic dilemma. If the arguments were equally persuasive, how did you, no longer a believer in fairness or justice, decide who won?

No one had ever explained to him how profoundly conservative the law is, lawyers are. Change is resisted, new arguments resisted, unusual clothes and haircuts and ideas resisted. Preservation of order is what law and lawyers are for. Predictability is all: It is the reason for having law. New and different are presumed evil until proven otherwise.

Like so many of Drew's first meetings, his with her was rocky. Fall semester, first year: Someone's study group was throwing a party in Woodley Park. He went with his study group. She was there, looking like Cat Woman: sharp dark eyes set in pale skin; shiny black hair cut boy-short; her eyebrows elongated and curved by mascara into something vaguely Spock-like. She moved about the apartment with an edgy self-awareness, and he watched her.

Reagan was discussed. He heard himself defending the tax cuts and the arms buildup. Whatever one thought of Reagan himself, he represented a healthy shift in emphasis, Drew said. (He did not mention that he had voted for Anderson.) There she was, standing almost next to him, staring with either amusement or hatred—he couldn't tell which. He stared back, expecting her to say something scathing, or introduce herself. He said something else to fill the space. A moment later he noticed she was gone, darted off to someone else's side.

In fact, though she hadn't said a word, he knew her name from orientation day, when each member of the entering class had been given a directory with photocopies of the photos they'd been asked to send in over the summer. He'd noticed her in the crowd, listening to the dean's welcome on the green in front of the library and had, even while the dean spoke, scanned the smudged portraits to find her.

Dana Raphaelson.

When she sat down next to him the first day of second semester, Criminal Procedure, he almost said the name out loud. Instead he kept quiet, wondering if she recognized him and still thought he was a dangerous reactionary madman. Just before class started he glanced over at her and she said, without returning the glance, "You look like you're from Los Angeles."

Since this could cut either way, he said simply (looking away from her), "I am."

"Drew Hopewell," she said as class started.

For the next hour he was so absorbed in the meaning of this tiny drama that he forgot to write down what "incorporation" was and had to ask her after class.

"You were sitting right next to me," she said. "*I* wrote it down. Weren't you paying attention?"

"No," he said. "I wasn't. I figured we both didn't have to."

"You figured," she said with genial contempt. They seemed to be walking in the same direction. "I hear you're a neo-Nazi fascist pig."

"I hear you're a wild-eyed feminist nihilist."

"Let's have lunch," she said. "I'll give you what you want."

He thought she wanted to go out, but they ended up at

her apartment near Thirty-first and P. The small kitchen was laden with cooking gadgets and implements and smelled richly of garlic and leeks and curry and other savory scents. They made small talk about politics on the way, he holding himself in check while she feinted and jabbed amusingly about Reagan (she described his hair as "E.T. orange"), but once inside he was left to himself while she bustled about the kitchen, preparing penne in a tomato sauce spiced with garlic and chipotle peppers, dressed with cilantro pesto and grated *queso blanco*. On the coffee table: *The New Yorker, Mother Jones, The Nation, Washington Monthly*. He wondered what he was getting himself into. At least, judging from the smells, she could cook.

"It'll be ten minutes or so," she said, emerging from the kitchen. "If you're starving I have some bread."

"It smells excellent," he said safely.

"It's a health issue," she said, reading his unspoken comment about feminists who cooked. "I'm vegetarian. And I like to eat and I like to cook. It's sexist to think that women shouldn't cook just because they've been chained to their stoves for hundreds of years, don't you think?"

"It smells good."

"I suppose you're going to go work for Ronnie the Gipman when you graduate," she said. "Or back to beach-bumland."

Drew shrugged. "Don't really know," he said. "What about you?"

She laughed. "Destroy the white patriarchy," she said, leaving no doubt in his mind that she meant it.

There was something thrilling about their adversarial posture; his desire thrived in the violent climate of love-hate. She was smart and beautiful and dangerous: someone to be tenderly smothered, subdued with the ecstatic thrusting of a big stiff dick. While they ate, their knees kept bumping under her tiny bistro table.

"I won't sleep with you today," she said as she served

him seconds from the big white earthenware bowl. The bottle
of red wine was half-empty.

"Do I look like that kind of guy?"

"Maybe tonight," she said. "We'll see if I feel like it."

He had never before heard a woman say quite these sorts
of things—suggest that she was as horny as he was. Trina had
been easy but submissive; she needed the touching, wasn't
driven by lust. He had always believed that girls were different
from boys in this respect, although, of course, like everyone
else, he had more recently been told that this belief was one
of the results of the sexist plot to deny women the enjoyment
of their bodies and keep them docile in their houses with
aprons knotted around their waists and children screaming at
their feet. Being with Dana, listening to her prod and tease,
was almost like being with another man: an equal, someone
who *understood.* Except that she had the other set of parts, the
right set, was a physical presence to which he was unreason-
ingly attracted. She was a she, after all, even if her words were
he words, even if her feelings and desires were what he un-
fashionably thought of as *he* feelings and desires, *his* feelings
and desires.

Living together is enough, at least for him, at least until the
psychological freedom of remaining a bachelor has palled (no
hint of this yet). The casualness with which they undertook to
move their things into the same apartment means, to him, that
those things can be moved to separate apartments with equal
casualness, if that should ever be found expedient. He cannot
even remember whose idea it was; she had basically been living with him since the new year, anyway, in the in-law apartment he rents from the ancient but indefatigable Georgetown
dowager Mrs. Dunwiddy. When her lease was up in June they
simply moved to Mrs. Dunwiddy's that small remainder of her
things which had not yet been moved.

After Trina, he decided that he ought to take up with

brainier women—or, at any rate, women whose lives seemed to run a little more closely to his own success track. There was no future, he thought, with someone you could push around, bully, dominate, who needed you; what was called for was an equal, a peer. Too many times with Trina he felt more alone than he ever had when he really *was* alone; he felt that while he understood her perfectly, she could not and did not know him. Chris is right, he would think to himself, although he never admitted this to Chris. I can do better.

Of late he is much preoccupied by his future with Dana. She is a peer and then some: founder and editor-in-chief of the *Women's Law Journal,* vice-president of the student bar association, a key organizer of the campus's feminist caucus and other left-wing organizations. (She graded onto law review but, in an open letter to the school newspaper, declined the invitation to join what she called a "white boys' club.") Everything Trina was and was not, she is not and is.

Part of his denial of the future is his clinging to the present, to the illusion that they will just go on this way indefinitely, always being law students, cohabitants, below-market-rent tenants of the immortal Mrs. Dunwiddy. The gales of adult life will not buffet them. Not that the present is all that great, but at least it is familiar. He is attached to his routines, to the knowable, and he is nervous about her volatility. Who knows what might happen to her in a change of circumstances? For all the imperfections of their relationship, the improbability of their being together at all, he is content and, lacking any reason to think otherwise, assumes she is, too.

Future shock: What will happen when they are no longer law students? Which comes first, her or the career? The two have become bound together in a tight knot he is not sure how to unravel. A choice is looming, a fork in the road in the dusk beyond graduation: Which job to take? What city? They will have to talk about it; he knows that, though the thought makes him uneasy. Even if they agree not to get married, even if they somehow agree to work in the same city, go on sharing an apartment and their lives—to remain unchanged, in other words, except for having graduated—the degree of commitment between them will still default to a higher level. The student deferments that shield them from growing up will expire; they will be young adults with professional jobs, big incomes, making investments, buying furniture, joining clubs. Society will expect that, sooner or later, they will get about the business of marrying, moving to the suburbs and raising children.

Never before has the subject of marriage—as in, an arrangement the two of them might join—even been alluded to. Adding to the shock is the fact that she opened the alluding. But it has been alluded to now, by her first, and the idea rings in his head with the rich resonance of timpani.

When they get home, Dalí, her tabby cat, is waiting by the door, meowing and whipping the tip of his tail back and forth. She bends down and he leaps into her arms.

"Puddy-tat," she says into his ear, and he rubs his face against hers. "I'll get you some food."

"Don't forget our food," Drew says. The apartment is redolent of one of her specialties, Latin lasagna, with Chihuahua cheese, her special hot sauce (of Anaheim and habañero chilis, ground to powder and blended with vinegar, garlic, cumin, oregano and lemon juice) and three kinds of fire-roasted Caribbean peppers. It has been warming in the oven since they left for the airport. His stomach growls, complaining about the lateness of dinner.

"Kitties first."

He feels like saying "People first," but knows that it is pointless, if not counterproductive, to interpose himself between her and Dalí, especially when the issue is food. One of her first nicknames for him was Robin, because, as she explained, he was like a baby robin, always sitting there with his head back and mouth open, waiting for a meal to drop into it.

Instead he goes to the refrigerator and busies his mouth with nibbles of the salad.

After dinner, while he is cleaning up (a gesture of atonement for his sexist oppression in letting her do all the cooking), she prepares food and water for her stray alleycats. These cats, too, are a point of contention. Dalí makes Drew's eyes itch, and Dalí is clean; God knows what filth these alleycats get themselves into. Moreover, Dalí himself dislikes the strays. This is one of the few issues on which Drew and Dalí find themselves in agreement. While she feeds them, Dalí crouches on the windowsill above the sink, hissing.

No matter. She sets down the bowls of cat food and fresh water, and two black cats immediately materialize from the darkness to sup. One she has named Margaret Sanger, the other Sarah Weddington. Her courtship of the creatures is already far enough along that Sarah, the smaller and younger of the two, will sit in her lap to be stroked. Drew scrubs away at the pots; Dalí bares his phantom front claws.

"You're feeding them," he calls out.

"I'm feeding them," she calls back in a singsong voice. "They're hungry."

"Let them eat rats."

"They need to be petted."

"They have fleas."

"Fumigate me."

"If I've touched you and you've been touching them, I itch."

"You're psychosomatic," she says dismissively, inspecting his work and finding two knives inadequately scrubbed. "You're doing a bang-up job here."

"Dalí can't stand them."

"Dalí," she says, "can't stand you."

"No," he agrees. Countless are the times when Dalí's fits of playfulness have left his fingers and forearms lined with little red tooth marks. Until Michael arrived, Drew had assumed

that Dalí simply hated other male animals. He had expected
the beast to put on his usual arched-back hissy show the instant Michael came through the door. So it was a bit of a surprise when Dalí could not seem to stop brushing against
Michael's legs, and took the first available chance to leap into
his lap. Drew had to remind himself that there was nothing to
be jealous about because he didn't like Dalí in the first place.
"Of course, Dalí really can't stand anybody."

"He is choosy," she agrees.

"Do you think it bothers him that she's as tall as he is?"
he says. Back to M&M. "Maybe she's even a little taller than
he is."

"Only you would have a fascist male chauvinist piggy
thought like that," she says, rearranging the precarious stack
of dishes he has erected on the dish-drying rack. "And FYI,
they're the same height."

"I wonder if it gives him a complex."

"The only complexes I noticed were yours."

Not until Drew was sitting in a Munich beer garden late on a
mild Friday night in mid-September, three months after graduation, arguing a theory of aesthetics with a prematurely bald,
young American student of pasta-platter face who introduced
himself by taking an empty seat at Drew's table and, in a matter of seconds, disclosing that he was a Writer waiting to be
discovered, did it occur to him how much he missed college,
how quickly the time had passed. Here, on another continent,
amid a people whose language he spoke fumblingly, the sense
of his own insignificance seized him. Homesickness wasn't the
problem; it was the ache of having been separated from his
life, his intimates—especially Michael and Chris. Especially
Chris.

He had come to Germany in the hope of avoiding this
very thing. Graduation with all its goodbyes was going to be
difficult, he had forecast long beforehand, and law school was

not an interval eagerly to be anticipated. Going abroad to live in a foreign culture would distract his attention from yesterday and tomorrow. It might give him an idea of what could be rather than what, barring a change of course, would be.

That, at any rate, was the theory of this interregnum year. It had seemed sound enough when he made the arrangements. It was only for a year. He was entitled to that much, wasn't he? To climb off the track for a few months and take a free breath or two before resuming? No harm could come of it.

Geoff had flown in for a visit soon after he'd arrived; they rented a Volkswagen and drove to Berlin, on which city Geoff professed some expertise. Part of the shipment Geoff brought from home was a packet of letters from Chris to Drew. It turned out that they had been written in the weeks immediately after graduation and mailed, weeks later, to the Hopewells' home in L.A. While Geoff (after making a weak excuse about "going for a walk") cruised the Tiergarten in broad daylight, Drew sat at a sidewalk café near the Kurfürstendamm to read Chris's oeuvre and try to absorb its meaning.

Despite the years of temper tantrums, the wars of silence, the snide underbreath cracks about Trina, the arguments about which classes to take (all, for Drew, vividly evoked between the handwritten lines), Chris was so central a feature of his life that his departure was like the opening of an air lock on a starship deep in space: an instant of screaming whoosh as the atmosphere expended itself in the void, then silent, frozen emptiness.

I really miss you, Chris had written. *I'm like Kirk on that fake* Enterprise *with no crew ("Mark of Gideon"; did you remember the title? Degree of difficulty 2.75.) I'm sick of being an alumnus and can't wait for fall quarter to begin.*

Reading those words—*miss you*—made him jump, as though the dentist's steely probe had touched a soft spot on one of his molars. He read on, telling himself it was nothing. Paragraph after paragraph, page after page, letter after letter the words flowed. It was almost embarrassing to be reading these thoughts, these flashes of unguarded emotion that could as easily have been written by him as to him. But it said something about the difference in their characters that Chris, not he, had written all this gush. Chris was not strong. Drew was strong. Still, only the comfortable anonymity of the strange divided city and the protection of its indifferent throng enabled him to read the letters straight through.

On the autobahn back to Munich, Drew drove while Geoff read the letters. He nodded and nibbled his lips while his eyes scanned the smallish, round, neat handwriting.

"I know how he feels," Geoff said when he had finished. "I felt that way, too."

"I wonder why he wrote it all down."

"He likes to write, maybe," Geoff said. Drew snorted. "Maybe he's trying to preserve the way he felt during those moments. Or to say stuff he couldn't say otherwise. It's easier to write a letter sometimes than to actually say something to someone. It's interesting what he leaves out."

"I thought he said everything that could possibly be said."

"Not even close," Geoff said. "It's so obvious, don't you see? Even though he never comes out and says it. The way he feels about you."

Drew glanced over at him. "The way he feels about me," he said.

"He's completely in love with you," Geoff said. "His heart is broken."

There was a long pause in which the tires whined and the wind whistled. In the rear-view mirror a huge blue Mercedes loomed, brights flashing on and off.

"He's just messed up about graduation," Drew murmured, returning his attention to the road, where the Mercedes flashed by them, doing well over a hundred. "We all are, sort of."

"I always thought he might be gay."

"Chris isn't gay," Drew said forcefully. "God. Only you would think something like that. You barely know the guy."

"Trust me."

"If you're right, why hasn't he told me?"

"He doesn't know how," Geoff said. "He's afraid you'll reject him if you find out the truth."

"Give me a break," Drew said.

"Don't say I didn't tell you."

"I won't."

Writer, having explained aesthetics, next turned his attention to the German character. Cold, brutal, unrepentant Jewhaters, he said, don't you think? Crude and rude, a country of money-grubbing, beer-swilling slave-drivers who should wash more often, don't you agree?

If he means to provoke, Drew wondered, why is he telling *me* this stuff? Why doesn't he stand up on a table, like Hitler did, and let everyone hear? Why not insult the Germans to their faces in their own language?

On carried Writer. He confided that he had recently enjoyed a sexual experience with a Dutch girl on the train to Vienna, where he had relatives willing to put him up. He had already, he said, written a story about it, which he would be glad to show Drew, who as another American expatriate might have a better grasp of its underlying Jamesian theme of American expatriates in Europe than would the unkempt German students who lived in his building, despite their fluency in English, which they always wanted to practice with him. Didn't he think? Should he send it to *The New Yorker?*

There was something appalling about this man, Drew decided, and before getting up carefully to begin his drunken progress into the street he called Writer "faggot" to his face. Then off, leaving behind a slack jaw, a plan in ruins, a bill.

It was impossible to associate Writer's loathsome flirtations with Chris. It was also impossible to associate Geoffrey's reckless trashing around in public parks (and God knew where else) with Chris. ("Going for a walk"! As if Drew hadn't heard about the Tiergarten, about Berlin generally.) Any insinuation about Chris, after all, was an insinuation about him, a suggestion that if Chris felt that way, then mustn't Drew? . . . hadn't they lived together all those years, in tiny crackerbox rooms with no privacy? . . . communal showers and all the rest? . . . spring breaks spent sleeping in the same double bed at his parents' condo in Rancho Mirage?

(Add two and two.)

No, it was not possible.

It is clear, after half an hour or so of preternatural calm (even Dalí is resting, waiting for the magical hour of three a.m. when he will begin his nightly ritual of batting around one of the several whiffle balls Dana has provided for him), that neither one of them is asleep, or even drowsy, although late-night sex usually knocks both of them out like a drug. The room roars with the sound of their careful, silent breathing.

"So why aren't you asleep?" he says at last. "What's your excuse?"

"You're not snoring."

"I never snore! I snore?"

"You snore."

"Dalí snores."

"You can't blame him for everything."

"You shouldn't have said that about getting married."

"It slipped out."

"Because now we're both fucked up."

"Maybe that's okay."

He clicks on his little reading lamp, and the shadows spring around them. "Not tonight," he says. "We're tired. I am."

"Tonight's as good as any other night. We probably should have talked about it a long time ago."

"I don't know about tonight. Not after guests."

"We can't sleep. What else is there to do?"

"Okay then. Let's talk about it. You brought it up, so you get to start."

"You're already hostile," she says.

"Okay, I'll start," he says. "Marriage. An off-the-wall idea. I'm free-associating. Everything's fine. You and me. Status quo. Why mess?"

"Do you love me?"

Ding-dong. Suddenly he feels as though he's drunk a pot of coffee. His heartbeat opens to full throttle. "What do you mean?"

"What do you mean, what do I mean? That's what I mean! I mean, we never talk about it. How we *feel.*"

"The topic is marriage."

"I'd say they're related topics, wouldn't you?"

"Not necessarily."

"What does that mean?"

"You know that's not a topic I discuss."

"Feelings."

"The undiscussable."

"If I were cynical," Dana says, "which I'm not, I'd say you were being evasive. I would interpret that to mean you don't."

"You're living with me in my apartment," Drew says. "With your cat."

"Is that proof?"

"Is this a trial?"

"Why are we living together?"

"Because we want to."

"Where are we going?"

"How do I know?" he says, trying not to be angry. "Do we have to be going anywhere?"

"Yes."

"I didn't know you were such a puritan."

"There's a lot you don't know."

"About you."

"About a lot of things."

"What is the big deal about the slip of paper that says, Now you're married? Now it's official. Who cares?"

"If you loved me," she says, "we wouldn't be having this stupid conversation."

"You keep dragging that into it," Drew says. "It's just a word. What about what I *do?* What about my actions?"

"You like to eat."

"Cheap shot."

"You're looking for a domestic servant you don't have to pay for."

"Right!" he says. "And so I'm living with a radical feminist law student who conjures fights out of nothing."

"And who can't figure out how she's gotten herself into this situation."

"One of the advantages of not being married," Drew says, "is that we don't have to stay together if we don't want to."

"You don't want to."

"It sounds like you don't."

"I'm saying we can't just drift along forever," she says, a little more calmly. "You remember *Annie Hall.* We have to work at this relationship. We have to try to make it better."

"It seems really weird to me that Mike and Meredith have somehow filled you with this urge to get married. Just by showing up. I mean, Jesus."

"I didn't say I wanted to. I said I wondered if we should."

"Now *you're* being evasive."

"There's nothing wrong with waiting until you're ready."

"So now you're ready?"

"It doesn't matter," she says, "because obviously you're not."

"I don't think either of us is," Drew says. "We haven't even graduated yet."

"A meaningless formality."

"Like a marriage license."

"Mike and Meredith have nothing to do with it."

"You weren't talking like this before they came."

"I was thinking it."

"Why didn't you say something?"

"I knew you'd say what you've just been saying."

"So why did you bring it up tonight?"

"Sooner or later we had to talk about it."

"I agree with that," Drew says.

"Are we getting somewhere?"

"That depends."

"On what?"

"On what you expect. If you'll tell me why marriage is no longer the fundamentally illegitimate, sexist, failed institution you're always saying it is, then we'll be getting somewhere."

"If I've given you that impression—" she begins carefully.

"You said it. 'A failed institution.' "

"I didn't make myself clear."

"I thought that was pretty clear."

"I stand by that statement," she says, a little uncomfortably. "But it doesn't mean that all marriages at all times are failures, or that the institution is completely unworkable. Anyway, that's not the real issue and you know it."

"What is the real issue?"

"The real issue," she says, "is that a year from now I don't want to be in this position."

"Which is?"

"No commitment."

Drew grunts as he falls back on his pillow. "You've been in law school too long. You see all this formalism as a substitute for reality. Words, licenses, bits of parchment—"

"Not a substitute. A reflection. If you really were committed you wouldn't be making such a big deal out of it. You'd say, yeah, we should, and that would be it. Admit it: It's obvious you're not committed."

"I'm stunned, that's what I am. Coming from you! I mean, you're the one who's always talking about gender roles and the need for flexibility and for people to explore themselves, how women are oppressed in society's traditional structures and all the rest of it. I hear it in my *sleep*. Now you're pissed at me because, what, I haven't fought back hard enough on behalf of sexism and traditional roles and failed institutions?"

"This has nothing to do with institutions," she says. "It has to do with you and me and planning what to do with our lives. What I'm telling you is that if this is going to be more than just some law-school thing, you and me, then we have to treat it like that. We're grown-ups. Grown-ups rely on each other. They raise children who have a right to expect that their parents aren't just casual about each other.

"Children!" Drew murmurs.

"I'm not saying I want them. Children or whatever. I'm just using it as an example. The point is that we can't just go on this way forever. I can't build a life with someone I don't *know* is committed to me, to the life."

"And marriage solves this problem?"

"It's not perfect," she says. "I admit that, okay? But it's a step. It helps. What good is it to talk about 'marriage' anyway? Every marriage is different. People shape it to their own needs, just like any other institution."

"I'm sorry," Drew says. "I just think this is all very premature."

"Mike and Merry—" she begins, before stopping.

"Mike and Merry?"

"I don't think this is all that premature."

"They *did* have something to do with this," Drew insists.

"All right, yes, of course, they did," Dana concedes. "Satisfied? I was curious about them, after all you'd said. I watched them. I learned something."

"They have nothing to do with us. We're not them. Everything will work out."

"You're so full of white-boy complacency!" she says. "Of course that's what you believe, because that's your whole experience of this society and the people in it. Things *do* work out for white boys, even if they don't try. You get paid for showing up. But I'm not a white boy and I have to *try* to get what I want if I really want it. I have to work for it."

"So now the issue is that I'm a white boy."

"Maybe we shouldn't get married."

"Why do you reduce every problem to these minority categories?"

"Because they matter."

"Even between you and me?"

"Even between you and me."

"It's crazy," he says. "You just got through telling me how this wasn't about institutions, it was personal between us," he says. "I don't get it."

"Of course you don't get it."

"Because I'm a white boy."

"Yes."

"And you're a non-white-boy revolutionary."

"Yes."

"Pushing to get married to a white boy."

"I'm not pushing, Drew," she says. "God, you can be such a *fucker*. I'm telling you that I'm not just some girlfriend you can dump when it suits you, like that poor slut from college. That was bullshit."

"I'd never do that to you."

"I wouldn't let you."

"Anyway that was mutual. She agreed. It was perfectly civilized. We had no future and we both knew it. I don't think you and I are in a remotely comparable situation. And she wasn't a slut."

"If that's your way of saying how much you care about me, it's pretty weak."

"I'm sorry. I'm not a poet."

"Tell me about it."

"Just because I can't say it doesn't mean I don't feel it."

"Neither one of us knows what you feel."

"I'm tired."

"Go to sleep," she says.

"Aren't you tired?"

"I'm tired of this."

There is nothing else he can think of to say. He shrugs and grunts and clicks off his lamp, careful to arrange his body so that none of it intrudes onto her side of the bed. Soon his breathing deepens, growing coarser and slower; she feels his back expand and contract against her. It is infuriating that he goes to sleep so easily, even after this. She kicks him once to stop his snoring, but he goes on snoring. For a long while she lies with her head on the pillow, staring at the wall, not seeing, just before her unfocused eyes, the single dark, curly hair on the sheet that is too dark to have come from him and too curly to have come from her.

"*Is that yours?*" *Meredith says to me. She means the dental floss. It isn't. Mine—which I ran out of—is waxed, hers is unwaxed. The spaces between my teeth are already filled with little shreds of guilt.*

"I don't know," I say. This is limp. "I guess not."

"You'll get it between your teeth," she says. "Here." She hands me a doll-sized box of waxed. "I brought this. I knew you'd run out."

She always knows. She smells of chlorine. She and Daniel have been swimming in the big pool in the courtyard, under the potted palms. The pool is one reason we chose this hotel; the other is that it's walking distance to campus. Which makes the rental car sort of overkill, except better safe than sorry. Plus the car makes it easier to get to and from the airport, not to mention into the city, where Drew is staying and where Chris still lives.

It could have been weirder, this little reunion dinner of

ours, but not much. It's hard to believe that ten years have gone by. It doesn't seem that long. It doesn't seem like people you knew really well (or thought you did) could change so much in that time. But here's Chris, dropping all these hints about leaving San Francisco, and here's Drew, working for some television production company in L.A.

I don't blame Chris. I think I'd leave, too, if I'd been through what he's been through. It was a hard story to hear, especially since I wasn't really ready for it, but I see why he felt he had to tell it to us. It's his story. When I relayed the details to Merry, as soon as I got back, she broke down and cried while I stood there. After a while she told me she'd known for a long time about Chris, so I guess it was easier for her to express her grief. I was, and still am, in shock, or at least I'm surprised about the whole thing. Looking back, I see the signs and signals, but there's a difference between wondering about your friends and actually thinking they are. Or knowing they are. I guess I've been trying not to think about it these last few years. None of my beeswax, but now it is. How do you comfort? What do you say?

I vowed to myself beforehand not to ask Drew about Dana, and I got all the way to dessert before I broke down. I was sure he was going to say, I've been waiting for you to ask me about her, you cur (or one of those other Drew words), but he kind of shrugged and said something about her getting married to some other guy and then, while Chris was in the john, told me that he was meeting Trina later tonight! The guy is just unbelievable.

You do not think, when you're about to get married, about whether the marriage will be good or bad, or that those categories will even apply to you. I didn't, anyway. Good and bad are vague words ("Meaningless," Drew would say, as he did earlier tonight, with respect to a variety of subjects) whose meanings always seem to be shifting. You just assume that it will be better than good, since both of you are. I always thought we had a good marriage, and I still think so, but sometimes I wonder if that just means it's been good for me, and if good for me just means predictable, or not bad, or not over.

Does she know? I'll never tell—it would do too much damage, probably destroy everything, for both of us. But that doesn't mean the answer is no. I think that it's yes, although how she knows, or whether she just guesses, or feels, or suspects, I have no idea. Maybe it doesn't even matter, because whatever deeds we've done cannot be undone. Dan cannot be unborn. He is my son, and I've loved him from the first moment she set him in my arms (and he whimpered). Even if he grows up to be a six-foot-four-inch lover of pasta and wearer of gold ear studs, that will not change.

When I am with Meredith, when her arms are around me, we belong to each other. It's that simple. If, before falling asleep, I sometimes think of what happened and what might have been, it's almost like breaking in on someone else's thoughts, the secret life of a man who isn't me. That's how remote it seems, but vivid, and I still can't forget her, or it.

There are all these different kinds of love, or maybe we shouldn't use the same word to describe all these feelings. The way I feel about Merry, for instance, and the way I feel about Drew and Chris; they're both strong feelings, but completely different. By the time the dinner was over and we were arguing over dessert (whether and where) and where to meet Saturday afternoon for the reunion tailgaters and the football game afterward, it was as though ten years had not passed and we had never been apart.

And still—for all the time I spent with these guys, for all the ease with which we stepped into the old ways, the bits of Star Trek dialogue and all the rest of it—I can't get away from the question of what it was that glued us together, and if there's any of it left. Drew always loved to say how men and women could never be friends, they were too fundamentally dissimilar, the *tension would never go away, blah blah blah, but Merry has been my best friend, really, from almost the day I met her.*

"You smell like chlorine," I say to her. "You reek."

"I'm just getting into the shower," she says.

"How's he?"

"Out like a light."

I peek out into the main room, where Dan is fast asleep in the middle of one of the two queen-sized beds. He, too, reeks of chlorine, but I don't awaken him to complain.

Behind me, while I slosh the Plax around my mouth and then start to brush, the shower beats steadily on her, and the air grows warmer and damper. From simple curiosity I turn to see what I can see, but the shower curtain is an opaque off-white, and I see nothing.

EAST is EAST

Drew's theory of love was that there was no such thing. Various affections were conceded to exist—for dogs, food, friends, "stuff like that"—and there was lust; but the two categories did not overlap. So he insisted. Never the twain shall meet. East is east. "It would be like mixing matter and antimatter. The annihilation of everything. Episode?"

" 'The Lazarus Syndrome,' " Chris recited.

"Correct."

Where Trina belonged in this scheme Chris could not figure. If Drew spent so much time with her (including all those nights), how could he not be in love with her? If he did not love her, why did he spend so much time with her? He longed to point out this paradoxical breach of the doctrine Drew himself had laid out, but he did not, because he knew what the answer would be. Your question is meaningless, Drew would say, in his annoyingly Spock-like way (probably raising the one eyebrow, just for spite), because there is no such thing as being in love. It's like dividing by zero.

The great weapon in Chris's arsenal of arguments—*but I love you*—was, like the doomsday machine in "The Doomsday Machine," unusable. It would bring the inevitable, crushing retaliation: *But we're two guys. You know what that means.* Of course, Chris did not know what *that* meant, though he saw what Drew was getting at. The whole topic was best avoided, especially as it pertained to the two of them. If Drew never actually *said* there was no hope, perhaps there was *not* no hope.

At first, when Chris began to recognize the strength of his feeling for Drew, he told himself that it was nothing more than an intense version of an ordinary friendship. He tried to ignore Drew's body, so casually displayed in the rooms they shared. Drew was always making cracks about fucking and jerking off, always pulling down his Jockey shorts or spreading his bath towel to flash Chris or moon him or just generally prancing around naked. He laughed when Chris swallowed and blushed. Thank God he thinks I'm just shy, Chris would think as he tried to will the thrill away.

By the middle of sophomore year, with Trina now attached like a barnacle to the hull of their lives, he admitted to himself that, no, it wasn't just an especially fond friendship: He was in love with Drew. He even wrote out the thought on a piece of notebook paper—*I am in love with Drew*—to give it some independent reality. He thought that might make it easier for him to see the basic preposterousness of it.

But that wasn't what happened. Instead, seeing the words on paper, written in green Bic Banana ink, made it clear to him that it really was true. He was in love with Drew. He tore the paper methodically to shreds and dropped the remains in his wastebasket. If writing it down confirmed the reality, maybe tearing it up would make the problem go away. It didn't.

Being in love with a roommate was wonderful when he had the roommate all to himself, as he had the first part of fall quarter, sophomore year, when it was possible to believe in the fantasy that life would always be like this, the two of them together in a small room, intimate, unself-conscious, uninterfered-with. But Trina was the needle that pricked the balloon, and he found himself holding the rubbery tatters in his hands while Drew was God knew where with her, night after night. It was impossible for Chris to fall asleep, despite hearty doses of beer and Sominex and NyQuil and warm milk.

Whatever his head told him, his heart could not accept that Drew would never be his. He could not give up. When, over spring break, Trina fever broke—Chris, Drew and Michael spent the week at the Hopewells' condo in the desert, and Drew announced he was going to spend the summer in Washington, D.C., as a congressional intern—Chris gritted his teeth at the gamble and agreed to live with Drew for another year. In the end, he was convinced—the cosmic order being fundamentally just—that he would be rewarded for his steadfastness.

He wanted to touch Drew. He wanted Drew to touch him. He wanted to run his hands over Drew's body and feel the warm muscles and skin press against his own. Sometimes he would return to their room unexpectedly and in stealth, hoping to burst in on some lurid scene of self-abuse. Just to see Drew acting as a sexual being was so exciting a thought that thinking beyond it to what might happen *then* seemed unnecessary.

It was in the desert that Drew told Chris about Geoff. Michael was asleep in the other bedroom; the two of them were lying in bed, flat on their backs, feeling the world spin beneath them. The trash can in the kitchen held the remains of the evening's amusement: a six-pack of Coors and two green-glass jugs of cheap California Chablis. Chris, feeling brave, thought that he would ask about Trina, but instead he heard himself saying something about Drew's hostility to homosexuals.

"Fuck," Drew said. "Brother's a faggot. I'm not hostile."

"Geoff?"

"Mmmm," Drew murmured. Of course Geoff. He was the only brother Drew had.

Chris felt like prey in the dark—prey to Drew's searchlight revelation, prey to the fact that he had always been attracted to Geoff. It was difficult to judge whether Drew was telling the truth or laying a trap for him to blunder into.

"Come on."

"I suppose you think he's cute," Drew said. "He does look just like me. Only older and grayer and wrinklier."

"Shut up. How do you know he is?"

"You mean, like, what are the giveaway signs? How can I spot fags a mile away?"

"You're really drunk," Chris said a little desperately, trying to wade out of the mess before he was spotted. "You'd better not puke in here."

"He told me," Drew said.

"Shut up and go to sleep," Chris said.

"No, I never slept with him," Drew said. "You were dying to know. I could tell. I read your squalid little mind and spared you the trouble of asking. No, we didn't. I feel that brothers shouldn't be anally involved."

Chris didn't hear this last bit because he had sandwiched his head between two pillows, praying to God almighty that Drew would drop the subject. Or? What if Drew said, I know you are, too. What if he said, I've seen you looking at me. What if Drew was curious? What if? What if? He tried to will himself to sleep but had to get up and pee.

It was becoming necessary to *act*. To do something. When Drew and Trina went their separate ways for the summer, Chris felt suddenly lighter of heart and freer to take some sort of step. He started pedaling his bike around campus late at night, looking for something but not sure what, ending up finally at the economics building, in whose open arcade *The Advocate* was sold from a newspaper machine. He would approach cautiously, careful not to be observed, blind to his conspicuous furtiveness but resolute in his conclusion that Drew or not, it was time for action, preferably of the pink-pages variety.

Drew had revised and redefined his relationship with Trina so many times that, when he announced one rainy January night that the two of them had agreed they should "see other people," Chris barely looked up from his Virginia Woolf. News along these lines had the same musty smell as their row house in damp weather, and was, Chris had recently decided, to be endured with the same stoicism. Tomorrow the sun would shine, the building would dry out and, no matter how Drew described his relation with her, they would be off screwing somewhere.

Saying "so what" was also easier, Chris had discovered, when you had something else to think about—as, since he'd met Wade, he had.

Drew's usual practice was to rush off on some bogus errand after dropping one of his verbal bombs, but not this time. After making his announcement and methodically stripping off his soaked clothes—"fucking Noah's flood out there"—he spoke again.

"Please," he said. "How can you expect me to cope with this boisterous exuberance?"

Chris looked up and nodded. "I'm sorry," he said. "I'll try to keep it down." He returned to his book.

"That's better. I did spot a bit of foam at the corner of your mouth."

Chris nodded again.

"It's true," Drew said. "We're going to see other people."

"I believe you."

"You don't have to bother being jealous anymore. I'm all yours."

They read for a while. Drew sat naked at his desk, underlining in Gibbon; Chris's concentration waxed and waned, caught between the plotless novel and the mesmerizing patter of raindrops on the porch roof, which extended from their window like a kind of rustic deck where, in good weather, they sunned. Every few minutes he snuck a peek at Drew, to see if the display of flesh had any effect, and he was elated to feel almost nothing.

"I don't suppose you're interested in her," Drew said after a while.

"No."

" 'Cause I wouldn't really mind."

Chris murmured.

"Do you think we'll ever be friends again?" Drew said to the wall. "I mean, as opposed to roommates for life?"

"We're friends."

"You act like you've been prepped for surgery. I want you to count backwards slowly from one hundred."

"I'm reading."

"You're reading. I see. Sorry to interrupt."

"I forgive you."

"What a relief," Drew said. "Maybe I'll read too."

Chris nodded. His stomach was already twisting, but not because of anything Drew was saying. Only seventy-five minutes separated him from *nine o'clock*. Nine o'clock: the hour at which Chris was to present himself at Wade's. Wade's roommate was in Los Angeles until Monday. T-minus seventy minutes and counting. *Tick-tock.*

Drew said something else, then got up and put on a pair of running shorts and a sweatshirt.

"I'll be in the showers," he said. "Maybe somebody will talk to me there."

Chris nodded and smiled blankly, strong in the knowledge that at the moment he didn't care what Drew said or wore or did or didn't.

Not too many days later, when Drew and Michael and a team from the house were playing mud football with a group of sophomores, there was a knock on the door. It was her, the dread one, in the flesh. She stepped into the room warily, like a cat examining new quarters, suspicious that some ghastly foe was about to leap out from behind the closet door. She seemed, although an inexpert Chris could not be sure, to be unhappily intoxicated in some way.

"You're alone," she said. "Right? I mean, he's not here. Drew, I mean."

"No."

"I'm interrupting you."

"Well, no," Chris said.

"Because I can leave."

"I'm not busy."

"You're surprised to see me."

"Yes."

"Drew didn't want to be with me here. He was always careful. He said it upset you. If I was here."

"He said that?"

"Yeah. And I've wondered about it. Like, why we seemed to hate each other right from the start."

"Hate is sort of a strong word."

"Okay. Whatever. You know what I mean."

"I guess so."

"Maybe we should talk about it. Do you want to? I do, because it's, you know, sort of bothered me all along."

"I'm sorry about that," Chris said.

"Like, even though we didn't know each other, we were enemies? Isn't that weird?"

"My fault."

"Because all he ever talks about is you. The things you guys have done and talked about and everything. Sometimes I had to tell him to shut up, I didn't want to hear any more."

"I'll bet he didn't."

She laughed, then fidgeted. "We agreed we should see other people," she said. "Did he tell you that?"

"Yes."

"Are you going out with anyone now?"

"Not really," Chris said after a pause in which he considered whether Wade counted and, if he did, whether that was mentionable.

"Do you think he would be mad if we went out? You and me?"

"He said it'd be okay," Chris said, wanting to be agreeable but wondering if this was going too far. "Sort of. I mean, he said something like that."

"Do you want to? Go out, I mean."

"I don't know," Chris said. "I don't think so. I mean, not now, anyway."

"That's cool," she said. "I can understand."

"It's nothing personal," Chris said. "It's just that—"

"I get the picture."

Chris shrugged and smiled.

"That's funny, because Drew's always saying how you're the most available guy he knows."

"He thinks he knows everything."

She laughed again. *"Definitely."* After a pause she said, "So what about Mike?"

"Don't know."

"You guys are so tight, it's weird. It's like one of you is never without at least one other one. There have been times, you know, when I've—should I say this?" She looked up at the ceiling, then out the window, as though guiding etiquette might be written in the clouds. "Jesus, sometimes I wonder about Drew and Mike. You know, like—do you know what I mean?"

"Not really."

"I mean, I know Drew likes girls and everything. We've never had any problem with that at all. Physically, I mean. Sexually in bed. But when you see two guys together that much, you sort of wonder?"

Despite himself, Chris laughed.

"Or you and Drew," she went on dizzily. "I mean, he talks about you so much. All the time. Sorry. I shouldn't have said that. I can't believe I did. But I've wondered. Sorry. Because, you know, you've always lived together and everything. It's not like you haven't had chances if you felt like it."

She looked at him, and he looked at her.

"I'm sorry," she said. "This must be really offensive."

Chris shook his head. "What about me and Mike?" he said. "Are we suspected?"

"*He'd* do anything," she said. "I don't know about you. You seem more uptight."

"Thanks."

She laughed with relief. "You're welcome!" she said.

"You think Mike's that wild."

"Oh God." She rolled her eyes.

"Really."

"The way he looks at girls. The way he's looked at me. You can just tell." She stopped talking for a moment to reach for a cigarette, then looked sheepishly at Chris and let her hands drop. "Sorry. Bad habit. You don't smoke, do you? No. Didn't think so. The reason I came over here in the first place is to say I'm sorry I messed up your friendship with Drew. Oh yes I did! I know it. Probably it's his fault and everything, but I didn't mean for it to happen. It was all because of me."

"No."

"Mostly."

"Partly. Not you personally, like I said. God, I feel like a dick. I don't even know you. It was—I don't know how to describe it."

"I hear you," she said.

"She was hitting on me," Michael said, during a break at the library.

"Hmmm," Drew said.

"Totally."

"Trina."

"Yes."

"She came by to talk to Chris, too," Drew said. "Last week when we were playing football. Sly little wench."

"This was at night," Michael said. "You guys were out somewhere. She must have known."

"The two of you alone."

"We didn't do anything," Michael said.

"I told her it was okay," Drew said. "We agreed we could go out with other people if we wanted to."

"I still think of her as being, like, yours."

"Hmmm," Drew said. "Women as property." He murmured something to himself. "You don't think she's attractive."

"Not at all," Michael said. "I mean, sure I do."

"So you thought about it."

"I suppose so. I mean, sure, sometimes. You know. I mean, there's Merry."

"Right." Drew's eyebrows rose.

"Mostly she wanted to talk, I think."

"About?"

"You. Me. All of us. You and Chris. What kind of friends we are."

Drew's eyes flickered blue.

"I don't know," Michael said uncomfortably. "It was a strange conversation."

"I'm sure. Chris said they actually spoke to each other. I sort of expected to see blood and fur all over the place, but he claims it was very civil. It's very bizarre."

"Are you still going to see her?"

Drew shrugged. "Suppose so. I mean, she's great to know in the biblical sense. Right?"

Michael nodded.

"She just showed up?" Drew said.

"She called," Michael said. " 'Meet me at the Union, it's

important.' I didn't even know it was her, at first. She didn't say who she was. So, there she was. We just talked."

"What kind of friends we are," Drew said. "What kind of friends are we?"

"Really tight and everything. That's what she said. She talked a lot about Chris."

"Always a fascinating subject."

"It was kind of off the wall," Michael said. "Like, what's the point of this."

"The whole conversation."

"Yeah."

"And?"

"I don't know. We just sort of sat there talking about things. And it got later and kind of uncomfortable."

"She thinks you and Chris are these two dark moons affecting my tides that she can't see. I told her that was bullshit but I don't think she was paying attention. She loves her little theories." He paused to lean back in his chair, stretching his arms over his head. "She gave me the third degree about spring break, you know. What did the three of us do in the desert, all by our lonesomes."

"Tons of drugs."

"That's what I told her," Drew said. "But no—she's convinced we were out there practicing our sodomy."

"You're *kidding*."

"I am not kidding. She's an extremely bizarre person. You're lucky you didn't do her."

"Why would she think that?"

"Who knows?" Drew said. "I've been plugging that girl's brains out for a year and a half."

"Do you have a green highlighter?" Michael said. "Mine's dried up."

Chris had Drew to thank for making the Wade liaison possible—Drew, who insisted that Chris come with him to a

party the history department was throwing to spice the undergraduate stew with some alumni savvy. Chris's complaint that
he wasn't even a history major was dismissed in a brief
phrase—"You should be"—and with the unflattering adden-
dum that bodies were needed to fill the count in case authentic
history majors failed to show up.

The entire enterprise seemed to Chris like numbing
drudgery until they got to the history building and climbed the
stairs to the second-floor lounge and gave their names to the
boy who sat at the courtesy table recording arrivals and
handing out name tags. He was, as Chris learned later, after
they had kissed for the first time, a freshman whose work-
study assignment was with the alumni association as a coordi-
nator of events that brought together undergraduates and
real-worlders.

After a few moments of on-and-off eye contact and nods
and smiles, but no actual exchange of anything other than the
name tag, Chris shrugged in the boy's direction and followed
Drew into the party. He did not want Drew watching, and there
was no reason to think that this enchanting boy was anything
other than a friendly freshman grateful to have been acknowl-
edged by a worldly upperclassman.

Making eye contact with boys had become Chris's favorite
sport, and he played it with bold skill and tenacity, up to a
point. No longer did he confine himself to the furtive glance
that would be abandoned at the instant of reply; now he stared
quite frankly until the other boy looked away.

Were these encounters nothing more than an exercise in
animal fascination? A vestige of the days before language,
when two beings communicated by intuition and grunts and
gestures? He wondered. For Chris, the stares he received from
other boys were unmistakably sexual, because his own were.
Every glance was an invitation, a plea—*please*—a gesture of
erotic promise. He could not imagine that anyone could miss
the obvious point he was making. Then one day an attractive

boy he had been staring at relentlessly in the library approached him (is this *it?* he thought, wild with fear and desire),
to ask if he was all right. Chris nodded mutely, looking down
like a dog that had just been reprimanded for peeing on the
rug, and the boy walked away into the rest room and did not
look back, even though the instant he passed, Chris fixed his
gaze on him once again.

Getting beyond eye contact was a problem he hadn't yet
solved. Because he had been raised to believe that staring at
people was impolite, even an exchange of meaningful glances
was an unsatisfactory basis on which to build further contacts.
You could not, after staring at someone and being stared back
at, simply start talking to him, as though the exchange of
stares had been a proper introduction. And yet, if you did not
stare at someone, catch his attention in some way, what hope
was there?

As a freshman, Chris had fallen in soundless love with a
boy he saw every other day in his Economics 1 class. Dogged
research in the froshbook yielded a name under a blurry but
recognizable black-and-white photo; the student directory gave
an address and phone number. Several times he started to dial
the number—five digits, six (hang up), finally all seven—but
before the first ring was over he lost his nerve.

It was easier to write letters, anonymous and passionate,
filled with proposals to meet in the library stacks or in a field,
at night, across campus, where no one could possibly find
out, than to risk the immediacy of the telephone. These letters
he wrote and mailed.

After each dispatch he came to Econ class the following
day wondering if his thoughts had been received, read, di-
gested, and if so, what discernible effects would they produce
in the object of his desire? Would he wear the green polo shirt
Chris had asked him to wear on Wednesday if he was interested in getting together? No. Perhaps he didn't own a green

polo shirt. Next time, mention an article of clothing you have seen him in before.

Desperation soon set in. The boy acted as though nothing had happened. Chris flirted with a daring step: writing his initials and address on the back of the envelope. Too risky; the consequences could be dire. He flirted again with the telephone, willing it to ring. It did, and it was always for Drew.

Eventually they wrote their finals and the quarter ended and Chris did not see the boy for many months—not until the spring, when he spotted him and a girl, sitting side by side on the lawn by the education building, staring at a blob of twisted metal rods assembled by an artist of the modern. He felt like shouting out, from the safety of his bicycle: Hey, *I'm* the one who wrote you all those letters. But he didn't.

Wade made it easy. He smiled and said, "Hi," when Chris emerged from the lounge, seeking fresh air. A shy-shocked Chris managed to nod and utter a syllable before averting his eyes and running his hands along the railing that lined the stairwell, feverishly trying to think of something more to say. He was about to ask the boy if he was interested in history when Drew emerged from the lounge and said:

"What a bore. Are we ready for warp maneuvers?"

"I guess. I needed a little air."

"A pretty sorry lot in there," Drew agreed. He glanced at the boy at the table. "And a regrettable shortage of drink. Shall we boldly blow this Popsicle stand? I'm psyched."

"Sure," Chris said. "I guess so."

So that was that, except that Wade called the next day. He introduced himself and explained how he had tracked Chris down (by a familiar method that began with his memorizing Chris's name from the name tag he had made for him the night before). Would Chris like to get together for coffee or something? There was no reason not to, even though it was odd to be sought out so aggressively as a friend by a freshman, who was certainly too young to have anything less than innocent in mind. As a freshman, Chris had had a few contacts with upper-classmen, but mostly he had remained within the boundaries of his class to make friends. This had seemed right and proper at the time, but he was glad Wade was less rigid.

The first night, after coffee, they took a walk in the foot-hills. It was clear and chilly, and when Wade suggested that they sit on the ground under a scrub oak to look at the stars, it was only natural that they would huddle together, pooling their heat. The casual brush of fingers across a neck or the resting of a palm on a blue-jeaned thigh was a thousand times more vivid than anything that had happened with Meredith or any other girl. Time seemed to slow.

How their mouths found each other neither could remember afterward; accident or instinct, it didn't matter. Years of hollowness melted in the fusion; years of wondering why girls did not set their hearts racing, of why they seemed to have slipped out of sorts with the boys they had grown up with and always known.

The second night was a week later—another chilly evening that smelled of woodsmoke and fog. This time Wade's roommate was away, and the two of them ended up writhing around on Wade's narrow bed. An author of sex manuals, had he been cataloging the action, would not have found much worth writing about; mostly it was the solitary technique the two had perfected over the years, modified to include the actual presence of the fantasy body, but to the lovers it was heartstopping. The sight of another naked boy upon whom you could lay your hands in the most intimate, the most secret places, was almost too much to stand.

"You smell funny," Drew said without looking up from his book when Chris returned. "And you're late. Report to sick bay."

Instead Chris locked himself in the bathroom, breathing in the smell of Wade as it rose from every part of his body.

.   .   .

Michael's growing attachment to Meredith made Chris feel glad and wistful at the same time. Glad, because their lives seemed to be merging smoothly and naturally (it could be done); wistful because what they were creating for themselves was not something he could imagine happening in his own life.

Even Drew, while circling the wagons around his contempt for the idea of love, was forced to notice that the two of them were, as far as anyone could tell (because they did not talk about themselves, and Michael smilingly shied away from the topic when she wasn't around), in love. He took a new tack.

"It's just like the Beatles," Drew said one day over lunch, just Chris and he; the happy couple were in San Mateo, having a picnic with the family for which she occasionally baby-sat. "John and Yoko. The group dynamic is ruined." The words were gloom-and-doom, but Drew spoke them calmly, as if even he, the love heretic, recognized the inevitable: that people, with luck and doggedness, bonded to one another, as Michael and Meredith were doing.

"Then I get to be Paul," Chris said.

"No way. I'm Paul. You're Ringo."

"George."

"Yes, better," Drew said. "I see you strumming a big guitar."

The first giddiness of the Wade affair convinced Chris that he was finally breaking free of Drew's grip, that he had achieved escape velocity. But the second time they had sex it wasn't much fun, and by the time Chris sat on the edge of the long, narrow bed pulling on his socks and tying his shoelaces, he knew that the only person he wanted to be with, ever would want to be with, was Drew.

Despite Trina's lingering at the edge of the scene, darting onstage at curious moments, disappearing before she could really be irritating, he and Drew were as close that spring as they had ever been. The world in which they lived had been boiled down to its essence, leaving the two of them in an intimacy Chris had spent months yearning for but now, sexually awake for the first time in his life, feared.

Without Michael on hand to complain to or Trina to hate or Wade to fondle, Drew drugged him with longing. Just a light prod to the imagination gave Chris the fantasy that they were lovers; when Drew wanted to spend a Saturday afternoon in San Francisco shopping for sweaters at Wilkes Bashford ("Ultra-faggy," he said as they left the shop empty-handed), it was as though they lived in the city and were recognized by everyone as the inevitable cute-boy couple they were.

Dangers lurked, some seen, some not. Mostly Chris feared the resurgence of Trina, the diversion of Drew's attention and emotional energy from its rightful focus—him—into the wadi that was her. The gulf of graduation lay in wait somewhere—like death, unavoidable but unimaginable, a prospect so remote he did not even try to consider it. Graduation would break them apart and carry them off in different directions to different places, friends, futures—unless there was a plan. But a plan required the conscious application of psychic energy, and Chris preferred to use his in sustaining the fantasy against everyday reality, even as the world tightened around them.

Often, when they were alone in their room or walking on a quiet lane to or from the gym or the squash courts, he felt the words rising in his throat: Just once. You should at least try it. Experience life. (There were many variations along this line.) If Drew would go to bed with him once, Chris was convinced, he would see the truth about the two of them. The sex would be apocalyptic, the melding of physical and metaphysical desires most people spent most of their lives trying to understand. There would be an answer.

Just say yes.

For Drew's twenty-first birthday, Trina gave him a pair of sheer white briefs with little red hearts all over them, and Geoff showed up to start an argument about sexual ethics.

Later, Chris and Drew ate Sara Lee birthday cake and got drunk on greyhounds, which, because Chris mixed them, wiped Drew out. Eventually, when they were lying in their beds—Drew in his new briefs, Chris trying not to think about how he looked in them—Drew raised the subject directly, jumping in from Geoff.

"It's not that I object, you know, to the idea of two guys making it," he said, "even though it is sort of gross. I guess all sex is, if you're not doing it."

"Are we still talking about Geoff?"

"What a total whore he is," Drew said. "But that's okay. I would be, too, if girls weren't so impossible about it. That's men, fine. It's that when you have two guys it can't be anything more."

"Like what?"

"Like babies."

"You hate babies!"

"I've never actually said that," Drew said carefully. "Besides, that's not the point. The point is that other people do like them, most people do, and they'll never accept fag stuff as equivalent. I don't care, actually. Fags can do whatever they want to. But it pisses me off when they say how unfairly they're treated when they give themselves these indulgences other people can't have. Geoff is really bad about it—he acts like it's perfectly normal, sleeping with somebody different every week."

"You're always saying how people need to be sexually liberated."

"There's a limit," Drew said. "Going to bathhouses is sick."

"He does that?"

"I'm sure he does. I haven't asked. I don't especially want to know."

"I don't think it has to be like that," Chris said. "You

know, homosexuals. They don't all go to the baths, do you
think?"

"He *claims* to know respectable faggots. Who own houses
and everything."

"Maybe he does."

"Who knows who he knows?"

"So you're saying it's impossible for two men to have a relationship," Chris said. "Other than sex."

"Yes."

"Or they can be friends."

"Like us."

"And you can't mix the two. Friendship and sex."

"Wrecks both. Who'd want to?"

"Did you ever feel like—um—that Trina was a friend?"

"Please."

"So it was just physical."

"Don't say *just* physical."

"It was *primarily* physical, then."

Chris thought he could see Drew squirm in the dark.

"She's so pathetically vulnerable half the time," Drew
said at last. "I suppose there was a certain degree of protec-
tiveness." He almost never said things like this, which made
Chris think he meant it.

"I think this would be a healthier society if we weren't so
hung up on gender," Chris said, feeling reckless. "I think two
people should be able to touch each other if they're close to
each other, even if they're both guys. Look at Mike. He's good
at it."

"He'll touch anything."

"It's natural."

"Hugging's okay," Drew said. "But friends don't suck
each other off."

"God," Chris said softly, sagging back on the bed.

"Cocksucking leads to buttfucking," Drew said. "It's just
like pot and heroin."

"That's the most ridiculous thing you've ever said."

"I feel unwell," Drew said, sitting up suddenly. "That cake."

"Just lie there," Chris commanded. "You'll be better."

"Sick bay," Drew said. "I'm on my way. Kirk out."

Chris heard the sheets part and saw a shadow move quickly but unsteadily toward the darkened bathroom. There was a wretched heaving sound that confirmed some sort of problem. Chris pulled himself out of bed and followed.

"You okay?" he asked, peering apprehensively into the darkened toilet. In a moment his eyes adjusted, and he saw Drew on his knees before the bowl, his hands gripping its sides and his head bowed. The sharp stink of vomit filled the air. Drew gave one more sad little heave and then sniffled several times.

"Flush," he said, without looking up.

Chris flushed.

"I'm getting the flu," Drew said.

Chris squatted beside him, slipping an arm around his shoulder to steady him. "Do you want to lie down?" he asked.

"I think so," Drew said, rising to his feet. Chris's arm fell away like an unwanted article of clothing. "I feel better," he said.

"It must be the twenty-four-minute flu," Chris said.

"I hate birthdays."

Slowly they walked back to Drew's bed. The bedclothes were in a tangle at its foot. Like a little boy Drew flopped onto the mattress and pulled the knotted sheets over him without bothering even to try to straighten them out. Chris fussed a bit, making sure he was fully covered.

"I like your shorts," he said.

"Do you?" Drew said. He lifted his hips, and in a moment the briefs were in his hand. "Here." He flung them at Chris. "You try them. They chafe me."

Chris swallowed, holding the undergarment uneasily. "You should wear something," he said. "It's January. It's cold."

"I'm fine," Drew said. He lay perfectly still, eyes closed, flat on his back.

Minutes passed. Chris stood there, telling himself that he was ready to help if Drew should need him again—although it was obvious that Drew had plunged deep into sleep.

Touch his fingers (nothing). Whisper his name (nothing). Brush back the hair from his forehead and brush your lips across the warm skin (nothing). With a sigh, Chris turned toward his own bed, the briefs rolled into a ball and tucked under his arm, like a teddy bear.

the CRACK-UP (1)

Drew reclines on the sofa, holding a wine goblet, with two fingers, at the point where the stem joins the bowl. The wine, a sweetish white zinfandel with noticeable fizz (Michael did the wine shopping this month), sloshes about precariously. Meredith silently asks herself if there is any club soda in the refrigerator, in the event of a spill on the off-white fabric. She cannot remember. Michael refills their glasses.

Outside it is a blizzard, a blinding blast of prickly snow that swirls in the orange light of the streetlamps, piles up on windowsills, tree branches, cars, people. In this winter wonderland, the evening of the day before Christmas Eve, all the airports have closed. Arctic air is on the way, forecasters agree: All the computer models of the atmosphere are converging. Soon the snow will turn to gray ice and the city will abandon its efforts to clear the streets and no one's car will start.

Drew called at about three-thirty, when, after a four-hour delay, the airline announced that all outbound flights, including his connection to the coast, were canceled. There was no way out of town until tomorrow morning at the earliest; he was to check back. Meredith told him how to ride the el into the city, and she met him at the station with their front-wheel-drive car.

"God, you look great!" were the first words out of his mouth. They were embracing each other—a little awkwardly; neither of them was sure how the change in circumstances between Michael and Merry affected the two of them, Drew and Merry, whose relationship had always been ambiguous anyway, flavored with a dash of unfinished business. So he liked to think. They looked enough alike that some people at graduation (mainly Chris's parents) mistook them for brother and sister.

"Michael's on his way home," she reported as they started on their way down the slush-bound street. "He was on call last night so he may be weird. FYI. Joe's driving them. It could take a while."

"Do I know Joe?"

"No. Classmate of Michael's. You've never met him. We have an extra bedroom, did I mention that? You're welcome to it. There's only one feather pillow. The other one is foam rubber."

"Hey, hard about!" he said. "Foam rubber. Forget it. Do I look like that kind of guy?"

"You look hungry. Like you need Christmas cookies."

"I do. Do you still celebrate Christmas?"

"Sort of," she said. "We call it the holiday season and leave it at that. Didn't you get our card?"

"I did."

"Next week we go east to see his and mine. Two birds with one stone and all that."

"Severe," Drew said.

Joe is only an hour gone, laden with a package of Meredith's cookies for his family. (They urged him not to drive through the storm, but he smilingly refused.

"I'll be careful," he had said. "The way I always am."

"You never are," Meredith said. "And you have rear-wheel drive."

"I think it's letting up," Drew said, peering out a window.

"Day after day after tomorrow," Michael said. "Be there."

"Aloha.")

"He looks just like you," Drew says to Michael. The conversation has drifted aimlessly back to Joe. "Schnoz, everything. The works."

"Did you tell this guy he's sleeping on the deck tonight?" Michael says to Meredith. "We do still have that sleeping bag somewhere, don't we? With the big hole that the rats ate in it?"

"Zipper's broken."

"And the pillow filled with gravel?"

"I told you he can be a little strange post-call," she says to Drew. He slugs down a good bit of his wine. "Mmm mmm good," he says. "Too fucking sweet for me. Have you ever heard of dry wine?"

"No."

"I've tried," Meredith says.

Drew pours himself more, nonetheless. "Do you ever hear from Chris?"

"Sometimes," Michael says. "We got a card or something last week. Didn't we? It's around here someplace."

"We saw him on our honeymoon," Meredith reminds Michael. "Remember? He and his roommate made us dinner."

"That was in August," Michael says. He is astounded at how easy it is to maintain this conversation when all he hears in Drew's voice is hers.

Already it is years. It doesn't seem like it. He still remembers the tiniest details of how it began. She was with Drew, waiting at the gate for Michael's flight into National, wearing a blue oxford button-down several sizes too large that probably belonged to him, and Aca Joe khakis. Perfectly nice, he thought to himself, perfectly innocent, sweet of her to come too, though Meredith was still hundreds of miles away at her parents' and he had felt the fire of Dana's glance lick him as soon as he stepped off the jetway. Her sex was pitched to his, a perfect harmony of lust; he did not need to sleep with her to know this.

Sometimes, when you have nothing better to do, you wonder about the sort of people your friends will end up married to. Drew had always been a mystery to Michael in this regard. It was far easier to imagine his *not* ending up with certain sorts of women than with them. He was a stand-alone type. Trina had been sweet and cooperative, but she never fully emerged from Drew's shadow when the two of them were together, and Michael knew, because Drew had told him so, that this was bothersome.

Even before they crossed the 395 bridge into the District, it was clear that being liable to eclipse was not Dana's problem; from the back seat she launched an argument about race relations and white-male privilege that got Drew snapping. She was aggressive and open, dark eyes shining with hostile curiosity in her pale face, around which her glossy black hair was cut close. She was there.

"I've already won this argument," Drew said, "so why do you persist? You'll give our guest indigestion."

"I thought someone was coming with you," Dana said. "Your significant other."

"Girlfriend," Drew said. "She's at her parents. Coming Friday. Am I right?"

"You're right."

"Don't forget it."

"No way, José."

"Don't encourage him," she said to Michael. "He thinks he always is."

"I am," Drew said. "Besides, you always think you are."

"I am."

"You argue with her for a while," Drew said. "It's pretty easy. Just ignore what she says. I'll be driving."

Michael took the banter as a sign that they were comfortable with each other. This made him feel comfortable with her, despite the smoky looks, and he settled into the back seat, half-listening to their argument as they carried it along like TV wrestlers: comic violence that did no harm.

It turned out that they were living together. Drew had not mentioned this, and Michael wanted to ask him what it was like, how it was going, but couldn't find the chance: Drew never seemed to be alone. Trina had never distorted Michael's vision of Drew as complete in himself, a figure of whom Michael had a full view and to whom he had direct access. Dana, more than distorting this vision, actually combined with Drew to create something altogether new: It was no longer possible for Michael to consider him without considering her, too—the two of them together. The recognition left him feeling vaguely uneasy, and he asked himself if he and Merry had a similar effect on other people.

For dinner they walked across the P Street bridge into Dupont Circle, where, after an argument about where to go that led into another hot Washington, D.C., political discussion in which Michael took a cameo part, Drew led them to a glassy little café along Twentieth Street that served a wide range of pastas. Several glasses of wine later they passed into the street in search of gelato. Michael found himself walking between them, and they bumped along like a herd of dizzy cattle.

Over cups of chocolate-hazelnut gelato Drew said to Dana: "So tell us again about Third World solidarity."

"Are you a right-wing pig like him?" Dana asked Michael.

"Does she look oppressed?" Drew asked Michael.

"No," Michael said.

"I am oppressed," she said. "All women are. It's built into the society."

"See?" Drew said to Michael. "I told you. Just like Old
Faithful."

"You probably have to study," Michael said. "I'm sorry."

"And you have to be well-rested for your interviews."

"While we walk home," Dana said, "I'll explain about oppression. You can't listen to him. He likes Reagan, he just
won't admit it."

It is six months now that they are married; almost a year since,
accommodating himself to the pressure of the inevitable, he
proposed; more than two years since Dana, from whom he has
never heard another word, crashed into his life. It was easy not
to talk to Drew, whom he has come guiltily to resent, and being
cut off from this dazzling, dangerous woman is an addictive
pain.

He and Merry had gotten sicker and sicker of commuting.
Weekends away were harder to arrange because of his being on
call and having to round on Saturdays, and when she came to
town she was so often by herself for so much of the time that
he felt guilty. Sometimes Joe, if he could, picked up some of
the slack, but a temporary arrangement that dragged on without end began to make them both miserable.

One truth—unspoken—was that he did not want her
moving to Chicago solely to be with him. That was too heavy
a burden for him to carry. She might hate the city and their life
in it. She might have trouble finding a job and they might be
poor. It would be an advance to a position from which orderly
retreat, if that became necessary, would be difficult.

Another truth was that there was no alternative, other
than agreeing that things were hopeless and giving up altogether. If they were going to be together, they might as well be
married. Everyone got married. Even if Dana were available,
he would have to ask himself if he would want to *marry* her.
Meredith was the sort of woman you married, the sort of
woman you could stand to be around. Dana probably was not.

In asking Meredith to marry him, he tried not to see any problem in the fact that deep in his heart there was another candle burning. Its warmth and glow made him a happier person, and didn't she benefit from that?

When he told his parents that he and Merry were engaged, they confined their open fretting to the children and made not a peep about his marrying out of the faith. He did not need to be told what this omission meant. Children would be an issue—even though none existed yet, or were even forecast—but he knew that his parents were fearful less of the hazy prospect that their grandchildren would not be born to a Jewish woman than of what the Frankels would think, and the Sarnoffs and all their other friends, about the marriage itself. Michael's break with expectation and solidarity was not unprecedented (the Lowenthals' son had married a Filipino; they lived in the Canal Zone) but still novel enough to give an unpleasant shock. Most disturbing, to the elder generation, was what the *idea* of marrying out portended: a future of mingling, confusion and chaos, in which the essence of Jewishness would be diluted and finally lost, its history and traditions forgotten or neglected.

The main gulf between Michael and his parents, in fact, is America. He is a Jewish American, not assimilated into America's secular, consumerist polyglot mongrel mess of a society but *born* into it. He is a native in the most profound way. It is all he has ever known and all that has shaped him. They are American Jews, holding clear memories of immigrant parents, bilingual households in which the old country and the new faced each other hopefully but sometimes with the confusion of missed signals. They are staunch supporters of Israel, people whose European cousins of the same age were murdered in Hitler's death camps.

At times Michael feels guilty at his utter Americanness. He went to Hebrew school, he owns a yarmulke, which he wears briefly during the High Holidays, he mutters "oy!"

whenever something goes wrong; but although he respects his past and that of his people, he seldom really feels it in his heart. Performing the rituals gives him a sense of belonging that he enjoys, but what he belongs to he could not say, other than what he has been taught it is.

Eventually they will have children, though the prospect does not particularly appeal, even beyond his parents' discomfort. He likes the idea of replicating himself, but he can't get over the fear that caring for a baby would take up still more of a life already short on free time. He has felt since high school that every aspect of his life has been tied to the professional goal. What has he given up to get this far (and he still is not fully trained!)? Too much even to contemplate, and of course you can't take back the time.

Instead of openly giving him the third degree about his seeing a blond Christian girl, his parents' preferred tactic had been to introduce him to the eligible daughters of their friends, who seemed to live all over the country, as if they were some sort of network, so that no matter where he went, a nice Jewish girl of reliable family was only a phone call away. Whenever he went home he was resigned to finding some young, dark-haired, dark-eyed woman sitting in the living room with his mother, chatting away as though they were already mother and daughter-in-law. He felt like an outsider.

It was after one such exhausting interlude, at Thanksgiving last year, that, on the train from his parents' to Virginia to spend half of Saturday and half of Sunday with Meredith before flying back to work, he made up his mind to ask her. The decision left him feeling flat—maybe because he had always known it would be made—but that did not discourage him. Surrounded by the madnesses of medicine and his parents and haunted by the steamy ghost of the shower, he turned to Meredith as to the soft blue blanket of childhood, the warm safe friend in the night. They were in her father's study; everyone else was asleep. She was drinking port from a lead-crystal snifter. Outside, the cold damp night smelled of autumn.

"I think we should do it," he said. "I think it's time."

She, walking around the room, looking at framed degrees and books on shelves, came to a stop behind him, behind the sofa on which he sat, and rested her hands on his neck. He squirmed with a pleasure within which it was impossible that she would say no. Vaguely he wondered if he should get down on one knee or open an expensive bottle of champagne, the way you were supposed to.

"I'm sorry I don't have a ring," he said. "I'll get one. I haven't planned very well."

She was pacing again, taking her warm strong hands with her. He turned his head around and saw her standing at the window, staring out the French windows into the night.

"You can pick it out," he offered. "I'd get the wrong one anyway."

"I don't care about the ring," she said. She moved around the couch and nestled herself beside him, studying his face until he felt like a Martian, until he became afraid that she really was looking inside him, seeing all those things he seldom permitted himself to look at. Seeing her. If he thought about the two of them much more he would inevitably reach the conclusion that he was unworthy of her, too short and not handsome or decent enough for a woman who seemed to him superior in every way. "Yes," she said, kissing him—a little awkwardly, because they were both sort of smiling and laughing and beginning to cry, too, all at the same time.

"She wasted me," Drew says. The bottle of white zinfandel is empty, but he holds it anyway.

Is that my fault? Michael thinks. My fault that this happened? Am I supposed to accept responsibility?

Later, in bed. The two of them alone.

"I feel bad for him," Meredith says. "I never thought I'd feel bad for Drew."

"He drank a lot tonight," Michael says. "Who knows what actually happened?"

"He seems so sad," she says. "I had no idea."

Earlier. Drew says, "Blam!" and jabs a fist into his open palm. There is a loud smacking sound. "I think she's a lesbian."

"Dana?" Meredith asks, after an uncomfortable moment.

Drew nods. Michael stares at him so long that the face before him no longer looks familiar. Who *is* that blond man? Dana a *lesbian?*

"Why do you think that?" Meredith asks.

"She moved in with her dyke friends," Drew says. "All these manhaters. She was always with them. No warning or anything. Just, See you later, I'm moving out, kiss my ass. I hate her. I really really do."

"She moved out?" Michael manages to say.

Drew nods.

"When did this happen?" Meredith asks.

"Long time ago," Drew says. "Two years. Something like that. Right after Christmas. Happy New Year!" His tone warns them that he is not to be regarded as pathetic.

Later.

"She did seem headstrong," Meredith says to Michael, in their private darkness. Drew is in the guest room, Joe's old room, snoring. Snow snow snow. It builds a fluffy white wedge outside their window. The north wind rattles the old wood frames, and the radiator gurgles and hisses.

"Like he isn't."

"Well, I suppose that's true. You don't seem very sympathetic. I can't believe she's a lesbian!"

"It's not really any of our business," Michael says. "It happened years ago. You heard him. Why is he bringing it up?"

"That's what happens when nobody comes along to take her place," she says. "It's all he's got to chew on so he chews on it. Besides, I don't think he understands what happened. I know *I* don't. She must have left for some reason." She pauses. "When Joe and Liz broke up you weren't so tough on him."

"That was different."

Indeed it was.

"We were living together," Michael continues. "I saw the guy every day. I saw how it affected him. Besides, that was mostly because his family drove them nuts. If you were Liz, you would have freaked too, I'll bet. Drew—God knows what really happened."

He rolls onto his side, horrified at what he is saying. There is Drew, sloshed and baffled, wondering what went wrong, can't get it out of his head; here is Michael, holding the answer. Not my fault, he thinks, but not quite believing it.

"They were weird together," Michael says. "She made Drew even more—I don't know. You know."

"Do you really think she's a lesbian?" she says. "I wonder if she was a lesbian before she met Drew or if, you know . . ."

"I have no idea," Michael says. This could be true, he reassures himself, even though it's not likely. He doesn't know that she *isn't*. Stranger things have happened.

Ever since Dana slipped into the shower with him, unannounced, the world has been spinning slightly off-center, like a child's top that lolls from side to side on the driveway concrete, making you feel dizzy if you stare at it too long. He has been staring a long time. To look at Drew is to see a competitor, friend, fool. Which is it? He cannot tell; the subject is uncomfortable.

Marrying Meredith was unrelated to the incident, he has often told himself. His feelings about her are deep and adult, constant emanations to which she is constantly responding.

Whether he loves Dana or not is a question that has no bearing on his marriage, and so he can admit that the answer to the question is, in a way, depending on what you mean by "love," yes. He is not sure what he means by that. He is glad no one is asking him.

The flat she shared with Drew was warm and dark, intimately close to the ground. He had gone to sleep on the futon in the living room serene in the knowledge that they would be up early and out the door to (her) class and (his) externship before the first faint stirrings of consciousness rattled inside his skull. Late in the afternoon Meredith would end the visit to her family in Virginia and join them, and they would fly to Chicago together the next day. In the meantime he looked forward to the luxury of long hours of quiet sleep, to be followed by that pink elephant of medical training, an afternoon of lazy solitude.

The shower curtain was translucent; when he opened his eyes he could see, through the streams of hot water and soap and the opalescent plastic, the line of bulbs above the vanity mirror, glowing distinctly, as if through a fog. Standing under the shower head, letting the hot water pound on his back, made him feel safe and relaxed. Maybe he would never leave this spot. His penis was half-hard from flitting images that lingered from the night, and from the simple sensual pleasure of the steamy flood.

Doing it in the shower still gave a small thrill. In high school it had been necessary, both to minimize the chance of being discovered and because the water would wash away the evidence, which in other circumstances had to be dealt with more elaborately. Doing it in *their* shower was especially naughty. He wondered if they ever did—or Drew. Hard to imagine Drew in this position—knees slightly flexed and legs bowed to prevent embarrassing collapse in the woozy aftermath—but you never knew. The simple fact of being naked in their bathroom excited him. Whose hair was in the drain?

Whose towel was whose? Whose toothbrush? It was over-whelmingly personal.

He had worked up a good head of soapy lather when the door opened with a squeak too muted to be heard above the rushing water. He did not see. He went on. Someone slipped into the bathroom. He went on, heart pounding in response to his imaginings. Not until the figure turned on the hot water in the basin, reducing the flow to the shower and turning its wet shroud cooler, did he open his eyes with a start and see a shadow standing there. An instant of paralyzed fear—the animal reaction to being caught off guard—subsided to an interval of watchful measure. Make no sudden movements. Escape is impossible, calling out hopeless. There is nothing to do but wait.

He stood there, waiting and watching as the blurred figure put its arms over its head to pull off its shirt. The shower curtain parted, and without a word *she* stepped in, pretending, for an instant, that she did not know he was there (as if the shower, like a high-tech coffeemaker, turned itself on at just the right minute every morning). He felt her body bumping against his, pressing against his, two sets of wet flesh slipping past each other. She had no business being there. What was she doing? She had already gone to class—he had heard the apartment door close. He felt like asking, but didn't, and each passing moment of silence made saying anything at all less likely.

He was almost ready to step out of the shower and towel himself down—having become convinced that he had misunderstood the entire sequence of events; apparently this sort of sharing was common practice (although he didn't picture Drew as the communal, sharing sort)—when her hand lighted on the back of his neck, pulling his mouth to hers. His still-swollen penis rose again, avid creature in the sweltering primeval jungle. They left the water running.

Afterward, his first feeling was that she would disappear, like a ghost, the two of them having exchanged no more than gasps and grunts and shudders and body fluids as they exhausted one hour, then two, locked together, pressing together, sliding together, then apart, then together another way, another time, on the bed she shared with Drew.

At least they didn't talk. It was all right if neither of them said anything; then no verbal memory would exist of what had happened. That he was used to; that was the usual way. Only words could pierce the delicate film of impersonality that lubricated the sex. Anyway there was nothing to say. They must get up and get dressed (but not before showering again, she for the third time) and return to the lives the world had prepared for them. The coffee grounds must be thrown away, the counters wiped, the sink scrubbed, the cat's water dish freshened.

"Drew doesn't love me," she said. She was lying on her back, staring at the ceiling.

"How do you know?"

"I just do."

He felt awkward. "You're wrong," he said. "I can see it."

"There's nothing to see."

"But you live with him."

She gave a sort of half-sigh, half-chuckle. "We've never done it like that. Never even close."

"That doesn't mean—"

"Oh, not by itself. But everything else. You can just tell these things. You know. You love her?"

"Yes."

"She's lucky."

"I don't know."

"You both are."

"This is strange."

"Talking about it."

"Yes."

"I'm not saying I want to marry him," she continued, her hand absently gripping his still-ticking dick. "It's just, you know, really a strange feeling to *know* you haven't reached somebody, even after living with him. You're different. Not all locked up inside."

That was one way of putting it. Michael did not know how to reply, or even if he should. There was nothing to say. The film that separated them was gone, popped like a soap bubble, and now they were exposed to each other far more than they were just by being naked together. Everything she said he understood and believed to be right. She knew Drew as he knew him.

"Oh God," she said.

"I wonder a lot whether likes or unlikes get along better," she continued. "Are you, you know, better off with someone who's just like you, so you know where the other person's coming from, or are you better off with an opposite, so you complement each other? I used to think Drew was exactly like me, and in his sort of sick right-wing way he is—sort of bellicose and rigid. But he's missing something inside, I don't know what it is, but I can feel it's not there. Your girlfriend isn't like you."

"Not really." At the mention of Meredith he groaned to himself and felt a little green swirl of nausea.

"I can tell. I picture you with someone sort of reasonable and, I don't know, mild, I suppose. Who doesn't get upset easily."

"She's blond," he said, more or less irrelevantly.

She shrugged without looking at him, then, with a smile, ran her tongue down the middle of his chest, over his navel, into the danger zone.

Generally he rubbed these sorts of episodes from his mind as soon as they were over, like steam from glass. Somewhere deep inside him another charge was posted on his guilt account to await the due date (if there was to be one), but in his conscious life it was as though nothing had happened. He was untouched.

His detachment made a stark contrast with the attachments that too often began to grow like tentacles from the other party. Too often had he heard the classic questions: "Do you

think we'll see each other again?" "Do you live by yourself?"
He had become an expert at the smile, the shrug, the see-you-
later that said, That's it. So long. Good life. *Ciao.*

So it was unexpected when she popped up from the bed
and, giving him a cursory peck on the lips, got ready for some
other class without saying more than a few absent words to
him. He thought she was being coy until she hoisted her backpack over her shoulder and said:

"See you guys at dinner."

"Okay," he said, feeling foolish for lying naked and exposed on the mattress but determined not to let it show by
clutching for a sheet. He forced himself to think of Meredith,
who was to arrive late in the afternoon. He took another
shower, half-expecting and hoping that the door would creak
open again, which it did not. In the solitude he thought about
things, waiting for the universe to fall back into its accustomed
order, which it did not.

On the plane to Chicago, as he and Merry flew over the
Appalachians and the flight attendants served roast-beef sandwiches, he thought about telling her what had happened. Like
popping a boil, it would be painful and messy, but it would
also relieve pressure and bring a permanent end to the problem. All it would take would be a brief declaration—"She seduced me"—and the needle would be in, the pus flowing.

Of course, this was impossible. Meredith would have to ask
if there had been others, and while he was prepared to lie, he did
not delude himself into thinking he would get away with it. Even
though all the other times were fundamentally different from
Dana—fundamentally meaningless—he knew that that particular
distinction would be equally meaningless to her. Admitting to
having been seduced was one thing, anyway; suggesting to your
lover that you were in love with your best friend's girlfriend—
whom you barely knew (not that that made a difference)—was a
crisis of far greater magnitude, even if you reassured her copi-
ously that you were still in love with her, too, as you were.

. . .

Next morning the snow has tapered to flurries, as the weathermen on all the TV channels agreed it would, and Drew is up early, working the phone, trying to set up the flight west. Michael steps into the shower slightly startled. Over the course of a night's sleep he has forgotten that Drew, the accidental guest, is still here.

This morning he is feeling better about Drew. At least he is out there sitting up straight, making sense when he talks, conducting the business of ordinary life with some proficiency. The memory of him lying there on the sofa, knocking back most of a bottle of bad wine, is like seeing the shadow of another person, someone who is not the friend of glittering invulnerability but a victim splashing around pointlessly in his sorrows and miscues.

The door swings open. It is Meredith, come to brush her teeth. She kisses him through the plastic shower curtain.

"He's calling," she says. "I think he's got a flight."

"Is there any more soap?" Michael asks.

"I thought I'd drive him to the airport," she says, handing him a fresh bar of Dial.

He opens the curtain but leaves the water running, so Drew cannot hear what he is about to say.

"You don't want to go all the way out to the airport," he says. "Not with all this snow. Let him take a cab. He's got money. The airline'll pay, anyway. Or," he says, retreating slightly from her puzzled look, "drive him to the el. That's the best thing for everybody."

"I'll ask him what he wants to do," she says, stepping out and closing the door behind her.

He has wondered, from time to time, but never seriously, about the two of them, Drew and Meredith. The official story is that Michael met her at the same party Drew did—her party—but if that weren't true would they tell him? If he were in Drew's shoes, he would say nothing. Drew could be coy. In

all those years when he went out with Trina in college, for instance, he left no doubt in Michael's mind that she was not the
only show in town, but who the others might be he never said.

And then there is Chris. He and Meredith went out for a
while. This is a matter of public record. Not much happened,
so the story goes; it didn't work out. If she went out with Chris,
is it possible she never met Drew? Is that even remotely plausible? No. So she *did* know Drew. She had to. She is lying. No
wonder she is so eager to drive him to the airport! Maybe they
will get lucky and become trapped in a snowdrift, alone together, with the fold-down back seat and the blanket he put in
the car at the beginning of November, because it was stupid to
travel by car in winter without one.

He towels himself off.

Breakfast is juice and oatmeal and bagels and cream
cheese and coffee. The two of them are at the dining-room table, still disheveled from the night, when he appears, dressed
and primped and combed.

"Yes, son, you can borrow the car tonight," Drew says in
a deep voice, glancing up father-like from the newspaper.
"Give him the keys, dear."

"The office is closed till noon," Meredith says, "so my
morning's free. His flight leaves at eleven."

"How are the roads?" Michael asks, taking a sip of the
coffee, to which she has added insufficient sugar. "Did you
call the state police? Are we out of sugar?"

"Better," she says. "Mostly clear. No we are not out of
sugar," she says, handing him the little porcelain jar. "Neither
are the state police."

"We've been talking about the best way to get you to the
airport," Michael says.

"I told him I'd drive him out."

"Oh," Michael says. "Good. That's great."

"If you trust us," Drew adds.

"Of course I trust you. I just—well, you know. Why drive if you don't have to in stuff like this?"

"I have full confidence in her," Drew says. "She redeems my faith that women should be allowed to drive after all."

"I'm flattered," Meredith says.

"I'm sorry, I didn't sleep well," Drew says. "Indian food gives me nightmares. She seems grouchy," he says to Michael.

"We're not morning people," Michael says. Something about the bagel is sickening—too much cream cheese, maybe, that low-fat Neufchâtel he is convinced doesn't taste the same, even if it is better for you—and he leaves half of it on his plate.

Crunching down the snow-covered sidewalk toward the Belmont station, he glances back at their building, as if he expects to see an answer written on its gray stone face. He felt funny saying goodbye to Drew just now, even though they shook hands and then embraced and said all the things they thought they were supposed to say. It felt funny saying all that when what he really wanted to say was, "Keep your hands off my wife."

Soon, after the ear-splitting thunder of the el, the pitch-and-sway roll downtown, he will be swallowed up again by his residency and will be relieved of the chance to think any more about the two of them. Rounds and note-writing, then at noon he and Joe are playing squash. Joe's family invited them out for Christmas Eve, but Michael made up an excuse so that he and Merry can go out to dinner alone, maybe rent a movie afterward. By then Drew will be gone and forgotten.

The face of his building stares back at him impassively, its windows dark eyes that tell nothing of the life inside. The sun, peeking shyly through the clouds, is just warm enough to make the snow good for packing, and as he walks he scoops, shapes and flips in one smooth motion. Splat goes the ball in the middle of the street, little chunks of it rolling away in a straight line, like asteroids.

TABLE for FOUR

Although neither of them can cook, they are giving a dinner party. Carl lobbied for days for a restaurant or a caterer ("at least they have pots and pans") but Chris wouldn't hear of it. For weeks he clipped recipes from the *Chronicle*, from *Bon Appétit* and *Sunset*, and studied them each night. A sequence of key questions arose: Could they get the ingredients (what was turmeric?)? If so, could they actually prepare the dish in question? If so, would anyone eat it? If so, would they not get sick?

Carl is feeling very insecure about the whole business, other than dessert and coffee, which he has voluntarily put himself in charge of. At least that will turn out, he thinks. Food for him has always been fuel, something you put in yourself so that you are able to do the really interesting things in life, like dance all night. The faster and more convenient, the better. Other than family holidays, the only times he has eaten at gatherings at someone else's house is when friends order out for pizza or mu shu pork. The idea that in a few hours the four of them will be sitting at the little round oak table Chris recklessly bought at a street estate sale, drinking wine from the green-glass Spanish goblets (same sale), talking about God knows what, is foreign and disturbing.

All he knows about the guests is that they are college chums of Chris's, just-married (to each other) straight people, out here honeymooning. His natural curiosity about the man, he hopes, will make the evening tolerable. So limited has been his contact with heteroland for so many years that he has come to see it as sinister, even threatening. Passing them on the street, riding alongside them in the Metro, is one thing; permitting them to enter your apartment is quite another. He does not take for granted that they will speak the same language or behave in a remotely civilized way. They could be fag-haters. Three nights ago he forced Chris to admit that he has never exactly told them—though he insisted they *must* know—that he's queer.

"I think she knows, though," he said defensively.

Bread will be broken at the apartment that appears to be Carl and Chris's but that is still really Carl's. Whether they should look for a new apartment or stay in Carl's was a topic they debated far more noisily than they had the knottier question of whether Chris should move in in the first place. For months Carl parried Chris's attempts to raise the issue with jokes and changes of subject. When these forensic tricks lost their punch, Carl suggested that Chris find his own place in the city so as to acclimate himself to his new surroundings rather than load the entire burden of an uprooted suburban life on their tender friendship.

To Carl this sensible idea had the added benefit of preventing their intimacy from getting out of hand, but Chris rejected it with the sharp and accurate charge that Carl, while talking about how the step-by-step approach would be better for Chris, was really thinking that it would be better for Carl.

"You're afraid," he would say. "You're afraid of me. Why should I move up here to live three blocks away?"

The unspoken words were unmistakable: Face it. Accept it. Stop denying reality. I am the future.

It was strange and irritating for Carl to know that this cherub-faced, innocent person was right (even if it was a lucky guess). He *was* afraid—of the change, disruption, of upsetting what was, for him, an ideal balance. Chris was around a lot, but when he wasn't (also a lot) Carl was free to do as he pleased, to act as the single man he had always been. But in the end he faced the reality that he was more afraid of losing Chris (and having to deal with the subsequent fact that his own emotional momentum was nil) than of having him around all the time. A transitional phase would have been better for them both, but it was not to be.

So Carl's apartment became, almost a year ago now, their apartment, despite its deficiencies, which include the small and slightly seedy kitchen (gray metal cabinets, seasick-green linoleum floors) in which Chris is at this moment unloading items from the grocery bags he filled at the markets along Clement Street. Soon he will be chopping, slicing and dicing all these exotic vegetables and meats, tossing them with sauces mixed from fluids packed in bottles they will probably never open again; and Carl will be dragooned into helping.

They have talked about moving—talks mostly initiated by Chris. We need more room, he argues; a guest room, another bathroom, a library, a terrace, a twentieth-century kitchen.

"No problem," Carl likes to say. "Just keep buying those Lotto tickets."

Although Carl goes along with the idea that they should find a better place, he is attached to an apartment he has thought of as his home for years. As long as they stay, it will not seem that his world will have changed quite so drastically as it already has. That is important in these days of enveloping terror: the maintenance of stability in those areas of life that are already stable.

While the old place remains their home, too, it remains possible for Carl to believe that he has not signed his life away for Chris's sake. They do live together in a new life, but beneath the shiny surface of these days lie the etchings of the old days, still recognizable, in which Chris was a guest. Chris is aware of this, and the awareness makes him squirm, but he has not yet forced Carl to acknowledge this psychological tax, which he, not Carl, pays.

Last week they went to the funeral of an old friend of Carl's, a business-school classmate who had come north at about the same time to take a job with Crown Zellerbach. Chris had not known the man well, but he was sad he had died, because he was one of the very few among Carl's friends who were not disco queens or full of drugs or fag talk.

After the memorial—attended mostly by good-looking white men in their mid-thirties to maybe fifty—Carl was remote and Chris was at a loss how to reach him. It wasn't even noon, so they went to Cafe Flore and ordered caffé lattés and Chris read the real-estate listings in the *Chronicle* while Carl sat there nibbling a croissant. It was a cool, sunshiny day. Market Street bustled with traffic and pedestrians and life in general. It was almost as if there weren't a war on.

They do not talk about what is happening around them. Carl switches off the TV whenever the newscaster announces that the subject will be dealt with after these messages. It is as though the eyes and ears themselves are portals to be guarded as potential routes of assault. No newspaper or magazine articles are clipped; no discussions are engaged in. Sometimes it seems to Chris that they live their lives as though they are surrounded by eavesdroppers—that they are free to talk about anything they want except the one topic they think about all the time, the one topic that matters more than any other, as if mentioning it will make it happen, and not mentioning it will keep it away.

Despite the shadow and the silence, Chris is serenely happy. At night, when he and Carl are in their big bed, the sheets become a warm safe nest where bad things can't even be imagined. Whatever is happening in the world out there, in the city around them, this is a separate place, made of, by and for the two of them alone. Here is where they belong.

For Chris, living with Carl means that the difficult loneliness of being a single adult has ended. No more solitary dinners of canned soup and saltines in front of the television; no more evenings wasted in bars like handfuls of loose change, waiting for a certain flawless someone to walk in the door and make dreams come true; no more wondering exactly what, if anything, is to be done about the paramount concern of sharing his life. The idiot job doesn't bother him anymore, because he has come to accept that what always mattered most to him was not so much a job or a career or a vocation but the discovery of that Other without whom life could be nothing more than a flitting shadow of promise.

If he has doubts about Carl, he does not allow himself to be aware of them. It has taken each of them some time to become accustomed to the other's presence—a process, Chris begins to see, that never really ends. Planning for two is logarithmically more difficult than planning for one. Even trying to decide what movie to see is an intricate dance of verbal and other clues, given over a period of minutes and hours (sometimes days and weeks), that, like democracy, often as not results in deadlock and frustration. Given the worthlessness of most movies, this is probably just as well. It often seems to Chris that he is subsidizing Carl's indecisiveness, that it is he, Chris, who makes most of the decisions, even those Carl ought to make (such as calling the landlord to tell him that the back stairway has rotted away to the point of collapse and litigation).

Still, like winter into summer, the weather gradually improves, and if there is the occasional overcast or blustery day, there are more and more in which the sun shines and the warm wind blows. They are now able to sleep more or less well in the same bed. This was never a serious problem for Chris, but Carl made himself sick with worry about it because, as he admitted, he was used to having the whole thing to himself and could never do more than doze lightly if his hegemony over the expanse of sheets was limited. The problem left him groggy and grouchy for the first few weeks, but exhaustion finally pushed him into sleep despite himself, and since then he has managed to do it, though sometimes he still complains about Chris's hogging the pillows and the blankets.

A few minutes alone in the kitchen—Chris has assigned him the task of chopping onions and garlic with the old steak knife while he makes an eleventh-hour dash to Safeway for another bottle or two of chilled wine—is heaven. He hacks and minces to the thump-thump of "So Many Men, So Little Time," a disco classic and therefore, to Chris, intolerable; Carl feels like Joel in *Risky Business:* a teenager whose stern parents have left him the run of the house for a bit. Outside it is still sunny and mild, although other districts of the city are already bound in the summer fog. The steady beat from the JBL studio monitors keeps his body moving, and he has refilled his wine glass twice (or three times) from the now half-empty bottle of chardonnay in the refrigerator.

An hour earlier he was genuinely nervous about the whole evening. How much more fun it would be to take them dancing, he argued to Chris—to the Endup or, if the secret was still to be kept, the Stud and its punked-out, ambi crowd. Anything but a proper bourgeois evening at home with proper guests, making proper conversation about the selection of wines and the procurement of exotic herbs and spices. Or, worse (since they were hetero), chat about babies and weddings and schools and PTA and baking chocolate-chip cookies for the neighborhood grade-schoolers' Halloween bags. Or, worst of all, real estate. Chris's assurances notwithstanding, Carl didn't doubt that the intersection of their worlds was bound to be too slender to support an entire evening of being together.

Relax, Chris would say. You'll like them.

That's not really the point, Carl would think to himself, but he couldn't say exactly what the point was.

The buzzer makes its nerve-jangling noise more or less in tune with the music, and Carl feels a little twist of frustration with Chris for forgetting his keys, as he does at least once a week. Fortunately Carl is not in the middle of a shower, as he was the last time. He clatters down the stairs and throws open the door, setting his face in a reproachful scowl.

"Hi!" says a good-looking young dark-haired man, beside whom stands a blond woman of about the same height. Low-key prep clothes, the both of them. "We were, ah, looking for Chris Halloran."

"You must be Carl," the woman says, extending a hand and a smile. "I'm Meredith Elliott."

"Michael Waldman," Michael says, shaking Carl's hand.

"Call me Merry," Meredith says.

"Mike," Michael says.

"I'm sorry!" Carl says. "I smell like onion. Phew. Don't cry. Chris went out to get some wine but he should be right back."

"We brought some," Michael says, holding out a brown paper bag, which Carl takes.

"Great," he says. "Terrific. Come on in! I didn't mean to keep you standing here."

Up the staircase the disco music reverberates.

"I'm sorry it's so loud," Carl says, wondering why he sounds as though he is apologizing. It *is* his home.

"I guess we're a little early," Meredith says.

"We took the subway," Michael adds.

"Up we go," Carl says, leading the way.

Chris arrives a few minutes later (the music having been

turned down to a whisper, but not off). He is muttering about recipes to himself as he bursts through the door into the living room, where Carl and Meredith are having an animated conversation about the neighborhood and its remarkable collection of restored Victorians and about real estate in general. Michael nods in agreement with most of what she says, but he looks distinctly relieved when he sees Chris.

"You made it!" he says, pushing himself up from the couch and toward Chris in one smooth motion. They embrace, despite the grocery bag Chris is carrying.

"Are you early?" he says. "I'm late. Merry!"

The unexpected fact of their presence makes him forget for the moment that he, like Carl but for different reasons, has been pondering this moment with a stomach-twisting admixture of excitement and trepidation. It is like Show and Tell, but he wants to show and not tell. He wants them to know, simply by seeing him with Carl, that he, too, is now a grown-up.

Years from now, he will think of these four hours as a child heading back to the first day of school remembers the Fourth of July: as the zenith of summer, not a care, a perfect fullness to life. He will remember what it felt like to say "we" in telling Mike and Merry—the ultimate we, the couple against whom all was measured—what he and Carl had done last weekend, where they were planning to go for the Labor Day weekend (the Russian River). He will remember the flush of pride he felt when he was sure, even before dessert, that, yes, *they noticed*. They knew. He will remember feeling, for one of the first and only times of his life, a sense of complete equality. Years from now, it will seem as though it never really happened.

There is food to be cooked. It is lying there in bowls and on plates, waiting for the master chef to begin his act of pan-juggling and skillet-jiggling and wok-tossing (Chris bought the Chinese pan at Macy's on Saturday and spent the rest of the day seasoning it; tonight is its first actual deployment), and almost immediately there is panic. Is that burner too hot? Who spilled on the recipe? *Where is the chicken stock?* Lemon-grass powder or curry, or would anyone even notice the difference? (What *is* the difference?) The sink soon overflows with dirty dishes, utensils, scraps of onion skin and chicken fat, and they have yet to eat a bite. Timing is all. The rice looks dry. He does not know what he is doing.

Carl leads the troupe into the kitchen, where he pours out more wine for everyone. Michael stands with his back to a wall, and Meredith helps Chris stir something that seems to be smoking.

"It smells delicious," she says.

"We eat like this all the time," Carl says.

"In smoldering chaos," says Chris.

Michael sends the bottle of wine around.

"I like your place," he says, in no particular direction. He is not sure whose place it is. "Do you own it?"

"Do we look like the sort of people who could afford this beautiful kitchen?" Carl says.

"Carl's rented the place forever," Chris says. "He knows the landlord so it's sort of cheap."

"We're obsessed by property ownership," Meredith says. "We've been looking around a little."

"We have?" Michael says.

"In Chicago?" Chris says, trying not to sound astonished. They do live there, after all.

"Just sort of window-shopping," she says. "It's fun living in an apartment—less to take care of, that's a blessing—but eventually we'll have to have a house." She glances toward Michael, who is staring in the general direction of a window.

"For the kiddies to play in, I guess," Chris says. "Right?"

"Plus we'll need the mortgage deduction," Michael says. "Eventually." He glances at her. "So says Mr. Tax."

"His father," Meredith explains.

Picturing Michael with a stroller or a dirty diaper isn't easy for Chris; your peers may have lots of sex, but they never get pregnant, and parents are middle-aged people of mild, middle-class habits and graying hair.

"Anyway," Michael continues, "nothing is imminent."

The food turns out to be edible, even tasty, although the stir-fry chicken's spicy sauce is unappetizingly murky, a brown-yellow goo. (Too much cornstarch, Chris concludes in a silent postmortem.) The chopped cilantro lightens it up a bit. Wine flows; Michael helps himself to large second servings of everything. By the time they reach dessert (a cheesecake from Just Desserts and Double Rainbow Ultra Chocolate ice cream) and coffee (decaf, expertly prepared in the French plunger pot), Chris feels entitled to congratulate himself for having pulled it off.

"I like Carl," Merry says to him while they are alone in the kitchen; Michael and Carl are at the stereo for a demonstration of the new compact-disc player. "It seems like I've known him a long time."

"Yeah," Chris says, trying not to blush. He manages to look at her steadily for a long moment, still struggling with the reflexive sense that any allusion to his private life is some sort of attack, but it is clear that she means what she says, and what she doesn't say—that she is happy for him.

"I told you things would work out," she says.

"You did."

"You didn't believe me."

"Not at the time," he admits.

"Sometimes it helps to be a little older."

"Just a little," he says with a laugh. "You seem very happy," he adds. "Loving it back there?"

She tosses her head back slightly and pulls a handful of hair behind her ear. "Well," she says. "That's really a question for Michael."

"Why?"

"Because he's the one under all the pressure. He's the resident. I'm just sort of a resident alien."

"But you're buying a house. In Chicago."

"Oh, not really," she says. "I just bring that little topic up sometimes to remind him how little he actually wants to stay. Inertia is very real, you know, have you noticed? It's almost easier not to change. We get set in our ways. Sometimes you have to rattle the various cages, including your own."

"You should move back out here," Chris says.

"We talk about it."

"I don't think I could ever leave," he says.

"Why should you? You've found where you belong."

He cocks his head in mute acknowledgment. "There are still so many things about San Francisco that make me sort of uncomfortable," he says. "It can be a very strange place. But being with Carl makes it seem like a new city."

"Have you lived here long? With him?"

"A year in September."

She nods.

"Does Mike know?" he asks.

"I've never told him."

"Should I?"

She shrugs. "It's not quite the same problem it was with Drew, is it," she says.

"You don't think I should."

"I didn't say that."

"He wouldn't mind, would he?"

"I'm sure on some level he knows," she says. "Carl isn't your uncle. I've only seen one bed! Michael isn't blind and stupid. But maybe everything doesn't have to be spelled out. Unless you think it should be. Do you want me to tell him?"

"I don't think so."

"I don't think I should, either," she agrees.

.   .   .

Half of the cheesecake (and all the ice cream) disappears, the flow of coffee slows to a fragrant trickle, and Michael insists on hearing one disco hit after another, as if to make up for a quarter-century of ignorance about this musical variant ("and I really hated *Saturday Night Fever,*" he admitted to Carl, who, with gracious silence, accepted the confession on behalf of disco queens everywhere). Carl is thrilled to have found a new devotee, and such a handsome one at that (Chris can see), even if he is a straight boy.

The usual effect of disco music on Chris is to carry him back to those choppy days and nights when he doubted he would ever be able to land Carl, when the swells of the gay sea threatened to swamp his little life. Tonight, he is deaf to the roar; he even tells Carl to put on "Without Your Love" by Cut Glass, which is the first song they ever danced to (he doesn't mention this).

For all the brilliance of Michael and Merry, he is glad he is not part of them, one of them. Marriage does have its privileges. It brings instant social acceptability and a downpour of gifts—some of them useful—that he and Carl will never receive even though they almost certainly need them more. (They still don't have a toaster oven.) It squares you with the law, so that, if something should happen to one of the pair, society's protective umbrella automatically opens over the other. It makes everything easier.

For all that, Chris at this moment would still choose to be gay and to be with Carl even if he were given the choice to make—even if he could choose to be other than he is. Watching Carl and Michael go through the heretofore hated library of twelve-inch dance singles while he casually leans his shoulder against Meredith's, listening to her say whatever it is she's saying, he finds it impossible to conceive that any two people, even these charmed two, can be any closer than are he and Carl, can have more thoroughly and profoundly opened their lives to each other than have he and Carl. They are not bound to each other by vows taken in front of a clergyman and their gathered families, or by a slip of paper filed at the registry of deeds, or by the constant pressure of the society around them, bearing down like the weight of the atmosphere itself, but by the simple, pure fact that they love each other, that they choose to be together and therefore are.

Does that mean their relationship is superior? He is almost startled to find himself thinking such a thought. He has never been in love with a woman, after all, has never been involved with anyone else, really; and in any case it is impossible to *know* what other people are feeling, as opposed to whatever feelings they choose to describe themselves as having. Only when you are involved with someone else, committed and consumed, do you become aware of the extraordinary solitude of life inside your own skull, of the impossibility of knowing anything for certain about anything or anyone outside yourself. Carl may have hurt you, and you know what that felt like, but you cannot say for sure that in the same circumstances Meredith would have been hurt by Michael, that she would have felt what you know you felt. You can only assume. So you don't.

Still, he's relieved to find that a life that wasn't supposed to be worth living not only turns out to be the opposite, but is in some respects even preferable to the standard arrangement. There are added bonuses and windfall profits, and given the heavy taxes of being gay (most of them levied early in life, before most souls are capable of paying them), he accepts them gladly.

"I didn't know you could cook," Michael says. They are all back at the table. "Megatron Man" plays on the stereo; it sounds odd at low volume, without a roomful of poppered people dancing around to its relentless, strobe-lit beat.

"I didn't know you liked disco music," Chris says.

"You forget the famous taco party," Meredith says to Michael.

"Oh, yeah."

"I hate Mexican food," Carl says. It is a reflexive statement he makes any time the subject comes up.

"We haven't been dancing in a long time," Michael says
to Merry.

"No."

"Because we go to bed so early."

"It's because of your meatloaf and mashed potatoes childhood," Chris says to Carl. "You're suspicious of spices. I'm
sure it's pathological. But you like guacamole. You remember
the big bowl of it at that party."

Carl shrugs. "That was different," he says. "That was
good guacamole."

"It was *yummy*," Chris says.

"You never said you *wanted* to go dancing," Meredith
says.

"It's not loud enough," Carl says. "It has to be really
loud."

"He means deafening," Chris says.

"We're too young to go deaf," Meredith says. "Aren't
we?"

"You're very young," Carl agrees.

"I have a gray hair," Michael announces, turning his head
so that everyone can see. "Right there"—he jams a finger into
his head behind his right ear.

"I don't see anything," Chris says.

"It's just the light," Meredith says.

"I get those all the time," Carl says. "I pull them out with
tweezers."

"You do not!" Chris says.

"I do. You're always ignoring my screams."

"Your father hardly has any gray," Meredith says to Michael. "I think you're panicking."

"He's heavy, though."

"So stop staring at the cheesecake."

"I got the smallest piece."

"Have some more," Chris says. "Carl paid for it."

"No," Meredith says. "Give it to Carl. He looks like he can use it. A lot more than you," she says to Michael. "You've gained five pounds since New Year's."

"Four."

"Somebody has to eat this cheesecake," Chris says. "I can't have it lying around here like a loaded gun. Please."

"I'm fatter than I look," Carl says. "I haven't been to the gym since last week."

"It's just so easy to eat too much," Meredith says. "And some of us don't believe in leftovers."

"I believe in them," Michael says.

"It's strictly a matter of faith," Meredith says, "because you've never actually seen any."

"I'm sorry. I work hard. I get hungry."

"Then you eat until there's nothing left. That's what wild dogs do."

"Here we go," Michael says. "Dogs."

"We've been thinking about getting a dog," Chris says.

"A black chow," Carl says.

"I told you they're vicious."

"I don't care. I want one."

"We should get something smaller. A terrier."

"I don't want a little itty-bitty dog. They're for old ladies."

"*She* wants a Bouvier something or other," Michael says, glancing toward Meredith. "I think it's actually a small horse. We'll need a barn."

"Bouvier des Flandres," she says. "But I will settle for twin girls."

"We'll find a barn."

"Bouvier des Flandres," she reminds him again later, on the way back to the hotel.

"I vote for goldfish," he says. "At least you can remember how to say it."

"They die."

"Well," he says, "what doesn't?"

The taxi whisks them up Market, toward their hotel on Nob Hill.

"I liked their apartment," she says.

"Too small. Bad kitchen."

"You're supposed to say 'cozy, with original kitchen.' "

"You've been reading too many classifieds."

"I liked Carl."

"He was okay," Michael agrees.

"They seem to get along well. He and Chris."

"Chris's mellowed out, I guess."

"So have you," she says, and sticks her nose into his ear. It tickles, and he laughs. "You don't really want goldfish."

"They're quiet."

"They remind me of dentists' offices," she says.

"We'll get a piranha."

"I want something I can pet and talk to."

"You have me."

"For when you're on call and I'm all alone."

"How old do you think he is? Carl?"

"Older," she says. "I'm not sure. Thirty or thirty-five or something like that."

"He lifts. They both do."

"He's built just like you."

"So you thought he was cute."

"I did," she says.

"You're actually admitting that?"

"I'm not allowed to notice if men are attractive?" she says. "I don't mind if you do."

"That's different," he says, a little stiffly, not sure what she means.

"Anyway I don't think he noticed me," she says. "He's a brunet-lover."

"Guess so," Michael says. "He had an earring just like Joe's."

"They were fun," Carl says. The last dish has been rinsed and set in the drying rack, the last serving platter scrubbed and dried and put away. The kitchen is, in its dingy way, immaculate. They walk down to the little store at the corner for a quart of milk.

"You sound surprised. I told you you'd like them."

"Well, I did. He's hot."

"I don't know," Chris says. It is embarrassing to hear such a thing said about Michael, whom he hasn't wanted to sleep with since freshman year. Michael is too straight to fantasize about.

"You can tell me."

Silence.

"But it was the other one, wasn't it," Carl says. "Drew."

"Drew."

"I know what you mean when you say it like that," Carl says. "You mean shut up."

"You want to go out?" Chris asks.

"Like for a drink?"

"Or dancing."

"You hate to go dancing."

"I feel like it tonight. All that disco you guys were playing. Where should we go?"

"To be honest," Carl says, "I'd rather go to bed."

"It's not even midnight."

"I drank a lot. Too much. Being brilliantly witty and charming to heterosexuals takes a lot out of you."

"Do you feel all right?" Chris says, brushing the back of his hand across Carl's forehead. "I'm *agreeing* to a disco ramble."

"I'm fine," Carl says. "Just don't feel like dancing. Not all of us are twenty-seven anymore. Let's go."

They walk several blocks in silence through the cool evening, now gauzy with fog. Around them the city and the world soften, as if the flowing gray mist separates them from the rest of creation. Chris slips an arm through Carl's, and they bump along together up the hill.

"It was kind of strange what she said about twins," Chris says as they approach their building.

"It was kind of strange what he said."

"Like he'd rather have the dog."

"Yeah."

"It's hard to believe they can actually do that," Chris says. "Make babies, I mean. You just decide you want one and bang."

"Bang-bang. Kiss-kiss first."

"Doesn't it seem like it should be harder?" Chris says. "Like you should have to get a license or pass some kind of parents' exam?"

"I haven't thought about it that much."

"We'd be better parents than a lot of people."

Carl opens the door and flips the light switch; they kiss, eyes open.

"I suppose I'd have to be the daddy," he whispers in a throaty voice.

"I'm serious," Chris says.

"Are you?"

"Yes."

"Have you missed your period?"

"I hate it when you talk like that."

"Because you're still uptight."

"Drew was always saying stuff like that. Just to shock me."

"You're so shockable. And you're still in love with him."

"Wrong. I'm in love with *you.*"

"Maybe the stork will just bring one."

"There's no reason gay couples shouldn't raise children," Chris says, feeling heated. "We could adopt."

"Let's try the dog first."

"I wish you'd stop joking," Chris says.

"I'm not joking. I think you're nuts. Adoption agencies don't farm orphans out to queers."

"Maybe they should. Besides, there are other ways."

"Turkey basters, test tubes, lesbians, wombs for rent, convenient terms."

"Yes."

"We have to brush our teeth."

Later. Darkness around them. Carl did not feel like fooling around, so together they drowse. The future. They will grow old together, look after each other. It doesn't seem so bad, maybe, children or no. Children would be nice, though, Chris thinks; raising them is something adults ought to do. Perhaps you need to be gay, to face a future in which, more likely than not, offspring do not figure, to understand how important a link they are to past and future, to the rest of humankind.

Children, too, look after you when you're sick or infirm or dying. Is it selfish to think that? he wonders. Maybe the real comfort is knowing that they will remain behind, tending the world, even as you leave it. The last thought he has, as sleep takes him, is amusement at thinking such a morbid thought at the end of what has been a lovely evening. All those strange spices are already coloring his dreams, but the stomach is calm, no sign of food poisoning. He is not aware, a short time later, of Carl's rolling out of bed in a shivery dash to the toilet.

CATS

The cats no longer come to the back door, but sometimes, late at night, when he is lying in bed, nuzzling the warm neck of sleep, just about to go under, he hears them in the alley. They wail like hungry babies, or wet babies, or babies with colic. Screaming fucking babies. They jolt him awake and keep him awake, pricking his anger so that he picks up a broom and charges out the back door (sometimes wearing shorts, sometimes not), ready to deal with them. They bound away when he appears, scurrying off behind trash cans, along the runways between houses, but often he sees their eyes glowing, as they take one more anxious, hateful glance back at this angry foe. He wishes his own eyes glowed back but knows they don't.

The wretched cats are part of her miserable legacy. She was the one who insisted on feeding them, who set out the bowls of milk and water and the Cat Chow every night, so that they became welfare cats, fawning and dependent and prickly. She loved it when they developed enough trust in her to enter

the apartment and rub against everything (they made his eyes
itch; Dalí had to be locked in the bathroom). Little tufts of
black fur marked their passage here and there as they roamed
the dwelling of their seductress and her shadowy mate. Drew's
few misconceived attempts to pet these black cats brought
hisses and arched backs, tails pointed straight into the air;
they leapt into her arms as though they were her familiars, and
she laughed.

"You're one of them," she would say. "They can tell. They
don't like you."

He felt like Korob in "Catspaw." "I don't like them," he
said.

So like spirits repelled each other, just as like poles of
magnets did. She was right about that and right about them,
though she never put it that way. Selfishness speaks for itself.
The experiment in sharing has made it clear. Sharing is un-
wise. Putting even part of your fate in the hands of another is
an invitation to disaster. Learn from cats. They are not stupid.
They fuck and kill without compunction. Their world, he
thinks, is in many ways superior to our own. It is not founded
on compassion or the common good or any of the other myths
humans have devised and clung to through the ages to convince themselves they are God's chosen—on anything other
than self-reliance. Cats survive, with claws and fangs and
soundless cunning.

Sleep is a precious commodity these days. For some reason he finds it necessary to stay up for *Late Night*. He could
easily videotape it to watch the next day after work, but the
show is meant to be watched late at night, and that is when he
watches it, even though he must rise at six forty-five to be out
of the house by seven-thirty to be at his desk by eight. He
walks to work, generally covering the distance between his
Georgetown apartment and the downtown office in about half
an hour. If he's late or it's raining, he cabs it.

Work is a drag, as Chris foretold freshman year. Like Chinese food, the portions are massive and unsatisfying. The firm, midsized and therefore unsure of its place in the changing legal universe, handles routine commercial litigation; Drew writes memos explaining why big corporate clients haven't violated antitrust laws. In Reagan's Washington, this is not difficult.

Every morning he showers and shaves, blow-dries his hair, brushes his teeth and puts on his tortoiseshell glasses (contacts being reserved for weekends and after hours); then the Jockeys and T-shirt, the conservative button-down, blue or white, from Woodie's or Brooks, the suit, blue or gray (he has four of each), the foulard or neat tie (making a good knot, with a proper dimple, no longer takes him five or six tries and ten or fifteen minutes, as it did when he first started). Heavy black shoes. A glance at the *Post* over cereal and juice. He snorts at the soggy liberal bilge on the editorial page.

Apart from the occasional furious outburst, he feels old. Everything is routine and endless. There is no natural break in life to look forward to, no graduation or end of internship. He could, in theory, remain in his present position for another decade, getting the yearly pay raise, an increased amount of authority and autonomy, yes, but playing no fundamentally different role while his hair turned gray and fell out, his arms grew thin and his ass flabby. Even the partnership hurdle is one of money rather than something *personal*. He is a lifer. He has peaked.

After Dana, which, for some reason, he told his mother about, his parents urged him to return to L.A. For once, he found himself listening to them. He had been away for several years, gotten a taste of the exotic East, where everyone was rude and aggressive; he had made the point to himself and his family that he was capable of surviving on his own a continent away. He had the law degree. He wasn't completely helpless. L.A., meanwhile, at once familiar and new, offered a change of venue he might benefit from. It would be easy to go back.

So he didn't. The firm from D.C. offered and he accepted. The money was fine, and the work didn't sound much different from the work he would be doing at any other law firm, east or west. It was easier not to move, though he did move out of Mrs. Dunwiddy's.

He lies in bed at night, half-asleep, dreaming up ways to kill the wretched cats. Drown them? Wring their necks? Put out bowls of food laced with poison? Shoot them? Call the SPCA and have them picked up (the most cruel and least unusual method)? Each amatory cry jangles his nerves. But it is not the cats that bring him out of bed this mild February evening. It is the telephone, ringing in the kitchen.

After a while the marriage madness seemed to subside. The wounds left by cutting words healed over, and the current of law-school routine swept them along. He assumed that Dana's outburst had been hormonal, a flush of feminine chemicals that dissipated as quickly as it had spilled out.

There was really no warning.

Over Christmas break he interviewed with a few L.A. firms, not because he was especially interested in them, or in L.A., but because he felt that he should have some other option than remaining in Washington. She had been noncommittal about her plans. He knew that she had interviewed with several firms in D.C. and over Christmas, he knew, would be interviewing with several more in Miami. He expected that, at some point, they would have to have a rational discussion of what was to be done. Miami was out, so far as he was concerned, and he was prepared to give his reasons when she finally got around to asking him if he'd be willing to move there.

Relations between them were the same and not the same. They still ate together, studied together, made love together, went to sleep every night in the same bed. But the old ordinariness was replaced by a watchful one, and his sense of dread grew.

Still, things might work out. He was a confident person, and this was what he believed. All the pieces were in place for a smooth transition to postgrad days. They both had but to take well-paying jobs in D.C., and the problem would solve itself. The jobs were already being offered; it was simply a matter of deciding which one to accept. He didn't doubt that once they had gotten around this obstacle of the first job, once they had relieved all the pressure that had been mounting behind it ever since they started out on this adventure almost three years ago, the world would seem much more pleasant, and all the nonsense about getting married, love and commitment and the rest of it, would seem less urgent, even to her. He had begun to look forward to law practice and its daily stateliness. It offered the promise of a foundation to life upon which you could rely.

"I have to tell you," she said. It was a snowy night in January, the beginning of their final semester. The city was paralyzed; even Metro could not move, its power rails having been glazed with ice. He was sitting on a vinyl-covered sofa in the lounge, watching the news and sipping coffee; she had just emerged from some errand in the library stacks. The lounge was deserted except for the two of them. It was too early in the semester for anyone to be worrying about schoolwork, especially at eleven o'clock at night with a blizzard burying the world. He looked at her, expecting a remark about the weather and how were they going to get home?

"I'm clerking in Miami next year," she said. "For a federal judge."

This did not register immediately. No foundation had been laid for her announcement; there had been no discovery, no negotiation, no pretrial maneuvering, no cross-exam. Just verdict. He felt the urge to say, "I object," or, "Move for a new trial." He said nothing.

"I'm sorry," she said.

"I'm sorry?" he said, cocking his head as if to signal he hadn't heard what she'd said.

"I just found out yesterday," she said. "He chooses late."

He got up from the couch and snapped off the television, as though its low background chatter had somehow been warping the conversation.

"You're going to Miami?"

"Yes."

"When?"

"I start end of August."

"For a year."

"Yes. Then Atlanta."

"Atlanta?"

"Eleventh Circuit." Another clerkship, with a federal court of appeals.

"Fuck," he said, and sat back down.

"I don't blame you for being angry," she said. "Raymond is coming down with his truck tomorrow. Rebecca's agreed that I . . . well, you know. She has that extra room since Cheryl graduated early. She's gone to Nicaragua, you know."

Drew neither knew nor cared. It was as if the roof had collapsed under the weight of the heavy, wet Atlantic snow. He ran his tongue over his lips, expecting to feel the flecks of icy wetness. He felt nothing.

Whenever the telephone rings he wonders if it might be her, calling to apologize or, more to the point, propose some kind of get-together. It could be that she finds whichever Southern city she's in at the moment (Atlanta?) too hot or crime-ridden or out of the way. (He prefers not to think about how Washington rates in the sultry-weather and crime-out-of-control categories.) It could be that she misses him after all.

At times, more so lately, he finds himself thinking of Trina, even of calling her. In his black address book her family is still listed (including phone number); and while he's never heard that she's living with her parents, he could probably reach her through them. He's written her notes, put them in envelopes, addressed them with the plea "Please forward"— but never mailed them.

That was part of the deal: that they would just forget about each other. Like most of the other terms of their breakup, it was one he insisted on, telling her it was for her own good.

"It'll be easier for you," he said. "It will be over and done with. You won't be sitting around thinking about it."

She didn't argue, but even as the years tick past he has not entirely lost the expectation that one day there will be a letter or a phone call. If he has been writing her notes (though not sending them) and looking up her parents' telephone number, then she—who was in love with him when he was not with her—must be doing the same.

Ring ring.

It will be Trina—or Dana, calling to say she is in town, can they please get together, Afterwords, forty-five minutes? Very forties. Sidewalk café, beautiful woman, late evening, neon, remembrance of things past. "Hello, Drew," she will say. He hates it when she says, "Hello." It sounds pretentious. "Hi" will do.

He picks up the phone and hears a voice that is far too deep to be hers. Hi, it says. It is a familiar voice. It is Chris's.

"I woke you."

"Not really," Drew says. "I was just listening to some cats fucking."

"I'm sorry," Chris says. "I can never remember what time it is there."

"Later than you think."

"I just called to say hi. I'll call back some other time. Go back to bed."

"No!" Drew says. "I'm wide awake now."

"I thought you hated cats."

"I do hate cats," Drew says. "So what's new?"

"Nothing."

"You sound tired."

"Do I? I am, a little."

"Me too. We work too hard."

"Yeah," Chris says. "My roommate has been sort of sick."

"Yeah?" Drew says. "I didn't know you had a roommate."

"Yeah. I do."

"Maybe you should get a new roommate."

Silence. Drew thinks about the word "roommate," whether it would have applied to Dana. Guys are roommates, he decides; students are roommates—like Chris and he had been. Friends are roommates. Your lover is something else. Are lovers friends? Brother Geoff uses the word "friend" with lewd promiscuity.

"You need a vacation," he says. "You should come out here for a week."

"I'd like to," Chris says, "but I really can't get away right now."

"You can stay with me," Drew says. "I've got a queen-size futon. Reasonable rates. I'll take off from work."

"I really can't leave him by himself."

"He'll be fine! Just get some Campbell's chicken-noodle soup and leave it out where he can find it."

"He's sick."

"Oh." A pause. "What's wrong with him?"

"We're not sure," Chris says, in a voice that, transmitted cross-continent, sounds slightly strangled.

"Maybe he should see a doctor," Drew says. "You shouldn't be sitting there worrying about it. Come out! Call now. Planes are standing by."

"He's been to the doctors."

"Speaking of which," Drew says. "Do you hear from Mike?"

"Um," Chris says, "No. Yeah. They were here in August. We had dinner."

"You heard about the kid."

"Yes," Chris says faintly.

"It's sort of hard for me to picture him as a father, you know? It's like one of us being a father. It doesn't compute. They invite you to the *Bris?*"

"Drew," Chris says, "Jesus. I don't know what to do."

"I told you. Get out for a week. I never see you. It'll be fun."

"*I told you,*" Chris says in a voice that shocks with hysterical harshness, "*I can't just leave him.* He needs me."

"Okay, then," Drew says, wondering why they are having this really weird conversation and trying to think of a polite way to end it. "Okay."

Like that, she was gone. A brief note set out the new address and telephone number and was signed simply, "D." In leaving, she had gone out of her way to make sure everything was neat; you could not tell from looking at the apartment that one of its two inhabitants had just moved out. The bed was made, the kitchen cleaned (even the nasty grease under the stovetop), the corners of the throw rugs laid flat.

The thud of her departure fell upon the dead plain of third year, which was both a blessing and a curse: a blessing, because no matter how bad the emotional trauma, it would have no effect on schoolwork that no one bothered to do anymore; a curse because without the consuming fear and effort of trying to learn the law, there was nothing to distract him from brooding on his woes and feeling sorry for himself.

On the whole, he was not as upset about the rupture as he might have expected to be. He suspected, without any proof other than instinct, that the commitment question was only part of the explanation for her leaving, and not even the most important one at that. There was something more, he decided after thinking about it in his water-rights class, during which he finished most of the *New York Times* crossword puzzle. It was this: When it came to the nub, she was more concerned about her transcendental politics than about him. It did not hurt to grasp this. In fact, in a cold way, he admired her for it—for what he thought of as her masculine rigor in pursuing her life's mission—much as he had admired her candid lust.

Didn't he feel the same way, after all? What would *he* have been willing to sacrifice to stay with her? The difference between them was that she was committed to a cause greater than she was, while he was a drone in a four-hundred-dollar suit. She *cared* about things in a way that left him breathless. He found energy in contempt and belittlement and was an expert in the shredding of others' ideals, but he lacked the push to imagine his own utopia. It was enough for him to let the stupid people of the world know they were stupid.

For several weeks they avoided each other. This was not difficult, with their slack last-semester schedules and their intimate knowledge of the other's likely whereabouts at any given moment. But one February night they bumped into each other at a small party in Dupont Circle a classmate was giving himself for having gotten a job on the Hill, and when he suggested that he might walk her home (the late-winter darkness having fallen and the party's liquor reserves dwindled), she said okay.

It was a clear night, unusually cold—the sort of winter night Drew still found exhilarating, while everyone else was dying for spring. That the weather should change so violently, season to season, day to day, amazed him, child of the mild Pacific, and he was cheerfully attentive to all the TV weather forecasts, the fronts draped across maps of the country and the big L's that indicated low pressure. Snow, in particular, captured his fancy—even city snow that had turned to gray ice and made walking treacherous. He nearly twisted his ankle as they crossed the P Street bridge into Georgetown. She extended an arm to steady him.

"I can't believe you just moved out," he said. "We never even talked."

"I thought it would be easier."

"Without talking?"

"Talking makes things worse sometimes," she said. "There are things you can't explain with words. You knew it had to happen."

"I never said I wouldn't get married."

"No," she said. "I thought about it and decided I didn't want to, either. You were right. Not now. There's too much to do."

"But that's fine," Drew said. "Is the choice marriage or nothing?"

"I don't want to stay here."

"Maybe I don't, either."

"I need a fresh start."

"Oh."

"It's nothing personal," she said. "I just felt like we've explored this territory. You know? You and me."

They were at her new apartment now; he followed her up the front steps, as if to make sure that disaster didn't strike at the last possible moment and not, as he did, to peek inside. He was ready to say goodbye, to disappear into the chill with her inconsistencies and paradoxes to ponder as he walked; but she took his hands in her own and rubbed them.

"You're cold," she said. "Come in for something warm to drink."

For an instant he hesitated, thinking not only about Rebecca, the terrifying cropped-hair lesbian roommate who openly loathed men (was she waiting inside with her chloroform-soaked rag and her razor blade?) but about the more serious danger of being in close quarters with Dana. Stuff could happen. If it really was over, let it be over.

"Why not?" he said.

She led the way in, and soon they were sitting in front of

the television with mugs of cocoa, watching the local news. In the pleasant warmth of the apartment, its cozy shabbiness (Rebecca was out), it was easy to believe that things were as they always had been.

"We don't belong together," she said, without looking away from the screen. "You know it and I know it. We are *total* opposites. It's incredible we got along at all."

"But we did."

"I can't be involved right now," she said. "With all these clerkships and everything. I just don't have the time."

"A few months ago you were demanding that we get married."

"Your friends had an effect on me, I guess," she conceded. "Even more than I thought. It was like: I want this, too. If they can, we can. But you were right. I was rushing. Trying to keep up. Rebecca says I'm too competitive."

So seldom had she ever told him that he was right about something that he could not suppress a blush of pride. Of course I was right, he thought, and isn't it just like you to leap from one extreme to another without even bothering to acknowledge the huge happy medium that separates them? On the other hand, he was not happy to find himself on the same side of an issue as Rebecca.

"This is very weird," he said at length, after the weather, during the sports. "This whole conversation."

"I wanted you to know where I'm coming from. That's all."

"I still don't really know."

"Oh God," she said, "I don't, either. Part of me wants the nice safe little life, but I've got all these things to do and I feel like I've got to get out of this creepy town if I'm going to live."

He was not inclined to rise to the defense of Washington. He had thought about getting out too, after all, of packing his things once again in the folded-up brown cardboard boxes he kept in storage in Mrs. Dunwiddy's cobwebbed garage and setting out to start life yet again, in another new place. One of his favorite theories was that America's decline, the general rot of her society, was the result of rootlessness, of people's bouncing here and there without ever really taking hold and helping to build a community separate and distinct from the national chains—McDonald's, Howard Johnson's, Century 21—that are the lowest common denominators of shopping-mall civilization. Itinerant workers, even those with college degrees and white collars, do not feel that they belong wherever they happen to be and have no sense of the body politic. Yet he, too, was a pilgrim, and he had shopped in malls.

"It's not so bad," he said, "but I know what you mean."

"I don't think you do," she said. "You're a much more content person than I am. You're not rash. I feel like I'm suffocating here, with everything. Do you feel like that?"

"No."

"See? I knew it. I want us to be friends," she continued. "I don't know, maybe we won't be. We're so different, basically."

"Is there someone else?" he asked, surprised to hear himself asking the sort of question that always got asked in the movies or television shows; he hadn't been thinking the question and wondered, briefly, where it came from.

"What makes you think that?" she said sharply. "Are you that competitive?"

"I'm sorry," he said. "Don't tell Rebecca I said that."

When pain and anger failed to strike, he told himself to wait; it was just a delayed reaction. When weeks passed and he saw her in the library—almost always with Rebecca; her bodyguard?—he waited for the dark mess of feelings that never came. He wondered if there was something wrong with him.

Since her there has been no one. Dates, yes, with daughters of his parents' friends, whom he takes out when he visits California (dates that usually end in decent sex); a few women he knows from school and work whose company he enjoys well enough but whom he does not think about if they are not around.

Although he did not say so on the phone (because telephone criticisms almost always come off more harshly than intended), he is annoyed with Chris. It is obvious that they can't keep living a continent apart without being diminished. The separation invites grave consequences. They are meant to be together far more than either one of them is meant to be with whatever woman happens to have sketched herself into the picture at any given moment.

More than ever, Drew is convinced of the rightness of his postulate that the gulf between physical and emotional intimacy is bottomless. He finds, as he approaches thirty and eighteen slips ever further behind, that he is more, not less, horny—and less interested in getting to know people as possible vessels of romantic investment. Camaraderie—that easy fellowship among fellows, or even the right sort of woman—is vastly preferable to the labyrinthine love game that strikes him as totally fake and worthless and a waste of time. Camaraderie and fucking, and not with the same person—that's the ticket.

If pressed when drunk, he would admit that he really doesn't *like* women. Their erotic mystique is real, but the basic core of femininity is as alien and baffling to him as it was when he was a college freshman, and he is not inclined, at this late date, when he is working no less than ten hours six days a week on the partnership express, to spend his energies trying to understand it. Men are just easier to deal with, as he explained to Chris when they were sophomores. He had added that if one of them had been a girl they would have gotten married on the spot.

"I'm not a girl," Chris had felt obliged to point out.

"Neither am I," Drew had said.

So that was settled.

Years later, the exchange persists in his memory. Setting aside the obvious obstacles, he and Chris would be happier together than most other pairs he is aware of (even rivaling that perfectly incandescent twosome, Michael and Meredith). Alas, the obvious obstacles aren't so easily set aside; they transcend the logic of individuals.

Even Drew recognizes this, though he regards as perverse the organization of human life around the forced bonding of deeply incompatible elements. The genders, on the whole (like the races), don't get along very well. There are the exceptions, of course (always held out in public discourse as the rule), but the great unspoken mass of truth is bewilderment and dissatisfaction.

He knows. It is what he felt when he was with Trina (windswept emptiness) and with Dana (like sitting on a munitions dump)—never with Chris. With Chris he was always completely at ease (even when Chris was being so obnoxious about Trina), free to say what he thought, confident that certain things were understood without his having to say them. Chris felt the same way, he knows, that sureness of the other he has never felt with anyone else, before or since, and does not expect to. You don't get that many chances at certain things in life. If you blow an opportunity at, say, building a best friendship, you are not automatically handed another.

On this point their thinking seems to have grown slightly discordant over the years and miles. It almost sounded, on the telephone, as if Chris did not understand what is at stake, how important it is to reunify their lives. A sick roommate is a burden and an obligation, it is true, but only up to a point; a best friend is a best friend. You can't tell me, he wanted to say, that your roommate doesn't have friends who can visit him while you are away, cheer him up, keep him company until he gets better. *You* don't have to be there all the time.

When she invites him to her wedding next spring ("and guest" the invitation will spitefully add), he will be tempted to go. Curiosity about the groom, Kirk Wiedenbeck, will draw him despite the humbling fact of his own lack of attachment, the fact that she shot the rapids of their failing romance to emerge downstream in the arms of another man, another WASP (a stockbroker!), while he has run safely but boringly aground. If there were justice, he will think, they would *both* be floundering in the white water.

But he won't go. The invitation itself will represent an obscure sort of validation, an acknowledgment by her that he is too important a part of her past to ignore even if the mere act of inviting him (to say nothing of his actually showing up) is distinctly uncomfortable. (The alternative explanation—that he is just another name on the list, no more likely to cause distress than Kirk's grandmother's sister—is suppressed.) He will remind himself again how lucky he is, basically, that Kirk Wiedenbeck's name, not his, is etched onto the invitations; that it is Kirk, whoever he is, who has volunteered to surrender his freedom and take up life with a capricious radical; the fool.

Not going, too, will prove the point that he is over her, doesn't need her or miss her, has better things to do, sorry (piss on you). She will notice the empty seat in the pews and at the reception, the absence of that central element of her life to whom she had very much looked forward to showing off her new prize. To make things seem casual, he will mark "try to" on his reply card, and he will fill in "2" for number in party attending. Maybe by then Chris will have broken his sick-roommate fixation and, in a fortuitous bit of timing, will be on a visit to the East.

What a scream it would be to show up with another man. *That* would make her wonder just who had stopped wanting whom, or who had ever *really* wanted whom at all, at any point. Chris would be his Rebecca; his presence would reopen the question of who had perpetrated the more glorious fraud. Two tuxed-out studs flushed with drink, talking boy talk with her new boy and making her crazy noticing the two of them, the three of them. They would go where she could not follow.

He peeks out the kitchen window, into the alley: A lonely bulb dangles an amber funnel to the ground through the night haze.

They are not visible, but he hears them, screeching and howling out there among the bushes and trash cans, making sure he cannot fall asleep (although it is not entirely their fault; he is still thinking about him, her, them). Making kittens.

She was always sentimental about the cats, and she worried aloud when she and Drew went away for a few days or weeks, as though without the dole of Cat Chow they would starve. This was an utterly misplaced fear. Once he watched in admiration as a housecat, a tabby with name tags, fat and (for a cat) sweet-looking, stalked a mouse: The cat stood perfectly still, as though frozen, only the tip of the tail whipping back and forth. The mouse grew increasingly uneasy; when it moved, whiskers twitching, the tabby slipped into a racer's crouch, and the tail stopped whipping. There was a stealthy, evil step forward, totally controlled. The mouse decided he should make a break for it, but too late. As he broke away, the cat sprang forward in a blur, front paws leading the pounce. Drew saw the cat strut by with the kill in its mouth.

He hated them both, cat and mouse.

He gets out of bed and goes to the kitchen, pulls a bowl down from the shelves and a carton of milk from the refrigerator. There's no way to know if these are the same cats, of course, although, since he is living only a block from Mrs. Dunwiddy, it's possible: No matter. Squalling cats are squalling cats. He pours milk into the dish and sets it just outside the back door, on the concrete steps. The shrieking stops.

He waits for a while, sitting there in the dark with arms wrapped around folded legs. Soon he sees a pair of green eyes glowing at him from the night, and a plaintive meow. It's not a true alleycat; they mistrust people. Probably a housecat some suburban person got tired of or became allergic to, took into the District and dumped from the car. A not-quite-streetwise cat: It is not as afraid as it should be of people. He feels a pleasurable twist in his stomach as the cat takes shape from the darkness, approaches the dish of milk, tail twitching. He sits motionless.

It is a thin, young-looking cat, black with a white belly. Life does not look to have been too easy lately; the tongue is swiftly thrust into the bowl, and Drew hears the sound of determined lapping. In only a moment the milk is gone, and the cat looks plaintively at him. He makes a meowing sound, and the cat replies. He does it again, and the cat responds by approaching, face upturned. Meow.

The creature jumps into his lap: warm and furry and pleasant against his bare skin. He has second thoughts. He strokes its head, rubbing his broad palm across the animal's skull, and is rewarded with a deep trill. He can feel the creature's throat vibrate against his thigh. He has third thoughts, fourth thoughts. Slowly he slides a hand around the cat's neck, gently, gently tightens his grip. The cat does not react. A little tighter. The trilling continues; the cat is comfortable and content in the warmth of his lap.

He reconsiders the plan. This is a sweet cat, not like the black hellions she used to trash around with; the ones who wouldn't let him near them, who hissed and arched their backs if he passed within twenty feet. The separatist lesbian nation cats. This cat needs affection and food, and he can provide both. The cat must have more milk.

He stands up as delicately as he can, reaching for the dish at the same time, but the cat screams in fear and claws his forearm as it bounds away and is swallowed up in the ink. Wait, he thinks, this makes no sense, I was going to get you more food, come back. He says it out loud, on the off chance that the cat speaks English.

But the cat does not come back. He refills the dish with milk and sets it out anyway, knowing that by morning it will be gone, sluiced off to some cat belly or other. Off to bed he slouches, feeling used and resentful, half-promising himself that the next time he will not be so sentimental, so easily seduced; that he will carry out the plan the way he made it, in the bracing chill of reason.

"*But why,*" *I say, "not?*"

"*Because I hate it, Drew.*"

Simple question. Simple answer. Simple girl. Classic, classic Trina. Why am I here?

"*Let's try it this other way,*" *she says, rolling me over, positioning my various parts. I feel like a lump of bread dough, but I don't complain. This isn't the sort of thing that I've been enjoying on a daily basis of late. Let's speak frankly.*

While we stood on the street after dinner, waving so long to Mike as he drove off in the rented blue Beretta to wife and kid, I explained to Chris why moving to L.A. would be salutory for him. It's warmer and sunnier and richer, I pointed out. You can stay with Geoff and me; we have an extra bedroom. We live in West Hollywood, for Christ's sake. (I didn't swear, though I felt like it.) Open ass, remove head. What more could you ask for?

"*Los Angeles,*" *he said, pursing his lips, like I'd said "Warsaw" or "Sverdlovsk" or some other pleasure camp like that.*

It is funny to be back, but it feels right, like completing a circle. I am tan again. I am relaxed, although not, entirely, about Geoff, whose little friends are forever trooping in and out—all blonds and all nineteen years old. This must be against the law. He is obsessed and narrow-minded, which I told him. He didn't agree, and we had a short, intense argument, but that didn't stop him from setting me up with the cousin of a friend's friend who knows someone on the inside, some kind of vice-president.

Working in the corporate counsel's office of a television production company is not exactly the future I glowingly described for myself on that questionnaire the university sent us last year. For one thing, it's not the movies (not yet)—but I wouldn't have put that down, either, even though, if I'd put down what I really wanted to, I would have. But it is a start and an in.

Going through my little divorce from the firm has turned out to be liberating. (Or maybe I should say "empowering" or "self-affirming." So many adjectives, so little time, but I'm quickly adjusting to the West-Coast-speak of the nineties.) At first I felt like machine-gunning the whole office, spraying the partners' conference room with dum-dum bullets, so that it would look like the garage at the end of The St. Valentine's Day Massacre. *Hey, and you have a nice weekend, rat-tat-tat-tat-tat. I was feeling a little hacked, I guess. Wade, et cetera. (Can that actually have happened?) But it was for the best. I needed to get out, but I see now, looking back—the best way to look—that I never would have done it on my own. The big salaries are a bribe; you become comfortable with your things and your habits until giving them up is unthinkable, even if you know you should.*

Back to Chris. Of course this evening was bizarre, in ways expected and not expected. It has been a long time, lots of water under the bridge and all that. I do not feel differently about him, still. It doesn't change the friendship. But I do think he's awash in self-pity and needs a change of scene. I explained this, and he nodded, but sort of like Gill in "Patterns of Force."

A move wouldn't kill Trina, either: Here she is, living in the same apartment she lent us for that graduation party where the three of us got drunk and stood around the pool. When I called her and she said, "Come on down" (just like on The Price Is Right*), I thought: What am I doing? But it's turned out to be just like old times, even better in a way, because the future seems to be less of a strain than it was in those days, and we are not buffeted by the turbulence of friends (naming no names). It's just the two of us.*

Women are astonishingly sensitive to the scent of other females in the lives of their men. It was almost as though she had talked heart to heart with Dana (assuming the latter had one) before I walked through the door. The story (my side) just spilled out. I had never really told anyone the whole thing before, and she sopped it up like a sponge, without any hint of becoming jealous. Not that there's anything to be jealous about: It's as over as it could possibly be. When, at dessert, Mike asked me how Dana was, I told him that I never hear anything from her and that the only thing I've heard about her since law school is that she's gotten married. Kirk Wiedenbeck, cha cha cha. (I snapped my fingers, but M. failed to laugh.)

Truth to tell, I would have preferred to spend the rest of the evening with Chris. He needs cheering up, reinforcement of the sense that life goes on. It was just the sort of evening—mild, clear, autumnal—in which we always liked to roam the city. Also: I think he's more interested in coming to L.A. than he lets on. If he wants to leave (and I don't blame him for that; San Francisco is a war zone these days, the walking dead and dying all over the place), where else can he go? He said something about his parents, home, et cetera, but as I noted, as tactfully as possible with respect to such a calamitous idea, that would put him in the Midwest, in the role of adult child living with

Mom and Dad. In the circumstances, I said, your circumstances, I mean, that's crazy.

I don't know, he said, in a tone that did not cut off further challenge. Catholic boy, he needs to be courted and persuaded. Maybe tomorrow I'll be sharper. Reminder: Tomorrow, call Geoff and ask him how to proceed. Even though he's an ass, he's an expert in this field and he was right about Chris all along and he may be able to say something useful about state of mind, et cetera. Maybe he can even talk some sense into C. (But don't let him gloat.)

She remembers exactly *where my neck develops that little knot of tightness: slightly right of center, just below the hairline. Dana never bothered to figure that out. I grunt to let her know I approve.*

Hometowns are weird places: You love and hate and are bored by them, all at the same time. They're very much like life itself in that way. All those years of pretending to love the Bay Area and D.C. have collapsed into this acknowledgment that I live in L.A. It's where I belong. I am an Angeleno. It's that simple. I'm blond and still look good in Jams and Ray-Bans and I drive a '66 Mustang convertible. So there. The white boy returns. Get over it.

And not a moment too soon. Being a visitor for the past fourteen years has made it easier to see the changes in progress; like a demographic version of time-lapse photography. The old neighborhoods aren't much changed—ours, for instance, or Mom and Dad's up in the hills—but when we decided one afternoon to give Geoff's Miata a road test in the desert, I thought we would never *get out of the subdivisions and kept asking myself, Who are these people and where are they getting their water and where are they putting their garbage and* where did they come from?

"You should at least think about it," I say, sounding the same reasonable note I sounded with Chris only a few hours before. *What is the harm in thinking about it, after all? These people need a fresh start. Are they going to move to New York City or one of those other dead brick shells back East? No fucking way.*

"I'll think about it," she says, managing, eerily, to say so with exactly the same words and in exactly the same tone Chris used just a few hours ago, making clear, somehow, that thinking about it is, other than actually doing it, the thing that is least likely to happen. But I'm not through with either one of them.

last SUMMER

June torched a white hole in the sky, and through it the heat cascaded, tumbling over the green heads of the mountains, bouncing off concrete and asphalt into the shimmering air, browning the foothills like toast. Summer's oven door had swung open.

June had always meant warmth and partings, but this June's unusual blaze was a signal, Chris thought, that these were not to be the usual partings, not little rips in the fabric of life that time would stitch back together. The sun and the heat, the persistently gusty wind, gave him a sense of apocalypse, and when he walked around campus, bobbing amid the throng of tank-tops and shorts and sandals and bare chests, zinc-creamed noses and Vuarnet sunglasses, he had the sense that everyone else, too, was waiting.

It had been like this at the end of freshman year, when undergraduate routine melted in the hot sun and the campus, the people, seemed overnight to have become foreign and unknowable. The school was not, after all, yours, and you did not, after all, belong to it. The arrangement was finite and mortal, and when it was over, you were on your own. On the way to the airport the three of them had eaten at Arby's, because Michael had coupons he wanted to use, and while they chewed their roast-beef sandwiches and talked the way they had always talked, Chris could not shake the feeling that he wasn't really there, that the life in which the three of them had been bound together was over, if only until September.

On the Tuesday after the last weekend of finals—at exactly the midpoint of that sweet, suspended interval when school was no more but the epic descent of parents, family and friends for the fest of graduation had not yet begun; when, the underclassmen having been shooed out of their rooms into whatever summer had prepared for them, the campus belonged solely to the seniors (as it had the first few days of freshman year, before the upperclassmen arrived)—Katherine and David hosted a small party at a winery high in the hills.

"Not that we know anything about wine," David said to Chris in extending the invitation to the three of them, plus Meredith and Trina.

"Except how to scarf it," Katherine said. "We've got that down."

Even knowing nothing about zinfandel grapes or tannin or French-oak aging barrels or all the other minutiae of winemaking that the guide gushed on about, it turned out to be fun sitting at the wood tables under the shade of a scrub oak that leaned into the abyss, sipping this one and that one and trying to persuade yourself that the first one had a good finish while the second tasted of berries and chocolate, with a spicy nose.

("Thank God she's paying for the whole thing," David confided to Michael after a glass or two. "Except the crackers. I brought those."

"They're delicious," Michael said.

Brie and Camembert were also offered.)

Just beyond their toes the ground fell away into nothing, reappearing in the far below as the flat bayside ledge of San Francisco and her Peninsula suburbs, silent and motionless under the breezy sun. The city itself, a prickly outcropping of white skyscrapers, sat in the distance on its bed of fog.

"It's like floating in the clouds," Meredith said, "except there aren't any clouds," and Michael almost burst into tears, not for lack of clouds, not because of the view, the hot, dry air scented with grape and earth and sea, his friends about him, not because he was in love with her, but because he didn't want to grow up and get married and become a doctor and have a house and children in some suburb. He wanted to stay here and drink cabernet sauvignon and zinfandel (or maybe something white and a little fruitier) and never get older, and if anyone had asked him, even her, he would have said so, but no one did.

"Like being high," Drew allowed.

"Attention, attention!" Katherine said, banging an empty bottle like a gavel on one of the tabletops. "*Achtung!* Just a few brief announcements. First, we accept MasterCard or Visa, or cash. No personal checks, especially from *you*," she said, pointing a finger toward a Top-Sidered, fraternity-house-looking boy Chris didn't recognize. "Cash preferred. Unmarked, small bills. Squire can make change." She glanced at David. "Second, just to confirm the rumors, yes. David and I are moving to the city, and no, we're not getting married. There will be another party to celebrate both of these developments in due course. Thank you. God save the queen."

She sat down to scattered applause and a flying cork or two.

"The city," Michael said. "What are you going to do there?"

"Live in sin," Katherine said.

"*For* sin, actually," David corrected her.

"Yes, you're quite right," she said. "More wine here." She poured. "We're going to rent a big truck and David's going to load everything into it all by his lonesome. Then I'll drive. Then sin."

"Get an automatic," Michael said to David. "You don't want to be shifting gears all the time."

Katherine nodded her head vigorously. "He's worn out two of Franz's clutches already," she said. "From now on I do the shifting in our family."

The plan of Katherine and David, however meager, was still far more plan than Chris had. He had, in fact, no plan. Sitting here on the roof of the world, nowhere to go but down, the sun beginning to slip from the sky, his head fluttering with too many sips, all of life seemed to have distilled itself into metaphors of decline, fall, departures, descents, farewell. They were all riding the pulse of separation—he, for all he knew, into the nothingness of temp jobs or waiting tables or living off his parents' dole, until they told him to get a life. At least David and Katherine were moving to San Francisco. That was something. That was exciting.

Time passed, no one really knew how much. The sun continued to lose altitude, its light fading to the color of old newsprint, but it was still hot. A large number of empty wine bottles stood on the tables, tastings and toasts and adjectives having yielded, at some point, to hearty swills. Trina lay in the back seat of Drew's car with an arm across her brow, listening to the radio, while Drew sat in the driver's seat, aimlessly shifting gears and mouthing orders about warp factors and photon torpedoes.

Michael and Meredith were touring one of the buildings, bumping and whispering as one of the vintners explained again about presses and barrels and the different kinds of grapes and where they came from. Outside, David and Katherine were in conference with the fraternity brothers.

Pairs, pairs, pairs and more, except for Chris, who wandered by himself among the trees, peering into the grape arbors, feeling woozily sorry for himself, feeling acutely that he alone was alone. He felt like going straight up to Drew and putting his arms around him and kissing him right on the mouth, so there would be no chance of his mistaking the gesture for some manly show of affection between two dudes. Just to make sure, slip him the tongue.

But even drunk, even with Drew drunk, he knew he wouldn't, couldn't do it. How many such chances had he already let pass by for fear of the consequences? Sweating with frustration and heat, he sat on the ground with his arms locked around his knees, so lost in the world he was staring out at that he did not hear Merry and Michael approach from behind.

"Tomorrow," she said, dropping down beside him, "we're going to the city to spend the day. Just the two of us. We thought you might like to come."

"Just us," Michael added, from somewhere in the westerly glare.

"I feel dizzy," Chris said.

"It's the heat," said Meredith. "We're all feeling it."

"I feel better," Michael said. "I can drive now. How about you?" he asked Chris, who looked at him blankly.

"We should dry out a little more," Merry said. "Think about tomorrow. It'll be fun."

"I will," Chris said, as though there were anything else to think about.

Drew had shrugged when Michael asked him, the week before, about the planned parting.

"It's simple," he said. "I'm going away and she's not. It's either this or get married."

Michael nodded. "No, it makes sense," he said, hoping to sound agreeably skeptical so that Drew would not guess how attractive this course was beginning to look to him. It was definitive. It left no loose ends, and he felt increasingly that he and Meredith were bound together more by loose ends than anything else.

Getting married was out of the question, even though he was pretty sure he loved her and even though she had avoided the mistake of bringing up the topic. The future was obscure enough without swirling a wife into it. For weeks the strongest urge he had been feeling was to simplify, simplify his life: peel away everything that was unnecessary so that he was more maneuverable.

Life without Meredith was unimaginable, but in a few weeks that was exactly what life would be. Was Drew right? Was it easier just to cut it off altogether, like cauterizing the stump of an amputated limb? The pain at that moment might be blinding, but over the long term it was easier and healthier than gangrenous rot.

He felt dishonest for thinking these thoughts when he was with her. At times he was on the verge of saying something, exhaling the question—*Is this it for us?*—but the words never quite found their way out. When she looked at him, talking of this or that, he wondered if she too was thinking along the same lines, wondering how to bring it up.

"So what are you going to do?" Drew said. "We've set up a pool on whether you'll break up or get married. Don't let me down."

"I don't know how you're betting."

"Let me put it this way," Drew said. "Chris bets that you'll get married."

Michael smiled and ate a french fry, touched, though he did not say so, by Chris's unwavering faith in the power of love.

"I'm betting you're smart," Drew continued, "because I know you are."

Late Thursday morning, Drew's brother Geoff drifted down from San Francisco, where he had been staying with friends, and set up graduation watch in a sleeping bag on the floor. Geoff was better-looking than Chris remembered, disturbingly similar to Drew—not quite as tall, darker hair. But he had the same nose and mouth, and made the same deep, honky laugh when something amused him.

The obvious difference was that Geoff was far more sensual: quick to touch one's hand or leg or the back of one's neck. Perhaps it had something to do with Geoff's being gay, of having overcome the stricture of men not touching men. Geoff touched anybody he felt like touching. Chris was drawn to him, and late in the afternoon, while Drew was away somewhere with Trina, and a *M*A*S*H* rerun was on the television, they ended up in each other's arms on the floor.

Afterward Chris wept, clinging to Geoff as the storm soaked them both. Geoff petted and murmured and soothed, and gradually the spasm broke into heaving breaths and wet sniffles; red eyes blinked uncertainly open.

"I just can't believe this is happening," Chris managed to say.

"You and me."

"Everything. You look so much like him. I never noticed. I can't believe college is over."

"You love him."

"I do," Chris said, "so much."

"Baby," Geoff whispered, fingers gently massaging Chris's scalp. "I know."

"I don't want to leave."

"I know."

They clung.

Graduation day was as sunny and hot as the week of days that preceded it. The class, swathed in black robes and tassels, assembled at midmorning in the basketball pavilion. There were instructions on the proceedings that no one paid attention to. At length they were released for the walk to the amphitheater, an open-air, man-made bowl of ground ringed by trees and sloping steadily up and away from a large stage, where an august assemblage of deans and professors gazed out benignly upon the masses.

An untold number of champagne bottles was being smuggled into the amphitheater. Chris could see the arms oddly crooked, the unusual distensions in the robes.

"I've got one, too," Drew announced. "I've been shaking it since last night. If I see"—he named an elderly professor of English who had given him a poor mark on a paper about Forster—"I'm going to waste the dude."

"I brought one for you, too," Michael said, a little sheepishly, as though anxious to disavow Drew's assassinatory plan. He handed Chris a cold green bottle. "We're saving most of the stuff to drink later. So fire at will."

Chris nodded, wondering at which luckless faculty member he would take aim if the vindictive urge struck. He gave his bottle a few tentative shakes before folding it into his robe. It felt cool and hard and comfortable against his side.

Like springing from a diving board, the plunge was beginning even as they reached the apex of college. Drew was leaving early the next morning, Michael later in the day. Their effects were already in boxes, on trucks, on their way back to their parents' homes. Two undergraduates working in New York for the summer were being paid to drive Michael's Fiat across the country. Tonight, after the taco party (for which Trina had volunteered her apartment), the three of them would say goodbye. They would shake hands and make a few lame jokes about getting old and promise to write and call, and the fault line upon which their lives together had been built would rupture catastrophically, carrying them, in a matter of moments, far apart.

The overture to *Tannhäuser* filled the hot air. Various academic officials paraded solemnly down the length of the amphitheater toward the stage, resplendent in their ceremonial garb, amid whoops and shouts and a few corks popping prematurely. Distinguished speakers said distinguished things. The black-robed mob was welcomed into the family of alumni. The president of the university quoted Adlai Stevenson:

> *Your days are short here;*
> *This is the last of your springs.*
> *And now in the serenity*
> *and quiet of this lovely place,*
> *touch the depths of truth,*
> *feel the hem of Heaven.*
> *You will go away with old, good*
> *friends. And don't forget*
> *when you leave why you came.*

Chris laughed and cried at the same time. They all did, because they did not know exactly what they were feeling or what they were supposed to feel. He heard shouts and popping corks all around him, like fireworks; he felt the cork popping in his own hands, the cool, tingly flow of foam. He splashed some on Drew, who sputtered, and lifted the bottle to his own lips—just as Michael doused him.

The courtyard of Trina's apartment complex was lighted by only a few pole lamps disguised as Victorian gaslights, but the swimming pool at its center glowed a phosphorescent blue, like a giant television screen embedded in the ground, rippling with test patterns.

Upstairs, many dozens of tacos were being assembled—from the bowls of Ortega-seasoned ground beef, shredded lettuce, grated jack cheese, sliced olives, diced tomatoes, guacamole, sour cream, salsa, corn tortillas toasted crisp in the shape of U's, most of which Chris had prepared—and munched. The first guests had been friends and classmates, grasping at one last chance to be seniors together outside the

defining presence of parents and family; but slowly those related particles appeared, crowding the shag-carpeted rooms
and the all-electric kitchen, drawing down supplies of food and
drink that only the day before had seemed wildly excessive.

Because there was no precedent with which to compare
Drew and Trina's announcement that they were officially broken up, there was no way to be certain that their clinking together two cans of beer to commemorate the moment was as
vulgar as it seemed to be—at least to Chris. In that instant,
even though they were smiling like newlyweds, he saw the long
draw of sadness in her face; or was it his own, being reflected?

Soon after, while the food was being dug into, he sat
cross-legged with Trina in a corner, holding hands, trying not
to cry.

"This is hard," she said. "I didn't think it would be. I
thought I'd be glad. And I'm not even graduating."

"It is hard."

"I think I'm going to miss you," she said, "more than
him."

"It's kind of a bummer," Drew said from his lounge chair at
poolside. He held an open bottle of champagne in one hand.
Michael held his head in both hands; Meredith had tactfully
remained upstairs, ostensibly to supervise the party. "Leaving
and stuff."

"Yeah," Michael said with a snuffle. He had drunk as
much champagne as he had ever drunk in his life, and the
very earth on which he stood seemed to be wobbling on its
axis. Fortunately, while he staggered and spun, his parents,
with Meredith's help, were already planning how to whisk him
off to the hotel and the second double bed, where they could
keep an eye on him until it came time for the ride to the airport.

"What do we do now?" Chris said with an uneasy laugh.
"Tomorrow morning I'm out on my ass." Not quite, actually:

Katherine had offered him the use of Franz to move his things
("but you have to *promise* not to ride the clutch"), and she and
David had said, separately and together, that he was welcome
to stay with them, wherever they were staying, until he had a
place of his own.

"A life of my own, you mean," he had corrected them, but
although he was nervous about sharing quarters with them—
however temporary the arrangement—he was also deeply
grateful. For one thing, their generosity kept him for the moment from having to return home, penniless and unemployed,
to throw himself on the mercy of his family. And it offered
some cushion to the reality blow that was about to fall: the departure of virtually everyone he loved. Even Trina was going
away for the summer—off to Thailand with Volunteers in Asia.

"Maybe tomorrow you'll meet the girl of your dreams,"
Drew said dreamily. "A beautiful brunet with a double major,
comp lit and physics, who works with crippled children. And
a nympho." The champagne bottle was empty and he threw it
into the pool. It floated for a while, slowly taking on water, like
a torpedoed battleship, before foundering. "God," he said, enraptured by his description.

"I'm really going to miss you guys," Michael said, sounding more weepy now than snuffly. He got up carefully and went
over to Chris and embraced him. The top of his head was
pressed to Chris's face; his hair gave off the coconut scent of
Nexxus Therappe. "Jesus," he said, "Jesus."

Chris looked over at Drew, who had risen from the
lounger and was standing a few feet away from them, looking
as though he did not know what to do. Chris held out a hand
and Drew took it, pulled himself to them.

"He's short, isn't he?" Drew said to Chris. Fissures gaped
in his flip tone. "Why do we like him?"

"Because," Chris said.

Michael had entirely dissolved into sobs and tears that
drained onto Chris's chest. Chris was moved by the smooth so-

lidity of the body and, at the same time, by the way it shivered and trembled with vulnerability: the essential, irresistible paradox of the human male. Drew managed to smile from his side of the mop of black curls; he laid a hand on Chris's neck and gently massaged.

"It's like the last episode of *Mary Tyler Moore*," he said. "We should all sing 'It's a Long Way to Tipperary.' "

"But no shuffling," Chris said. "We'll end up in the pool."

Like a baby, Michael shifted his attention from Chris to Drew, who with surprising grace took the shorter, stockier figure into his arms.

Thus Meredith found them some moments later: Drew and Michael locked in a wordless embrace; Chris standing beside them. Gently Drew broke away, guiding Michael to her.

"All yours," he said, and she nodded. He cupped a hand over her hair and kissed her lightly on the cheek. "Y'all take care," he whispered with a tiny smile.

"Goodbye, Andrew," she said. "I'll miss you." And, locking her arm in Michael's, she led him back upstairs.

The sea breeze sighed around them.

"Well," Drew said. He looked away from Chris, toward the blue pool. "I feel funny," he said.

"Me too."

"Not drunk, really."

"No."

"He went completely to pieces," Drew said. "I didn't know he was so sentimental." He paused.

"Neither did I," Chris said. He wondered if this was the moment God had appointed. If this was the big chance. Say it now. Blurt it out. Tell him the truth about yourself and, at the very zenith of the friendship, a few hours beyond which lies nothing, make him wonder if he ever really knew you.

"Don't die, please," Drew said, and although he was looking the other way, suddenly his voice was choked so tight that the words could scarcely escape. He reached out to Chris, who pulled them against each other. Drew was crying—silently but hard, his eyes squeezed shut and his face distorted from trying not to, his body shuddering. Chris stroked his hair, thinking, I have wanted this for so very long. This big, beautiful man helpless in my arms. *Drew is crying in my arms.*

"You're not going to kiss me, are you?" Drew said in between deep, damp breaths, as if he'd been reading Chris's mind. "I suppose I can't stop you. It's a free country. Just make sure no one sees. And no tongue."

"Don't worry."

"It's weird," Drew said with an unpersuasive chuckle, "that you're the sentimental one and I'm the one who's crying."

Chris could not think of anything to say. He could not feel.

"I still think we should live in the same city and become old, crabby bachelors together."

"I'll be here," Chris said, almost inaudibly.

"Don't really want to go to Europe," Drew said. "Or law school. Washington. Fuck. I *hate* the East."

"Maybe you'll like it this time."

"I won't."

"Don't go."

"Have to."

"Why?"

Drew shrugged. "Just do," he said. "Parents'd kill me."

"You're a grown-up."

"They've got all the money."

For what seemed like hours to Chris, they stood together by the pool, arms looped around each other, gently rocking back and forth as if to music only they could hear. Overhead, a starry, starry night; up the staircase, a chorus of voices still rising and falling. Gradually Chris became aware of a figure standing by the edge of the pool's glow. Geoff. He approached, step by gingerly step.

"Mom and Dad are looking for you," he said, laying his hands on Drew's shoulders.

"Tell them Chris and I are running off together."

"You can tell them that," Geoff said with a low laugh.

"I guess this is it," Drew said. Chris nodded, his hands still outstretched as Drew slipped through them, away—arms, hands, fingers. The cool night air. The hands, emptied, fell back to his sides.

"Take care, Chris," Geoff said, a little bittersweet smile bending one corner of his mouth. He bent forward quickly and pressed his lips against Chris's cheek.

"I will."

"Miss you," Drew said. Abruptly, as if taking a cue from Geoff, he leaned over and kissed Chris on the same cheek. Then they were gone.

the CRACK-UP (II)

"Hi," Michael says, peeking in the open door. It is a small office, with two tall, narrow windows that look northeast onto the lake, a framed Monet print on the opposite wall, a bookshelf filled with heavy professional volumes, a desk, and several easy chairs set around a low wood coffee table. There is no couch. Dr. Oldenburger is clean-shaven, has a full head of hair, and is not smoking a cigar. Michael knocks on the doorjamb, to reinforce the "Hi."

"Hello," Oldenburger says, glancing up from the papers at his desk. He is young—mid to late thirties, Michael guesses—and seems to be perfectly normal. No Viennese accent. Apprehension subsides. They shake hands. "Dr. Waldman."

"Dr. Oldenburger."

"Call me Peter."

"Mike."

"Have a seat, Mike," Oldenburger says, indicating a chair

in front of the desk, to the other side of which he returns. He shuffles the papers. He is not an organized person; this is obvious. Something has gotten misplaced—"Ah!" he says, finding it; a translucent yellow sheet of paper with computer holes along each edge. "I was just pondering how to clean things up in here," he says. "I was away all last week, and you know what *that* means. Any time I've been away from the office, I spend the night before I come back in sleepless *dread* of what I will find. Piles and piles of documents. That is what bureaucracies are for—document shuffling."

"Yeah."

"I'm sorry," Oldenburger says with a smile. "I'm getting carried away. I'm glad you're here."

"I feel funny about it."

"Oh yes. Many people do. They feel as though they are confessing something terrible about themselves. Perfectly normal to feel that way. Not unusual at all."

"It's not that I'm depressed or anything," Michael says. "I mean, nothing unusual. Just the usual up-and-down stuff. You know. Thanks, yes, tea," he says, as Oldenburger indicates a choice of beverages from the serving table in the corner.

"I find that young doctors often become very upset when they cannot say exactly why they are not perfectly happy, even though none of them are," Oldenburger says. "*I'm* that way! I think it has to do with the kind of training we go through—winnowing all the facts and all our observations to an inescapable conclusion. We have a hard time sometimes accepting that there isn't always *an* answer, and therefore *a* solution. I'm writing a paper about this."

"The kind of training we receive."

"The precision of science. Yes or no, black or white, zero or one. Professionally we live in a world that prizes this sort of binary exactitude. But the rest of the world is fuzzier."

"Professionally—I don't know," Michael says.

Oldenburger gestures to the easy chairs, and, tea in hand,

they settle in. Michael thinks of an English men's club, old Tories poured into their leather armchairs, gin-and-tonics conveniently positioned nearby.

"Professionally," Dr. Oldenburger says. "You don't know."

"Do you ever wonder why you're a doctor?" Michael asks.

The older man nods, sipping his tea. "Certainly," he says. "Of course. Who doesn't?"

"I do all the time."

"Why *are* you a doctor?"

"I have no idea."

"Mmmm," Dr. Oldenburger says. "Well, the easy answer is that you studied to become one. That's one answer. Maybe there are others. Do you *want* to be a doctor?"

Michael squirms. "That's what I'm not sure," he says miserably. "I feel like, you know, I've reached this point and I can see how I got here and everything, but I can't remember why I started out on this path."

Oldenburger nods.

"You know. I mean, you decide when you're fifteen or something that this is what you want to do, and suddenly you're married and thirty and you've got a little kid and you realize you're still living this decision you made in tenth-grade biology or whatever. When you didn't have a clue about anything. You see what I mean."

"I think I decided in ninth-grade English," Oldenburger says. "Yes. It is one of the epiphanies of adulthood that we begin to see how our choices echo down the years. Proof that the past is real. What's your child's name?"

"Daniel."

"I like that."

"It was my dad's dad's name."

"The past," Oldenburger says. "You respect it."

"I guess so. I never thought of it that way."

"Did you enjoy tenth-grade biology?"

"I got an A."

"Is that the same thing?"

"I didn't really like high school," Michael admits. "It's like, no one knew who they were, all these groups and cliques and everything. I studied a lot."

"You did well."

"I did well," Michael says. "A's. A couple of B's."

"Your parents were proud."

"*Oh,*" Michael says, "they were proud."

"Even of the B's."

"They were in phys ed and one in social studies, I think, stuff that didn't count."

"To you or to them?"

"They knew what they wanted for me," Michael says.

"What did you want?"

"No clue," Michael says. "Probably whatever they wanted me to want."

"What did you *not* want?"

"What's the difference?"

"I don't know."

"I don't remember that much about high school," Michael says. "Just that I was glad to get out."

"You went to college out West, didn't you? California." He glances at a file on his desk, nodding to himself.

"Yes."

"Made a break for the sunshine."

"It rains," Michael says with a small smile. "Sometimes."

"College was when I had my one big professional crisis," Oldenburger says. "So far, at any rate! I took a class in basic Western philosophy to satisfy some kind of requirement—I was a sophomore, I think—and I absolutely loved it. Wrote my family, this was what I want to do, what I'm going to do. Be a philosopher. They nearly died, of course."

"That never happened to me!" Michael exclaims. "I never had a class like that. I waited and waited."

"What were you waiting for?"

"What you just said. To be excited by a class or a professor or something."

"Did your friends feel the same way?"

"I don't know," Michael says. "We didn't talk about it much. Meredith got into some of her classes, but they were art history and stuff like that."

"Meredith was—?"

"The girl I went out with junior and senior year."

"Are you still in touch?"

"She's my wife."

Oldenburger throws his head back and laughs. "Of course," he says. "I'm sorry. I knew the name was familiar! It's in the materials here." He shuffles his papers industriously. "What is she doing these days?"

"She was working at the Art Institute before the baby. Part-time now. Plus she does some free-lance design stuff at home."

"Married how long?"

"Four years."

"And the baby is—?"

"Two."

"Oh, an exciting age," Oldenburger says. "Yes indeed. I remember when my daughter was two. We couldn't leave her alone for an instant."

"Dan's that way," Michael agrees.

"But Meredith is with him most days."

"Most," Michael says. "We have a regular sitter for the days she works."

"Busy lives," Oldenburger says.

The day Meredith and Daniel came home from the hospital—a damp, chilly November Saturday; the baby was wrapped in layers and layers of blankets, like a piece of crystal being shipped cross-country—Joe showed up with a box of home-made chocolate-chip cookies and a Gund bear. He was goofy in that post-call way, but the baby seemed to have a settling effect on him and, when Merry slipped the bleating bundle into his arms, he had the same effect on it.

At first, Michael found it difficult to relate the child to himself, to think of this little mass of red flesh, with its tiny translucent fingers and thin straggles of dark hair, as his issue, something he had helped to create. In part, he supposes, this was because Meredith's pregnancy was so uneventful—was hardly noticeable, in fact (other than when she was naked) until the last six weeks. By then all he was thinking about was labor, what kind of anesthesia she should have, if any, the delivery itself, and where he would be during it—at her side, holding her hand? Was that allowed?—and all the rest of the traumas that attended birthing.

The baby, when he first saw it and was allowed to hold it, seemed foreign in the generic way of babies, which, like sheep, look more or less alike to grown-ups. The tiny creature, eyes shut, squirmed and grunted and kept opening and closing his empty hands; Michael wondered if he was holding him badly. When Dan finally fluttered his eyelids and looked at him, Michael wondered what the infant saw. His blue eyes were blank with curiosity. Here was a human being who knew nothing, understood nothing, could say nothing, was only a few hours old, and yet came from him, was part of him, was every bit as human as he was. Or: He had been just like this, twenty-eight years ago. Intellectually he grasped this fact, but there was no reflection in his heart. Instead he saw Meredith, wan and tired but happy after the ordeal, and he felt a surge of relief that despite the arrival of the baby, she was still there, still the same.

Dan cried, and he handed him back to her, afraid that a change of diaper might be in order.

Whether and when to have a baby were questions they deferred for more than a year after the wedding. But when midway through the residency it became clear that Michael's department was going to want him to stay (the main signal being his designation as chief resident for a six-month term), the clouds of uncertainty that had been hanging over their future lifted slightly, and they agreed (he not without reluctance) to go ahead.

Reluctant was not the picture he liked to' see of himself, face to face with fatherhood, but he could not stop thinking about how much money a baby was going to cost and the responsibility and the loss of freedom, the acceleration of trends that had been gathering for years. On the morning of Dan's first full day home, Michael looked at his face in the bathroom mirror and was startled to see his familiar self staring back. Part of him had expected to lay eyes on a more fatherly figure, one with a slight paunch and tufts of gray at the temples and crow's-feet about the eyes, as if being a father were impossible without these physical characteristics, or as if becoming a father would produce them overnight. It was hard to think of himself as a father. Fathers were older, grayer, blander, heavier.

There was something different about Meredith, about the two of them. The baby was a paradox between them: a tiny, helpless bundle around which they wrapped their protections and themselves tightly, united in purpose; also a tiny, helpless bundle whose huge emotional mass now reshaped the space between them. When he saw Merry and Dan together, she sitting on the little sofa in their bedroom, he attached to her bare breast, suckling, he felt like an outsider, an interloper, a coarse creature who had purveyed his sperm and was no longer needed. Male honeybees died after mating, but young chief residents went on and on, and so he went on and on, tending to the sick and to the junior residents and the medical students, learning the hospital's administrative routines and hierarchies—all as before, as if the patterns and feel of life itself, *his* life, had not shifted so remarkably.

"Cute kid," Joe said to him the following Monday.

"Thanks."

"I like the dark hair."

"That's her side of the family."

"I figured. She looks great, too."

"Yeah. It wasn't as bad as we thought it was going to be."

"I wouldn't trade places with them for anything," Joe said. "Women. What a drag, having to go through that."

Michael nodded, thinking of how happy she had looked in her depletion. She looked the way you were supposed to look after hard work and a job well done. Were men lesser creatures, he asked himself, for never knowing that pain, never sweating and grunting and straining and hurting for life? Men sweated and grunted in making war or playing football, but when it came time to perpetuate the species women did the real work.

His wife's body had always spoken to him in tones that were either erotic or warmly comfortable; watching her face contort with the agony and effort of pushing Dan into the world revealed the grit that made her just like him. She too, he saw, was a mass of muscle and bone and fluids who, under pressure, could look awful and determined at the same time. While he held her hand during the last stages of labor, he began to imagine that the pain she was feeling was flowing to him, too, jumping the gap between their neurons like blue arcs of electricity. He felt the burning twist shoot up from his gut, spending itself in a hot flush on the tip of his nose and in his ears. Everything he had ever felt for her was distilled into a rush of sympathy and a hopefulness, which he willed along his nerves into hers, that the suffering would soon end. Which it did, leaving her with a glow in her face and a baby in her arms.

"I hope that doesn't sound sexist," Joe said. "It's just the truth."

"It is tough," Michael agreed.

"That black hair's going to curl," Joe says. "I can tell. He liked me, don't you think?"

"I can't even tell yet if he likes *me*," Michael said.

"He loves Merry," Joe said. "Of course, she feeds him."

These days, Dan having grown from a blurry-eyed infant into a miniature person, complete with a wardrobe of miniature Reeboks and Bears sweatshirts, Michael feeds him too—chops his hot dogs and roasted potatoes and mounds of linguine into edible bits. This makes him feel as though he has reached some sort of parity with Meredith. The boy eats a lot and has already grown shockingly tall, Michael thinks, and the dark hair has thickened and curled nicely, as Joe predicted.

"I feel like I'm not as close to him as I should be," Michael says. "I feel like we're not close enough."

"What's close enough?"

"Close enough is when you feel you're close enough."

"When is that?"

"I'll know when it happens. I don't know. It's just something I'll feel."

"What do you feel now?"

Michael hesitates, suspicious of this easy question. "I feel like, I don't know," he says. "Like I'm really the same person I was before he was born."

"Who else should you be?"

"I expected, you know, to feel different somehow."

"To be transformed by fatherhood."

"Maybe not transformed," Michael says. "Something. I mean, I don't *feel* like a father."

"But you enjoy being one."

"Oh yeah. We have a lot of fun. He's the happiest little kid, I think. He laughs a lot, anyway."

"You play with him."

"Whenever I can."

"And you take care of him."

"I try," Michael says. "I work these crazy hours, you know. She's the one who's always there for him. I'm not sure how I feel about that. I mean, it's not like we have a choice, you know? I have this career and everything. I can't very well give it up."

Oldenburger nods, tapping a pen lightly on his knee. "Have you thought about giving it up?"

"Should I?"

"Only you can answer that question," Oldenburger says. "I think you know what the answer is."

"I don't think I do."

"How do you play with Dan?"

"He likes to pretend he's an airplane," Michael says. "He spreads his arms out and I pick him up and fly him around. Joe is taller—my friend Joe—so they, you know, soar a little higher. He loves to scream when we land. Dan, I mean. Joe screams when he drives. We all do, actually."

"Joe's a resident?"

"Yeah. Surgery. We were lab partners first year. Roommates for a while. Before I got married."

"How did he feel about that? Your getting married."

Michael shakes his head. "He gave us a bottle of champagne and a soup tureen," he says.

"He and Meredith get along."

"Great. No problem. Why are you asking me this?"

"Just filling in a few blanks," Oldenburger says. He scribbles something on a sheet of paper.

"Joe's Dan's godfather," Michael says. "If anything, you know, happened to me, he'd be there. That's important. I wanted it that way."

Oldenburger nods, scratching some kind of note on his little pad. "More tea?" he says.

"None for me, thanks. I'm not here because of any of that stuff." He pauses, waiting for the question that does not come, except for Oldenburger's looking at him. "I'm here because I want to be a good father to Dan."

"Are you not a good father?"

"I try."

"You sound as though you think you're letting him down in some way."

"I want him to be tall," Michael says, after a short, difficult pause. "I want him to be a good basketball player."

"Why?"

"Because I wasn't. I ended up on the wrestling team."

"Was that bad?"

"Everyone smelled. Men should be tall."

"And smell nice."

"Like Joe. Six-two, he could play forward."

"Is Dan small for his age?"

"He's tall for his age, actually. So far. But he's only two."

"You're not short," Oldenburger says, "unless I am, too. We're about average for American men, I think."

"Of course Meredith is as tall as I am," Michael says doubtfully, as if to himself. "I'll tell you," he says, returning his attention to Oldenburger. "I want him to have the best, you know, of everything. Including heredity."

"You can't control that."

"That's what's so frustrating."

"Your son is healthy, happy, and taller than average."

"I didn't say I was being rational."

"Heredity isn't everything," Oldenburger continues. "There is the environment. The quality of parenting, pure and simple. For what it's worth, I think the fact that you've come here to talk to me, express these doubts, speaks pretty highly of your dedication as a father."

"The funny thing is," Michael says, "I don't even like basketball. Boring! And they smell bad, too. It's not like I want him to grow up to be the Jewish Michael Jordan."

Before Michael first knocked on Dr. Oldenburger's open door, he walked around the block three or four times, talking to himself. His stomach churned. Counseling services were part of his benefits package, so it wasn't the money; the fact that they were provided at all was proof that there was no shame in using them. Other young doctors, too, must have felt the need. Still. To see a counselor was to concede, if only to yourself, that you had things on your mind you weren't sure you could deal with on your own.

Orbiting the high-rise like a satellite in the dank gray of midmorning, he reminded himself that, although Oldenburger was a psychiatrist, he was not Oldenburger's patient—he was to be counseled, listened to, not *treated.* This was a key distinction. During his psych rotation third year he had seen the real cases—the minds smashed into bits of schizophrenia, the chronically depressed, the addicted, the compulsives—who ended up, more often than not, on drugs or in electroshock treatment or in programs of psychotherapy that stretched to eternity. For them there was no true hope, only a faint prospect of melioration. He was not one of them. What he needed was not jolts of electrical current in the brain but the chance to talk to someone who could listen with interest and disinterest, help him sort things out. That was all. For him there was hope.

Since the arrival of Dan and their buying the Wrigleyville row house so they would have a garden (though a tiny one) for him to play in, the fluid of life in which he moves has thickened: Sometimes he feels as though he's underwater, struggling to breathe against the pressure on his chest. Change is slow-motion. With a family and a house and a prestigious job that pays six figures, he has nothing to complain about—except that he is not sure he is living the life he wants to be living.

It is almost ten years since he met Meredith and fell in love with her. Together they have made a life and a home and a baby; they are happy together. Why, then, is he unable to flush from his mind the pesky fantasy that *she* is out there somewhere, Dana, the brilliant vixen, who with a bang and a flash will reshape the future and carry him into it, away from this proper world of grays and browns and grocery bags and bills and dirty diapers and being so exhausted that they go to bed after *The Nine O'Clock News?* From the world of eight to six, where he knows his place and everyone else's?

Drew drops the occasional note (never mentioning her), but he doesn't have much to say and Michael finds it impossible to respond, other than to sign his name to the holiday card from the Art Institute they send out to a long list of acquaintances the first week of every December. No one, knowing all the facts, would blame Michael for what happened, for their breaking up—not when Dana was as volatile as she was, Drew as impossible; they were the impossible couple—but still. She practically confessed to him, when they were lying there afterward. Their parting of the ways was certainly inevitable, but he almost certainly sped things along.

As the years pass, these thoughts, while shrinking to tiny vivid images, become concentrated and more intense, gaining enough psychological mass to affect the balance of his life. So much of what has happened to him over the course of years he has let go of; memories have been carried away by time. But not Dana, not Drew without Dana, for which he knows he is responsible. Drew is alone because of Michael's uncontrollable hormones. He has tried to pitch any thought of her or them overboard, but they refuse to take the tumble. He cannot wipe them away. At times he dreams of himself in clothes stained with something blood-red, and the stains will not come out despite the most determined, furtive washings and scrubbings and bleachings. He is marked.

Meredith does not see, thank God. She could not possibly. He has never said a word (and does not talk in his sleep, in which mode people do not spill their dark secrets anyway, he has learned), never has palpitations when she mentions Drew or Washington or Drew's love life. There is no way she could have any idea, and she does not need to know.

He is clear about that, because her innocence is what sustains their marriage: her faith that he is worth being mar-

ried to and that the marriage is worth preserving. It's because
she believes; the belief is part of her. He *wants* to believe, but
he is smart enough to understand that this is not the same
thing. His faith rests, instead, piggyback, on hers. If he knocks
her down into the mud, what will he be riding on?

"She's having an affair."

Oldenburger's face remains impassive. "Meredith?" he
says. "How do you know that?"

"I do."

"With whom?"

"Joe."

Pause. Now Oldenburger is looking at him with that same
mask of calm perplexity that was on Kennedy's face in the
Zapruder film, right before the final shattering bullet.

"Your friend Joe?"

"Joe. My friend Joe." He spits out the phrase with satisfying bitterness.

"How do you know *that?*"

"It's so obvious," Michael says. "Haven't you been listening to what I've said? Where do you think Dan got his dark
and curly hair?"

"You have dark and curly hair."

"Joe. Six-two Joe. Dan is too tall."

"Michael, he's a two-year-old infant. Too tall, who's to
say? He'll grow up to be your size. How big were you when you
were his age?"

"Not that big," Michael says, making a mental note to research this question.

"Maybe you were. Even if you weren't, this strikes me as
not the sort of evidence you would go to court with. Michael,
do you hear what you're saying?"

Michael stares at him.

"You know these kinds of things," Michael says after a

moment. "When your partner is trying to hide something. You can tell. They can't hide it. You just feel it."

Oldenburger exhales, glances up at the ceiling. "Well," he says at the end of a reflective moment, as if he is not sure how to proceed, "let's assume this is true. Tell me what you think about it. What you feel. What does it mean?"

Michael shrugs. "What it means is—I don't know," he says. "Maybe nothing. There's not anything I can do about it."

"No?"

"I don't have hard proof, no, excuse the pun," Michael says. "I haven't caught them in the act or anything like that, found their love letters. It might even be over, for all I know. But it definitely happened and I can feel it and that's why we have Dan. You can tell, you know, about your partner's past, something a long time ago that they think is forgotten? You can feel that kind of thing."

"What do you feel?"

"Hard to describe. I've never tried. It's just this sense, I guess, that there's part of them you don't see—they don't *want* you to see."

"Does she see all of you?"

"No."

"What is she not seeing?"

"Lots of things. My work, for one. That's my world, not hers. We don't talk about it that much, and when we do, I'm pretty sure she doesn't really see what it's like."

"That's an evasive answer," Oldenburger says, in the same even tone of voice, as if he were reading off bingo numbers. "Are you having an affair?"

Michael swallows hard, trying to look Oldenburger straight in the eye, wondering why it is so difficult to do this when he is telling the truth. He is *not* having an affair. No. Not now. The times he has broken his wedding vows were not affairs; mostly they have been one-night stands at out-of-town conferences and seminars, with a few liaisons of slightly longer duration, but none of them in the last six months.

Dana, strictly speaking, doesn't even count, because he and Meredith weren't yet married when it happened. Is his subsequent schoolboy pining to be scored against him? Even though he hasn't heard of her in years, never touched her after the one explosion, does the moral code of the universe condemn him for what he would have done again if he'd had the chance, but didn't do, because there has been no chance?

"No."

"I see."

"I've slept with other women since I've been married. But no affairs."

"You see a difference."

"The difference is that I don't get *involved* with any of them," Michael says. "They were just romps. And nobody got pregnant."

"As far as you know."

"As far as I know."

"Do you think she knows?"

"I've been careful."

"Have she and Joe been careful?"

"Pretty careful," Michael concedes.

"Yet you sense their intimacy. Why do you think she doesn't have the same sorts of intuitions about you?"

"Because there's nothing to have intuitions about. I just, you know, fucked them. I don't even remember most of their names."

"And you didn't tell her. You withheld. You don't think she's aware of that."

"She knows," Michael concedes at last. "Of course she knows. She knows about Dana, too. Why else would she do this—with Joe? I mean, I *know*. I get the message."

"Who's Dana?"

"Oh God," Michael says. "I don't know if I can talk about it."

"You don't have to."

"I think I do." He takes the plunge. "She was Drew's girlfriend. Drew's my best friend from college. One of them. They were in law school together in D.C., he and Dana were. I was out there visiting them, oh, five years ago or something like that. Before Meredith and I got married, but we were going out. It just happened. Meredith was at her parents'. They broke up right after I left—well, not right after, but not long. Dana. I've never talked about it with anyone. I couldn't. Who could I tell? Merry? I thought about it. Drew? No way. Chris lives in California. So I didn't."

"You can tell me."

"Jesus," Michael says. He wrings his hands, stopping in mid-gesture when he sees what he is doing. "I didn't think it was that big a deal. It just happened. Why does it stay with me?"

"I don't know," Oldenburger says. "Why does it?"

"The more I try to forget about it, the worse it gets. I have these fantasies—she calls, she's on some Caribbean island, her rich dad's left her a fortune, come live with me. Like this will ever happen! Like I could do something about it even if it did."

"What would you do if you got the call?"

"What do you think I'd do?"

"Tell me."

"What *could* I do?" Michael says. "Leave Merry? Walk out on Dan? I have a job here. A career. I own a house, for God's sake. I have a mortgage."

"You fantasize about her being rich. Let's say she is. Let's say she pays off your mortgage and you never have to work again."

"Oh," Michael says, a single raw syllable "That still leaves Dan and Merry and the career."

"She takes care of your alimony and child support. Dan's not your son. Your wife's been unfaithful and gotten pregnant by your best friend. Your parents made you be a doctor. You've never known what *you* really wanted to do."

"Stop."

"Okay," Oldenburger says.

"I couldn't go," Michael says. "No matter how much money she has."

"No," Oldenburger says. "You're right. Face it. It was over long ago. It wasn't anything."

"I know."

"You've let it corrode you."

"Should I tell Merry?"

"No. Accept your life for what it is, what it has been. You have a strong marriage."

"I do?"

"You do. You just can't see it. If you didn't, you wouldn't be here. You wouldn't care."

Michael ponders.

"I want you to come by next week, same time, and talk to me. If it's still on your mind we'll talk about it. Or we'll talk about something else, whatever you want. Let it go. It's past. It's got nothing to do with your future or your family's. You're lucky."

"I am lucky," Michael says, trying the phrase on for size. The session is over; he feels as though he's leaving the dentist's office after having been told that, no, the deep pain in his molar is nothing, everything is fine. An updraft of relief and wonder carries him onto the elevator and out of the building.

Outside it is gray and cold, although one of the TV weathermen has cautiously forecast partial clearing and broken sunshine (but still cold) by sometime this afternoon. Michael will not go back. He knows this. There is nothing more he wants to say to Oldenburger. It is enough to have given voice to the problem, pricked the bubble of his discontent.

As he walks along the sidewalk, loafers clack-clacking under his feet, the world settles itself into its familiar position on top of him. The exhilaration of telling has already melted away. His life hasn't changed, except that Dana, formerly a shining icon, is suddenly a small dull figure he can't see clearly across the distance.

For years he's yearned for a resolution to this and other issues, for a final accounting and judgment: about Dana, Dan, Merry and Joe, medicine. Between now and sometime in the future, he believed, lay a definite dividing line between what is—a series of messes, ambiguities, paradoxes, hidden conflicts—and what would be, which would be what should be. In life, he has always believed, everything sorts itself out.

Except that today, for the first time, he understands that this isn't necessarily so. Not all questions have answers; not all problems have solutions. He loves Dan. It is that simple. Dan is his son, even if. Meredith is his wife, even if, and he loves her, too. (Who could throw stones at her, after all? Not Michael in his glass row house.) He is a doctor, period. All of it is acceptable, some of it even wonderful. It is his life, made by him; it will go on a while longer, whether he figures it out or not.

Meantime, patients. Lunch with Meredith at the West Egg. Buy the model 747 for Dan; see if they can wrap it for Christmas, or Hanukkah, whichever comes first.

LIFE after DEATH

STUDMUFFIN, 21, blond, gd-lkg, strt-actg-appr, hot to the touch, sks smlr for safe h(e)aven. No fats, fems, drugs, smokers, marrieds, positives. Inexp, bi OK. Photo a must.

The personals. The eyes linger. Let your fingers do the walking. Ah. *Studmuffin.* An image forms. Yes. He finds a pen and a blank sheet of paper and starts a reply.

Hi—

Read your note.

Wait. Stop. The photo business. Let's get real, please. There is no chance he will send a picture of himself to an unknown self-advertiser who could as easily be sixty-one as twenty-one; who could be a serial sex killer, for all he knew— one of those psycho queens who hung people upside down in the basement and pumped them full of drugs and fucked them for days with broom handles.

Plus he photographs poorly. Plus he hasn't felt like having his picture taken in a long time, and it hasn't been.

I apologize for not including a photograph. I'm new to this and kind of shy, I guess.

New to this? Kind of shy, I guess? Well, he is still shy, he guesses. And he is new to the personals, at least to actually making use of them. It is not a complete lie. It is not as though Studmuffin is going to give him a polygraph test, although there's no point lying about age. He can't pass for twenty-one anymore. Instinctively one knows that mentioning that one is thirty will bring catastrophe. Better to sound vaguely late-twenties, without getting too specific, too soon (although he has heard that there are boys who like their men a little older).

Studmuffin naked, willing, sprawled invitingly on a big bed; he wonders who it is, really. Someone he knows? How many twenty-one-year-olds does he know these days? *If* Studmuffin is, as advertised, twenty-one. Since he is ready to lie, it is only fair to assume everyone else is, too. Would it be embarrassing if they met?

The pen twitches in his hand, hovering over the paper like a honeybee over a blossom. Words fail, but not desire. Funny thing, that; not at all what he had expected. No matter the darkness or danger and despair, the hormones still flow, like the mail or the Mississippi: a mile wide even in drought.

Perhaps writing letters isn't the thing. Perhaps something else. He picks up the telephone, dials. Busy. Thanks to the automatic redial, however, it is usually possible to get through in a matter of minutes on one of the free lines. Disembodied voices. More lies.

Twenty-six.

Bi.

Anything.

Contra Costa.

At her parents'.

Lift every other day.

Before I got up this morning.

Just a little on my chest.

A T-shirt.
White.
Blond.
Clean-shaven.
Real *close.*
Dan.
Mike.
Pete.
Bill.
Rob.
Todd.
(Hard, smooth masculine pebbles; like talking dirty to a
baseball team.)
I'm looking to get together with someone.
I can't, Chris always says. *I have a lover.*

He feels the silence—when he wakes up in the morning, goes
to sleep at night. It lies cold and empty beside him. Sometimes
a foghorn, sometimes the wail of a fire engine, quivers in the
terrible perfection of stillness, but they're smudges of sound
easily wiped away by sleep. Lots of sleep.

Silence is good for writing letters, bad poems, fragments
of half-assed novels. There are no distractions from concentration, from the sight of mute paper on the desktop, awaiting
the scratches of articulacy. Sometimes it is a gift he is able
to give—most often in letters he folds carefully, puts in envelopes, but does not send.

> *Dear Carl—*
> *Do you get tired of hearing how dull my todays*
> *are? (Not to mention* Today!) *I did not know rewrit-*
> *ing bad English could be so exhausting. The paradox*
> *is that prolificacy is directly related to true awfulness*
> *of style. My desk is like a landfill where the garbage*
> *piles up faster than I can process it. (Incineration! I*

dream of it. Recycling. Even ocean dumping. For Christmas I want a shredder, industrial-strength, like Ollie and Fawn's.) It's strange that although I cannot understand what I've translated, even after I've translated it, the flow of words washes my mind clean. I'm not aware of anything else, except the occasional hunger pang or need to visit the john. At one time I suppose I would have thought this was a good thing, being reduced to one dimension. Manageable. Now I'm not so sure.

Do you get tired of hearing how much I miss you? Please don't, because I can't stop saying it, writing it, feeling it. It seems to help somewhat. Purging, I guess. I do miss you. Love you so much.

Chris.

(How can I go on?)

How it all began. So, so quietly, so innocently. Like a sympathetic reaction to all the hysterical articles in the *Chronicle*—the grim statistics, the horrible checklists. Safe. Possibly safe. Unsafe. The Do's and Don't's of Love—already too late, of course, for almost everyone, the horse having galloped miles from the barn by the time people began to be aware that something was amiss. *Clop clop clop*—like the sound of the burial cart creeping through the streets of plague-stricken medieval towns.

Almost everyone. Not *every*one. Not us, thank God, Chris told himself. We haven't done anything wrong. We haven't trashed around, gone home with the wrong people, hung around the Asylum or the Brig or Ringold Alley or any of those other nightmare places of desire south of Market.

A step or two slower, a moment or two more to get out of bed in the morning. At the time it seemed like nothing; maybe just an increment of age they happened to notice. A little cough, a few pounds lost, an upset stomach that wouldn't settle down.

"And I'm not even on a diet!" he said lightly, although inside they were both sick with terror. Constant probing of the lymph glands in the neck—were they swollen?—became a subconscious tic, like cracking your knuckles waiting for the dentist. It was impossible to detect any change.

"Hmm," the doctor said when he lost five more pounds and the cough wouldn't go away, nor the diarrhea, and he sweated in the night. "Hmmm."

"We have to talk," Carl said when he came home from that visit. "I think I've got it." The flat voice, prairie voice: He could have been talking about another parking ticket.

"Got what?" Chris said, wishing, wishing, eyes squeezed tight, heels clicking together, like Dorothy in *The Wizard of Oz.* It must be something else. It must be. Let it be. He clicked three times. A hundred times. A hundred zillion trillion times. Not that. Not it. *No.*

"What we're going to do," Carl murmured.

David is coming by at two. Chris is convinced he is having an affair with Wade, but David smilingly denies it.

"Not my type," he said the other night, over Chinese at a place out in the Avenues.

"Not married to a woman, in other words," Chris said.

"Please," he said. "Don't remind me."

Ross and Katherine are rarely seen nowadays. Chris gets a Christmas card and a birthday card from them every year; David has coffee with her "about once every six months, when he's taking depositions in Pago Pago"; but mostly they keep to themselves, moving in the Pacific Heights social circles that flow from their jobs. They have a son named Timothy; there had been an announcement of his birth three years ago. The rest is mostly silence.

"Someday he'll crack," Chris said. "Don't worry."

"I keep wondering if I'll ever see him, you know, *out*," David said. "But I guess he's become the model father."

Chris shook his head.

"Maybe he really *isn't* gay," David said.

"Only his hairdresser knows for sure."

"*He* doesn't even know. I tricked with him a few months ago. That was my pickup line."

They will have a little brunch on the deck and discuss Wade. Chris is feeling prosecutorial as the hot water flows down his back. He has no objection to David's fooling around with Wade, even falling for Wade (and vice versa); he does, however, feel a proprietary interest in Wade, who was the first boy he ever slept with, and he persists in thinking of Wade as a freshman, even though he's only three years younger, will himself be thirty (and more!) in not so very long. Wade must be married off properly.

Anyway, he thinks to himself as he towels off, I'm not going to let him say nothing is going on.

When David arrives they embrace. It may be that Chris clings. The muscles ripple in David's back and arms, and there is a faint whiff of Boss on his neck. He is solid and real.

"You're awfully frisky today," David says, gently disengaging himself.

"Like you're ever not."

"Must be the sunshine."

September. A cloudless sky, light cool breeze. There is a pot of coffee, fresh-squeezed orange juice, toast, yogurt, berries.

"A feast," David says. "You've outdone yourself."

They sit shirtless on the deck and look at other shirtless men on their decks, looking at them. They look at each other.

"Hot."

"All right," Chris says. "Seriously. Wade. Let's hear it."

"You're obsessed."

"Yes, I'm obsessed."

"I like him."

"What does that mean?"

"I know what you're thinking," David says. "Lewd thoughts."

"Only because I know you."

"And him."

"You're avoiding."

"Well, things are strange," David says. "He's talking about graduate school."

"Elsewhere?"

"Yes."

"I thought I heard something about that," Chris says.

"He wants to get out of here," David adds. Further explanation is not needed. More coffee. A clone on a deck a few houses away, up the hill, trains his telescope on them.

"At four-thirty," David says, trying to keep the uncertainty out of his voice, "I'm helping these guys make dinner. Shanti. You know."

Chris blanches, although it's invisible in the bright sunlight. He and Carl had a Shanti volunteer to help them and be with them. The man even came a few times afterward, to make sure Chris did not disintegrate. His own obituary was in one of the gay papers about six months ago.

"I thought, you know, if you wanted, you're welcome to come along," David adds in a near-whisper. "If it's not too weird, I mean. I'd be glad to have the company."

The weight fell away, like chunks of wet plaster. He looked bony and drawn, a reincarnation of one of the Union prisoners at Andersonville, their withering preserved forever in Civil War photos. Fade to black and white. His skin felt cool and dry, not quite alive.

Sieges of diarrhea, night sweats, coughing. Every lesion, every pimple, scratch, and wart, was examined and fretted over. Then: a rally. Appetite returned, weight following.

Strength, color. Out of the hospital. Cruel hope. He looked only forty-five instead of sixty (he was thirty-four).

Chris felt the world collapsing on his shoulders. He dreaded going to work each morning, leaving Carl to take care of himself as the attackers reorganized, regrouped, prepared their next stroke out of sight, out of range.

One February night, a Pacific storm shrieking in the flue, the wind and rain beating on the windows, Carl sleeping, he called Drew. To hear that voice, he hoped, to hear it saying anything at all, would comfort him across the miles, would keep him, for at least a few minutes, from pondering the imponderable horror of what was happening in the next room.

He needed Drew and wanted him to come visit, to lend aid in this desperate hour, to help him bear the burden he could not bear alone. Who else could do that but his best friend forever, who had known him all these years?

Yet the conversation went badly. Drew was no longer Drew. Chris was no longer Chris. He could not utter what was in his heart, what he wanted, what he needed, and Drew went on and on so maddeningly about Chris's leaving his "sick roommate" to visit him in Washington that Chris eventually screamed something into the mouthpiece. He hung up feeling utterly isolated.

For a long while afterward he sat there staring at the telephone, willing it to ring, to be Drew calling back, offering an apology, comfort, solace, the news that he was coming to visit after all. With the world going dark around him, the present in ruins, the future canceled, what remained except the past, of which Drew was custodian? There was nowhere else to turn.

The phone sat silent. Chris sat silent. From the bedroom, wheezes and murmurs and groans; the sounds of a body shifting uneasily on the bed. Please, Chris thought, don't have to go to the hospital again tonight. Please, God, if you're there, let him stay with me tonight.

Feeling a hundred years old, he got up and went into the

darkened, stuffy bedroom, where he spent the next hour or two or who knew how long, who even kept track anymore, holding Carl's hand, brushing his now long, unruly hair off his forehead, remembering, remembering, whispering in his ear of all the light and warmth and hope and love and devotion he could find in his heart to whisper of.

Then he went into the bathroom and cried, a small shuddering ball crouched alone in the dark next to the bathtub, the tiles cold under his bare feet. *I need you so much,* he thought, *I love you so much.*

I am alone.

The flat is on Pine, near Divisadero; they park on Divisadero. The building is a renovated Victorian; the door to the second floor is locked.

"I have a key," David says. "Not the greatest neighborhood. 'Lower Pacific Heights' but it's really close to the Fillmore." They proceed up the groaning stairs. Chris feels claustrophobic, feels that something dreadful awaits at the landing.

"Martin is the one who's sick," David explains.

"What's the friend's name?"

"Bruce."

Chris nods. Of course.

"He's positive too," David is saying. "But so far he seems to be okay."

The buzzer sounds. The door opens. Chris recognizes Bruce, and he does look okay—at least recognizable—although rings of fatigue darken his eyes. David embraces him, pats him gently on the small of his back, introduces Chris.

"My sous-chef."

"I'm awfully glad you're here," Bruce says. "Both of you. We've been having quite a time of it lately."

As if sizing up a patient, Chris evaluates Bruce in a quick glance. He and his hair both seem a bit thinner, but the glands in the neck are unobtrusive. No cough. Eyes clear, skin clear, mouth clear; he seems, as always, languidly coherent. The bloom is definitely off the rose of youth, but that is to be expected. Otherwise, physically, he looks fine.

A clench of pity and of uncomfortable sameness—who would ever have thought that fate would plop them down side by side in these abysmal front-row seats?—nonetheless makes Chris look away, around the room, as if the print on the far wall or the view through the window of the apartment building next door is remarkably fascinating.

"I'll say hi to Martin," David says.

"Yes," Bruce says. "He may not be awake."

David lets himself into the bedroom.

"I'm glad you came," Bruce says again. His tone is distracted, but his gaze is disconcertingly and discordantly sharp. "It's been a while."

Yes. Not since the memorial. Chris finds himself unable to say this; he nods instead.

"I like your apartment," he says. It is the wrong thing to say. The apartment is a possession in common, part of the life they have built together and now, like everything else in that life, about to be lost. Why did I say that, Chris silently asks himself, when I had to move afterward too?

But Bruce's expression has gone blank, as Chris knows his own has been so often, when the world no longer seems quite real, and the only refuge from the siege of grief is not to pay attention to anything at all. Without speaking, Chris reaches for his hand and holds it gently between his own. For a while they sit there like that.

David emerges from the bedroom, his expression artfully composed. Chris stifles an impulse to ask about Martin. He does not want to see Martin. It is too much.

"It's pretty bad today, I'm afraid," Bruce says, releasing Chris's hand and lighting a Gauloises cigarette with trembling fingers.

"I think he recognized me," David says.

"Yes," Bruce says, meaning nothing in particular.

They could be talking about an aged, addled relative in a nursing home. Martin is forty-one.

"We'll start dinner," David says. "You must be getting hungry."

"A little," Bruce says.

Chris isn't really hungry.

Conversation with a dead man:

Why did this happen to us?

It just did.

It doesn't seem fair.

It isn't fair.

How can you be so matter-of-fact about it? About being . . .

Dead. Say it.

I don't want to say it! And not just that, either. (Angrier now.) About our being apart.

I'll always be with you, if you want me to.

That's so glib. (Still angry, but cracking.) I can't even tell my mother.

You ought to tell her. She'll understand.

She'll worry. Is that fair?

You're obsessed by fair. There is no such thing. Ask your lawyer friend Drew.

Drew?

How do you know what's fair for her, anyway? You don't. It's just an excuse. You have to do what you need to do. You have to tell her what happened, about you. She has a right to know. She has a right to comfort you. You are her only son, after all.

(Weeping now, but trying to hold it back.) I want *you* to comfort me. I want *you* to come back.

I wish I could. I think about you all the time.

What's it like there?

(Pause.) *Pretty much like there. Quieter, I guess.* Great view. *It's not so bad.*

(Shivers.) I'm only thirty.

I know, baby.

I mean, we were going to have so many years. The house in Napa and the dogs and the famous people for dinner and evenings in the garden, watching the sunset. (Starts to cry again.) I don't want to do them by myself.

You don't have to. (As gently as he can.) *You're still young and voluptuous . . .*

I know what you're thinking.

Well, it's true. Life isn't over. Life goes on. You go on with it. You can't live like a monk, feeling sorry for yourself for the next half-century. You're a young man with human needs. So meet them!

I love *you.*

And I love you. *But that doesn't mean you can't love someone else, too.*

I don't want to.

But you need to.

(I don't know how.)

They are both somber after taking leave of Bruce and Martin. During the little meal Martin called out incoherently from the bedroom, where a mad scene invisible to the rest of them played itself out before his fevered eyes. During the salad, Bruce got up and went into the bedroom; his presence seemed to settle Martin down. Chris and David awkwardly remained at the table, reluctant, for some reason, to keep eating while a grotesque decline was in progress a few feet away.

"I'm not feeling too good about him," David says as they step into the cool evening air. "He's a lot worse than he was last week."

"Bruce seemed okay."

"Yeah." He takes a deep breath. "How about you?"

"I handled it."

"You did. This whole thing," David says, clenching one fist inside the other, "makes me so fucking mad. You know. I mean, this shouldn't be happening. *Should not be happening.* We've put men on the moon, for Christ's sake. It's these dick-fuck Republicans."

"I don't know," Chris says. David's anger surprises him, and he asks himself if he feels guilty that he isn't equally furious. His anger burned itself out long ago, along with Carl. It's a disease. It makes people sick and then they die. There have been many such diseases; there will be many more. To scream into the void about the unfairness of it, of holocaust and genocide—the virus isn't listening, he wants to say. It doesn't care.

". . . the government," David is saying, "doesn't listen. They don't care. The policy is pure homophobia. Let the fags die. It's all deliberate."

Chris takes his hand and holds it as they walk to the car.

Toward the end, Carl's mind had failed much as Martin's seemed to be failing—in little bits at first, like tiles breaking off the space shuttle, names forgotten, days, conversations that suddenly made no sense. Then long passages of incoherence and bafflement, imagined hostilities, gaping emptiness, as the ship of the mind plunged from the heavens in a splintering fireball.

By the time Carl died, it seemed to Chris like months since he'd actually left. He's never admitted to anyone the relief he felt at that moment, when Carl, on a sunny afternoon, the window of their bedroom open for fresh air, simply stopped breathing. Such a tiny, almost imperceptible change that he didn't notice it for several moments. So that was the difference between life and death! For an instant it did not seem so terrible, no more terrible than the last six months had been. Except that once Carl was gone, reclaimed by his family for burial in Iowa, all that remained to Chris was the memory of someone who had been young and handsome and vibrant. Then the difference seemed as sharp and bitter as the edge of a butcher's knife.

"We should," David says, "get out of here."

"Okay with me."

"I told Wade we might meet him for a drink. At the Sun, eight-thirty."

"You're such a conspirator," Chris says, although he is deeply pleased at the prospect. It is a rare moment when he feels sociable, but the plunge into Bruce and Martin's death-bound flat has given him a bounce as if from a trampoline, and he feels more alive than he has in many months. He doesn't mention how eager he is to observe the two of them together, they who deny anything is going on. As if anyone could believe that.

It is early; they park on Noe between Seventeenth and Eighteenth. People are about, groups of men, two, three, four, in and out of restaurants, card shops, bars. The Latest Scoop is gone. Jaguar Books is gone, replaced by an espresso bar. They jaywalk across Eighteenth to the small black portal in the steel wall.

It is the same San Francisco, the same Castro, and not the same. A plague city in which stubborn life refuses to sur-render. The bars are still full, the baths replaced by jerk-off clubs, the business cards and napkins with notes written on the back of them still exchanged—but there is a note of *piano* in the erotic symphony that was not there when Chris and Da-vid first moved to the city. Then sex was *fortissimo*, full speed ahead, all you can eat. Now it is hip to be square, or at least cautious.

Underneath the veneer of continuity lie layers of doom, gloom, grief, hysteria. In how many of the people on this street, Chris wonders, is the time bomb already ticking? In how many is it *not?* It is possible they will all die. The strain is palpable, the anticipation, the dread: a siege with no siegebreaker in sight. Even so, the community reorganizes; the sick and dying are cared for; the anger and desperation channeled out, purged, directed at external targets against which the attack is invigorating. Anger flushes out the psychic toxins, if not the virus itself.

Entering the bar is like slipping into the tent of a sheikh: through a door, then a black curtain, into the warm darkness. It is almost empty at this early hour. A few people are sitting at the bar, or along the opposite wall; the center of the room is open. Although they have arrived ten minutes early, Wade is earlier still. Chris sees him in the far corner, talking to someone he recognizes as Chaz. Chaz is talking rapidly, hands gesticulating; Wade listens, nods.

"You want a beer?" David says.

"Sure."

"I'll meet you over there."

When Chris approaches they suspend their conversation, and Wade embraces him. He feels big and strong in Chris's arms; he is a man now, grown up. Chris feels oddly paternal, as though he has had some hand in Wade's turning out so well. Chaz is fluttery and twitchy. He is *just* on his way out the door, spending the weekend in Woodside with a friend who lives with a television producer, they have Nubian goats.

"I keep telling him to switch to decaf," Wade says when Chaz has scuttled out the door. "I worry when he drives."

"He's still driving?" Chris asks.

"We think in a bumper car," Wade says.

David appears with three beers. They drink, watch a few videos.

"Do we have any real interest in staying here?" David asks after a while. "It's like a tomb."

"Let's go," Chris says.

"I'm up for it," Wade says.

"I hear you're going to graduate school," Chris says to Wade as they step into Eighteenth Street.

"Thinking about it."

"I squealed," David says. "I'm sorry."

"It's okay. I'm not keeping it a secret."

"Not that you don't keep secrets," Chris says.

"He's convinced we're having an affair," David says.

"With *that* old thing?" Wade says to Chris. "Get real, please. He's at *least* thirty and *tired*."

"You're not sweet sixteen anymore, honey," David says, in a kidding tone that does not quite conceal his distress at having someone point out that he has graduated from the golden twenties. Chris is shocked to hear them speaking fag. He again forces himself to remember that Wade is no longer a freshman; that he lived in New York for two years after college; in San Francisco ever since. He is actually twenty-seven. He is not a child, not the naïf of that fumbling first night on a creaky dorm bed.

"I'm thirty, too," Chris says. "So watch it."

"There's no point having affairs here anymore, anyway," Wade says.

This is a sobering thought, and they walk along in silence for a time. Where, none of them knows. Enough just to stroll through the warm evening, checking people out.

"Do you ever have sex anymore?" David asks Chris suddenly.

"I just love your manners," Wade says to David.

"No."

"I don't mean to be rude," David says. "I was just curious."

"I hardly have sex anymore, either," Wade says. "You know, it's so complicated, like launching a spaceship, all the safeguards and vigilance and everything. It's not really worth it."

"We were going to get stoned," David says. "You want to come?"

"We roll our own," Wade adds. "In rubbers. Safe."
"Sure," Chris says.
They walk on.

Entry from an abandoned journal:

They never tell you, when you fall in love with
someone, about all you stand to lose at the end. They
never tell you there will *be* an end—that it's inevitable. (Who are "they," anyway?) I think it would be
easier to break up with someone; at least he remains
a part of the world, and the part of you that remains
with him remains a part of the world, too.

I said goodbye, but I don't know if he really
heard me. When he still could hear, and understand,
I didn't have the will to say it. It still seemed impossible that doing it would be necessary. That would
have been admitting what was happening. He was
still there, still Carl. Then he wasn't. It didn't matter,
after all, whether I had the strength to admit it. *I*
didn't matter.

I regret all the times I got angry with him—
always about the most trivial things: mold behind the
bathtowels, a strawberry stain on the cutting board,
his drinking three glasses of wine at dinner and
cruising the waiters and the busboys—all the times
I refused to say "I love you" when we talked by
phone in the middle of the day because I was pissed
off about some tiny thing. Even then, the thought occurred: What if I don't see him ever again? What if
he gets hit by a runaway bus or trolley on the way
home from work? But of course he didn't.

Things unsaid, gestures unmade—this is what
haunts you. This is what you can't get over, what you
will carry into eternity yourself, hoping to make a

belated delivery in the hereafter. *Here, these are for you*—feeling like the idiot mailman who loses the payoff check from the lottery, shows up with it twenty years later, after the bankruptcy and the foreclosure.

Now I think a lot about why we let ourselves in for all this trouble. If you never fall in love with someone, never share your life, you do not face the eventual dismantlement of that life. Loving someone with your life is like building a house on an active fault: You may have ten years of peace, absolute tranquillity, twenty or forty or fifty or more, but at some point the earth *will* convulse, 8.3 on the Richter scale, the Big One, and your life will be a little heap of rubble. Maybe you'll only have three years—just enough time to make the rest of your time on earth look like a limitless waste, the urge to rebuild checked by a too-soon vision of what must happen again eventually.

We do it because we do it. Because our hearts tell us we must. Because life will end sooner or later anyway, and isn't it foolish to turn down the joys of today when grief comes tomorrow regardless of what you did today? Are we supposed to live in preparation for death? Are we supposed to spend our three score years and ten getting ready to give them up? Grieving? That makes no sense. Not natural; not healthy. I can't accept that. No. We live in defiance of death, just as we live in defiance of earthquakes; we pretend they aren't going to happen, and go about the business of building up lives—lives, we tell ourselves, that are permanent. That is what life is.

Sometimes I feel like a ghost, someone who's here but not really. I can be touched and talked to but not *reached.* I watch television and read books and talk to my mother and wonder what will I do to-morrow? the next day? when all the days look the same to me. The city has lost its magic: I look at the sights and do not see them. I do not even see him anymore, not unless I look at the pictures. And they are just pictures in an album, mementos from an-other life whose outlines I can no longer quite make out. I am numb, and I am glad.

They are laughing, laughing, laughing. Chris wonders why they are laughing. No one is really *trying* to be funny. He feels as though his head has been shrunk, as though it is the size of a pea on a man's body. He must stifle the urge to find a mirror and make sure that his hair is in place.

Wade lives near Eighteenth and Eureka, in a small one-bedroom apartment on the second floor of a converted Victo-rian mansion. The bay windows in the living room admit a lovely cool breeze that stirs but does not entirely dissipate the fragrant cloud they have raised. There is a nature show on KQED; in stereo but no sound. Beneath the TV screen the VCR is lit up like a Christmas tree—blue lights and green lights and red lights. It is just impossible even to begin figur-ing out what they all mean. David shifts on the sofa, his arm around Chris's shoulder. After a while they stop laughing, and Chris folds himself into the warmth of David's chest.

"The thing is," Wade calls out from the kitchen, where for some reason he is pouring cans of warm beer into an ice-filled pitcher, "I'm just a whore. I need sex constantly."

"I thought you said you don't have sex anymore," David replies. "Didn't he say that?" he says to Chris.

Chris shrugs, smiles. He feels safe and comfortable; doesn't care what they say.

"*Hardly* ever, I said," Wade says. "But that doesn't mean I don't need it."

"Do you ever write anything anymore?" David asks Chris. "I thought you were going to write a novel or something."

"Just junk."

"Well, nobody reads anyway, so I guess it really doesn't matter."

"No."

"I thought we were both going to be writers," Wade says, returning from the kitchen with the pitcher and a clutch of paper cups. "Like the Beats."

"The beat-offs," David says, and starts laughing uncontrollably again. Chris cannot help joining him even though he agrees with Wade, who dismisses David's joke as "weak."

"Iced beer?" David says.

"It wasn't cold."

"I'm hot." He winks broadly. "Wink-wink, nod-nod, nudge-nudge."

"You know where they are."

David nods. As gently as he can he shifts Chris's weight to an arm of the couch. "Be right back," he says.

"Like he cares about writing," Wade says while David is in the next room, riffling through the library of videotapes. "The barbarian."

"You're not really a whore, are you?" Chris asks.

"One key difference between us," Wade says, "is that you *lived* with someone and I've never had a boyfriend for more than a week or two. To answer your question: No, not in the *strict* sense. I have never accepted remuneration."

Chris casts his glance inquiringly toward the bedroom, where David is muttering, "Where is the fucking thing?" over and over. Wade laughs, shaking his head.

"Silly boy," he says. "Rooting around mindlessly."

Then David reappears. "This was hidden *under your bed,*" he says triumphantly, holding up an innocuous-looking videocassette. "Almost as if you didn't *want* me to find it."

"You found it," Wade says with a smile at David. "I just knew you would."

"I call this session of sexual congress to order."

In the harsh light of the television monitor their skin is a ghostly pale blue, weirdly shadowed, as it is in the strobe lights of the discos that they hardly ever go to anymore. Their clothes are arranged more or less neatly on a chair by the window, the little tub of Lube set among them like a candle at the center of a dining table. David sits upright, legs crossed yoga-style; Wade's back is pressed against the sofa while he rests on his right side, left knee bent in the air (also he's left-handed, Chris notices; David seems to be ambi, always switching back and forth). Chris lies flat on his back between them.

Sex among friends. It violates all the rules, except Drew's. Chris imagines that he would heartily approve of the scene's spirit if not its casting. The room smells of Lube and groins and darkness, nakedness, lust. They gaze at the screen, then at each other—shyly at first, with frank interest as the moments pass.

"Don't you dare get it on my rug!" Wade says as David groans and grunts to himself and just generally seems to be on the verge. David does not reply.

Afterward, the tape still running through scene after scene (all of which have a strong military flavor), they snuggle together on the unsoiled rug, under a blanket Wade drags in from the bedroom.

"That smell still drives me wild," David says. "One whiff and I'm wired." He rolls Chris onto his stomach and starts to rub his back, teasing the muscles and skin slowly, sensuously with the base of his hand. "If I could write poetry I'd write a poem about it."

"Fortunately you can't," Wade says.

The intimacy, physical contact, sexuality are spontaneous and natural, as if all the neurotic forces of human civilization had, for this one unexpected moment, aligned themselves in such a way as to be canceled out, leaving in effect only sweet animal impulses.

"The worst part," Chris says quietly, "is that sometimes I still smell him. In the sheets or a shirt or something. It reminds me of when we met. I smelled him all over me. Even after a shower. That's how I knew that it was serious."

David thinks grimly of Ross—identical phenomenon. Wade says, "I know what you mean," and starts to knead one of Chris's hands.

"I mean, eighty percent of what we perceive in the world we *see*, but smell brings memories back instantly. It's like the whole part of my life flashing before me."

"Proust," Wade says gravely. "The triggers of memory."

"You haven't read Proust." David's tone is a gentle scoff.

"Not the whole thing," Wade concedes. "But I got that part. The madeleines and everything." In fact the professor of the course for which Wade read "Swann's Way" had brought a plate of madeleines to class one day to make sure his students had at least some pleasant association with Proust. "Anyway, you haven't read *any.*"

"I can't figure it out," Chris says. "What's going on with you guys."

"What's to figure out?" Wade says. "We trap people for three-way circle jerks."

"Anyway he's leaving," David says. "Back to K.C. in January—great timing!—then grad school somewhere."

"You're really leaving?" Chris says. Secretly he is pleased at the modestness of the link between them (two people who offered themselves to him), but he tries to sound perplexed that Wade would abandon the promised land. This is tricky because he is himself, he recognizes suddenly, drawn to the idea.

Wade rubs his neck with his long fingers, scratches his scalp; David is working on his ass, the backs of his thighs. The massage gives deep, irresistible pleasure; not the white-hot flash of orgasm, but a slow steady burn, like a fire in a peat bog.

"I can't stand it anymore," Wade says. "It's like, everybody here is just waiting. Like Hong Kong and the Chinese. You can't make any assumption of permanence, of any future at all, really."

David looks up for a moment, as if to argue, but he says nothing. They have all heard the gruesome numbers: fifty percent infected? Eighty? Ninety? No one knows for sure. Would any of them recognize the city in ten years? Would they be alive to recognize it?

"You can't imagine how important what you do with Shanti is," Chris says, the words catching deep in his throat. Gratitude. Sorrow. The pleasure of David's rubbing his toes. He rolls onto his back to provide a better angle.

"Watch the balls," Wade says.

"I have to do it," David says. "I can't leave. The whole thing just pisses me off."

"I know," Wade says. "I can't stay."

"I know."

—and Chris understands he's hearing just a part of a conversation that began long before tonight and will run on long past tomorrow. He doesn't mind listening, so long as they keep touching him, scratching him, reminding him with pleasures and the triggers of memory—sweet and sorrowful—that he is still alive.

WEST is WEST

Thirty came and went—a day, a blur, forgotten. A card and a check came from his parents. Geoff phoned. He deposited the check into the mutual fund he keeps for a down payment on a house. A condo in Dupont Circle, perhaps, or Woodley Park; or a townhouse in one of the suburbs along one of the Metro lines? There seems to be little point in owning a house—or even an apartment—as a single person. To rent means to be temporary; it promises change. Although he has awaited change now for several years, watched for a sign that his life has not taken its final, all-too-ordinary form, he sees nothing but signs that it has.

At work, his secretary, whom he shares with another associate, a black woman from Harvard named Angela, presented him with a homemade German-chocolate cake, and the associates from his class crowded into his office to sing "Happy Birthday." He was touched and embarrassed and wondered how he would account for the elapsed time—which was certainly not billable—on his time sheet.

He and Geoff didn't have much to say to each other.

Chris sent a Far Side card that came three days late.

Although he does not *feel* older, it has become more difficult to get out of bed in the morning. A paradox: He seems to need less sleep, stays up most nights for Letterman, maybe a movie. Or he reads. Physical exhaustion is not the problem; it is emotional. There is a dearth of psychic energy. The days, all the same, run together, like faces in a subway station glimpsed through the windows as the train accelerates. He remembers no better what he did last night than what he did two months ago last night. Or what he did at work.

Work. A suitably plain, Anglo-Saxon word. The law sucks the life out of him: Its calmness, detachment, the skeins of awful writing are powerfully enervating. By the time he left law school he had come to terms with the idea that law was the religion of secular society, its sacred texts pondered and cited like Scripture, its rules, rituals and myths preserved through the generations. Lawyers, like priests, spoke in Latin phrases they didn't understand, cloaking pedestrian thoughts and common-sense principles in shrouds of antique gobbledygook.

This, at first, did not bother him. He was trained to do it. He took a job in a good, medium-sized firm that handled commercial litigation and some international law, and he earned a comfortable, although not top-drawer, salary. Soon after he started, he moved from Mrs. Dunwiddy's shabby Georgetown palace to a small, one-bedroom apartment a few blocks away. The work was dull but doable and not overwhelming in volume; he rarely stayed past six, even more rarely found himself in the office on Saturdays.

But the tedium. The *grayness* of it, of the people around him—bright, well-educated, unadventurous, vanilla folk. He began to wonder, as thirty approached—a time of reckoning, the last molting of youth—what he was living *for*. To become a partner? Handle the PepsiCo account? Anything at all? Conferment of the law degree was the last step along the path he had so carefully plotted. He has gotten where he planned to go. So now what? The heart still beats, plan for tomorrow or no; the bills still come.

The suspicion gnaws at him that he is missing something, that his life is not complete; and while he is able persuasively to rationalize that the feeling is perfectly *normal*—nothing wrong with it, dissatisfaction is a human constant; so he was fond of saying in college, when he was not dissatisfied—he is not quite able to persuade himself that *his* dissatisfaction is simply something that must be lived with.

Today he is having lunch with his supervising partner, Webster. The meeting is preliminary to his performance review next week, at which time they will formally advise him of the likelihood of his making partner. Does he want to be a partner? All he needs to do is persist, persist, persist, bill those hours—and his gray-flannel future at a second-tier firm, a perfectly respectable firm, is assured.

He decides, while brushing his teeth, not to wear the gray-flannel suit today. Dark blue instead.

Geoff arrived for a four-day marketing seminar in mid-June. Drew had offered him a place to stay but "the agency gets a great deal at the Ritz-Carlton," Geoff explained apologetically. "Besides, I don't want to put you out. You don't have that much room."

"I could find room," Drew said, but he knew the discussion was superfluous. The Ritz it was.

They got into an argument about politics even before the head of foam had subsided in the two glasses of champagne Geoff poured from the portable bar in his room. A crack about Geoff's "yup drag" (he was now an account executive at an ad agency in Long Beach) got them going.

"Like you wear blue jeans to work," Geoff replied. "You

know, you're sounding a lot like Dad these days. Sorry, I spilled a little. Like, you're not really a man until you wear a suit to work every day. Or a stethoscope."

"Don't tell me," Drew said. "Deep down you'd still rather be out saving the whales and the pandas and the snail darters and the caribou and the spotted owl. Have I forgotten anything?"

"Lots. The atmosphere and the oceans and the rain forests. Fine. We'll just drill for oil in your neighborhood."

"If the choice is between having enough energy and knowing that somewhere lichen are happily flourishing free of our interference," Drew said, "I choose energy."

"We could use less. We could be a little less greedy."

"You and Jerry Brown," Drew said. "The moonbeamers. Small is beautiful." He chugged about half the champagne.

"Jerry Brown was right about almost everything, the voters just couldn't accept it," Geoff said. "And since when have you become such an Orange County fascist?"

"At least my views have *evolved*," Drew said. "I'm not sitting there spewing out stale hippie bilge from the sixties."

"Devolved, you mean. Green isn't hippie bilge. It's the great political issue of the 1990s. Even the love of your life, Maggie Thatcher, understands that."

"So how's the new car?" Drew asked. "A Miata, isn't it? Dad told me he helped you find one."

"It's nice," Geoff said stiffly. "It's fun."

"They're cute," Drew said. "Sort of . . . unisex," he added with a lift of his eyebrows.

A certain taste for battle ran through both branches of the family, but the brothers understood that their ideological arguments transcended mere intellectual belligerence. They reflected another, almost-never-mentioned tension: Geoff's *life-style*, as Drew referred to it, and Drew's concern about it. Unease about it. Inability to understand it.

("And, you know, you hate everything you don't under-

stand," Geoff had said to him when he'd revealed he was gay,
years ago, before either of them had much of an idea what it
would come to mean over the years.

"Which isn't much," Drew had replied.)

"So how are things in L.A.?" Drew said.

"Same."

"Mom and Dad?"

"He got her a Range Rover for her birthday."

"With a big red ribbon tied around it, I'll bet."

"A bull bar, actually. I told them it was silly, but they've
gone totally English. Every time I step in the door these days
I'm handed a cup of tea. You should see all the chintz!"

"Speaking of seeing. Are you? Anyone?"

"You know," Geoff said with a smile that imperfectly con-
cealed his unpreparedness for the question. By tacit agreement
they did not discuss their personal lives. Drew, having
breached the agreement, felt like a law professor zeroing in for
the kill. Geoff said: "Here and there. You?"

"Nothing."

"Not since you broke up with . . ."

"Dana."

"Right. That was quite a while ago."

"Years."

"Prospects?"

"Not really."

"You don't sound concerned."

"I'm not."

Geoff poured more champagne.

"You ever lonely?" Drew asked.

"Not really."

"You don't miss having someone there?"

"I'm not a monk," Geoff said. "You know. Besides, I lived
with Donald for almost a year. That was enough for me."

"Yeah." Drew paused, fingering the rim of his glass.
"Sometimes I wonder if bachelorhood or whatever runs in the

family. The instinct to be alone. You know, like Dad didn't really want to get married but just did it because that's what you did then."

"That's always been your theory, hasn't it?" Geoff said, pouring out the rest of the champagne, which they chugged. "Even in high school. Men are predators. Solitary hunters. Right? Am I misstating?"

"It's just funny to think of your own family that way. Like you. 'I'm not a monk.' I quote. I just can't picture you, you know, picking people up."

"I do, though."

"You've never said how."

"You don't want to know."

"I do."

Geoff sighed and laughed at the same time. "Bars are bars," he said. "They all operate on the same principle."

"So you pick them up in bars?"

"Mostly."

"But not always."

"No. Not always."

"Like in Berlin. 'I'm going for a walk'!"

Geoff smiled. "I did go for a walk."

"Some walk."

"Well . . ." He shrugged. "I walk, therefore I am."

"I want to know," Drew said. "Show me."

"God, Drew."

"I'm curious."

"You can meet people anywhere. Don't you meet women just walking down the street?"

"Not often enough. Besides, you still have to talk to them and make all this effort like you're really interested in their personalities. It isn't just like . . . Where do you go?"

"Some places are better than others. If you want," Geoff said, draining his glass, "I'll show you."

. ▪ .

It strikes Drew as unjust that Geoffrey's life should be so difficult to distinguish from his own. Here they are, two thirtyish bachelors, good-looking, with good jobs and comfortable apartments in desirable cities. (Geoff's has two bedrooms and an extra half-bath off the kitchen.) Except Drew planned. Drew went to law school. Drew is *straight*. He resents being made to feel resentful, but even more he resents the apparent fact that Geoff is at least as content and successful as he is.

In high school, Drew made all the right academic moves— AP English and history—while Geoff bumbled through, but they both ended up going to the same college. As undergraduates, Drew's GPA was 3.927, Geoff's 3.6—something: there was a certain vagueness; Geoff majored in communication. Drew went to law school and was an editor of the law review. Geoff spent a few months abroad teaching English, then lived at home for two years after that; he waited tables and wrote a screenplay. Then blam! the job at the ad agency. (Thank you, Dad. And for the Miata!)

The sex business particularly rankles. The ease with which, among gay boys, it is agreed upon and carried out; the lack of any personal entanglements to slow the pursuit of pleasure or hinder the search for more. First names are optional.

"You don't even have to bother with one-night stands!" he said in amazement after they returned to the hotel from the park. "They're just stands."

"Yeah," Geoff said, laughing. "Or leans."

"Are you going back there? After I take off?"

"Oh, gentlemen never tell."

"You're not a gentleman."

"Fuck you."

"Aren't you afraid?"

"I'm careful."

So Drew trudged back to his Georgetown apartment after detouring for a cup of gelato from one of the little shops along Connecticut, his mind all the while fixed on an image of Geoff getting blown under the trees; of finding and completing a sexual assignation in the matter of seconds it would take him to finish his ice cream. The sugary butterfat suddenly seemed poor consolation. Part of him refused to believe it was so simple. He considered the possibility of returning to the hotel to reconnoiter. Geoff could be making up these stories to tease him—that would not be out of character—although he had seen the men with his own eyes, prowling the dark, wooded ravine like hungry predators.

"Ah," Webster says, dipping a spoon into his minestrone. To Drew's eyes, he looks *exactly* the way a forty-three-year-old lawyer should look: noticeably bald, slightly overweight, horn-rimmed glasses, pallor, expensive bland suit and tie.

They are at a little Italian bistro on Wisconsin, not far, in fact, from Drew's place. If the lunch goes on long enough, he might be able to cut the rest of this empty Friday afternoon and go straight home. He dips into his own cup of soup, not lifting the spoon to his mouth, however, until the waiter finishes opening their bottle of Pellegrino water and walks away.

"Do you like your work?" Webster asks. It's the sort of question a parent might ask after a glass or two of wine. Drew looks at him, sees his eyes fixed on some point behind Drew's shoulder.

"Sure," he says. "I mean, yeah. Of course. No one's ever asked me before."

"It's probably the sort of thing people should be asked more often. Especially when they're younger and they haven't made their major life decisions."

"Do you like *your* work?" Drew asks, feeling emboldened for no particular reason. He has always been at ease with Webster; they have gotten along well and worked smoothly together.

"Hmm," Webster says, studying the minestrone. "There are things I like and things I don't like."

"So being partner isn't all fun and games."

"Not even close." Webster breaks off a chunk of bread and spreads ricotta cheese on it. "Especially not lately."

"Oh." Something is up; Webster is not in his usual steady-as-she-goes mood. He doesn't say things like that by accident. Slowly he works his way through the minestrone, the chunk of bread, the glass of iced Pellegrino with the twist of lime. By the time the pasta comes, neither of them will be hungry. Drew says nothing, waiting for the older man to come to the point, as he always does, in the end.

"We're not a huge firm," Webster says at length. "And we're not a boutique." He pauses. "In fact it's not clear what we are. We're somewhere in the middle. Pretty big, but not big enough. But too big to be really agile."

The pasta comes.

"When I was your age," he continues, "I'd never heard the word 'rainmaking.' We didn't worry about revenues, billings—it was vulgar. Part of me still feels that way, but you know, law *is* a business, just like any other, when you get down to it."

Drew nods, wondering why the food has no flavor today. Perhaps it needs salt.

"Nobody ever used to think in terms of cutbacks," Webster continues, "downsizing or whatever the term is these days. We're not automakers! Well. I should get to the point. There is a point. What I'm trying to say," he says, again looking at that magical focus beyond Drew's shoulder; now directly at him, "is that—"

Don't say it, please, Drew thinks, suddenly seeing disaster in Webster's eyes, like seeing a set of headlights veer into your lane at the crest of a hill, *because I don't want to hear.* So this is why Webster asked him to lunch: to tell him he's not on the partnership track. He will not, three years hence, be asked to join the firm. Instead he will become a "senior associate," a permanent drone, employee for life, educated labor. Mom and Dad will be shattered. His first thought: I've failed, finally. Of course, this isn't that unusual these days; firms all over the country are having to thin the herds lumbering toward partnership. There are too many young lawyers, not enough money to make them all rich. It's almost a relief.

"—is that . . . Well." Deep breath. Is he having angina? "I'm terribly, terribly sorry. I really am, but it's not my decision to make. In fact I was scarcely consulted." He harrumphed. "This is it, then. I'm sorry. The firm, er, are going to have to let you go."

Like thunder that trails a distant flash of lightning—count the seconds between the bolt and the boom and you can estimate how far off the strike was—these words do not register in Drew's mind until several moments after Webster has so painfully uttered them. He is still thinking about not making partner when Webster launches into the explanations of why he is out the door altogether: how the decision reflects no discredit on Drew's skills as a lawyer or his performance as an employee; how it is a matter of simple economics, too many mouths to feed from the shrinking legal pie; how he is telling Drew early, so he can make plans. Things are tough. The firm has lost its way; it must streamline if it is to survive.

"I'm not sure even that's going to be enough," Webster says, relieved to have unloaded the burden the other partners laid on his back and anxious to say a consoling word. Five other associates are also out. Drew is not alone. Feel better? "There are some serious merger talks going on."

Although it is barely two-thirty when they finish, Drew does decide to walk home, leaving Webster with the bill and the cab back to the office.

The longing for California that lies, sometimes latent, sometimes not, in the heart of each of that golden state's expatriates, can awaken for any number of reasons, not the least of which is losing one's dreary job in the never-beloved grimy East. Images flash through his mind for the rest of the afternoon: the beach and the sun, the palms along Sunset, the smell of jasmine in the desert and the eerie howl of the Santa Anas blowing down Topanga Canyon.

He has never particularly liked L.A. Often, in his exile, he has made lists of the reasons why, as if to remind himself why he remains in the East. The smog, earthquakes, traffic, water shortages, real-estate prices, serial killers. The ever-mounting horde of Mexicans, Vietnamese, Cambodians, Hong Kongers, Japanese, who transform the very face of the place. His parents and brother—he loves them, yes, but takes comfort in the emotional distance that the breadth of the continent provides.

For some years his understanding of the California mystique—the appeal that transcends the rational—has been deepening. Even as the quality of life in the Southland slips (each visit home is a startling glimpse of the extent to which West comes to resemble East—crowded, smelly, impolite, polluted, Third-Worldish: The twain meet), its grip on his imagination and his emotions tightens. Even though he has never felt altogether comfortable there, not altogether as though it was the place where he was supposed to have been born, it draws him.

He certainly doesn't belong in the nation's capital, although no one else seems to, either. Everyone is from somewhere else, is young, good-looking, well-educated and blow-dried, works on the Hill for a member of that bloated whale, Congress, or clerks for a federal judge or wants to write for the *Post* or produce a political talk show. Northwest Washington is like a campus for just-out-of-college-or-grad-school-or-something adults.

At first this was attractive: a sea of people you would enjoy knowing or at least sleeping with, quite a few of whom you did indeed know or had indeed slept with. The population's high levels of sophistication and physical attractiveness made it easier to overlook the general rootlessness, including his own.

But, like all the other little gleams of magic in his life, this one too seems to have flickered and gone dark. The conversations he has with friends from school and work in the cafés of Northwest seem as stale as week-old bread. Their lives are the same: They are filled with work and, in what little leftover time there is, the search for a partner. They are dull. And they don't seem to belong here, either, or anywhere else. How, among such people, is he to refresh the sense of his own life, he wonders, of its possibilities? To feel as though he is feeling again?

Scorn is his usual response to these sorts of gauzy complaints when others make them. He has long been in the habit of telling people that cities themselves aren't different enough from each other to affect the quality of one's life; that it is the quality of one's friends and of one's work that govern a man's measure of satisfaction. You can be content anywhere (the states of the Old Confederacy excepted)—so he has always said. McDonald's and Holiday Inn and Safeway, even Brooks Brothers and Saks, are everywhere these days.

Yet Washington itself, most self-preening of cities, begins to disappoint. It is not a real metropolis; it has no real character other than the marble-pillared bureaucracy and the stark and increasingly terrifying schism between the races. It is a city of façades and artifice—which, because they were polished façades and he was from unpolished Los Angeles, impressed him at first. But now, having become a resident of the imperial capital, having made it the place where he lives and works, he dips his toes beneath the glossy surface of the city and feels nothing but the cool post-prep emptiness that seems too much like what he feels inside himself.

Almost exactly three months to the day after Geoff arrived from California, Drew stands naked in his bathroom, primping. A muggy Friday evening. Nine o'clock: the sun not far beneath the western horizon. He blow-dries his hair with a little mousse to hold it in place above the ears; dabs some Paco Rabanne on his cheeks. His stomach churns, but not because he suddenly has no job.

("The trouble with straight relationships," Geoff had said the night before he left; they got smashed at a bar in Adams-Morgan, "is that men and women basically don't like each other."

This was an accurate observation, Drew thought, his own, in fact, but coming from Geoff it seemed to be an indirect attack on heterosexuality so he replied: "Hostility feeds desire."

"But most women are so coy. Even when they want it, they try to keep it secret because they know you want it worse."

"Why are you rubbing it in?"

"I'm not rubbing it in. I'm saying what you've always said."

You're not allowed to say it, Drew thought, because it's not your problem. You just go to your park or wherever and ten minutes later your problems are solved.

"Somewhere out there have got to be women who aren't so uptight about sex," Drew said, "who understand it's just an appetite that needs to be satisfied without drawing up lifetime legal obligations around it. *Somewhere*. I refuse to give up hope."

"You should have been gay."

"Thanks. Prick."

"Why did you break up with Dana?"

He shook his head. "Her idea," he said.

"Couldn't talk her out of it?"

Drew shrugged.

"Boy, you don't like to talk about her."

"You don't like to talk about Donald."

"No. Well, I guess that's right."

"Because they're over and done with."

Geoff nodded.)

Drew shakes his head to make sure the mousse is hold-ing. His hands are shaky, as though he's drunk a pot or two of coffee; he concentrates on quelling the sense of nausea. For the first time in a month of Saturday nights, he does not know what to expect. Just where to go. He thinks briefly of Webster, home safe in Potomac with the cars in the garage, the televi-sion on, the wife tucking in the children.

No underwear. No job.

The evening is mild and fragrant with the scent of im-pending rain as he steps out the door in sleeveless T-shirt and black 501s, in the left front pocket of which his Swiss Army knife—better safe than sorry, he tells himself—makes a bulge so negligible as to be virtually invisible. The sidewalks are filled with people strolling, discussing, laughing, on their way to or from dinner, eating ice-cream cones, carrying books from Kramer or Lambda Rising. He feels, somehow, conspicuous among them, as though they all know what he is thinking, planning, where he is going, when even he is not altogether sure.

The P Street bridge. He crosses into Dupont, glancing back occasionally as if to reassure himself that he is not being followed. The darkness is invigorating. Right at the corner, then along the sidewalk. He hears, but does not see, a cat slip through the underbrush in pursuit of prey.

Being fired turns out, eight hours later, to being a sense of renewal. On Monday, he will get the official word. The firm will give him ninety days, will let him use its resources to find another job, will pay him for his unused vacation days and keep him in the group insurance policy until the end of the year. Angela will not be fired: She is not expendable. The last thing the firm wants is their only black woman lawyer bringing a civil-rights suit for wrongful discharge and racial discrimina-tion.

The *idea* of his being let go while she stays on would, a week ago, have infuriated him as exactly the sort of blind-to-merit decision that is killing the country. Tonight he knows that he still thinks that, somewhere in his brain, but he doesn't care. He feels as though he's just been paroled, shown the door of a place he never wanted to be in the first place. Life again pulses through him.

Five minutes later. There is no sound except the cracking of twigs underfoot, the rustle of leaves, the muted groans and peeps of traffic edging through the intersection of Twenty-fifth and P. No voices except the wind's, breathing danger and desire. His hands are clammy; he feels the sweat gathering on the small of his back.

It is difficult to see anything. The mercury-vapor streetlamps along the park's perimeter leave the regions beneath the trees soaked in darkness. Shapes move restlessly along the hillside, following the paths that lead into the depths of the unseen. The terrain is treacherous, the trails broken by tree roots, and he does not stray beyond the fragile woody crescent near the street where he has stationed himself. Men move by him, behind him, alongside him, casting brief, intense glances before vanishing.

One comforting fantasy: that all these people are lusty young women who long for a good, quick crank. Who will, at a word or two, allow their blouses and jeans to be unbuttoned, who long for the rush of hands over their soft, warm skin. Who derive an erotic charge from doing it outside, where someone might see, or watch.

He is not really afraid of gay boys, but he is disgusted by the thought of sex between men. Imagining the acts makes him queasy but also, unpleasantly, fascinates him. He cannot altogether keep the thoughts out of his mind. When he was younger he took the fascination as a sign of latent homosexuality—just as Freud said!—and the recognition struck him cold with fear. But he has come to believe that it is nothing more than a transferred interest in one's own body. Even the most remorselessly heterosexual boys jerk off at least one cock in their lifetimes. It's only natural, then, that your own sex should hold some interest. Like looking in a mirror.

Then there is the thrill of the hunt. He feels the energy of this sexual fox-chase even though he is nothing more than an observer—a voyeur. He peers without moving a muscle while one man sucks another in the groin of a tree a few yards to his right. He considers the possibility of moving in for a closer look but decides not to leave the safety of the tree against which he's leaning. To contain the evening's anxieties, he talks quietly to himself, explaining why he is here, the thirst for something out of the ordinary, something *new*. He expects to leave any minute now. He should have had a drink or two before doing this.

His mumbled monologue fails to dispel the attentions of a tall, possibly handsome boy who walks slowly by him, staring with frank interest. Drew tries not to stare back. He hopes the boy will leave and must stifle the impulse to look after him to make sure. The boy ambles off a way down the slope, then stops, back turned. Then away.

Drew is convinced he is gone, prowling the bowels of the park, when he glances the other way and finds that the boy is leaning against a nearby tree, hands hitched in front pockets. They stare at each other. Drew moves his head once, up and down, a twitch of nerves and nothing more, but the boy approaches, sidling up to him, and almost brushes Drew's hip with one of his own.

"Hi," the boy says in a rough whisper. He is actually a young man, Drew concludes, with a stenciling of heavy whiskers on the cheeks and a well-developed frame. About his own age, he guesses.

Drew nods, this time with intent. The air seems to be thin; the darkness tightens. He feels as though he has heart disease. The first, as-if nod was fatal, as he knew when he made it: It set him playing a game whose rules he can only guess at.

The boy's head seems to be dipping down, like a divining rod. Is he whispering something? One knee buckles; the rest of the boy slides downward. A hand runs toward the buttons of Drew's fly but is intercepted short of the goal.

"Not here," Drew hears himself saying.

The boy's lips press against his ear. Drew resists the sensuousness of it. "I live just across the bridge. In Georgetown," the boy says with just his lips. The words are superfluous: The heat of his breath is a universal constant.

Saying no more, they emerge from the thicket onto the lighted sidewalk. It is like returning to your own world from a fantasy voyage, or waking from a nightmare. Drew feels his heartbeat and his breathing slow, but not quite to normal. They are walking together, toward where the boy lives, just across the bridge, in Georgetown. He is going home with a guy he picked up in a park. A guy. A park. Picked up. Despite himself, he has an erection.

"I'm Drew," he says, feeling the need to say something.

"Wade."

They walk a few more steps, onto the bridge over Rock Creek, without looking at each other.

"What are you into?" Wade says, in a tone of voice that suggests a choice among ethnic foods.

"I, um," Drew says, trying to think of a way to put what he wants to put. Which is: "I'll be honest with you. I've never done this before."

"You're married," Wade whispers. "Oh God, that's so sexy."

"Actually, no," Drew says. "I'm not really into guys."

"I'm not either, really," Wade says, as they keep on walking. Cars slow as they pass, their drivers leaning to ogle.

"Then what are we doing?"

"Going to my place for a drink."

"What do you have?"

"Well, water, for one," Wade says. "There's some wine, too, I think. Maybe some light beer."

"Lead on," Drew says, letting it unfold.

Wade lives in an English basement apartment, one large room under a town house on a one-way side street. The ceilings are low and beamed, like a ski chalet's; the light is dim. In one corner there is a large bed and a television with VCR. The front of the room contains a sofa and low table and a few chairs—a parlor with three walls. Glasses of wine in hand, they sit in the chairs, in the front, semi-facing each other, away from the bed. Wade—if Wade is his real name, which seems unlikely—looks pale and nervous, Drew thinks, like Nixon giving a speech.

"So," Drew says, "what are *you* into?" Along the top of his thigh he feels the light press of the knife in its cotton cocoon. Wade smiles nervously and drains his glass.

"I don't know," he says in a rushed gaspy voice. "Safe stuff. You know. You look like a top."

"A what?"

"You like to fuck?" Wade asks.

Drew nods.

"Ever fuck a guy?"

"I thought you were safe."

"I've got rubbers. Or just let me suck you off."

Drew considers. His insides are calm now; the nervous frenzy of the park has worn off. There are a number of ways to proceed. "I thought you weren't into guys," he says.

"Well," Wade says, "sometimes. These days . . ."

"You like getting fucked?" To Drew this is unimaginable and almost unspeakable: a gross violation of the self from which recovery would be impossible.

"Yeah. I do. But it hardly ever happens anymore."

"What if I said I'd like to?"

"Would you?"

"I didn't say that. I said, What if."

"I'd say, first, you sound like a lawyer. Then I'd say okay."

"Even if I don't want to wear a rubber."

Wade gnaws his lip, plainly unhappy. "Goddamn. That's hot," he says, spreading his legs slightly and unconsciously flexing the muscles of his rear. "I'd be very tempted."

"I didn't ask if you'd be tempted," Drew says. "I asked if you'd do it."

Wade smiles and tips his glass in Drew's direction. "If I said yes, would *you* do it?"

"Do you say yes?"

"If I did, would you?"

Drew is surprised, although less so than when he agreed to come back here in the first place, to hear himself say, "Yes." He wonders if he means it.

Wade drains his glass. "I'm really turned on," he says. "I'd love it so much if we did it that way. But we can't."

"I'm clean."

"I believe you. But that's not enough."

"Do you ever think you're paranoid? About, you know, that? Body fluids et cetera?"

"Oh, all the time," Wade says. "But I should be. I've had friends die. Maybe I'll die too."

"You look fine," Drew says, feeling curiously sympathetic. Wade will not die. Geoff will not die. He is confident. They are too young, too healthy. It is ridiculous.

"Why were you at the park?" Wade asks.

"Just wandering through."

"So you didn't know what was going on?"

"Not right away."

"But you didn't leave when you figured it out."

"Now *you* sound like a lawyer."

"Sorry," Wade says. "I guess there's something I'm not getting here."

"I got fired today," Drew says.

"God," Wade says. "I'm sorry. What do you do?"

"Lawyer."

"Lawyers get fired?"

"That's the same question I've been asking myself all day," Drew says. "Yes, they do. This one did. I'm sort of freaking about it at the moment."

"Do you like being a lawyer?"

"No."

"Then maybe it's a good thing."

"Maybe."

"It is. Definitely," Wade says.

"Are you a lawyer?"

"Grad student."

Drew grunts. "Biz?"

"Ph.D. Comp lit."

Drew grunts again.

"It's not *that* bad," Wade says. "Come on."

"My brother's gay," Drew says.

"Does he live here?"

"L.A."

"Cool. Is he a movie person?"

"No," Drew says. "Everybody there isn't, you know."

"Everybody I know in L.A. is," Wade says. "Is he cute, your brother?"

"I'm not sure," Drew says, trying not to sound stiff, trying to make clear that it is a question he can consider impartially. "He thinks so."

"Because if he looks anything like you, I'd love to meet him."

You probably already have, Drew thinks darkly. "He's got dark hair," he says.

"I love dark hair," Wade says.

"After you get your doctorate," Drew says, "then what?"

"Write movie scripts."

Drew shakes his head. "Then why are you slaving away for a Ph.D. in comp lit, of all things?"

Wade shrugs. "I wanted to," he says. "But I dream of L.A."

"I do, too," Drew says, to his surprise. He sees now that he's talking to himself through Wade. "I always wanted to work in the movies."

"Go for it," Wade says. "But get your Ph.D. in comp lit first."

"Why did you ask me if I was married?" Drew asks.

"I don't know," Wade says. His expression is part rue, part hope. "It's kind of a little thing of mine, lately."

"I am straight, though." He wonders why he is bothering to say this, when it ought to be perfectly plain that he is.

"That's cool," Wade murmurs.

And now the silence refuses to yield. They sit, conscious of each other. Wade sticks a finger in his mouth and, eyes fixed on Drew, draws it out slowly through the sliding seal of his lips. He smiles a small smile, still looking at Drew, who looks back at him while slowly getting to his feet.

"Carl died of AIDS," I said.

When my mother heard me say that word, years ago now, the first time I managed to say it in the same sentence with his name without gagging, she broke down in tears, while I sat there beside her on the sofa, trying awkwardly to comfort and console. I patted her arm and nudged encouragingly at the cup of tea in front of her. Months of crying myself to sleep every night had drawn down the well of my own grief, and I asked myself, while she wept, What could make me cry like this? But even today, I'm not sure what broke her that afternoon: my loss, her loss (of a happy future, or possibly any future, for her son), simple shock and horror. I omitted the details, but still—it's on prime-time TV movies and in the newspapers. People know.

When I told Michael and Drew, they sat there as though frozen by a trumpet blast, looking at me. Drew might have said, "God." I couldn't be sure. If they were waiting for me to say something more, they waited in vain. I looked at them and *shrugged my shoulders. I am older than they are. They will learn. How do you explain that? The waiter refilled our water glasses.*

I glance at the clock and read 12:21. Sleep teases, then withdraws. There is the anxiety of moving, of feeling life itself slip and shake under your feet. The older you are, the more difficult it gets; you fall out of practice in uprooting yourself. Inertia is psychological as well as physical, inclining us to stay where we are, coping with the known, unless we are given a terrible push.

There is the wondering about Drew. The answer is clear to me now—obvious, even—as I lie cool and alone in the dark. Why we are strangers to each other. It's because we never slept together. But I couldn't say that to him. It would have sounded as though, even at this late hour, I am still interested, which I am not.

Thinking of your peers as adults isn't easy. I remember that Michael always had a pimple or two on his shoulders and one on his forehead; in the showers, after lifting or squash, I would make a brief inventory, thankful that my own skin behaved better. I don't think we thought of ourselves as either boys or men, just guys, independent units, away from our families, unattached. Now Michael has a son, a walking, talking, thinking little person that he helped to create. He is a man, an adult, a father, a husband, a homeowner, a grown-up. He lives in a different world, is linked to life in every direction.

This campaign of Drew's to get me to move to L.A.! At first I felt like laughing, but then I understood he was serious. *He really means it, and, knowing him, he will pursue it until he is soundly deflected—a task I don't know if I'm up to. Hints, innuendo, subtle stuff, even if laid down in saturation bombings, won't do the trick: He needs it right between the eyes, pointblank.* No way, dude.

There is something about sex, even the garden-variety bad kind, that brings two people closer together in a way nothing

else can. You cannot touch all of another person's body, draw
out its most intense pleasure and give back your own in return,
see him as God sees him, primally nude, acting on the primal
impulses God gave him, without being moved and touched and
bonded. It's basic and essential. I still remember the names of
everyone I've ever slept with, faces, voices, bodies and their telling details, bits and pieces of stories told on the edge of sleep,
and I care about them all, or pray for them if they're gone. Seeing an old fling or trick (or even an old friend of Carl's) in a
bar or on the street fills me with an urge to run up and throw
a hug and a kiss and say, "I am glad to see you." Sometimes
I even do it.

 I cannot do that with Drew. There is a low ceiling above
us that keeps the friendship from standing up straight. In the
old days, I was determined to find a way to burst through that
ceiling, and I was convinced I would. But I didn't, and now I
know it will never happen: It is an inconvenience I am too old
either to set right or put up with. It isn't worth the discomfort,
the two of us standing there, hunched over inside, making each
other old and sour, wondering what's left.

 Because the truth is: not much, and that's just the way it
is. Maybe friendships in which less is invested initially wear better over time and distance; I know that I'm looking forward to
seeing Mike and Merry again regularly, if not often. Just before
Mike got into his car he wrapped his arms around me the way
it's always been so easy for him to do, and he was the same
body, the same warm sweet smell I've always loved and always
will. It is natural. But I never wanted him the way I wanted
Drew, so there was no bottom to fall out.

 It was my persistent, impregnable fantasy, of course, for all
the years until I met Carl, that one day Drew would come to his
senses and we would fall apocalyptically into bed and live perfectly ever after. I ask Carl, as I often have in the past, not to
be jealous about this fantasy, but he seems to be resting comfort-
ably tonight, or else has heard me say this so many times that

he is no longer interested in talking about it. He has always been too sweet and gentle to tell me what a stupid fantasy it really was, my believing that sex, so desperately sought by an inept undergraduate, would lead magically and inevitably to a lifetime together.

"I'm so sorry," Drew said, when it was just the two of us over decaf espressos. "I didn't know. You never told me."

"I'm sorry," I said. I tried to tell you. You wouldn't listen. I couldn't say this. "I'm sorry." Then I took a sip of his (too much sugar), just to prove that we had not drifted as far apart as we both knew we had.

Tonight I don't know why I'm asking myself this stuff about Drew, anyway, because I accept that it wouldn't have worked out. Yes, all right, Carl, you're right, it wouldn't have lasted. But something would have come of it, I think, some enduring glow that would have kept warm some kind of feeling for each other over time and space. Drew was always so sure that sex and love were unrelated, but he never understood (or at least never talked about) sex and friendship. I didn't, either, and now it is much too late.

Where is home? Here no longer. These days I look at the bridges, the tangerine dream of the Golden Gate, the hills, the skyline, and I do not see them. I look around the apartment, with its white walls and bleached oak floors, a few prints still hanging, the lonely Wassily chair in the corner, the old sofa I must try to sell, and I see emptiness. I think about my life in wonder at its fragile, beautiful hollowness and ask myself if it really belongs to me, if it ever really has.

Outside my window the webbed mantle of glitter falls on the shoulders of Twin Peaks, twinkling agreeably in the night. For the first time in a long time I see the city lights and am surprised to be touched by them. They keep the room from becoming too dark; they will cradle me while I lay me down to sleep.

Continuing your reading journey

As well as Quick Reads, The Reading Agency runs lots of programmes to help keep you and your family reading.

Reading Ahead invites you to pick six reads and record your reading in a diary to get a certificate **readingahead.org.uk**

World Book Night is an annual celebration of reading and books on 23 April **worldbooknight.org**

Chatterbooks children's reading groups and the **Summer Reading Challenge** inspire children to read more and share the books they love **readingagency.org.uk/children**

Why not start a reading group?

If you have enjoyed this book, why not share your next Quick Read with friends, colleagues, or neighbours?

The Reading Agency also runs **Reading Groups for Everyone** which helps you discover and share new books. Find a reading group near you, or register a group you already belong to and get free books and offers from publishers at **readinggroups.org**

There is a free toolkit with lots of ideas to help you run a Quick Reads reading group at **www.readingagency.org.uk/quickreads**

Share your experiences of your group on Twitter

🐦 @Quick_Reads

Discover the pleasure of reading with Galaxy®

Curled up on the sofa,
Sunday morning in pyjamas,
just before bed,
in the bath or
on the way to work?

Wherever, whenever,
you can escape
with a good book!

So go on...
indulge yourself with
a good read and the
smooth taste of
Galaxy® chocolate.

Proudly supports

Stories about real life

Stories to take you to another time

Stories to make you turn the pages

For a complete list of titles visit
www.readingagency.org.uk/quickreads

Available in paperback, ebook and from your local library

The Other
Side of You

The Other Side of You

Amanda Craig

ABACUS

To my sister, Constance,
gardener and guide.

ABACUS

First published in Great Britain in 2017 by Abacus

3 5 7 9 10 8 6 4 2

ISBN 978-0-349-14172-5

Typeset in Stone Serif by M Rules
Printed and bound in Great Britain by
Clays Ltd, St Ives plc

Papers used by Abacus are from well-managed forests
and other responsible sources.

Abacus
An imprint of
Little, Brown Book Group
Carmelite House
50 Victoria Embankment
London EC4Y 0DZ

Distributed By:
Grass Roots Press
Toll Free: 1-888-303-3213
Fax: (780) 413-6582
Web Site: www.grassrootsbooks.net

Chapter One

There was a knife, and blood, and the thud of a door. There was the taste of blood in my mouth, and the sound of feet. Down the stairs, two steps at a time, almost blinded by sweat and fear, the knives coming for me.

Have you ever had a dream about being chased? You run and run, and no matter how hard you try, you can never get away.

But my chase wasn't a dream. It was real.

I wasn't going to wake up safe at home in bed. I didn't have a home any more, or a bed. All I had were my legs and my feet, and they were pounding the street as hard as they could. My shoes didn't fit properly, and my lungs hurt like they were on fire, and I felt sick. But I had to run. The BANG Gang were after me, and when they came for you, it was run or die.

The BANG Gang ran my estate. Even if you wanted to stay away, even if your mum begged you, they sucked in all the kids. Nobody could escape. Nobody wanted this life. It just

1

happened. It was normal not to go to school. It was normal to go to prison, like it was normal to deal drugs, carry a knife, bang any kid smaller than you. How and why I pissed off the Gang big time is another story. All that mattered was what kind of fear I had.

There are two kinds of fear. There's the kind that makes you stand and fight. There's the kind that makes you run, and keep on running. Either can get you killed. On my estate, there is no right or wrong. There's only live or die. Sooner or later, most died. Even if you got to the top, and became the Boss, you died. Another guy was always waiting to take your place.

My estate was famous all over the city. Not for any good thing, like a rap star or a lottery winner. It was famous for killing. Every two, three months, somebody got shot, or stabbed. Often, they weren't anything to do with the gangs. They could be walking some place, or sitting in their flat, trying to stay out of trouble. Made no difference. BANG stood for Bullets, Anger, (K)nives, Guns. Also, bang as in steal. Bang as in kill. Bang as in rape. Nobody was quite sure what it meant. All of these, and more, but most of all the noise a gun makes.

Many years ago, before I was born, my estate was known to be bad, dangerous, but nothing

like it was now. The police never came near it, unless there'd been another stabbing. The social workers: jokes. It was crim central. Nobody could be inside the law and survive. Nothing good happened to anyone there, ever. Some people, like Aunty May, bought a lottery ticket each week. Like anything was going to change, ever.

Everyone young, including the girls, carried a knife. Everyone except me, that is. I'd been beaten up so many times, but I knew that all a shank – a knife – would do was get me stabbed, as well as punched and robbed. If you went to school, you were a target. I'd stayed in school, right up to sixteen. Aunty May said, 'You have a good head on those shoulders, Billy. Use it.'

Aunty May – I couldn't think about that. I was half-crazy with fear, but I used my head. I ran.

The estate had been my whole world for seven years. I hadn't been out since I turned eleven, except to go to school down the road. But even that was dangerous. Across the road on the next estate was the other gang, the Bulldogz. Sooner or later, they saw you weren't a little kid any more, and mashed you up. Any excuse would do. You learned to keep looking over your shoulder.

I knew every twist and turn. I knew where there was a bin so you could jump up on to the walkway, and where there was a small passage. I knew where there was a gap in the wire of the mugger – that's the Multi-Use Games Area, the caged football pitch where nobody played games. Or not games it was made for, anyway. I knew where the bushes were in the bit of green where people brought their dogs to dump. It was one big dog turd. I knew which places you could squeeze into and wriggle through, and which places were dead ends.

Trouble is, so did they. Stickz, Gazza, Lipz and Raffle had all grown up on the estate, just like me. Just like me, they had mums who wanted the best for them, but that meant staying out of trouble. But trouble would still find you, or the Gang did. We all knew the price of a bullet. They did some stealing and dealing. They carried knives. They got little kids to deliver drugs into school and they put the fear into people. Even if you joined them, you were afraid. When you saw them up to no good, you looked the other way.

Chances were, somebody was watching what was going on right now, but if I got stabbed it would turn out everybody was blind, and deaf, as well as dumb. You didn't tell on the BANG

Gang, not unless you wanted to be shanked too. Besides, it was the middle of the night.

'Hey, Beasty!' I could hear Gazza hiss. 'You come now, boy, we ain't gonna cut you so bad.'

He had nunchuck, two metal sticks joined by a chain. They might not look much, but if he got near me I'd find them wrapped round my throat in no time. The others had shanks. Big ones, with jagged edges, like you might skin a rhino with. Lipz had a gun. I didn't have so much as a twig. My mum made me promise I'd never carry.

'Having a gun isn't life insurance, Billy. It won't make you any safer, no matter what they say.'

I needed to catch my breath, so I hid in the doorway of a shop. It wasn't a real shop. It was what they call a business unit, boarded up and empty like all the shops on the estate. Nobody could run a business. If anyone dared open a shop there, first week the BANG Gang would be round asking for money. Second week, you'd be robbed. Third week, you'd be banged for disrespect. Result: you had to go on a bus to get to Iceland just for a pint of milk. Not that any of the bigger kids went. Iceland was off the estate, and that was out of bounds for the brothers of the BANG Gang. If you went into

another gang's territory, somebody would make a call.

I knew this, but I also knew that if I didn't make it off the estate I'd be killed anyway. I was hoping, this time in the morning when it was cold and dark, I might not be noticed.

But I couldn't stay where I was. For one thing, the longer I stayed, the more cold and scared I became. For another, the Gang was getting closer. I could see the glint of gold round their necks shining in the fizzing orange street-light, and I knew that, before long, they'd find me. They found everyone. I felt alone, and dead scared: scared so I might drop dead of fear. I was so thirsty! The thirst was worse than the hunger, worse than the anger, worse than the sorrow. If the BANG Gang didn't get me, the thirst would.

What could I do? I had to send them in a different direction, away from me. How was that possible? I couldn't be in two places at once.

Or could I? There was a big steel trash bin about twenty feet away. It was full of rubbish. The binmen mostly didn't bother to come. Mostly, it was set on fire, but the firemen didn't come either. I scrabbled around for something to throw. The concrete wall beside me was

cracked. I pulled at it, quiet as possible. A chunk came away, with a slight noise.

The Gang stiffened, like dogs.

'Over there!'

I threw the stone at the bin as hard as I could. It made a loud, metallic thump. The Gang stopped, like one creature with five heads, and turned. Something moved in the shadows. A cat, or a rat maybe, but it did the trick.

'There!'

They ran one way, and I the other. My feet pumped the pavement again, and then, at last, I was out. The estate was behind me. The wide road lay like a river of darkness before me. It might be ten times more dangerous being out in the open, but I didn't wait. I ran.

Chapter Two

I was halfway across the road when the Gang burst out behind me. They knew as well as I did that the CCTV cameras there were bust. They'd bust them. Cars came along sometimes, but they drove fast, and never stopped. Everyone knew not to stop.

In the days when we had a TV, I sometimes watched nature films. There was one about a herd of deer trying to cross a river, and on either side, there were crocodiles waiting. They didn't look like crocs. You saw these things that looked like big logs in the water, floating. The deer go as fast as they can. They know there's danger, but they can't see it yet. Then one of the logs splits open, and it's all teeth. It's the croc! Big as a nightmare, grinning. The teeth grab and snatch and a deer goes down. Then it's crunch, crunch, crunch, the croc tearing and gulping, blood in the water. Only sometimes they pick the wrong one, and the deer jumps away.

It was like that now.

There was a metal barrier halfway across the road, and that was the crossover point between my estate and the others'. That was the line we never crossed. No matter how mad the Boss was at me, Stickz, Gazza, Raffle and the rest would stick to this side of the line, and the Bulldogz would stick to theirs. If you crossed over to the other side, it was war.

I should have jumped right away. The barrier was only waist-high, and guys like me, we could jump, even if we had had nothing to eat all day but a bag of crisps. We could jump as if springs were in our heels, just like those deer. But something made me stop, and look back.

Maybe I knew that this was the last time I'd see the estate. I had nothing and nobody to go back for. My mum was dead, and Aunty May too now. She'd hated me. I'd hated her. She was always on my case. She was the first to call me Beasty.

'Boy, you so ugly and dirty, you look like a beast,' she'd say. 'Look at yourself! Dirty hair, dirty claws, bad smell, bad skin. Ugh! When you last brush your teeth? Where is the good Billy from school?'

'Gone to hell,' I answered.

I knew that would make her angry enough

to reach for her cane. She had a cane – maybe she'd brought it all the way from Jamaica. It was real bamboo, and you could hear it sing through the air before it landed on your ass. Man, did I hate that! Only now she'd never make me yell again.

I looked back, and that was when the Gang began to whoop and call.

'Yo, Beasty! Keep runnin', B! They goin' to love you.'

Suddenly, I understood what they were doing. They were trying to draw the Bulldogz out, so they'd shank me instead. The more noise they made, the bigger the danger. Someone would hear, then someone would come and see. They'd think I was crossing the line for a dare. I had seconds to get over the road and disappear. Where to run in a place I'd never been to and knew nothing about? They'd know I was a stranger. I might as well have had a big X on my back.

I had never felt so lonely, or so afraid.

'Beasty-Boy! You can run but you can't hide!'

Run, said a voice. *Run now!*

By now, it was so dark that I could hardly see who had spoken or where I was going, and maybe that helped. Or maybe it was the rain that suddenly fell down like a sheet of

plastic. Everything was behind a grey, crackling blur. The pavement was slick and the gutters gurgled. We were all blinded.

Behind me, I heard a gunshot. Then another. I ran, and my heart was going so loud I couldn't hear any more. Nothing hit me, only raindrops as big as bullets. I was soaked in seconds. Things went past me, big buildings, cars, trees, street lamps, signs. It was an endless maze. I had my mobile, but it was out of credit and out of juice. I had no idea where I was. I had never, apart from when I was a tiny child, been more than half a mile from my home.

All I knew was that I'd been born north-side, across the river. Any good memories I had were from that time, memories of grass and trees. So I tried to head for the Thames. At some point I found it, though it was so wide I thought it might be the sea. It smelled salty, and mist was rising off it, but then I came to a bridge. I crossed that, and by now I couldn't run any more.

How long I walked for, I don't know. It was still night. I kept stopping and looking over my shoulder to see if I was being followed. I've done that all my life. I didn't even know I was doing it.

I knew I must hide. By now, there were more

11

buses about, all lit up and carrying people to work. The idea of sitting down somewhere was tempting. Only I couldn't try it. I had no money, no family, no home – nothing.

Besides, I wasn't alone.

Chapter Three

I don't know how I knew that somebody else was there. I wasn't looking, yet I also knew I wasn't alone. Somebody was on the other side of me. I couldn't make out who it was. It wore a hood, like me. No matter whether I ran or walked, it kept up. I didn't know if it was a man or a woman, only that they were there. My feet had long since stopped throbbing and started bleeding. Somewhere, I had a cut on my arm, and another deeper one on my back. Gazza had made those as I ran past. They would bleed, and dry, and catch, and then bleed again. I had a feeling like I should stop and lick them, like an animal. I knew I was losing a lot of blood from deep inside me.

Clean it later. Find the safe place first.

How could I find the safe place when I'd never been here before?

You will, the person said.

I had felt this person beside me ever since I hid in the shop door. It was their idea to throw

13

the stone at the bin. When I stopped in the middle of the road, it held out its hand and pulled me across. Each time I stopped, tired and hopeless, it spoke.

Keep going.

I couldn't see who it was. Sometimes I thought it was a man, sometimes a woman. I did know that I could trust the voice. It sounded friendly. The sun was rising, and the air was all white, like when you put soap on a window. Things weren't there until the last moment, when suddenly they became real and solid. Once, I found myself walking into a lamp-post. Jokes.

By now, I was away from the river, and well away from my estate. I wished I had a bike, even though the bikes we had were all tiny kids' bikes. Little kids get bikes, but bigger kids never. So we banged the tiny ones, and rode about, knees up to our chests. Better than nothing.

I'd never walked so far. My trainers had given me so many blisters that I hardly felt them. My top was still soaked, and I was getting the shakes from cold. I walked, down a hill and up a hill, down a hill, the pavements punishing my bones. I turned off a big road into a street of shops.

Even with their shutters down, you could tell

they were open. Lights were on. Some weren't shuttered at all, but the glass wasn't broken or boarded up. I saw takeaways, a chemist, a hairdresser, a hardware shop, a greengrocer, a newsagent, a post office, a bakery, a Poundland, a library. It was like a street in a kids' book. I didn't know streets like that really existed.

'Posh,' I muttered. It was a word my mum had used. I hadn't known what it meant, but I did now.

When I left that street, I was in a place with old houses all lined up together. The houses had trees in front, and small gardens. There was no rubbish. There were pots with flowers. The cars weren't new, but the front doors were all different colours. I came into a square. When I was little, I had gone to places where there were other old houses, so I knew enough about London squares to know there should be grass in the middle, with railings. Instead, there was this big wire wall.

It was three times as high as a man. At the top was barbed wire. Behind the wire, I could see only trees, more trees and thorns, and some kind of building. It would be the perfect hiding place, if I could get in.

The gates had a chain, and a huge padlock on. No give.

Climb up, said the voice.

The sun was rising, and I knew that I must get over the wire fence right away. Soon people would be waking, and I needed to get out of sight. Me covered in blood would not look good to whoever lived here. There were signs warning this was a Neighbourhood Watch Area, with Smart Water, whatever that meant.

I took a running jump at the fence, and climbed. The trick to climbing any wall is to do it like a fox – fast. It all has to be one motion. If you stop and think, you're lost.

Right at the top, I kicked my feet into the air. I almost made it. Only, my bad arm let me down. The barbed wire sank its rusty teeth into my skin.

Unlike the knife, it hurt at once. I knew, even as I fell, that it'd be bad. But the place into which I fell wasn't like anything I'd seen before.

You will be safe now, said the voice, and then, quite suddenly, I was alone.

Chapter Four

At first I could see nothing but tall, thin, grey trees. They stood up like spears. I was lucky not to have landed on top of one. I pushed forwards, holding on to them to stay upright.

There was a house behind the trees, but it wasn't an ordinary house. It was all glass, and it sparkled in the rising sun as if it were made of diamond.

I'd never seen a glass house before. I went forward, carefully, and peered through the panes. Inside, there were more plants. It was weird. I wondered if it was skunk. They were the only plants I'd seen before, and that had been in a flat where lamps were on day and night. Only those plants were all the same, and these were all different.

Maybe the plants were drugs. Or maybe poison. I didn't want to touch them, in case. If I hadn't been hurt bad, I'd have turned round and got out. But that meant climbing the wire

wall again, and by now I was feeling bad. So I went in.

It was warm. That was the first thing. Not cold, not hot, just right. There was a smell, sweet but not too much. Better than Mum's perfume, which is the best smell I know. It came from some white flowers like little stars.

Yet each plant was different. Some were so big, they looked as if they came from dinosaur-time. The one with the white flowers had twisted itself all the way along the roof. Another had big bright red trumpets. There were trees, too, with bright shiny green leaves like plates. Some had fruit that looked like oranges. Some had bananas. Some had green pears. What *was* this place? Even though my arm was hurting almost as much as my belly, I wondered.

I felt like an explorer in the jungle. There were flashes of wings – pink, blue, green, brown. Soft, fluttering noises, and trills. Otherwise, it was quiet. Not a bad kind of quiet, when people are dead. A good quiet. I could almost hear those plants growing. I could feel the roots spreading, the leaves swelling, the flowers opening.

You will be safe here, the voice had said.

For the first time in many hours, I began to

relax. I was far away from the BANG Gang and my estate. I didn't need to keep looking over my shoulder. Whatever this place was, it was different. I knew nobody could climb that wire wall unless they were desperate.

Anyway, it was just a glass house. Nothing to steal. Just plants, and bits of rubbish. Candles and plastic pots and racks with a few packets of seeds. A metal bucket with a grille. Plastic bags with brown stuff in that some creature had scratched open. Paper bags with black stuff. None of it drugs. I found a till – empty – and some leaflets about a garden centre. This must be the place. It looked as if it had been abandoned for months, maybe years.

I was hungry, though. I was always hungry, like my belly was trying to eat itself. Most days, I didn't get more than a bag of crisps to eat. Aunty May cooked sometimes, and those were good days. Rice, beans, sweet potato, food that fills your belly. But I wouldn't be getting her cooking any more.

Right in the middle of the glass house was a sink, a kettle and two cupboards. From the dust and mess, I didn't expect anything, but I turned the tap. Out came a gush of cold. I let it run, in case the water was bad. It went on flowing, so I drank. It was the best drink ever.

Then I looked in the cupboards. Maybe I'd find coins or gear. But I found tins. Tuna, beans, tomatoes, pineapple, milk ... No tin opener. I was so hungry, I could have cried. All that food, and locked up so I couldn't eat. But then I looked in the dim dawn light and saw that each tin had a ring on top. Pull the ring, the tin opened.

In a moment, two tuna and beans were gone. I don't even remember eating. I hadn't had so much food for a long time. Then I had some pineapple. It was sweet and sour and syrupy. The pineapple was in chunks, so you didn't have to cut it up. There was a box of something called Quaker Oats, which looked like sawdust. I wanted to eat more, in case the food went away. But I felt sick again, and if I ate more, I'd be sick.

I could rest, then think what to do. I was so tired, I wasn't sure what was real any more. My arm was still bleeding, and I had deep scratches from the barbed wire. I had to clean the cuts before I slept. I washed them with water. It wasn't enough, I knew. Both were going red and angry.

My hands were dirty. Aunty May was right. The sink had a bottle of liquid by it. I sniffed it, and it was soap. It smelled funny, but OK, so I

washed the cuts, and looked for a first aid kit. Anybody who left food like this must have one.

There was a green box with a white cross. *Thank you*, I thought. Inside were bandages, antiseptic, painkillers. By now my head was spinning. I smeared antiseptic on the cuts and tied the bandage on my arm, swallowed painkillers. Close by I saw a heap of old cloth. I fell on to this. I passed out.

Chapter Five

When I woke, I felt terrible. So terrible I even forgot to think about the Gang hunting for me.

I was weak, and hot all over. My throat and head were raw. The cuts were red and felt like they were burning. My arm was swollen. I swallowed more painkillers. I drank water. It didn't help my throat, but I slept again. Each time I woke, I did the same. I got up only to drink and piss.

Aunty May was in most of my dreams. She'd taken me into her flat when Mum died: it was that, or social services. I think she got some money, child benefit, for me until I turned sixteen. She didn't care for me, nor I for her. But she was better than being in care, for sure. She never knew what brought the BANG Gang into her home, to stab her where she sat.

All I wanted was to mind my own business. Only that was the one thing you couldn't do.

By the third day, my head was clear and the cuts were no longer puffy. I was hollow with

hunger, but better. I ate more tuna, more beans, more pineapple. After a couple of days, there were none left.

The only thing I hadn't tried eating was the oats. The instructions said to just add a cup of water or milk, and microwave. Then add salt or sugar. I didn't have a microwave, but I did have hot water from the kettle, and sugar. It tasted disgusting, but it was food.

Still nobody came. The glass house really was abandoned. Life went on beyond the wire walls, but inside it was just plants and birds.

It was dirty. Not bad dirt, just the dirt of city air. At night, I had a little light, from the street lamps and the houses, but nothing to do. It was warm and quiet. Mostly, I slept.

When the oats were gone, I began to look at the plants. Could those round orange fruits on the trees be oranges? Maybe. I picked one, and peeled it, then tried a piece. It tasted sweet, and a bit sour. Just like the ones Aunty May sometimes bought, but I couldn't live on oranges.

The bananas were still green. I was tempted to try to eat one, but was afraid of getting pains in my belly. The green pears were still hard as rocks – and I had no knife to cut them open.

I looked at the bags. The brown stuff was

called compost. It was for planting seeds in. The black stuff was for a BBQ, and so was the metal bucket with a grille. It would cook food – or it would if I could find matches. There were none.

I had to get out. I wasn't strong enough to climb the wire again. I had to make a hole.

The wire wall was only around three sides. On the fourth was a tall brick wall with no windows – the back of some housing. I found a weak spot, down by the ground where the brick wall was, hidden by a bush. From the smell, a fox had found it before me. I made it bigger, but not by much. I got down on my belly, and wriggled through. My clothes and hands got even dirtier. I didn't care. I was a beast, like Aunty May said.

Outside, I was scared again. It was still winter, and cold. I'd spent long enough in hiding to feel odd at being in the open. I kept looking over my shoulder again. I still couldn't believe the BANG Gang weren't there.

I got lost twice, then found the street of shops. I waited until they were shut, and then I climbed over a back wall, found their bins and went through them.

All kinds of food gets thrown out, every day. If you aren't too worried by it being cold and a

little bit old, it's fine. I was glad to have half a pizza, and some chicken nuggets.

Once or twice, I saw a fox, going through a bin like I was. Maybe it was the same one that had lived behind the wire wall. It wasn't afraid of me, and I wasn't afraid of it. We were both scavengers.

I took care to be seen by as few people as possible. Even if, as days and weeks went by, I was less scared of being found by the BANG Gang, it turned out that Aunty May's name for me was like a curse.

I had become a beast.

Chapter Six

I had never been good-looking, but I knew I was ugly now. I had healed where the cuts were, but my skin was sore and crusty. It had once been smooth, like toffee, but the need to scratch was terrible. Bit by bit, I could feel my flesh melting. I had some disease. Maybe it was the itchy, scratchy one I'd had before as a kid, when my skin flaked off and Mum stopped giving me milk. Eczema, it was called. Maybe it was a new one.

My hair hung down in long dreads. My teeth were scummy. My breath stank. All of me stank. My nails grew long, like black claws. I never washed. Why should I? Nobody cared about me. My mum and Aunty May, both were dead. My teachers, they never knew my name. All I had ever had was hard hands giving me hard knocks. You live that way, your heart becomes stone.

I kept expecting someone to come in and kick me out of the glass house. Surely, this had to belong to somebody?

I found some red bills in a drawer. A Mr
Engels hadn't paid council tax – but the bills
were from months ago. Maybe he'd done a
runner from the glass house, like I'd done a
runner from mine.

'Thanks,' I said aloud. Just in case Mr Engels
was, you know, dead. 'I'll look after it.'

How did the glass house stay warm? The glass
helped, but there was even electricity. I flicked
a switch, just to check, and almost jumped out
of my skin. Someone was talking out of a dusty
old radio. I turned it off, sweating. But nobody
came by to check. It was as if I had become
invisible.

I could have sold the radio, but I didn't know
who to sell it to. So I began to listen to it. At
first, I nearly went crazy. No music, just voices.
Boring! It was stuck on 92 FM. I had to listen
to the news, and programmes about all kinds
of things – politics, health, books, food, plants,
money, women's feelings, law, history, more
politics. I couldn't understand most of it, to
start with, but I began to learn stuff. Most was
how little I knew.

Those voices ... I thought of the voice I'd
heard when I was running for my life. That
kind, wise voice I had trusted.

'Where are you, man?' I whispered sometimes,

just to hear myself speak. If I didn't use my voice, I was afraid I might never find it again. 'Who are you? Are you here?'

There was never any answer. Sometimes, I thought he – I was pretty sure it was a he – had been a fever dream. Aunty May would have said it was my guardian angel.

'Everybody has one. You too, Billy. You do a bad thing, they see. And you do a good thing, they see that too. But your guardian angel is there for you.'

I was lonely. Even if I had no family, I'd always lived with other people. At Aunty May's we'd slept four to a bed, sideways, me and the other kids, all our feet sticking out. People shouted, screamed, fought but they were there, banged up with you. When those kids left, I stayed, because even an old witch with a cane was better than being alone with nowhere to go. Here, I was on my own. I was surrounded by people, but outside their world. The wire fence had so many things growing up it – trees and creepers and things – that nobody looked through to the other side.

I didn't want them to look.

I kept myself busy. I found that the black BBQ stuff was fuel for a thing called a fire-pit. This was a metal bowl on legs, and if I could

find matches, I could cook on it. Mostly, I ate oats, with water.

The glass house garden was giving me food. It was almost dropping into my hands each day, now spring was coming. I knew nothing about trees and plants, but I went through the garden centre's book about them. It took me a long time to read. How to make seeds and cuttings grow into plants. How to give plants water, food, sun, but not too much. How to train them so they grow the right way. How to give them love, just like they were people.

It was the last part that made me think. I never thought that love was like food. Or that it mattered to plants. I'd never had anyone or anything to love, once Mum died.

But I loved those plants. It sounds crazy, I know.

At first they were all the same – just green stuff that got in the way. Pretty soon, though, I saw the leaves were even more different than I first thought. Before long, I knew what they were called.

There were plants outside the glass house, too. Some was ordinary stuff like grass. Others were taller. These ones looked like sticks with claws on. I saw other kinds of thorns mixed in with them, like they were strangling the claw

sticks. I knew what these were. Brambles. In all my estate, they'd been the only things that grew.

There was a pair of gloves in the glass house – stiff, grey, dirty but thick. I put them on to protect my hands, and pulled the brambles out.

The earth was soft and black, and soon a bird flew down. It hopped and pecked at the ground. It was a little brown bird with a fat body and tiny thin legs. I'd never been so near one. It put its head on one side, and let out this sound, as if asking me a question. When I didn't answer, it hopped closer again, and pulled at a worm with its beak like it was eating spaghetti. Then it made this cheeping, whistling sound, like it was laughing. It was a cool bird.

'Hi,' I said. 'What's with you?'

It made the cheeping sound.

'Are you asking me to pull up more?'

It looked at me, with bright black eyes. It was a friendly look, as if it wanted to play.

All that day, the bird stayed beside me. It had no fear, although I could have crushed it with my hand. Every now and then, it would pull out a bit of dried grass, and fly off. I saw it was disappearing into the same place. I wondered if it was eating the grass, and then I realised: it was building a nest.

I wanted so much to see that nest, but something warned me that if I came near, the bird would fly away. So I respected it. It seemed to like hanging out with me. That was the first good thing.

I thought of feeding it some of the seeds in the packets. But it wasn't interested in these, so instead I tried putting some into little pots with compost, just to see what would happen. Nothing happened for a week, but then the second good thing happened. Every pot suddenly had tiny plants in it. Each began with two simple leaves, but then something different grew out of them. Before long, I had dozens of new plants. I didn't know what they were, only that they must be some of the flowers I'd planted. In the heat of the glass house, they grew fat much faster than the packet said. I reckoned they shouldn't sleep four to a bed as I had. Before long, each plant had a pot of its own.

Next was that the sticks by the wire wall weren't dead. As it got warmer, they began to have bumps on them. The bumps grew, and split open into leaves – and more buds.

I looked at the pictures in my plant book, and found the sticks were roses. All over the wire wall, roses were folded up tight in green shells.

It rained and shone and rained, and then the shells split open. The flowers unfolded.

Nothing in my life had been as good as that moment. I'd seen a rose once, in a cartoon called *Beauty and the Beast*. Maybe that's why I loved them. But I'd never seen one in real life – deep red flowers, like nests of silk with crowns in the middle. They smelled of honey. They smelled of happiness. They smelled of love.

They didn't care that I was ugly, and my skin was covered in scaly lumps. I knew each one. I dug in something called bone-meal, which my book said was food for them. I gave them water on dry days. I picked greenfly off them with my fingers. I watched the bees kneeling on them, like people praying. They were mine, and a miracle. If anybody ever picked one of my roses, I'd rip them to bits.

Chapter Seven

Even with the fruit the glass house gave me, I needed more to eat. That feeling of my belly eating itself was pain. I was a beast, and a beast needs meat. So I did what everybody did on my estate. I found a kid on the way to school.

He was on his own. One look told me all I needed. Small, weak, white shirt, black rucksack. He even wore glasses.

'Money. Mobile,' I said, stepping up and pinning him against the wall. I didn't have a knife but I didn't need one. All I needed was to be bigger and stronger than he was, with my scarf round my face.

'Wh-what?'

'Hurry up.'

I breathed into his face, and he said, 'I only have £2.'

He handed it over.

'Don't piss me off. Give me the rest.'

He gave me his mobile. It was one of those old grey Nokias. It wasn't even for emails. Just

calls and texts. Anybody would feel shame to have it.

'You this basic?'

'It's all I have.'

I couldn't believe a kid in a neighbourhood like this could have so little.

'You not got another mobile?'

'No. My mum says—'

'What?'

'She says even a mugger wouldn't be—'

'Wrong,' I said.

So, I kept it. Fully charged, it might be useful. I turned it off though, just in case.

Two more little kids, acting like they've never been robbed before. Easy money. Soon, I had £12. I didn't wait to hang around. One of them might tell their mum, or teacher. Even if I was still more scared of the Gang than the police, I didn't want more troubles. Most everybody I knew had done time. Nothing happens to you in prison, but three meals a day. That's what they say. Only prisons are full of gangs, so I didn't want to go there.

I wanted to spend my £12 on getting high. To stop the bad feelings I still had when I remembered Aunty May with blood all over her. Only I didn't know who sold weed here. There was always someone, even in a place like

this. But word might be out to look for me and, if I ever saw another guy in a hoodie, I turned and walked away.

There was the Poundland on the high street. I got twelve things – a pot with a lid, a mug, wooden spoons, a grater, a tin opener, more tins, eggs, matches, more porridge oats. The one thing that I couldn't get was a knife. I didn't look eighteen, had no ID. In the end, I bought scissors, took them apart, sharpened the blade, and used that. I needed them to chop onions. I'd found these growing outside the glass house in a kind of box of earth. It had taken a while to understand it was the root that mattered, not the plant, but the little bird had kind of given me a hint. Onion and eggs made a big difference to the hunger.

Of course, I was lonely. All around me, people were doing their thing. It was weird. I'd listen out for them. And that was how my life changed again.

Chapter Eight

I knew that taking the kids' money was a risk. These weren't like the ones on my estate. They had people looking out for them. They were legal. Already, I'd seen a police car going round my new home, very slowly, as if looking for me. That scared me, so I hid for three days.

But when I was hiding, I was also watching my roses. I knew every one of them.

And because of my roses, I saw the girl, Padma.

Each day, she would walk to school with a friend. They'd come down the alley from the high street and into the square. I could always hear them coming. They'd be laughing and chatting. I knew Padma was beautiful, just from her voice.

'Really, Anji, how could you?'

She was teasing.

'Are you honestly not interested?'

'No, all I want is to finish my studies and go to uni. They know that.'

'But if your family is planning to take you home, Padma—'

'India is not my home. It's theirs.'

I didn't know what they were talking about. I listened to her voice. It was like the voice of deep water over stones.

I peered through the wire wall, past the bright new leaves of the wood, and saw them go by. Two girls, their long hair tied back. Padma's was in a single shining plait. It fell to her waist. I wondered what it looked like, untied.

I'd never seen anything like her. I had done it with girls, because if you don't on my estate, you're gay. If you're gay, you're dead. It meant nothing. The girls there have babies like we go to prison. It just happens. Even though they love the babies, they know: if it's a boy, he'll be like his babyfather. If a girl, she'll be like them. On and on, the same pattern. I never thought about whether girls liked me or I liked them. I only hoped they wouldn't laugh at me.

Anyway, Padma and Anji were not like that. These girls were like people from the radio. They were *people*. I listened and waited.

I wanted to see Padma's face.

Chapter Nine

As it got warmer, I got bolder. I'd work out of doors with my shirt off on a warm day, though I always hid behind the trees. My scars still itched and pulled, especially the one on my back, and I didn't want to scare the girls. They always walked to school together at the same time, chatting. I'd never heard so much chat! It made me smile, as if I was listening to birds. I learned that Anji, her friend, was the daughter of the chemist in the high street. Padma was the daughter of the newsagent. Both their parents had come from India.

Anji was working to become a lawyer, and Padma to become a doctor. They did difficult subjects at school – sciences, maths, history. Sometimes they would imitate their fathers and mothers, saying, 'Good job!' before giggling.

When they giggled like this, I knew they were trying to keep stuff inside them that most people didn't know about.

Maybe they didn't want to be doctors and

lawyers, or maybe they did. I knew what doctors and lawyers did, more or less. Sometimes, if you were lucky – or unlucky – on my estate, you got to see one of them before you got sent to hospital, or prison. I wondered what you needed to do to become one. I couldn't imagine it. It must take a lot of school, even more than sixth form.

School had been one of my favourite things. I liked learning things. I read slowly, but if I got told something, I never forgot. I liked being in another place. No dogs barking, or music blaring, or people shouting. I wanted to get to college. I wanted a better life.

So I kept trying, until I kept getting mugged. I had gone crying back to Aunty May's, and she'd put stuff on my cuts. Then I went back, until the BANG Gang began picking on me, more and more. They hated that I was wearing a white shirt and not doing drugs. It was like everybody had to be like them, even if nobody could.

Of course, I was picking on kids here. I didn't like thinking about that. I had myself to look after, didn't I? Besides, I didn't hit them or do any of the bad things that had been done to me, like making them strip or taking their shoes or showing them my knife. I didn't need

to. It was enough just to be the beast, big and stinky and scary. They handed over their lunch money.

I needed it more than they did. They had homes, and clothes, and food and stuff. I had nothing. Everything cost £1 at Poundland, but if I didn't get those £1s, I couldn't eat. Even if Aunty May hadn't fed me much, I'd never thought about all the gear she needed just to *begin* feeding me. She must have collected that as carefully as the little brown bird had collected the grass. I needed that gear now. The pot, the spoons, the cooking oil, salt, rice, beans and spices. And meat. I was desperate for meat because I was growing.

I had never thanked her, never understood what a struggle it was. I'd just gulped it down like the beast that I was becoming, and blamed her for my bad skin.

There was no meat here, not unless I trapped squirrels and cats, and how could I without a knife? I kept buying the tuna, and sardines in tomato sauce. Mostly, what I ate was porridge, twelve packets for £1, enough for a week. But as the days grew brighter and warmer, I found I needed to buy food less.

The glass house fed me its pears.

The pears now had black, bumpy skin like

dinosaurs'. I tried biting into them when they softened, but that didn't work. Then I tried peeling them. Inside was a soft green flesh, and a huge pip. The flesh tasted like nuts. With a little salt, it was good and filling, like the bananas. However much I picked, there always seemed to be more. Everything grew so fast there, in the heat and light, it was like magic.

Bit by bit, I was making the glass house into a home. I got a mattress, rolling it up and sliding it through the hole in the wall. Maybe a dog had pissed on it before I found it, but it felt like luxury. People put things out on the street that they didn't want – shoes, newspapers, old pots, old china, old clothes, dust-sheets. I took what I could.

I went out most nights, like the foxes. Sometimes, I saw other human foxes around. They'd be breaking into cars to look for loose change. The next day there would be cries of sadness and anger, and the sound of glass being swept up, *tinkle-crunch*.

'Two hundred pounds of damage for two quid!' I heard one of the people who lived in the square say.

He was a teacher at the school where Padma went. His girlfriend was going to have a kid, I could see. Of all the people living on the

square, they were my favourite. I could see through the window of their basement flat because my foxhole was right opposite, and they often didn't draw the curtains in the evening. They were so gentle to each other. I didn't know people could be like that. He was called Ian and she was Katie. Sometimes, when I was coming back from Poundland, I'd pass Katie. She always smiled and said, 'Hi!' but I never knew what to say back.

I was worried about the cars. I had a feeling that people might know I was living in the glass house, and think it was me. I was even more worried because I sometimes thought the guys looked like they might be in the Gang. But how could anyone from there be here?

When I went in or out past the wall, I was even more careful not to be seen.

Padma and Anji made me think for the first time how I must look. Now that it wasn't freezing outside, I didn't have to wear everything at once. So I peeled off my clothes. It was weird being without them, like taking the skin off one of the black pears. I felt shivery.

All that I had was in rags. You live in the same clothes, day in day out, they'll fall to bits. Mine were beyond stinky and also full of holes. I needed new socks, new T-shirts, new hoodie,

new jeans. Most of all, I needed new trainers. My feet were the only things I could depend on if I ever had to run again. But I didn't have what even the cheapest trainers cost.

Padma and Anji, they were so clean, they seemed to shine. I knew that if they ever met me they'd probably wrinkle up their perfect noses, not because they were mean but because it was so long since my clothes and I had been washed.

The little brown bird came down to see if I had anything for him and his mate. I didn't even have some boiled rice.

'Right,' I said. 'I'd best get sorted, then.'

Back to Poundland. Each T-shirt, each pair of socks, was another kid without lunch money. The cashiers had stopped giving me looks like I was going to steal from the shop. I spent £1 on a toothbrush. Another £1 on toothpaste. My hair ... But Poundland didn't have shampoo for dreadlocks. I bought rice instead.

I listened to the girls, walking to and from school. On the way they were in more of a hurry, but on the way back they seemed to slow down. The reason was that they liked my roses.

'Mmm, smell that!'

'Oh, wow. Look at the blossom. It's a real little wood in there.'

'It's such a weird place, Padma. You know, nobody knows who owns it?'

I pricked up my ears at that.

'People have tried for ages to discover why it's been abandoned.'

'It wasn't always, was it? I'm sure I remember some old guy in there.'

'Not for ages. People don't know if he was squatting or trying to run a business. It looks a mess, doesn't it?'

'Can't it be knocked down? Turned into a park, maybe?'

'My dad says not,' said Padma. 'The greenhouse is listed or something. It used to be a garden centre.'

'More like a garden jungle.'

Their voices were full of laughter.

'It doesn't look so bad now all the roses are out.'

'No. I've never seen them so big. And look at the morning glories! Such deep blue.'

'It makes me think of Tamil Nadu,' Padma said, in a dreamy voice. 'Whole mountains covered with flowers.'

'Do you go home every Christmas?'

'You know we can't afford that. Do you?'

'No. Every three years. But each time we go, one of my sisters comes back married.'

They were silent.

'And you?'

'I dread that. To be married to some stinky old man with no education, just so he can get a passport and my parents some money. I want to go to uni.'

'My *amma* says, I can continue schooling after I get married. Only I may get a husband who does not wish me to do that.'

'To be trapped ...' Padma said, and I could hear the shiver in her voice.

'We all know it's illegal. But has anyone been prosecuted for it, ever?'

I didn't understand what this was about. Where I came from, nobody got forced to marry. Almost nobody *got* married. But these were different people, with different religion. Maybe that was it. I couldn't understand, though, why if you had a daughter as smart as Padma and Anji, you wouldn't want them to be free. Why you wouldn't trust them. They weren't like the girls I'd known on my estate, girls so angry and broken they could never be free.

I hadn't been free either, until I came to the glass house.

Padma and Anji didn't talk much about this. I had the feeling that it made them unhappy,

45

and what made Padma unhappy made me unhappy too.

My friend the bird was the lucky one. He'd made his nest now, and every so often his mate would come out and sing, like she was teasing. Then he'd sing back, and fill his beak with my cooked rice, hop over, and feed her. It was a game, but not a game. When she'd had enough, she'd fly off to their hidden nest.

My glass house felt more and more like my own hidden nest. I had food – more and more of it as the garden grew. Only I had no mate to feed.

Chapter Ten

Sometimes, before I went to sleep, I'd see Aunty May. Not how she looked the last time, on the floor. How she used to be. A big woman, wearing many colours. When she laughed, it was like lightning. When she shouted, it was like thunder.

I heard her thundering now.

'Wake up, Billy!'

I woke with a jump. It wasn't Aunty May. It was the wire wall. It was shaking because some old guy was touching it. He was picking my roses.

I roared my fury.

'YOU!'

I gripped the guy's fingers through the mesh so hard, I almost broke them. He shrank back.

'HOW DARE YOU BANG MY ROSES, THIEF.'

I didn't think that I was a thief, too. I could see them in his hands, a big bunch of them.

He almost passed out.

'So-so-sorry, sir. I thought this place – was empty.'

I roared again.

'WRONG!'

'Please – please don't hurt me.' He was shaking. 'They were a present for my daughter.'

I growled, but stopped twisting his fingers so hard.

'What is her name?'

'P-P-Padma.'

'Does she love you?'

'Yes – yes. She's a very good girl, sir. I only wished to please her.'

'Sure . . . ' I let my voice snarl with sarcasm. 'Then in return for my roses, she can come here for tea.'

I had no idea what made me say that.

'Sir, I cannot let my daughter do that,' said Padma's father. He was shaking all over, but very firm. 'For a young woman to be alone with a – a—'

'A beast?'

'A male person,' he said, hurriedly. 'It is not permitted. I will pay you for your roses. I will—'

'You have disrespected me. She must visit, but she can bring her friend.'

I showed him my teeth. The rest of my face

was in shadow, from the trees and my hoodie, and they were probably all he could see.

'I'll ask her.'

'You do that. And if she doesn't come – I know where you live.'

I didn't of course, but it was likely he lived over his shop. I'd prowled past it late at night while scavenging. I had seen this man before, because he delivered newspapers very early in the morning – not on foot, but in his car. I was glad of the papers when they were put out in the recycling bins. They were useful in many ways, from starting fires in the fire-pit on cold days to toilet paper. I could read them, too, when I got bored.

Mostly, though, I was too busy to be bored.

Now that I would be getting a visit from Padma, I wanted to make the glass house look as good as it could. That meant throwing away tins and rubbish from my meals. It meant clearing up my mess. It meant cleaning up myself.

I found two broken chairs and mended them. I found a wooden table underneath stacks of pots, and cleaned that too. It looked really nice. My new plants were coming into bloom. I swept and washed down everything.

I didn't want to live like a beast. I didn't want to look like a beast either.

49

My hair was the worst thing. It hadn't been washed for months, and I knew it must smell like an old towel. There was an itch in my scalp that was driving me mad. I hoped it wasn't bugs.

If you have locks like mine, you know what a business it is to get it clean. Hair that kinks, splits and breaks needs so much oil that it seems easier to cut it all off. But my hair had always been in dreads. It wasn't a religious thing, but it felt like something that made me different from the Gang. Aunty May had dreads too. She put wax on hers, but I had nothing, not even coconut oil. So I opened the big plastic jerry-can of soap, and got another surprise. Peppermint! It didn't smell like any soap I'd ever sniffed before, but maybe that was a good thing. I wondered whether Mr Engels had made it himself.

By now, I'd worked out that he must have done some smart things. The electricity, for instance: I was pretty sure that some of the panes of glass in the roof were solar panels, even though they were transparent. I'd heard of stuff like this, and people selling the energy they didn't need, so maybe he'd set up a system which paid for other things, like water and council tax. Aunty May had always worried so

much about those, and I knew that there would be no water if it wasn't paid for. Even so, I was nervous about using it, just like I was nervous of using the electricity.

So far, I didn't seem to have upset whatever it was that looked after the glass house, and me.

I stood in a plastic tub and poured water over myself, then began to soap. I was cold at first, but then it was good. I squeezed my hair like a sponge, gently, and kept putting a little more of the soap on to my scalp. Then I emptied the grey water, and began rinsing. It felt so good. All the itchiness of my skin fell away. I thought: *I am washing away the fear. I am washing away the Gang. I am washing away what happened to Aunty May.* Even if I was still an ugly beast, my skin didn't hurt so much.

Padma had said, *I don't want some stinky old man.* I wasn't old, and I was no longer stinky. The smell of mint from the soap was amazing. *Maybe I could rig up a shower,* I thought. Now it was almost summer, I could wash every day. I didn't want to think about winter, or whether I'd still be here then. I had been living from minute to minute, then hour to hour. Only now I could think about the next day, too. About the new plants in my pots, and the flowers opening in them.

I wondered if I should buy biscuits, or if fruit would be OK. Did girls like milk in their tea? I hoped not. I didn't want to have to keep taking lunch money. I wished I had something to sell, so I could be lawful and honest. But I had nothing.

I knew that it was stupid to take money off kids. I also knew it was wrong. I had things in my head, now. Things Aunty May tried to teach me. She tried so hard. All the mums tried. They did all the work, long hours and two or three jobs, and got us to go to school, and church, and tried to help us become good men. It wasn't their fault we turned out as we did.

Sometimes I had bad dreams about being back. Those rows of tall buildings. Everything grey, everything sad, the rubbish blowing about. The kids hanging around, scoring or stealing. The junkies, the dealers, the graffiti, the burning trash bins. No trees. Everything broken.

Then I'd wake up in the glass house, and it was like I was in heaven. I'd see the green leaves, and smell the flowers and hear the birds. Each week, I'd sow more seeds. Outside I had tiny carrots, and potatoes, and lettuce. It felt as if I was helping the glass house, just as it was helping me.

I had stopped worrying. People left me alone. Nobody in the houses all around seemed to notice I was there, living in the middle of them. Now that I'd even cleaned it up, I felt it was mine.

Only it wasn't, of course.

Chapter Eleven

I waited and waited for Padma and her friend to stop by. They didn't. Not only that, but they no longer passed the glass house. Padma's dad must have warned her, or maybe stories about my mugging kids on the way to school had put them off.

What could I do? I'd gone to all this effort, and it hadn't worked. I got mad.

I really wanted to see Padma. Not to do anything, or even say anything. Just to look at her face. But if I wasn't to frighten her, I had to do something.

Before I could lose my nerve, I slipped out. I'd made the entrance and exit to the fence bigger, so I no longer had to crawl. You couldn't see that a part of the wire hooked back on to itself unless you looked very carefully, right next to the brick wall. How I'd ever climbed that fence when I was wounded, I still couldn't understand. Maybe my mysterious helper had given me wings.

I wished he was here now. Because I was almost as scared of meeting Padma, face to face, as I'd been when I was on the run. If I could have put on a mask, I would have. I wanted to hide inside my hoodie as if it were a cave. Yet if I did that, chances were she'd be even more freaked out.

I had done everything to seem OK. I was smelling minty-fresh, my teeth were clean and my clothes were different from when I was mugging the kids.

It was the middle of the afternoon, and kids were coming back from school. It felt strange to walk out into the tree-lined streets in the sunlight, just like a normal person. If I were legal, I could be one of those teenagers. I was still young enough. I could be thinking about homework, and a future, and not about every tiny thing just to survive. I could even have some mates, instead of just the little brown bird that kept me company.

The newsagent was open. The name, BV Moulik, was on the sign. I'd been into one before, a long time ago. I knew it sold all kinds of stuff – newspapers, Oyster cards, chewing gum, lottery tickets, soft drinks. Not replica guns, like back where I came from. The mums had demonstrated against ours, with signs

saying: TAKE BACK OUR COMMUNITY –
NO GUNS. But nobody took any notice.
There was the usual sign saying: NO PRAMS
OR PUSHCHAIRS. NO MORE THAN TWO
SCHOOLCHILDREN AT ONCE. They all said
that. It almost made me feel at home again.

I walked up to the woman behind the
counter.

She had an angry look on her face – not
because she saw me, more like a permanent
expression. But beside her, sitting on a high
stool, was Padma. She was bent over a book.

'Hello, can I help you?'

'I – er – I'd like—'

Padma looked up, and I couldn't speak. It was
like my bones had gone out of my body.

She was wearing school clothes, but her
mum was in a weird dress, like one long scarf.
I remembered what this was called: a sari. She
had a red dot on her forehead. It made her look
like she'd come from another world. Padma,
though, was more beautiful than the moon. I
stared at her, and she stared back.

'Yes?' said her mum. She glared at me, like I
was a piece of trash.

'It's OK, *Amma*. He just wants to buy a
Galaxy bar, and a lottery ticket.' Padma turned
to me. 'Don't you?'

I nodded. I still couldn't speak.

'That will be £3.'

It was all the money I had. I needed it to buy more tins of tuna, but I handed it over. In return, I got some chocolate, and one of the tickets I'd seen Aunty May fill out every week. I'd never bought a lottery ticket before.

'Thanks.'

'I need your name, and mobile number. Just in case you win.'

I knew I wouldn't win a thing. People like me never do. But right now, the only thing that mattered was being near Padma.

I wrote 'William Grant'. Then I stopped, because I couldn't even remember my mobile, and it was out of battery. I couldn't think of anything but her.

Some schoolchildren came in, hustling and bustling. The mum was distracted, telling them off in a voice like a steel wire. Padma bent over me and murmured,

'I don't *really* need your name and number for the ticket, you know.'

It seemed impossible she might like me, but I nodded. She smelled of the white flowers in the glass house. I'd found an old plastic label with a picture of them, and the name. Jasmine.

'Can you speak, Will?'

I liked her calling me that. Not Billy. Not Beasty.

'Yeah.' My voice sounded husky. 'Sorry.'

'My father said—' She glanced at her mum, still busy with the kids. Then she said, in a low voice, 'He said you wanted a visit, in return for the roses.'

'I look after them. The roses. He was picking them, and I got mad. Will you come?'

I knew it was stupid.

She said, 'OK.'

I didn't let my jaw hang open with surprise. I just nodded, and said, 'OK.'

'Tomorrow.'

'Sure.'

I turned to go, grinning all over.

'Wait!'

Her mum was watching us now. Padma said, 'You've forgotten your lottery ticket.'

I came back, and reached over the heads of the kids to take it.

One of them looked up, into my face. It was the kid whose lunch money I took – the first one.

Chapter Twelve

I wasn't as scared as I should have been. He was just a kid. What could he do to me? Yet seeing him in Padma's parents' shop made me see him as a person. He'd probably lived here for ever. Padma and her mum would know him. All it took was one word, and my new life could be over.

He was looking at a chocolate bar just as I'd looked at them when I was his age. Maybe the £2 I'd taken off him wasn't for his school lunch after all. Maybe it was for sweets. I didn't want the chocolate, so I held it out to him.

'Here.'

'Don't you want it?'

'Mate, sugar isn't good for you.'

I walked on, pleased I'd given him something he wanted.

'Hey!'

It was the kid, running after me. He must have felt safer in the open, all the shops and people.

'Wait!'

I couldn't be running away from a kid half my size. I scrunched my lottery ticket up into a ball in my pocket.

'What?'

'It's you, isn't it?'

'What is?'

'You're the one who takes—'

I turned away.

'Wrong person. D'you understand what I'm saying?'

'No, wait! My mum says—'

I turned on him suddenly.

'What does she say?'

'She says, there has to be another side to you. She says, if you're hungry there's food—'

I knew what he was going to say. I hated people like this, with their charities and shit. Like I was a beggar, or stupid. If we hadn't been in the middle of the street, I'd have hit him.

'Piss off.'

He shrugged, and ran back to his mates. Next time I found him, I wouldn't just take his money. I'd take his shoes, his pants, his house keys. I'd make him sorry he was born.

Boiling with anger, I walked on. I'd seen Padma. I'd talked to her. But even this didn't make me feel OK. I forgot about looking over

my shoulder. I forgot about looking in front. I forgot about being in danger, pretty much from everyone. I was almost caught out. But I did glance in one of the shop windows – the shiny big windows that still amazed me, just by being there. They were like mirrors, reflecting the street. I didn't want to see myself. I just looked – and there, behind me, were two figures I knew all too well.

They wore the same clothes, the hoods with caps over them, the baggy jeans, the scarves, the trainers. I'd once dressed like that, only without the jewellery, trying to look normal. Here, it was weird. Nobody went around wrapped up that way. They stood out. But all I needed to see was the walk. That rolling, bouncing walk like they were sizing up who to bang next.

Gazza and Lipz.

Chapter Thirteen

I ducked into a shop, and watched them through the glass. They drifted past, and I was sweating with fear in a way I hadn't for months. I peered at them through the stuff in the window – brooms and bins and doormats – and pretended to be interested in some mothballs. The shopkeeper was giving me the evils, like I was going to nick them. Like I even had enough clothes to need mothballs.

What were they doing here, in the north? Had they moved? They had to be either looking for me, or on some job. Whatever, they were up to no good.

Most guys, they're drawn into the gang before they are twelve. They start off having fist-fights, then they get knives. When they get knives, they get ideas. Because they're kids, they get work as run-men, bringing drugs from the dealers. They look so small and innocent, they never get nicked, but the slightest thing gets them hotted up. They've got no self-control, and

they're full of rage. If they don't make enough money, they can turn on anyone and kill them.

Aunty May said they were the children of parents who are children themselves. The gangs are their family. You've got to stay in the gang or you're on your own, and either way you need protection. Sure, you get found with a gun, it's five years in prison, but it's that or no life. Often they're the smart ones who, if they had a better chance, might be rappers. But some just get off on it.

Gazza and Lipz, they were the last kind. The crazy, mean kind that would shank you, even if you never met them in your life before. You look into their eyes, it's like looking at a black hole. No pity, no laughter, no anger even. Mostly, they made their money killing drug dealers so as to take their cash.

It was crazy, but I began to follow them. I wanted to see if they knew where I was hiding.

They didn't look over their shoulders as I did. They had never needed to, perhaps.

As I followed them, I thought about Aunty May, and how they'd killed her. They'd kicked in the door to her flat, and gone for her in her kitchen. She'd been sitting down at the table, glasses on, reading. I hope for her sake it was her Bible.

It was always out of order to kill mums. They were the ones you felt sorry for, when someone had shot or shanked their son, or you said you did. They were the ones who tried to keep the community together, to keep kids in order, to make things better. They campaigned and complained and got their hearts broken. Some had been in girl gangs themselves, before having a child changed the way they saw things.

'Once you have a child, it's like your heart leaves your body to live some place else,' my mum used to say. 'All you care about is the child, not your own self.'

Aunty May wasn't my mum, and she wasn't involved in anything other than her church, but it made no difference.

I'd stayed out of the BANG Gang, even though I'd dropped out of school. Those GCSEs, I'd done them, all six and with good grades. I'd been set to be one of the few kids to continue at the academy. Only it was more and more hard. I had no money, and Aunty May needed my help. She'd looked after me when Mum died, so it was my turn to look after her when she got sick.

That's why she was in the flat when Gazza and Lipz broke in. She didn't have anything to

steal, except the one thing. They took that just as I came in through the door.

One look was all it took to see she was gone. One look, and I was out, running, then hiding for my life. I'd hated myself as soon as I was myself again, but for those hours ...

To my relief, Gazza and Lipz didn't go anywhere near the square with the glass house. They went on down the road, towards the bus stop. Maybe they were just up for the day, like going on holiday. Maybe they had relations in another estate nearby. I didn't know, or want to know. I hoped they'd stay away.

Though in my heart, I knew they'd be back.

For now, I was relieved, not just for myself. I liked this new place. I didn't know most of the people, but I had looked in through their windows at night, and they seemed, somehow, kind. Some had jobs, and some didn't. Some were in council flats, some weren't. Only, they looked out for each other.

The teacher and his wife, the old couple next door, the retired postman and his sons, the woman in the wheelchair, the single mum and her daughter – they all talked to each other. Nobody got into fights or arguments. They picked up rubbish. They recycled rubbish. They helped each other with heavy shopping, and

took in post for neighbours. They had cats, and little dogs like cats. They planted flowers in their front gardens, and even made raised beds round trees. There were ball games, but no dog crap in the street, no people shouting and banging guns. In fact, the only crime as far as I could see came from me.

Me, and whoever kept breaking into the cars.

I wondered if it could be Gazza and Lipz. It seemed too low-level, even for them, but each time I heard the crash of glass and a car alarm going off, I huddled deeper into my blanket.

In any case, as long as Padma was coming, it didn't matter. I didn't want to think about my old life, and all those itchy, scratchy times. I wanted to live with the trees, and big windows full of light and happiness. I wanted to live in a place where kids went to school, and people had families, and gardens.

Every one of the green leaves in my little wood was her eyes.

Chapter Fourteen

'So this is where you live?'

'Yes.'

'It's like a palace.'

Padma was staring all about her. I shuffled my feet, embarrassed, but smiling.

'I'm glad you like it.'

'I do. This place, the white cast-iron, it reminds me ...'

'Of India?'

'No! Well, maybe a little. But more of something that I once copied from a photo in school once – a building called the Crystal Palace. A man called Paxton designed it.'

'A Victorian?' It was a guess.

'Yes!' She looked pleased, and a bit surprised, as if she expected me to have no education at all. 'Only that was huge.'

I opened the door of the glass house for her, and she looked surprised.

'Thank you. You are polite.'

'My aunty told me to always let a lady go first. Where is it?

'It burned down. It was built for the Great Exhibition, over a hundred and fifty years ago.'

I had no idea what she was talking about, but nodded like I did. I wished I had an iPhone, so I could look these things up. I looked things up all the time, when I could. School of Google, school of Wikipedia, that's me. But now I had no laptop, and my mobile had died, and I had no charger for it. The only thing I had was the old Nokia.

'So, man of mystery. You live in a crystal palace, you have good manners, you like knowing things. Do you also look after these plants? They're amazing.'

'I try to,' I said. I was blushing.

'You must have green fingers. Did you grow these?'

'I grew the new, small ones. Not the big old ones. They give me food.'

'Oh wow, avocados!' Padma picked up one of the black pears. 'You know, in some countries, that's all babies eat, they're so good for you. They're like nuts, full of protein. I didn't think avocados could be grown in Britain.'

'I eat a lot of them,' I said. I still felt shy, but it was easy talking to her. 'Do you want to try one?'

'I don't want to take your food.'

'No, do. It's OK.'

Padma thought they were delicious. The best she'd ever eaten, she said. I couldn't help being pleased. She said the big, smooth-skinned green fruit turning red was mango: we shared one of those. The small fruit with furry skin was kiwi fruit. It had bright green flesh with a perfect ring of violet seeds inside.

'This is the best fruit I've ever had,' she said. 'Even Indian fruit isn't as good.'

'Do you miss India?'

'I love it, but it's not my home,' she answered.

We talked and talked. I thought it would be difficult, never having talked much to a girl before – to anyone before. But it was easy. I told her about running away from my home. I didn't say why, but when I said the name of the estate, she nodded.

'I've read about it in the newspapers.'

'You have?'

She smiled. 'You work in a newsagent's, you read the papers. It sounds terrible. It's notorious.'

'It's not all that. There are good people there too. Only, it's like a maze. Everybody gets lost in it.'

'But you got away.'

'If I hadn't, I'd be dead.'

I hoped she hadn't read about Aunty May's murder. Or that I'd done it. I'd probably be a suspect if I ever turned up.

'I was trapped there with bad people.'

'Believe me, I know what that feels like.' She shivered.

'But you'll go on with your education, at least.' I wanted to know if the stinky old husband was still a possibility.

'I hope so.' She looked sad. 'It's what I most want – and I'd better go. I told my mum I was studying with my friend.'

'Anji?'

'How do you know her name?'

'I listen when you go by. You didn't see me, but I saw you.'

Padma laughed. 'We knew you were there.'

'You did?'

'Yes. I saw you first.'

'I hope I didn't scare you.'

'Why should you?'

'Because – because I'm so ugly, and you are so beautiful.'

I hadn't meant to say that, but it came out.

She stared at me. 'Will, you aren't ugly.'

I thought she was joking. 'I wish I weren't. It's like, something I have to live with.'

She looked at me with an odd expression.

'You aren't ugly. Some people look great on the outside, but are horrible on the inside.'

She was being kind, or maybe blind.

'I wasn't always like this. It's like my curse. I think my aunty cursed me.'

I hadn't put it into words before, but when I thought of how she'd shrieked at me on the day she died, that was what it felt like. She'd shrieked because I went out without doing the washing-up. She'd been half-crazy with rage, but even so ... Aunty May, with her beaded dreads, her necklaces, her fluttering clothes – even the Gang were afraid of her.

'Why would you think that?'

'I did some bad things. Stole some money off her for food. She was angry, and then – I wouldn't help her when I should have.'

'Whatever you did or didn't do,' Padma said, 'I am sure you are a good person. A gentle person. You could not have made this garden bloom if you were bad.'

It was the nicest thing anyone had ever said to me.

'I think you are a good person, too. I hope you'll come again,' I said.

'Yes, I would like that. Only—'

'What?'

'Why don't you sell some of your plants, the

little ones in pots? I'm sure people would buy them.'

She looked at me, and I knew she knew about my taking money off schoolkids. I was so ashamed. It was like a burning wave going through me. She didn't say anything, but just knowing that she thought it wrong made me decide right there I would stop. I would stop being a beast, and try to become a person.

'Who would buy them?'

'A lot of people. Like I said, you have green fingers.'

After she'd gone, I looked at my fingers. They didn't look green, just the same as always. But they were different.

Chapter Fifteen

The lumpy, bumpy skin on my hands was gone. I couldn't believe it. My nails were no longer torn and bleeding. My palms were not cracked. The back of my hands, which had once been almost as rough and stiff as gloves, was now smooth. Having my hands nice again made me want to cry. I'd never thought any bit of me might be nice to look at, but they were.

What had brought this miracle about? Was it the minty soap? Maybe. But I thought I knew. It was the glass house and its garden, and the food I ate from it.

These days, I hardly bought anything, apart from the tinned tuna and the porridge oats. I didn't need it. The garden gave me all the fruit and vegetables I could eat, and then some. Things that the seed packets said took six weeks took half that. I'd even started eating tomatoes, aubergines, courgettes, green beans, carrots.

You put anything in that soil, and it would grow. Even I was growing.

Padma kept visiting. Maybe she liked getting away from school and home. Maybe she enjoyed talking to me a little bit. We talked about so many things. Sometimes it was grey and wet outside, but when she was there it was as if the sun was shining. She knew everyone, like Ian and Katie opposite, because she'd lived there for ever and Ian taught at her school, but we had to be secret.

'My parents think everything is dangerous. There's been a few burglaries round here, so everyone is a robber or a rapist. I love them but they're so old-fashioned, it drives me mad.'

I knew I had nothing to offer her. I had no money, no education, nothing but what the glass house gave me. I might be evicted at any moment. I didn't even have £2 to spend, because of that stupid lottery ticket.

'Why don't you put some pots in the wheelbarrow, and go out on Saturday to the high street to sell them?' Padma asked.

'I wouldn't know what to ask.'

I was terrified of talking to anyone. I was even more terrified of being seen by Gazza and Lipz, even if they didn't usually get up until late afternoon.

'Ask £1. Most people will buy something for

that. Go next to the chemist, that's a good spot.'

She was a shopkeeper's daughter, after all.

I did as she suggested. It wasn't easy getting the wheelbarrow out through the wire wall, and then my thirty little pots of plants, all in bud or starting to bloom. But I managed, and by ten o'clock I was there.

People hardly looked at me, they looked at my plants. At first, I was so nervous. I couldn't believe it when people stopped to buy. But they did. Even away from the glass house, my flowers seemed to gleam and glow with health. They were bushy and glossy, bright and colourful. The more people bought, the more other people wanted some. In one hour, I made enough money to keep me for two weeks.

'They are lovely, and so cheap!'

'Do you grow them yourself?'

'Yes, I do.'

'Oh, I wanted that salvia! Was it the last one?'

'I can bring more.'

'I hope you'll be back next week.'

'Yes, I will.'

One of the people who stopped was the kid whose lunch money I kept taking. He was with his mum. He didn't say anything to her, but

when she got out her worn leather purse to buy two plants, I shook my head.

'No. I owe your son.'

She paused.

'Thank you. I'm glad you're turning over a new leaf.'

Was that what it was? When I walked back with my empty wheelbarrow, I was grinning. It was an amazing feeling, to have earned money instead of stealing it.

I should have known, it wasn't that easy.

Chapter Sixteen

The next week, I was back with even more plants. I took a rack of shelves on wheels to bits, and brought out a hundred. All my pots seemed to be putting on an extra effort. I wondered why people who bought from me didn't sow their own seeds, but they all said they didn't have the time.

Or maybe they didn't have the glass house.

It was so full of flowers that the scent was almost too strong. When I opened the door, I felt drunk. A new plant had opened, with flowers that hung like creamy angel wings. They were the ones with the amazing smell. They made me think of Padma. But then everything did.

I kept everything neat, clean, watered, fed. I loved it, and the plants loved me back. I was afraid of running out of seeds, until I thought of keeping back one or two healthy plants to make more. But there were enough to last me all summer, if I was careful. Some plants even

grew new plants out of little bits of themselves. I read how to do this in the garden centre book. If I'd stayed on at school, I thought, I'd have liked to study plants.

My friend, the brown bird, never had to look far for worms to feed his family. I could hear them cheeping away, now they'd hatched out. I wished I could see them. Maybe when they grew up, I'd get to see them fly. But he came to see me often. I could talk to him, and he'd cheep back. He'd even sit on my finger to peck boiled rice. I liked the feeling – the tiny peck on my palm, and the trust.

All the time, I was looking out for Padma. But she had exams, she told me when she next came by.

'I can't do anything until they are over,' she said.

'I'm sorry. I miss seeing you.'

'I miss coming here, too.'

I didn't know whether it was me or the glass house that she missed. I hoped it was me.

'Is everything OK?' I asked.

'I hope so.'

We were sitting deep in the thickest part of the garden. It was so quiet. There was no sound but birds and trees. The trees all around were rustling, and the red roses tumbled over the

wire wall, and the angel flowers were breathing from inside the glass house.

We never touched, not once. However often I dreamed of burying my face in her soft skin, in her long shining hair, of even just holding her hand, I knew it was forbidden. I would horrify her, and she was taking a big risk just visiting me, alone.

'Anji knows,' she said. 'I had to tell her, so she could cover for me when I'm supposed to be studying with her. I'll be in such trouble if my parents find out. We weren't even allowed to do sleepovers at each other's homes when we were little girls.'

My little brown bird hopped over. Padma brought me one or two things like rice from home; it was easy for her, she said. Her mum didn't notice stuff like that going missing. She was too busy running everything and making her family scared of her. I didn't need much, but it was nice. I had over £100 in a tin box. I had never had so much in my life.

'That's a pity,' I said. There was such a gulf between my life and Padma's. 'But she won't tell, will she?'

'No. Anj has my back and I have hers. Though I'm afraid ...'

'What is it?'

'My parents had an arranged marriage. To them, it's normal. I don't want to disappoint them. But I am not a *thing*.'

'No, you could never be that.'

'To them, what matters is money, and caste. Not whether there is any deep feeling or friendship.'

She explained to me about caste. How if you were Hindu, you were born into a level of society – scholar, warrior, merchant or untouchable – and could never leave it or marry anyone else who wasn't from the same caste. If you did, your family would never see you or your kids again. The worst, the lowest of all, were the untouchables. They did all the worst jobs, like street cleaning and rubbish, and they had the darkest skin.

I was shocked.

'So it's like, racism?'

'Not exactly. I don't believe it anyway. I love many things in my culture, but not that.'

'Would I be a merchant, now I'm selling plants?'

'No. You aren't Hindu.'

I knew, from the way she said this, that I would never be accepted. But it was no good knowing this. It had grown up inside me, like one of the seeds, and I'd never even noticed it until it was too late.

80

Chapter Seventeen

As the summer came, I tried very hard not to think about Padma, and it should have been easy. Every moment of every day was about studying. She wasn't going to waste any time she had left.

If I were at school, I'd probably be doing the same. I listened to the radio, and I sometimes read the newspapers I picked up from the recycling bins at night. Ian and Katie were best for these. They were a crazy mixture – some full of serious stuff, and some all headlines like ROLLOVER EURO MILLIONS SEARCH, or KIM'S BUM IMPLANTS SHOCK.

I knew that this wasn't the same as an education. But the more I read, the more I hoped that I could buy a laptop with the money I had hidden away. I needed to find out so much.

Ian's wife had stopped work. She was too pregnant to do much but water her garden, which meant she was often out in front.

'Hi there!' she said when she saw me.

I had to say hi back.

'I was wondering whether you do gardening work as well,' she said. 'I need some branches cutting in the back.'

'As long as you pay me.'

'Of course. Say – £20 for a couple of hours?'

I would have done it for half that.

I hadn't been into someone else's home for a very long time. Her flat wasn't fancy. It was no bigger than any on my estate – in fact, quite a bit smaller. It had books on the walls, so many I couldn't believe anyone read that much. Messy, but clean. Old furniture, a big sofa covered in a blanket, an armchair, a brown wooden table with four chairs, a lamp. A bedroom with a big bed overlooking the garden, a little bathroom and a kitchen. All on the ground floor. Flimsy locks, no hinge bolts , no London bar across the lock, no security glass on the windows.

'You should get bars on the windows, you know. And a gate across the passage.'

'Ian says that too. But we've got nothing to steal, and I don't want to live in a prison.'

I shook my head, worried for her.

'Everybody's got something.'

'Not us.'

I saw the TV, and the laptop on the table,

about three years old but still. There was an iPhone charger, so they must have an iPhone. Those weren't nothing. What did she think got nicked? Gold bars? A radio was on in the kitchen. She listened to the same channel that the one in the glass house was stuck on. I could hear familiar voices murmuring quietly in the background about Ancient Greece.

'I like that programme,' I said. 'You can learn so much from it.'

'I do too.'

I could see she wanted to ask why I wasn't at school if I liked finding stuff out, she could see I wasn't eighteen, but was too polite.

Katie not only paid me, she gave me a drink of homemade lemonade and a big sandwich when I finished. I learned she was American. She worked on a political magazine, which is why she had so many newspapers delivered. Her boyfriend was away in the country for a couple of days, she said, helping his grandma. She was trying to tidy up before the baby came. I asked if she knew Padma, just to have the pleasure of saying her name to someone. She did.

'Such a bright, lovely girl. Ian has taught her.'

I said nothing. I was afraid she might know about Padma's visits, and tell her dad.

'I wish I could go back to school,' I said, suddenly.

'What's stopping you?'

'I – well, I don't think I could. I'm not from here, and I don't have the money.'

'Lots of teenagers drop out of school for a bit, then come back. Maybe you could talk to Ian, if you'd like.'

I shook my head. 'No, thank you. People like me, we're not helped.'

'Everyone can be helped, if they ask for it,' Katie said.

I nodded, though I didn't believe her. She was so smart, but she knew nothing of the world I came from. I felt even more sad. When I'd first come here, it had been enough to get well and find food to eat. Now, I wanted impossible things. I wanted to get educated. To be worthy of Padma. To have a real home. Even if I sold a hundred plants a week, more than I could grow, I couldn't do it, and if I tried to I was afraid the police would come for me.

But the police came anyway.

Chapter Eighteen

My little brown bird had a hungry family. I often heard the chicks cheeping, like, 'Mum, I'm starving!', 'Mum, I'm bored!'

Then my friend would pop out of the bush, and fly down to peck up something to bring back. He had a worried look on his face, just like a dad.

'OK, OK,' he seemed to be saying.

It made me laugh, however sad I was. You didn't have to speak Bird to know that kids are all the same.

I found a bit of paper in my pocket, and flicked it over to him, just in case his kids liked to play football. That was what some dads did with their kids, I knew, even if I'd never known my own father. Mum told me he'd been a soldier. I couldn't remember my dad, but I remember her telling me that. It made me proud, though maybe it was just a story to make me feel better about him not being there. She was white and he was black,

and maybe that was even harder than Padma and me.

The bird pecked at the ball of paper, picked it up and flew away. I didn't think his family could eat it, so maybe they would play with it.

'Good luck, mate,' I said.

I wondered if I'd ever have a family of my own. Some guys my age, they already had kids. I couldn't see anything like that happening with Padma. I couldn't see anything whatsoever happening with Padma, but it didn't stop me hoping. Sometimes, I thought she liked me that way too, but sometimes I thought she just wanted to get away from her family and school, and be some place else. I was just part of that – that otherness.

I told Padma how I'd come to the glass house. How I'd been led here by somebody I could never quite see.

'Maybe it was a ghost. Or an angel. Or maybe I'm nuts,' I said.

Padma thought. 'No, there are cases like this. I've read about them. There was an explorer, Shackleton. When he and his team were almost dying and trying to get across the Antarctic he was convinced that they were helped by an invisible friend.'

'And were they?'

'Nobody knows. People's minds can play strange tricks when they're under a lot of stress.'

'So maybe I am nuts. Yet I was so sure this person was there.'

'But you couldn't see their face?'

'No. I thought – well, I thought it might be Death. I had a bad cut. Look.'

I knew she'd be interested, if only as a future doctor. I pulled up my T-shirt and turned round. I could hear her draw in a breath.

'That's a big scar, Will. Close to your heart.'

'Yeah. The B— the people I was running from, they don't mess about.'

'Why didn't you tell the police?'

'The police don't do nothing.'

'Are you sure?'

'Yes. Look, it's a different world. Someone like you could live a few feet away and never know what it's like.'

'But the law is the same for everyone.'

I didn't believe her. So many kids on my estate had been stabbed or shot. Nothing ever changed.

'Will the law protect you, Padma?' I asked. 'You don't want to be made to marry someone you've never met, do you?'

Her face closed. 'No, I don't. But ... My father

borrowed money from a man in Tamil Nadu to come here, many years ago. It's his brother they want me to marry.'

'You said you aren't a thing. They can't make you.'

'Yes, they can. What do you think will happen to me if I disobey? Where could I live?'

'You'd lose your home? Come and live here, with me.'

She laughed, sadly. 'Oh, Will. You have no money, and neither do I. You know the winning ticket actually came from my father's shop? It's driving him crazy, not knowing who has it. Enough money to free anyone for ever, and he wants his shop to be famous. As if that mattered!'

She didn't mind that I was so ugly, and I didn't care that all we could do was talk. I wished we could stay in the secret garden, in the glass palace for ever. I wished that time would stop.

'I don't think it was Death,' Padma said. 'I think whatever it was helped you stay alive.'

I found comfort in that thought.

Chapter Nineteen

All this time, I was keeping an eye out for Gazza and Lipz. I couldn't believe they just happened to be around when I saw them. But now I wasn't scavenging in the middle of the night, I slept. Such deep, deep sleep!

I never had any trouble sleeping in the glass house. The trees and flowers felt like friends looking out for me. The bush with enormous white flowers that hung down made me dizzy with its scent. Sometimes, I thought they *were* angels, floating in the darkness. I didn't want to sleep right underneath them, but I liked having them there.

What woke me was the voice.

Up! it said, just as it had before.

I sat up, rubbing my eyes. I thought someone had got into the glass house, or that I was having a dream. Or maybe that a fox was screaming, as they sometimes did.

It wasn't a fox, though. It was a woman.

'Help!'

Padma! I thought. I was completely confused, but I shot out from under the wire wall without even putting my shoes on.

Then I realised, it wasn't Padma's voice I had heard. It was Katie's.

'No!' she shrieked.

I didn't stop to think whether her husband was there, or if she was on her own. All I could think about was when I'd heard another woman screaming, and had rushed in to find Aunty May. I'd had nothing in my hands then, and this time I didn't even have shoes on my feet, but I grabbed a bottle out of the recycling bin. I wished I had an iron bar, or a screwdriver, but it was better than nothing.

Katie's flat had a passage all the way through to the back garden. The door was locked, but I ran round the back. Just as I thought, the patio door was kicked in.

Inside was Lipz, holding his knife to Katie's throat.

He didn't hear me, because he was looking at Gazza.

'Where's the money, bitch?'

'I told you, I don't have any. You've looked in my purse.'

That was all I had time for, because I raised the bottle and smashed it across his neck.

Lipz fell over in a shower of glass.

'You leave her alone.'

Gazza was looking at me. 'Beasty-Boy. So this is where you been hiding. This your bitch?'

'No.'

'So why you here?'

'I was passing. I heard her cry out.'

'Lipz and me, we'll make her cry more.'

'Come on, man. Leave her. She's got no money. She gave it to me.'

Katie was looking from Gazza to me in horror. 'You know these two? Is that why they're here?'

'Yes. No. I ran from them before. They killed my aunty.'

'Jesus.'

Katie's face was pale above her huge belly. A trickle of blood was going down her neck. Lipz was trying to get up, groaning. I kicked him in the head, and he went down again, on top of his knife. But now Gazza had his own knife out. I wouldn't be able to protect Katie if he went for her.

'You leave her, I'll give you the money she gave me.'

'You that dumb, Beasty?'

'She hasn't got anything. I do.'

I could see his little eyes. Whatever happened to Lipz was no concern of his. He just wanted

money. He was either on drugs, or wanted them. I had to get him away from Katie before he stuck his knife in her.

Katie suddenly pitched sideways, on to the sofa. She looked like she was praying, face down in the cushion.

'Fainted,' I said. I hoped she had, so that whatever happened to her, she wouldn't feel it. I took a step towards her, across the glass of the broken bottle, and turned her head to one side, gently.

'Come on. You want that money? Look, I got no weapon, no shoes, nothing.'

'You'd better not be messing with me.'

I turned my back on him, and walked out. It sounds simple, but it was the hardest thing ever. I could feel the tip of his knife pricking my back. I couldn't feel the splinters of glass in my feet.

Outside, everything looked the same. Same quiet houses, same quiet square, same quiet trees. Nobody else had heard Katie's cry.

There was the tall wire wall that had protected me for so long, and the trees, and the glass house. I didn't want to show Gazza my secret hideaway, or the entrance, I hated doing it with everything in my body. But it was the only way I could get him away from Katie.

Chapter Twenty

'Nice,' Gazza said.

We'd both gone through the wire. He was looking at the glass house.

'So, you growing weed?'

'No. I grow flowers. I'm legit.'

He laughed at me. 'You always were a sad little Beasty. So give me the money.'

I hadn't hidden it any place special. It was inside a tin.

He counted it out, and put the money in his pocket. Then he glanced around.

'See you've made yourself comfortable here. Think I'll move in myself.'

I couldn't stand the idea of Gazza invading this place. It'd destroy everything. Not only the glass house and the garden but the whole area. All the people who had lived in peace and kindness would go, and it would become another place of thorns and concrete. I prayed then to go back to being a beast. To tear him with my black nails and roar in his face. But

however hard I tried to call my rage, it wouldn't come.

'Why couldn't you stay with the Gang?' I asked, bitterly. 'Why did you have to come here?'

'You haven't heard? The Gang got broken up. Raffle got shot, and some of the Bulldogz. Some new kids took over. Lipz and me, we moved on. Got on the tube, started doing some stealing and dealing up here.'

'I heard there'd been a lot of break-ins.'

Now that he had my money, Gazza seemed almost friendly. He'd forgotten about Lipz, knocked out in Katie's flat, and having tried to kill me. He yawned and asked,

'Don't you want to get some gear?'

'What?'

He was standing underneath a great white flower from the angel-tree. The perfume that came from it was making even me dizzy.

'Who is that?' he asked suddenly.

'What?'

'Who is that, on the other side of you?'

I turned to where he was looking. 'Who do you mean?'

Gazza was shaking.

'There, over there. You! Why don't you say something?'

My skin was crawling. What could he see? What I could see were blue lights flashing, silently, but he was staring at something else.

With a cry, Gazza suddenly threw his knife. It missed me, but he wasn't aiming for me. He was aiming at the other side of me, where there was nobody.

Chapter Twenty-One

Padma came to see me after the police took Gazza and Lipz away. I was almost taken away too, but Katie told them I had saved her. She said nothing about my knowing them from before. They were arrested for a number of crimes, including assault – but not murder. Aunty May was alive. She'd been found, and taken to hospital. All this time I'd thought that she was dead, and she'd thought that I must be.

She wasn't exactly overjoyed.

'You can come back, Billy.'

'Thanks. I'll think about it. Like, if I want to get shanked again.'

We couldn't meet on the estate, but she could travel out of it. I was glad she was alive, and I knew she was glad I was alive. Even if you don't get along with a person enough to want to live with them, you can still care.

'Your choice. But you should go back to school.'

'I know.'

Having the police come to the glass house was not a good idea. My secret hideaway was a secret no more. Someone told the council, and the next thing I knew, I was in trouble for squatting there. Nobody knew who owned it, or what had happened to Mr Engels, only that I shouldn't be there.

Katie told me. 'The garden centre, it's an anomaly.'

'A what?'

'Something that shouldn't be there, but is. They can't knock it down, because it's listed. That means, it's protected because it's part of history.'

'Padma thought it might be by the Crystal Palace man. Paxton.'

A flicker of surprise crossed Katie's face. She said, 'It might be. But they can't find who owns it either. Mr Engels, well, if he left a will, nobody has found it. He went abroad last winter, and died there.'

'When?'

'Sometime in January.'

That was when I'd escaped from the estate.

'Did someone kill him?'

Katie grimaced. 'No, he died of natural causes. There was a picture of him in a

97

paper – he was quite well known as a botanist. I'll show you on my laptop.'

She tapped a few buttons and up came the face of an old man. I couldn't be sure – after all, I'd never seen the face of my guide – only, it felt like it might have been him.

'So I've got to leave the glass house?'

'Not right away. But I expect so, eventually. They'd rather have somewhere empty and falling down than brought back to life.'

I didn't want to leave. If I had somewhere to go, just a room where I could live and study and earn, it'd be so different. I'd got back the money Gazza stole – he'd dropped it just before the police came. But it wasn't enough. I had nowhere else to go.

Still, I was alive.

'It was weird. I kept expecting to be shanked but Gazza was in a dream,' I told Padma. 'Something made him change his mind.'

'He was standing under a Datura plant on a hot night.'

'What's that?'

'Those big white flowers have a toxin. It's what South American Indians dip their arrows in to make them poisonous.'

'Do you know everything, Padma?'

'Not everything, no. But if you breathe in

Datura dew, you can die. At the very least, it will give you some weird thoughts.'

'I wouldn't like to be in your husband's shoes.'

I was lying, of course.

'Don't joke about it.'

The glass house had protected me once more. Or maybe it had been the ghost of Mr Engels. But it couldn't protect Padma. She'd come back to say that she couldn't see me again.

'It's not acceptable to see you again.'

'I know I'm too ugly for you.'

'Will, you aren't ugly. I don't know why you think you are.'

'My face, my skin ... '

'There's nothing wrong with your face. You're not ugly, Will. You're ... the opposite.'

I stared at her.

'I wish everything were the opposite!' she said, suddenly. 'I wish you were rich, I wish you were rich enough for it not to matter to my parents that—'

I could hardly speak.

'Why do you wish that?'

'Because ... because ... '

She burst into tears. I put my arms round her.

'I'll do anything for you, Padma. I'm going to go back to school if I can. Katie and Ian are going to find a way to help me.'

'Do they have money?' she asked, sniffing and half-laughing.

I laughed. 'No. Hardly anybody good ever has money, haven't you noticed? But there has to be a way. Even if we have to build a nest out of grass and feathers.'

I looked at the brown bird, hopping about under the roses. He kept pecking at something with his beak, very crossly, and cheeping.

'What a fuss that bird makes!' Padma said. 'What's he doing?'

'He's just playing with a ball I made,' I answered.

She was looking at it intently.

'Where did you get that piece of paper?' she asked.

'I've no idea.'

Padma stooped, as if pouncing, and the little bird flew off. She picked up the paper ball I had made, all those weeks ago, and unrolled it.

There, crumpled but perfectly clear, was my lottery ticket.

THE END

Afterword

There are many recorded instances of what has been called Third Man Syndrome. This is when people in great danger are convinced that they are being helped and guided by a person who turns out not to be there. The famous explorer Sir Ernest Shackleton described how he and his surviving men were led to safety in the Antarctic by such a figure. His account inspired a passage in T.S. Eliot's great poem, *The Waste Land*, from which the title of this book comes.

One of the few people to escape the flames in the Twin Towers also says he was guided through them to safety by a friendly voice. Many soldiers, pilots and others have experienced this.

It may be a stress response of the human brain. Or it may be something more mysterious.

About Quick Reads

Quick Reads are brilliant short new books written by bestselling writers. They are perfect for regular readers wanting a fast and satisfying read, but they are also ideal for adults who are discovering reading for pleasure for the first time.

Since Quick Reads was founded in 2006, over 4.5 million copies of more than a hundred titles have been sold or distributed. Quick Reads are available in paperback, in ebook and from your local library.

To find out more about Quick Reads titles, visit

www.readingagency.org.uk/quickreads

Tweet us 🐦 @Quick_Reads

Quick Reads is part of The Reading Agency,
a national charity that inspires more people to read more, encourages them to share their enjoyment of reading with others and celebrates the difference that reading makes to all our lives.
www.readingagency.org.uk Tweet us @readingagency

The Reading Agency Ltd · Registered number: 3904882 (England & Wales) Registered charity number: 1085443 (England & Wales) Registered Office: Free Word Centre, 60 Farringdon Road, London, EC1R 3GA The Reading Agency is supported using public funding by Arts Council England.

We would like to thank all our funders:

LOTTERY FUNDED

has something for everyone

Stories to make you laugh

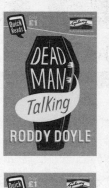

Stories to make you feel good

Stories to take you to another place

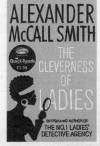